# Janna was knocked breathless.

By the time she could react, it was too late. She was flat on her back, pinned to the hot earth by the weight of Ty's big body. He caught her wrists and held them above her head, imprisoned in his hands.

"Don't you think it's time that you and I had a little chat?" he drawled.

"Let go of me!" Janna answered.

"Promise you won't run?"

Janna twisted abruptly, trying to throw Ty off. He simply settled a bit more heavily onto her body.

"I'm bigger than you are, if you hadn't noticed," Ty said. "A little thing like you doesn't have a chance against a man of any size, much less one as big as I am."

Janna started calling Ty the same names her father had used when the wagon mules wouldn't move. "You misbegotten whelp of a cross-eyed cow...."

A big hand clamped over her mouth, cutting off the flow of her invective.

"Didn't anybody ever tell you a girl shouldn't use such language?"

The muffled sounds from beneath his hand told him that Janna wasn't listening.

Dear Reader,

The holidays are upon us and Harlequin Historicals is celebrating with a quartet of keepers!

First, *New York Times* bestselling author Elizabeth Lowell brings us *Reckless Love*. Janna Wayland is as untamed as the wild horses she trains. But when Ty Mackenzie comes into her life, her unbridled passion forces her to make a painful choice.

Margaret Moore, author of the Warrior series, takes us back to the age of Norsemen in her latest release. *The Viking* is Einar, a warrior whose decision to take Saxon woman Meradyce hostage changes his life forever. Filled with adventure and romance, this is a *must* read.

In *Providence,* Ananiah Snow—a woman with a scandalous past—risks everything when she hires handsome sea captain Sam Colburn to find her missing father. Yet losing her heart to Sam proves the greatest risk of all. Another swashbuckling, romantic tale on the high seas by popular author Miranda Jarrett.

And rounding out December is *Counterfeit Laird* by Erin Yorke. This charming tale about the people in a small Scottish village who trick American businessman Creag Blake into believing he is the long-lost laird is sure to please readers—especially when the sparks begin to fly between Creag and the old laird's granddaughter, Jeanne....

All of us at Harlequin wish you a happy and safe holiday season and best wishes for the new year!

Sincerely,

Tracy Farrell
Senior Editor

# Elizabeth Lowell

# Reckless Love

# Harlequin Books

TORONTO • NEW YORK • LONDON
AMSTERDAM • PARIS • SYDNEY • HAMBURG
STOCKHOLM • ATHENS • TOKYO • MILAN
MADRID • WARSAW • BUDAPEST • AUCKLAND

ISBN 0-373-28799-2

RECKLESS LOVE

Printed in U.S.A.

# Elizabeth Lowell

is one of romance's most versatile and successful authors. With over five million copies of her books in print, she has been named on numerous lists, including the *New York Times* bestseller list. With her husband, Evan Maxwell, she has written mysteries and romantic suspense.

# Chapter One

Heart pounding, body flattened to the hot earth, Janna Wayland peered down the brush-covered slopes and watched the tall stranger run naked between a double line of Cascabel's renegade Ute warriors.

*He'll never make it,* Janna thought. Her heart turned over in pity for the man as blow after blow rained onto his powerful body, staggering him, sending him to his knees. *No matter how big or how strong he looks from here, they'll kill him. They always kill the white men they catch.*

Crimson streaks appeared on the man's broad back as he struggled to his feet and began to run once more, doubled over in pain, lurching from side to side between the two lines of half-drunk warriors. When he reached the end of the gauntlet he straightened unexpectedly and surged forward, his legs driving hard, his head up, running with the power and grace of a wild stallion.

The laughing, jeering Utes remained unconcerned about their prey's apparent escape. Other men had run the gauntlet before. Most of them never reached the end before being knocked unconscious and clubbed to death. The few prisoners who managed to survive the gauntlet had provided great sport for the renegades as they tracked their bleeding quarry through the rugged canyons, plateaus and mountains of the lower Utah Territory. Whether they found their prisoner a hundred yards away or a mile, the end was always the same—torture and a death that was no more merciful than the red-rock desert itself.

*Go to the left,* Janna prayed, her slender body vibrating with intensity. *Don't take the first side canyon that offers itself. It's a death trap. Go left. Left!*

As though he heard her silent pleas, the man passed up the brush-choked entrance of a small ravine and ran on. For a few more moments Janna watched him through her spyglass, assuring herself that he was running in the correct direction. Despite the crimson blood staining his skin, the man ran smoothly, powerfully. Janna's breath caught and then wedged in her throat as she watched the stranger run. Every line of his body proclaimed his determination to survive. She had seen nothing so beautiful in her life, not even Lucifer, the black stallion every man pursued and every shaman said no man would catch.

The stranger disappeared around a bend in the dry wash, still running hard. Janna collapsed the spyglass, stuffed it into her hip pocket and began wiggling backward out of the brush that had concealed her from the warriors below. As she moved, she automatically smoothed out signs of her passage and replaced stones or twigs that her body overturned. She had survived for years alone in Indian country by being very, very careful to leave few traces of her presence.

Once Janna was out of sight of the warriors below—and of the guard on the rimrock at the head of Raven Canyon, where Cascabel's renegades had their camp—she began running on a roundabout course that skirted one of the many prows of rock that jutted out from the sloping base of Black Plateau. She crossed a dry wash by leaping from boulder to boulder, leaving no trace of her passage. Then she set off on a course that she hoped would cut across the stranger's trail within a few hundred yards.

If he got that far.

Despite her urgency, Janna used every bit of cover along the way, for she could do the man no good if she were caught by renegades herself. After five minutes she stopped, held her breath and listened. She heard nothing to suggest that the renegades had begun pursuing the stranger. Hope rose a little higher in her heart. She resumed running, moving with the grace and silence of fire skimming over the land. It was the silence of her movement as well as the rich auburn blaze of her hair that had caused the natives to call her Shadow of Fire.

Just before Janna reached another dry wash, she saw the stranger's trail. She veered left, following him, wondering which hiding place the man had chosen of all those offered by the tiny finger canyons and rugged rock formations that riddled the base of the plateau. Not that hiding would do him much good. He tried to conceal his trail, but he was bleeding so much that every few feet bright crimson drops proclaimed his passage.

Janna slowed and began rubbing out the telltale drops, using sand or dirt or brush, whatever was near at hand. When his blood trail began to climb up the slope, she noted with approval that the man had passed up obvious hiding places where the renegades would be sure to look. In spite of injuries and the certain knowledge of pursuit, the man hadn't panicked. Like the elusive Lucifer, the stranger relied on intelligence as well as raw strength for his survival.

Yet it was the man's determination that impressed Janna while she followed his twisting trail up the steep, rocky flank of the plateau. She realized that he was hiding in the most unexpected manner. He was taking a route up the plateau's north face that was so difficult the warriors wouldn't believe their prey could possibly have gone that way. The renegades would search the easier escape routes first, perhaps wasting enough time that darkness would fall before the stranger was discovered.

It was a long chance, but it was the only one he had, and
he had been smart and tough enough to take it.

Janna redoubled her efforts, moving quickly, wiping out
signs of the man, doing everything she could to help him
elude the warriors who were sure to follow. The farther up
the flank of the plateau she climbed, the more her admiration for the stranger's determination and stamina increased. She began to hope that he knew of an ancient
footpath to the top of the plateau, a path that had been
abandoned by the Indians, who now rode horses.

The farther up she climbed, the more she allowed herself
to believe that the stranger would make it to the top. Up
there was water, cover, game, all that a man would need to
survive. Up there she could hide him easily, care for his
wounds, nurse him if he required it.

Hopes high, Janna levered herself over a rockfall, only to
find a stone cliff cutting off all possibility of advance or escape. At the base of the cliff, piñon and rocks grew in equal
profusion.

There was no one in sight.

But there was no way out of the rugged little canyon except the way he had come, and she certainly hadn't seen
anything bigger than a rabbit. He had to be somewhere in
the piñon- and rock-filled hollow behind the landslide—
unless he had spread spectral wings and flown from this trap
like a shaman.

A frisson went over Janna's skin at the thought. If any
man could have flown like a pagan god, this one could have.
He had taken a beating that would have killed most men,
then he had run three miles and threaded his way to the head
of a nameless rocky canyon over land that had tried even
Janna's skill.

*Don't be foolish,* Janna told herself firmly. *He's as human as you are. You've looked at enough of his blood in the
last mile to swear to that on a stack of Bibles as tall as God*

Intently Janna stared at every foot of the sloping hollow. Despite her sharp eyes, it took two circuits of the ground before she spotted the stranger lying facedown amid the low, ragged piñon branches. She approached him cautiously, unwilling to make any unnecessary sound by calling out to him. Besides, he could be playing possum, waiting for her to get within reach of those powerful hands. He wouldn't expect to be followed by anyone but a renegade Indian out to kill him.

A few minutes of silent observation convinced Janna that the stranger wasn't lying in ambush. He was too still for too long. Janna began to fear that the man was dead. He lay utterly motionless, his limbs at very awkward angles, his skin covered by blood and dirt. In fact it was the slow welling of blood from his wounds that told her he was still alive. She crawled beneath piñon boughs until she was close enough to put her mouth next to his ear.

"I'm a friend. Do you hear me? I'm a friend."

The man didn't move.

"Mister?" Janna whispered, touching his naked shoulder, shaking him lightly, calling to him in her low, husky voice.

There was no sign that he heard.

Carefully Janna sat on her heels next to the man, letting fragrant piñon boughs brush over her. She slid her hand around his neck until she could press against the jugular... and breathed out. Her first impression was of fiery heat, then of the strength in his muscular neck, and then finally she felt the slow, somewhat ragged beating of his heart. From the size of the lump on the side of his head, she was surprised that he had remained conscious long enough to get this far.

"You're not going another inch, are you?" she asked very softly.

The man didn't disagree.

With gentle fingers Janna probed his head wound. Though it was puffy, there was no softness of crushed bone beneath. Nor was blood pooling in the dirt anywhere around his big body, which meant that none of his wounds were bleeding him to death.

Once Janna assured herself of that, she didn't waste any more time checking injuries. The stranger's extraordinary efforts had ended up defeated by a dead end against a stone cliff, but his original plan was still good—take such a difficult route up the side of the plateau that Cascabel wouldn't think to look there for an injured man. All Janna had to do was backtrack, thoroughly wiping out the man's trail as she went. Then she would lay a false trail in another direction and sneak back up to the stranger to make sure that he kept quiet until Cascabel tired of the game and went back to camp.

Slowly Janna worked back down the man's trail, doing a thorough job this time of removing all signs that anyone had come this way. Where blood had fallen onto loose stone, she picked up the stained rock and substituted another of like size. Where the man's feet had disturbed earth, she brushed it flat once more and sifted dust and plant debris over the surface.

She worked in this manner past several places where he could have chosen other routes to the left or right, up the slope or down. When she came to another place where he had a choice of directions, she pulled a knife from the sheath at her waist, gritted her teeth and cut her arm until blood flowed.

Using her own blood, Janna laid a false trail, concealed it so hastily that it could be detected readily by a warrior with sharp eyes, and began a long, slanting descent to the base of the plateau, heading away from the renegades' camp. As she went, she made more obvious attempts to conceal her direction each time there was a logical choice in routes to make. The closer to Mustang Canyon she came, the less blood she left behind, for she wanted to suggest to the renegades that their quarry wasn't badly wounded; that, in fact, he was bleeding less and less with each moment. Hopefully, when the blood spoor disappeared, the Indians wouldn't be suspicious.

Just as Janna reached the broad mouth of Mustang Canyon, she heard Cascabel's men. They were behind her—and they had just discovered the trail of their prey.

# Chapter Two

Trapped by Mustang Canyon's high rock walls, the cries of the renegades echoed eerily, making Janna feel surrounded. She redoubled her speed, running hard toward the head of the wide, deep canyon. As she ran, she pulled the bandanna from her neck and wrapped her arm so that no more drops of blood would fall to the ground.

By the time Janna found the tiny side canyon she had been headed for, she was breathing raggedly. Even so, she took great care to mask her trail when she turned into the twisting slot that opened onto the floor of Mustang Canyon. The feeder canyon she had chosen was extremely deep and narrow. The creek that lay in the tiny canyon's bottom was dry, for it carried water only in the wet season or after summer cloudbursts.

No more than six feet wide as it opened onto Mustang Canyon's broad floor, the slot was a hundred feet deep. Only if the sun were directly overhead did any light reach the bottom of the finger canyon. Thirty feet up the sides were marks of previous floods—brush and small trees wedged into crevices, water stains, small boulders perched precariously in water-smoothed hollows. The floor of the feeder canyon was a dry wash paved with boulders and fine deposits of silt and dried mud, all of which angled steeply back into the body of the plateau.

Leaving no trace of her passage, Janna leaped from boulder to boulder up the slot canyon's floor until it became so narrow that she couldn't extend both arms out from her sides at the same time. At this point the top of the canyon—which was the surface of the plateau itself—was only fifty feet away. Farther on, when the red stone walls pressed in even more tightly, she turned sideways, put her back against one wall and her feet against the opposite wall and inched up the chimneylike opening. The top was only thirty feet away, but her progress was dangerously slow. If one of Cascabel's men should happen into the tiny side canyon, she would be discovered within minutes.

In the distance came shouts from the renegades. Janna ignored them, concentrating only on climbing out of the slot canyon and onto the relative safety of the plateau beyond. By the time she reached the top, she was trembling with the effort of levering her body up the narrow opening. She heaved herself over the edge and lay flat, breathing in great gasps, trembling all over and stinging from the scrapes and cuts she had gotten from the stone walls.

*What am I complaining about?* she asked herself tartly. *He suffered a lot worse and kept going. And if I don't do the same, he's going to come to and thrash around and groan and Cascabel will find him and spend the next four days torturing him to death.*

The thought galvanized Janna. The stranger was too strong and too courageous for her to permit him to die at Cascabel's cruel hands. She pushed herself to her feet and began trotting across the top of Black Plateau, whose rumpled forests, meadows, and crumbling edges she knew as well as any human being ever had. The plateau was part of the summer grazing territory of Lucifer's band.

Janna had spent five years following Lucifer's band, caring for the sick or the lame, taming those animals that hungered for human companionship or easy food, leaving free those horses that could not accept anything from man's hand, even safety. One of those horses had become Janna's only companion in the plateau's wildness, coming to her freely, staying with her willingly, carrying her on wild rides across the rugged land. It was that horse Janna hoped to find now. The band often grazed this part of the plateau in the afternoon.

She found Lucifer and his harem grazing along one of the plateau's many green meadows, some of which ran like a winding river of grass between thick pine forests. A tiny creek trickled down the center of the sinuous meadow.

Janna lifted her hands to her mouth. Moments later a hawk's wild cry keened over the meadow. She called three times, then went to one of the small caches she had scattered across the plateau and surrounding countryside for the times when Cascabel amused himself by pursuing her. From the cache she took a canteen, a handful of rawhide thongs, a leather pouch that was full of various herbs, a blanket and a small leather drawstring bag that contained some of the gold that Mad Jack insisted was her father's share of his gold mine. As her father had been dead for five years, Mad Jack simply paid her instead.

After a moment of hesitation, Janna removed a knife as well, the last item in the small cache. It took just seconds and a few lengths of rawhide thongs to transform the blanket into a makeshift pack. She slung the pack diagonally across her back and looked over to where the wild horses grazed. Lucifer was staring in her direction with pricked ears, but he was not alarmed. Though he had never permitted her to come within fifty feet of him, he no longer ran from or threatened to attack her. He had come to accept Janna as a particularly slow and awkward horse that showed up from time to time carrying delicacies such as rock salt and grain—certainly no threat to his band despite the man odor that accompanied her.

By the time Janna filled her canteen at the small stream, one of Lucifer's mares had come over at a trot, whinnying a welcome. Zebra was dust colored with black mane, tail, stockings, ears, muzzle, and a black stripe down her back. Cowboys called such horses zebra duns and prized them above all others for stamina, intelligence, and the natural camouflage that allowed them to pass unnoticed where other horses would be spotted by hostile Indians or equally hostile outlaws.

"Hello, Zebra," Janna said, smiling and stroking the dust-colored mare's velvety black muzzle. "Ready for a run? It won't be far today. Just a few miles."

Zebra nudged her muzzle against Janna with enough force to stagger her. She grabbed a handful of mane and swung onto Zebra's back. A light touch of Janna's heels sent the mare into a canter, which rapidly became a gallop. Guided only by Janna's hands, heels and voice, the mare took a slanting course across a corner of the plateau, then plunged down the hair-raising trail used by the wild horses to climb up or down the plateau's north side.

This particular route was one of the most difficult ways to ascend or descend the plateau. That was why Janna chose the route. To her knowledge, none of Cascabel's men had ever used it. They gained access to the plateau through one of the two western trails or from the southern edge, leaving the northern and eastern areas of the plateau pretty much alone. That suited Janna very well; a slot canyon that opened up from the plateau's eastern face was as close to a home as she could ever remember having.

Twenty minutes after Zebra attacked the precipitous trail down into Mustang Canyon, she slid to the canyon's floor and stretched out for a good run. Janna let her go until she was as close to the stranger's hiding place as she could come without making her destination obvious.

"That's it girl. Whoa, Zebra. This is where I get off."

Reluctantly Zebra slowed. Janna leaped off and smacked the mare lightly on her dust-colored haunch to send her on her way.

The mare didn't budge.

"Go on," Janna said, smacking Zebra again. "I don't have time to play anymore today. Next time, I promise."

Abruptly the mare's head went up and her nostrils flared. She stood motionless, drinking the wind and staring off down the canyon. Janna didn't need any more warning; she faded back into the rocks and clumps of brush. Zebra stood for a few moments more, then quietly withdrew back up the canyon. Within minutes she was all but invisible, protected by her natural camouflage.

Moving quickly, silently, camouflaged by her own dusty clothes and earth-colored hat, Janna retreated along the canyon bottom until she could turn and climb up to the small hollow. Wiping out her traces as she went, she approached the stranger's hiding place from a different, even steeper angle, scrambled over the rock slide at the hollow's entrance and immediately looked toward the tangle of piñons and rocks at the base of the cliff.

The stranger was gone.

Janna ran across the hollow and went into the piñons on her hands and knees. There was blood still fresh on the ground, as well as signs that the man had dragged himself deeper into cover. She followed his trail, wiping it out as she went, crumbling and scattering earth and the debris that piled up beneath the piñons. She found him in a dense thicket that crowded up against the cliff. Bloody handprints on the stone told her that he had tried to climb, only to fall. He lay where he had fallen, facedown in the dirt, his hands still reaching toward stone as though he would awaken at any moment and try to climb once more.

She bit her lip against unaccustomed tears, feeling as she had once when she had found a cougar with its paw wedged into a crack in the rocks. She hadn't been able to approach the cat until it was nearly dead with thirst. Only then had she been able to free it—but she would never forget the agony of waiting for the magnificent cat to weaken enough to allow her close.

*"Pobrecito,"* Janna murmured, touching the man's arm as she settled into place beside him. *Poor little one.*

The swell of firm muscle beneath her fingers reminded Janna that the man was hardly little; he was as powerful as the cougar had been, and perhaps as dangerous. He had shown a frightening determination to survive, driving himself beyond all reason or hope. Perhaps he was like Cascabel, whose ability to endure pain was legendary. As was his cruelty.

Was this man also cruel? Had it been savage cunning and coldness that had driven him to survive rather than unusual intelligence and courage and determination?

Shouts floated up from the canyon bottom as renegades called to one another, searching for the man who had run their gauntlet and then disappeared like a shaman into the air itself. Janna shrugged out of her pack, untied the rawhide thongs and spread the army blanket over the stranger. An instant later she removed it. The solid color was too noticeable in the dappled light and shadow of the piñons. As long as there was any chance of Cascabel finding the hollow, the man was better off camouflaged by random patterns of dirt and dried blood.

Slowly, silently, Janna shifted position until she was sitting next to the man, his face turned toward her. She looked at him intently, trying to guess what kind of man lay beneath the bruises and dirt. If she hadn't already had ample evidence of his strength, his body would have convinced her of his power. His shoulders were as wide as the length of an ax handle, his back was a broad wedge tapering to narrow hips, and his legs were long, well muscled, and covered in black hair that was repeated in the small of his back and beneath his arms.

Gradually Janna realized that the stranger was very handsome and intensely male. There was a regularity of feature in his face that was pleasing. His forehead was broad, his eyes were set well apart and thickly lashed, his cheekbones were high and well defined beneath the black beard stubble, his nose was straight, his mustache was well trimmed, and his jaw fully reflected the determination he had already shown. She wondered whether his eyes were dark or light, but his skin gave no clue. Faint lines of laughter or concentration radiated out from the corners of his eyes. Beneath the dust and blood, his hair was thick, slightly curly, and the color of a raven's wing. His hair tempted her to run her fingers through it, testing its depth and texture.

More voices floated up from the canyon, freezing Janna in the act of reaching out to stroke the stranger's hair. Cascabel's men were closer now—much too close. They must have seen past her efforts to obscure the trail.

The man's eyes opened. They were a deep, crystalline green, and they burned with the savage light of his determination to live. Instantly Janna put her fingers over his lips and shook her head. Her other hand pressed down on his back, urging him not to move. He nodded his understanding that he must not speak or make any motion that might give away their hiding place.

Frozen, barely breathing, they waited and listened to the sounds of Cascabel's renegades searching the rugged land for their prey.

Gradually the sounds withdrew. Apparently the Indians hadn't believed that their wounded prey could climb the steep side of the canyon. When the voices failed to come back again, the man let out a long, broken breath and fell unconscious again.

Janna bent and stroked the stranger's hair in a silent reassurance meant to soothe the animal awareness that had awakened him at the first sound of pursuers. She understood the kind of life that resulted in a division of the mind where part slept and part stood guard. It was how she slept, alertly, waking often to listen to the small sounds of mice and coyote, the call of an owl and branches rustling against the wind. She accepted the dangers of a wild land, thinking no more about their presence than she did that of the sun or the wind or the brilliant silver moon.

After it had been silent for an hour, Janna cautiously opened the leather pouch she had brought. One by one she unwrapped the herbs she had collected at different times and places as she roamed the Utah Territory. Some of the herbs had already been made into unguents. Others were whole. Working quickly and quietly, she treated the wounds she could reach without disturbing the stranger's sleep. His feet were a collection of cuts, thorns and bruises. She cleaned the cuts, removed the thorns, applied a thick layer of healing herbs and wrapped his feet in strips she cut from the blanket. Not once did he stir or show any signs of waking. His stillness would have worried her had it not been for the strong, even beating of his heart and his rhythmic breathing.

When Janna could do no more for the stranger, she pulled the blanket over him, sat next to him and watched the sky catch fire from the dying sun. She loved the silent blaze of beauty, the incandescence and the transformation of the sky. It made her believe that anything was possible—anything—even her fierce, silent hope of someday having a home where she could sleep without always waking alone.

Only when it was full dark and the last star had glittered into life did Janna put her arms around her knees, lower her forehead to them and sleep, waking every few minutes to listen to the small sounds of the living night and the breathing of the man who trusted her enough to sleep naked and weaponless at her feet.

# Chapter Three

Tyrell MacKenzie awoke feeling as though he had slept beneath a herd of stampeding steers. Despite the pain lancing through his head with every heartbeat, he didn't groan or cry out; his instincts were screaming at him that he had to be silent and hide. The Civil War had taught Ty to trust those instincts. He opened one eye a bare slit, just enough to see without revealing the fact that he had returned to consciousness.

A pair of moccasins was only inches away from his face.

Instantly memories flooded through Ty's pain-hazed mind—Cascabel and his renegades and a gauntlet of clubs that had seemed to go on forever. Somehow he had gotten through it and then he had run and run until he thought his chest would burst, but he had kept on running and trying to find a place where he could go to ground before the Indians tracked him down and killed him.

Another memory came to Ty, that of a thin boy with ragged clothes and steady gray eyes warning him to be silent. Ty opened his eyes a bit more and saw that the moccasins belonged to the boy rather than to one of Cascabel's killers. The boy had his head on his knees and was hugging his long legs against his body as though still trying to ward off the chill of a night spent in the open.

The angle and direction of the sunlight slanting between the towering black thunderheads told Ty that it was early afternoon rather than early morning, which meant that he had slept through yesterday afternoon, all of the hours of darkness, and most of the day, as well. He was surprised that the cold hadn't awakened him during the night. Even though it was still August, the countryside wasn't particularly warm once the sun set behind Black Plateau.

The boy turned his head until his chin rested on his knees. Ty found himself staring into the clear gray eyes he remembered. Such a steady glance was unusual in a boy so young that he wouldn't need a razor for a few years. But then, Ty had seen what war did to children. The ones who survived were old far beyond their years.

The youth raised his index finger to his lips in a signal for Ty not to make a sound. Ty nodded slightly and watched while the boy eased through the underbrush with the silence of an Indian. Despite the aches of his bruised and beaten body, Ty didn't shift position. That was another thing the war had taught him. The man who moved first died first.

While Ty waited for the youth to return from reconnoitering, he noticed that there was a blanket covering his body, protecting him against the chilly air. From the look of the corner covering his arm, the blanket was as ragged as the boy's clothes. Ty realized that the blanket must belong to the boy, who obviously had stood guard throughout the cold night and the long day as well, protecting a helpless stranger, giving him the only cover.

*Hell of a kid*, Ty thought. *Wonder what he's doing out here alone?*

It was the last thought Ty had before he drifted off into a pain-filled, fitful sleep.

He was still dozing when Janna returned through the brush as silently as she had come. Even so, his eyes opened.

Like a wild animal, he had sensed that he was no longer alone.

"You can move around, but we can't leave yet," Janna said in a low voice. "Cascabel and his men are still searching for you, but they're on the east side of Black Plateau."

"Then you better get out while you can," Ty said hoarsely. He shifted position with cautious movements, grimaced with pain and kept moving anyway. He had to find out what his body would be good for if he had to run again. And he would have to run if Cascabel were still searching. "I left a trail a blind man could follow."

"I know," Janna said softly. "I wiped it out as I followed you."

"Won't do any good," Ty said in a low voice that was more like a groan. He forced himself into an upright position despite dizziness and the excruciating pain in his head. "Once Cascabel sobers up, he'll find your sign. He could track a snake over solid rock. Go on, kid. Get out while you can."

Janna saw the stranger's pallor and the sudden sweat that covered his face. She wanted to tell him to lie down, not to move, not to cause himself any more pain; but she knew that he might have to move, to run, to hide. Better that they find out now how much strength he had so that they could plan for his weakness rather than being caught by surprise.

"I laid a false trail to a blind keyhole canyon way back up Mustang Canyon," she said softly. "Then I climbed out. I'd stopped bleeding by then, so I didn't leave any sign of where I went."

"Bleeding?" Ty looked up, focusing on the boy with difficulty because pain had turned the world to red and black. "Are you hurt?"

"I cut myself," Janna said as she unwrapped the bandanna from her arm. "Cascabel knew you were bleeding. If there weren't any sign of blood, he wouldn't believe the trail was yours."

The last turn of the bandanna was stuck to Janna's skin by dried blood. She moistened the cloth with a small amount of water from the canteen, gritted her teeth and pulled the bandanna free. The cut oozed blood for a moment, then stopped. There was no sign of infection, but she dug in the leather pouch and sprinkled more herb powder over the cut anyway.

"You all right?" Ty asked thickly.

Janna looked up and smiled. "Sure. Papa always told me that cuts from a sharp knife heal better than cuts from a dull one, so I keep my knives sharp. See? No sign of infection."

Ty looked at the long red line on the back of the unmuscular forearm and realized that the boy had deliberately cut himself in order to leave a trail of blood for Cascabel to follow.

"Your papa raised a brave boy," Ty said.

Janna's head came up sharply. She was on the edge of saying that her father had raised a brave *girl*, when she caught herself. Other people had mistaken her for a boy since her father had died, especially after she had done everything she could to foster the impression. She bound her breasts with turn after turn of cloth to flatten and conceal her feminine curves. For the same reason she wore her father's old shirts, which were much too big, and his old pants rode low on her hips, hiding the pronounced inward curve of her waist. She wore her hair in thick Indian braids stuffed beneath a man's hat, which was also too big for her.

Being taken for a boy had proven useful when Janna went to the few ranches around to trade her writing and reading skills for food, or when she went to town to spend a bit of Mad Jack's gold on store-bought clothes or rare, precious books. Being a boy gave her a freedom of movement that was denied to girls. Because she loved freedom as much as any mustang ever born, she had always been relieved when strangers assumed she was a boy.

Yet it galled Janna that this particular stranger had mistaken her sex. Her first reaction was to make him look beyond the clothes to the woman beneath. Her second reaction was that that would be a really stupid thing to do.

Her third reaction was a repeat of her first.

"Your papa didn't do badly, either," Janna said finally. "Cascabel has killed more men than you have fingers and toes."

"Don't know about the toes," Ty said, smiling crookedly as he sat upright and examined his feet. The sight of the bandages made him look quickly at Janna.

"Oh, you've still got ten of them," she said. "A bit raw, but otherwise intact. It's going to hurt like the devil to walk on them, though."

Ty hissed softly through his teeth as he crossed his legs and sat Indian-style. "Don't have to wait until I walk. Hurts like hell right now."

Janna said nothing because her mouth had gone dry. When he had sat up and crossed his legs, the blanket had fallen away, revealing a broad, bloody chest and muscular torso. Crisp black hair swirled around his flat nipples, gathered in the center line of his body and curled down to his loins. There the hair became thick and lush as it fanned out, defining and emphasizing the essential difference between male and female.

Abruptly Janna looked away and forced herself to drag air into her aching lungs, wondering if she were going to faint.

*Why am I being such a goose?* she asked herself fiercely. *I've seen naked men before.*

But somehow cowboys washing off in lonely water holes and dancing Indians wearing little more than strings and flapping squares of cloth weren't the same as the powerful man sitting naked and unconcerned just a few feet away from her.

"Hey, kid," Ty said softly. "You sure you're all right? You look kind of pale."

Janna swallowed hard, twice. "I'm fine," she said huskily. "And my name is . . . Jan, not 'kid.'"

"Jan, huh?" Ty said, unwrapping his right foot carefully. "My mother's father was called Jan. He was a big Swede with a laugh you could hear in the next county. Mama used to say I took after him."

"Well, you're big enough," Janna said dryly, "but I'd keep a tight rein on the laughing until Cascabel gives up."

Ty hissed an obscenity under his breath when the strip of blanket refused to come off the sole of his foot. After a moment he added, "My name's Ty MacKenzie." He looked up at the long-legged, thin youth and smiled. "As for big, don't worry, ki—Jan. You'll start putting on height and muscle about the same time you think you need to shave."

"And pigs will fly," Janna muttered beneath her breath.

Ty heard anyway. He smiled widely and gave Janna a brotherly pat on the knee. "I felt the same way when I was your age. Thought I'd never catch up with my older brother, Logan, but I finally did. Well, almost. No one's as big as Logan. I've had one hell of a lot more luck with the ladies, though," Ty added with a wink.

The news didn't sweeten Janna's temper. She could well imagine that women would swoon over a cleaned-up version of Tyrell MacKenzie, because the beaten, dirty, naked version was giving her pulse a severe case of the jump and flutters. And that irritated her, because she was certain that she hadn't had the least effect on Ty's pulse.

*You'll start putting on height and muscle about the same time you think you need to shave.*

Grimly Janna told herself that one day she would think back on this and laugh. Someday, but definitely not today.

A small sound from Ty made Janna glance up—way up, all the way to his eyes, which were narrowed against pain. He was sweating again and his hands were pressed against his forehead as though to keep it from flying apart. Instantly she forgot her pique at not being recognized as a woman and reached to help him.

"Lie down on your back," she said, pushing against Ty's chest and supporting his head at the same time.

It was like pushing against a sun-warmed cliff.

"If you lie down, it will be easier for me to tend your cuts," Janna pointed out. "I could only get to your back last night. If I don't clean up your front, you'll get infected and feverish and be no more use in a fight than a half-starved kitten."

Ty shook his head slowly, then grimaced again.

"How's your stomach?" Janna asked, giving up for the moment on making him lie down. With deft fingers she rewrapped the bandage on his right foot. "Do you feel sick?"

"No."

She stared into the crystalline green of his eyes. Both of his pupils were the same size.

"Look into the sun for a second," she said.

Ty gave Janna a long look, then glanced overhead, where a piece of sun was peeking between thunderheads. When he looked away, she stared at his pupils intently. Both of them had contracted in response to the sun's light.

"Well? Do I have a concussion?" he asked, his voice low and amused.

"With a skull as thick as yours, I doubt it," she retorted.

"Is that a professional opinion, doctor?"

"Pa was the doctor, but he taught me a lot before he died." Janna looked at Ty's pupils again, fascinated by the clear midnight circles surrounded by such a gemlike green. "It's a good thing Indians collect scalps, not eyes. Yours would be a real prize."

Ty blinked, laughed softly, then made a low sound of pain as his own laughter hit his skull like a hammer.

"You sure your stomach is all right?" she asked.

"Yes," he said through clenched teeth. "Why?"

"You should drink to replace the blood you lost, but if you're going to throw up there's no point in wasting water. The nearest seep is a quarter mile from Cascabel's camp."

Silently Ty took the canteen Janna held out to him. He drank slowly, savoring the cool glide of water over his tongue and down his throat. After several long swallows he reluctantly lowered the canteen and handed it back. Janna shook her head, refusing the canteen. "Unless you're nauseated, drink more."

"What about you?" he asked.

"You need it more than I do."

Ty hesitated, then took a few more swallows and handed the canteen back.

"Here, chew on this while I clean the cuts on your chest," Janna said.

As she spoke, she dug a piece of beef jerky from her shirt pocket. Ty took the tough strip of dried meat, automatically reached to his waist for a knife with which to cut off a bite and realized all over again that he was naked. Before he could say anything, Janna handed him the long-bladed hunting knife she had taken from the cache. He tested the edge, nodded approvingly and sliced off a chunk of jerky with a swift, controlled motion that spoke of real expertise in using knives.

Janna cut off the cleanest corner of the blanket she could find, moistened it carefully with water from the canteen and reached toward the broad expanse of Ty's chest. At the last instant she hesitated.

"This will hurt."

Ty gave her a sidelong, amused glance. "Boy, there isn't a square inch of me that doesn't hurt."

*Boy.*

The corners of Janna's mouth turned down in displeasure, but her hands were careful as he cleaned the blood-encrusted cuts on Ty's chest. Two of them were ragged, puffy and already inflamed. She bit her lip against the pain she knew she must be causing Ty despite all her care.

"Sorry," she whispered helplessly when he grimaced.

Ty heard the distress in the youthful voice and felt like gathering that slender body into his arms and giving comfort. The thought both surprised him and made him uncomfortable. He definitely wasn't the type of man who liked boys. Abruptly he grabbed the narrow wrists and held them away from his body.

"That's good enough," he said brusquely.

"But I'm not fin—"

Janna's words ended as though cut off by a knife. Into the taut silence came the sound of a rock bouncing and rolling down the slope.

Ty's hands shifted with shocking speed. In an instant Janna found herself jerked over his body and then jammed between his broad back and the face of the cliff.

Naked and weaponless but for the knife, Ty waited to see what scrambled up over the rockfall and into the piñon-filled hollow.

# Chapter Four

A soft nicker floated through the air as a horse scrambled over the last of the rockfall and into the hollow.

"What the hell?" whispered Ty.

Janna peeked over his back. "Zebra!"

"Boy, can't you tell a horse from a zebra!"

"Better than you can tell a girl from a boy," Janna muttered.

"What?"

"Let me out," she said, pushing against Ty's back.

"Ouch!"

Instantly Janna lifted her hand and apologized. Ty grunted and moved aside so that she could crawl out over his legs. Zebra walked up to the edge of the piñon grove, pushed her head in and nickered again.

"Hello, girl," Janna said softly, rubbing the velvet muzzle. "Did you get lonesome without me?"

Zebra whuffled over Janna's fingers, nudged her hands, and kept a wary eye on Ty all the while. When he moved, her head came up and her nostrils flared.

"Be still," Janna said. "She's not used to people."

"What does she think you are?"

"A bad-smelling horse."

Ty laughed softly. The sound made Zebra's ears twitch. He began talking in a gentle, low voice.

"You've got a better nose than my daddy's best hound ever did," he said. Without looking aside he asked Janna, "How long have you owned her?"

"I don't."

"What?"

"I don't own her. She likes me, that's all. Some horses enjoy people, if you approach them the right way."

"And some horses damn near get people killed," Ty said. "I was about ten seconds away from dropping my loop on Lucifer's neck when Cascabel jumped me."

Janna's heart hesitated, then beat faster. Despite Lucifer's refusal to approach her, she thought of him somehow as her own horse. "How did you get so close to him?"

"I'm a fair tracker when I'm not half-dead," Ty said dryly.

"The shamans say that no mortal man will ever capture Lucifer. He's a spirit horse."

Ty shook his head. "That old boy is pure flesh and blood, and he sires the best colts I've seen west of the Mississippi. Lucifer's my ticket to the future that the Civil War took away from the MacKenzie family. With him I'm going to found the kind of herd that my daddy always wanted. He would have had it, too, except for the war. The four MacKenzie brothers rode off to battle on his best horses. They saved our lives more than once."

Janna saw Ty's mouth harden. He shrugged as though to throw off unhappy memories. Into the silence came the rumble of distant thunder and the scrape of branches stirring beneath a wind that smelled of moisture.

"Hope it rains soon," Ty said, looking up at the massed thunderheads. "Otherwise that big dog's tracks are going to lead Cascabel right to us."

"It will rain."

The confidence in Janna's voice made Ty turn and look at her intently.

"How do you know?" he asked.

"I just…know," she said slowly. "I've lived with the land so long that I know a lot of its secrets."

"Such as?"

"Such as—when the air over the Fire range gets an odd sort of crystal shine to it and then clouds form, it always rains about two hours before sundown. It rains hard and cold and sudden, like an ocean turned upside down and pouring back to earth. After an hour or two some of the finger canyons run twenty feet deep with water." Janna pushed away the mare's muzzle and looked at Ty. "Are you still dizzy?"

Ty wasn't surprised that his occasional dizziness had been noticed. He was discovering that not much escaped those clear gray eyes.

"Some," he admitted. "It comes and goes."

"Do you think you can get over that rockfall if I help?"

"Count on it, with or without your help."

Janna looked at the determined lines of Ty's face and the latent power in his big body and hoped he was right. The rocky hollow had been useful, but it would become a lethal trap the instant Cascabel scrambled up and found his prey. The sooner they left, the better it would be.

There was only one haven Janna could think of. It lay on the southeast side of Black Plateau, at the edge of Cascabel's ill-defined territory. It was a spirit place avoided by Indians, whose legends told of a time when the mountain had roared in anguish and split open and thick red blood had gushed forth, spirit blood that made everything burn, even stone itself. When the blood finally cooled it had become the dark, rough rock that gave Black Plateau its name. There, at the foot of ancient lava flows and sandstone cliffs, Janna had found a keyhole canyon snaking back into the solid body of the plateau. Once past the narrow entrance, the canyon widened out into a parklike area that was thick with grass and sparkling with sweet water. It was there she wintered, secure in the knowledge that no warriors or outlaws would see her tracks in the snow.

It had been her secret place, as close to a home as she had ever known. She had shared it with no one. The thought of sharing it with Ty made her feel odd. Yet there really was no other choice.

"Soon as I get you patched up," Janna said, turning to her bag of herbs, "we'll go to a keyhole canyon I know about. Nobody else has any idea that it exists, except maybe Mad Jack, and he hardly counts."

"Mad Jack? I thought he was a legend."

"He's old enough to be one."

"You've actually seen him?"

Janna dug out the herbal paste she had made during the long hours of daylight while Ty had slept. "Yes, I've seen him," she said, and began dabbing the paste on the worst of Ty's cuts.

"I've heard he has a gold mine hidden somewhere on Black Plateau."

Her hands paused, then resumed slathering on medication. "Whatever Mad Jack has or doesn't have is his business."

Ty's black eyebrows lifted at Janna's curt words. "Ouch! Watch it, boy, that's not stone you're poking."

"Sorry," she said in a tight voice.

For several moments Ty watched the gray eyes that refused to meet his.

"Hey," he said finally, catching Janna's chin in his big hand, forcing her to meet his eyes. "I'm not going to hurt that old man no matter how much gold he might have found. I'm not a thief or a raider. I'm not going to build my future on bloodstained gold."

Janna searched the green eyes that were so close to hers and saw no evasion. She remembered Ty telling her to leave him and save herself, and she remembered how he had put his own body between her and whatever danger might have been coming into the hollow. Abruptly she felt ashamed of her suspicions.

"I'm sorry," Janna said. "It's just that I've had men follow me out of town when I buy supplies with a bit of gold I've found here and there. It's usually easy enough to lose the men, but it hasn't given me a very kind opinion of human nature."

The surge of anger Ty felt at the thought of a child having to lose white men in the rocks as though they were Indian renegades surprised him. So did the protectiveness he felt toward this particular child. Uneasily it occurred to Ty that beneath the shapeless old hat and the random smears of dirt, the youth's face was . . . extraordinary.

*My God, I've seen women a hell of a lot less beautiful than this boy. Maybe the men weren't following gold, after all.*

Ty snatched his hand back as though he had been burned. The sudden movement made Zebra shy away violently.

"That damn horse is as spooky as a mustang," he said, rubbing his hand against his chest as though to remove the tactile memory of soft skin and delicate bone structure.

Janna blinked, wondering what had made Ty so irritable. She wished that he would put his hand beneath her chin again. His palm was warm and firm, his fingers were long and gentle, and it had been years since she had felt a comforting touch from another human being.

"Zebra is a mustang," Janna said huskily. "When she's not with me, she runs free."

Ty's head turned toward the mare with renewed interest. He studied her carefully, especially her hooves. They had been trimmed by stony ground rather than by a pair of steel nippers. She was sleek without being fat, strong without being big. Nowhere did she show the marks of man—no brand, no ear notch, no shoes, no rubbed places on her hide where bridle or saddle had rested.

"Do you ride her?" he asked.

"Sometimes, when it's safe."

"When is that?"

"When Cascabel isn't around," Janna said simply. "He's been around a lot the past six months, which is why Zebra is so lonesome. I guess the Army is making life hard for Cascabel."

"Or Black Hawk is tired of being blamed for Cascabel's raids and is clamping down," Ty said. "Black Hawk is a war chief and a leader. Cascabel is a butcher and a raider. Hell, I'm surprised that renegade hasn't tracked you down and cooked you over a slow fire just for the sport of it."

Janna shrugged off the implicit question. She had no intention of telling Ty that to most Utes she was Shadow of Fire, *una bruja*, a witch who walked with spirits. Ty thought of her as a boy, which was both irritating and quite useful—especially as long as he was sitting around stark naked while she rubbed medicine into his cuts.

The renewed realization of Ty's nudity brought heightened color to Janna's cheeks. It took every bit of her willpower to keep her hands from trembling as she smoothed the herb paste over his skin.

Ty noticed the fine tremor in the slender fingers and swore under his breath.

"Sorry, boy. I didn't mean to scare you," he said gruffly. "Once we get free of Cascabel, I'll take you to the Army post at Sweetwater. You'll be safe there."

Janna shook her head and said nothing, concentrating on keeping her hands from revealing the uncertain state of her emotions.

"Don't be silly," Ty said. "You might have survived out here in the past, but it's different now. The Army has been fighting Black Hawk for nearly three years, since the end of the Civil War. They've had a bellyful of fighting Utes. There will be a big campaign before winter. The Army figures to have it all wrapped up by Thanksgiving and to have Cascabel's ears in the bargain. Between Black Hawk and the soldiers fighting each other, and Cascabel killing everything that moves, it won't be safe for man nor beast here, much less a boy who's as skinny as a willow switch."

"If it's so dangerous, why are you here?"

"Lucifer," Ty said simply. "I figured this was my best chance. Once the Utes are quiet, every man with an eye for prime horseflesh will be trying for that stallion. Even if no one gets him, sure as hell some money-hungry mustanger will put a bullet through his black head just to get at his colts." Ty looked at Zebra again. "He sired her, didn't he?"

"Yes."

"It shows in her long legs and well-shaped head. The barb blood in Lucifer comes through no matter what he breeds with. Does she run with his bunch?"

"Yes."

"How did you get close to her?"

Janna wiped her fingers on her pants as she looked critically at Ty's cuts. "Her mother was a runaway ranch horse. She liked salt and grain and human company. Zebra grew up with me petting her. There are others like her in Lucifer's bunch. They accept me. After a time, so do some of the true mustangs. I take care of their cuts and scrapes and scratch the places they can't reach, and they tell me when there are men around. That's how I've kept away from Cascabel. Lucifer can smell him a mile off."

"Does Lucifer let you pet him?" Ty asked intently.

"He's as wild as a storm wind," Janna said, not answering the question.

"So is that one," Ty said, looking at Zebra, "but she followed your trail like a tame old hound dog. Will the next horse through that gap be Lucifer?"

"No. I've survived by being inconspicuous. Anyone standing next to Lucifer would be as conspicuous as lightning."

Thunder belled suddenly, but Ty didn't look away from Janna's face.

"Have you ever tried to get close to Lucifer?"

"No."

"Why not? Is he a killer?"

Janna shrugged. "Wouldn't you try to kill a man who wanted to put you in a cage?"

"Horses have been bred by men for thousands and thousands of years. It's a partnership, like men and dogs."

"Not to a lot of men."

"Those same men are cruel to other men. I'm not. I don't fight for the pleasure of it, but to get the job done."

Janna looked at her knife, which Ty kept within easy reach at all times. She remembered how he had held the knife—as a weapon, not as a tool. There was no doubt in her mind that he could "get the job done" better than any man she had ever seen, except Cascabel.

The realization should have frightened her, for despite Ty's injuries he was far stronger than she was. Yet she was no more frightened of him than she was of Lucifer. In the past her instincts had proven to be very good at picking up the presence of senseless viciousness or cruelty; she sensed none in either Ty or the big black stallion so many men longed to own.

*But what if I'm wrong this time? What if Ty is just another man greedy for whatever he can get from those weaker than he is?*

There was no answer to Janna's silent question but the obvious one—if she took Ty to her private refuge and discovered there that she had been wrong about his essential decency, she would have made the worst mistake of her life.

And probably the last, as well.

# Chapter Five

The sudden downpour of cold rain was like a blow. In spite of that, the rain was welcome, for it would wash away Ty and Janna's trail.

"Ready?" Janna asked.

Ty nodded grimly. He was still angry at having lost the battle of the shrinking blanket. Over his objections Janna had cut the blanket up into a breechcloth, bandages for his bruised ribs and a makeshift poncho. He hadn't objected to the breechcloth, had given in on the bandages, but had been damned if he would wear a blanket while a child ran around with no more protection against the thunderstorm than a ragged shirt and pants.

Yet here he was, wearing the blanket; and there the kid was, wearing only a shirt and pants.

"Stubborn as a Missouri mule," Ty snarled, but his words were drowned out by thunder.

Zebra took the lightning, thunder and pelting rain with the indifference of a horse born and raised out in the open. She watched with interest as Ty and Janna negotiated the rocky rubble at the head of the hollow. While the mustang wasn't completely relaxed around Ty, she no longer shied at his every movement.

It was a good thing. Ty made some very sudden movements as he clawed over the rockfall, hobbled by his injuries and the increasing slickness of the rocks. Though he said nothing, he was grateful that his ribs were bound, despite the fact that it made breathing deeply impossible. He was also grateful for the small, surprisingly strong hands that helped to lever him over the tricky places—although he had nearly yelped with surprise the first time he had received a firm boost from behind.

Janna passed Ty just beneath the crest of the rockfall. She motioned with her hand for him to wait. When he sank into a sitting position, she peered through a crevice between two rocks. All but the first two hundred feet of the slope was veiled in sheets of rain. In the stretch of land that she could see, nothing moved but rain itself. She turned and went back to Ty.

"How do your feet feel?"

He gave her a slanting glance. "You saw them. How do you think they feel?"

"Worse than your ribs and better than your head," Janna said succinctly.

Ty grunted and began to struggle to his feet once more.

She bent, put both of her hands around his right arm just beneath his shoulder and steadied him as he came to his feet. The hissing intake of his breath, the pallor of his skin and the clenched iron of the muscles beneath her hands told Janna just how painful it was for Ty to stand on his raw feet. There was no help for it, though. There would never be a better time to exit the hollow without attracting Cascabel's notice.

By the time Janna and Ty had climbed up and over the rockfall, both of them were sweating in spite of the cold rain pouring over their bodies. Though Ty was breathing hard and fast, he didn't suggest a rest. The slope was too exposed. One of Cascabel's renegades—or a bolt of lightning—could find them at any moment.

Behind Ty and Janna came the clatter and slide of stones as the mustang scrambled over a slope Ty would have sworn

a donkey would refuse. But then, he had watched in disbelief while Lucifer's band took worse countryside at a dead
run in order to escape from men, including one Tyrell
MacKenzie. The horses that weren't fast enough were
caught. The remainder ran free to give birth to another
generation of fleet, agile mustangs.

When the steepest part of the slope had been negotiated,
Janna stopped and looked over her shoulder. Zebra was
following close behind, watching the humans' progress with
interest, pausing from time to time to sniff the strange mixture of sweat and herbal odors that Ty gave off. On the
whole, the mare was rather intrigued by his smell.

"She likes you," Janna said.

"She ought to. I smell like the warm mash Daddy used to
give his favorite brood mares."

Janna smiled. "Can you ride bareback?"

Ty gave Janna a disbelieving look. "What do you think I
am, a greenhorn? Of course I can ride bareback."

"Let me rephrase that. Can you ride Zebra without a
saddle or a bridle?"

"Boy," Ty said, shifting his position in a vain attempt to
ease the searing pain in his feet and the throbbing in his head
and ribs, "this is a piss poor time for me to be breaking a
mustang."

"I've ridden Zebra a lot. She likes it."

Ty looked skeptical.

Janna made an exasperated sound, dropped her hold on
Ty and went to the mare. She grabbed a double handful of
thick mane and swung onto Zebra's back. The horse didn't
even switch her tail, much less offer to buck. When Janna
urged her forward until she stood next to Ty, the mustang
responded as placidly as a plow horse.

"Pet her," Janna said.

Zebra flinched at the strange hand reaching up to her
neck, but Ty's low, reassuring voice and gentle touch soon
calmed the mare. After a few minutes she sighed and low-

ered her head until she could use Ty's chest as a shield
against the cold rain. Smiling slightly despite his pain, he
rubbed the base of the mare's ears, scratching all the itchy
spots a horse couldn't reach for itself.

As Janna watched Ty's big, careful hands caressing the
mare so skillfully, an odd feeling shimmered in the pit of her
stomach. She wondered what it would be like if he stroked
her half as gently as he was stroking Zebra. The thought
brought a tingling that spread out from her stomach to her
fingertips, making her shiver. With a quick motion she slid
off the horse. In her haste she landed so close to Ty that she
had to catch her balance against his bare, rain-chilled thigh.
Instantly she snatched back her hand.

"I'll help you on," Janna said, then added quickly, "I
know you could do it alone, but there's no point in putting
any more strain on your ribs than you have to."

"Five will get you ten that your mustang bucks me off
into the rocks," Ty said.

"She's never bucked with me."

"She's never had a man on her back instead of a skinny
boy."

*Boy.*

"Listen," Janna said through gritted teeth, very tired of
hearing herself described as a boy, "it's at least twenty miles
to my winter camp. You can walk, you can ride, or you can
freeze to death right here while you make smart remarks
about my lack of muscle."

"Easy, girl," Ty said softly.

For an instant Janna thought he was talking to her; then
she realized that he had taken a good grip on Zebra's mane
and was looking over his shoulder toward the "skinny boy."

"Well?" Ty asked. "You waiting for me to freeze to
death?"

"Don't tempt me," Janna muttered.

She braced herself, cupped her hands to make a stirrup
and prepared to help Ty onto the mare. A few seconds later

Janna was looking up at him in surprise. He had moved so quickly that she had barely felt his weight before it was gone. Zebra looked around in surprise as well, for she had been expecting Janna's light weight. But instead of mounting the horse, Janna stood with her hand on Zebra's muzzle in a steady pressure that was a signal to stand quietly. The mare snorted uneasily, then stood still, adjusting to the strange weight on her back.

"You're very quick for such a big man," Janna said.

For the space of a few breaths Ty was in too much pain to answer. When he did look down he had to fight the impulse to cup his hand caressingly beneath that delicate chin. The eyes looking back up at him were as clear as rain and a lot warmer... the eyes of a woman experiencing the slow unfolding of desire.

*Pain is making me crazy,* Ty told himself in disgust. *That's a boy looking up at me, not a girl, and he's got a bad case of hero worship. Poor kid must be lonely as hell, living with only wild horses for companionship.*

"And you owe me ten dollars," Janna added.

"What?"

"Zebra didn't buck you off into the rocks."

"You'll have to collect from Cascabel. He stole my money along with my hat, boots, guns and clothes."

"And your horse."

Ty's mouth flattened. "He shot Blackbird out from under me. That was the only way Cascabel caught me. Blackbird was half-thoroughbred and all heart."

"I'm sorry," Janna said, resting her hand on Ty's leg in an impulsive gesture of comfort.

At first touch his skin was cold, yet within moments the vital heat of him flowed up and warmed her palm. After a time Janna realized she was staring up at Ty, and had been for too long. She snatched back her hand and turned away, heading down the steep slope to the flatter land beyond the plateau's face. She would have to take a looping route to her secret canyon, for the base of the plateau itself was too rugged to travel along in anything approaching a straight line.

Zebra followed Janna without guidance, which was just as well. After the first four miles Ty was no longer in shape to give directions. The pounding in his head alternated with twisting strikes of agony from his ribs. The blanket was some protection against cold, but not nearly enough. He was shivering before a mile had passed beneath the mustang's agile, untrimmed hooves.

During the first hours Janna turned and looked over her shoulder every few minutes to reassure herself that Ty was all right. The farther they went, the more he slumped over Zebra's neck. Janna kept on going because there was no other choice. She had to get Ty to a place of safety.

Rain pelted down in an unceasing, cold barrage. Behind the clouds the sun slowly set, its passage marked only by a gradual lowering of the level of light. A wind sprang up soon after sunset, tearing apart the storm until only brief, hard showers remained. Through great rents in the clouds a brilliant half-moon shone forth. The wind concealed and then revealed the moon again, weaving intricate patterns of darkness and light.

Shivering, tired, worried about Ty's strength and his ability to endure any more pain, Janna forced herself to keep going, knowing that that was all she could do to help him. She walked quickly despite her own weariness, using the familiar silhouettes of buttes and mesas looming against the night sky as her landmarks. The moon had crossed more than half of its arc before she stopped and looked toward the bulky, ragged outline of the plateau whose north and east flanks she had been skirting through the long hours of darkness.

The long, sloping outwash plain glittered with rills and shallow streams as Black Plateau shed water from the recent storm. A branch of that network of shifting, gleaming temporary streams led to her hidden canyon. She hoped that there would be enough water in that temporary stream to hide her tracks, but not so much that it would be dangerous to go through the narrow slot that led to the concealed valley. She hoped, but she had no way of knowing until she got there. Everything depended on how much rain had fallen on this side of Black Plateau.

Until now Janna had made little effort to conceal her trail, hoping that the violent, intermittent showers would wash out enough of her tracks to confuse any pursuer. But now she was within four miles of her hidden valley. She could take no chance that a wandering renegade would come across her tracks and follow them to the tiny slot carved by time and water into the side of Black Plateau.

Resolutely Janna turned toward the nearest shallow wash and began wading. Zebra watched, then calmly paced alongside—beyond the reach of water. Janna waded farther out. Zebra kept walking along the edge of the runoff stream. Finally Janna waded back toward the horse.

"Ty?"

There was no answer.

For an instant Janna's heart stopped. She ran up and saw Ty slumped over Zebra's neck, his hands twisted into her mane. He seemed to be asleep.

"Ty?" she asked, pressing against his arm. "Zebra has to walk in the water."

Slowly he straightened. She looked up at him anxiously. As she watched, he began to slump again. Obviously he wouldn't be able to guide the mustang. Nor could Janna lead her; she had never put a rope on Zebra, so the mare wouldn't have the least idea how to respond.

"I hope you don't mind riding double," Janna said to Zebra. "Stand quiet, girl. It will be a big load for you, but it's the only way I'll be able to hide your tracks."

Janna grabbed the horse's long mane in her left hand and tried to swing around Ty and up onto the mare's back. It was an awkward mount that was saved from disaster only when Ty wrapped his arm around Janna and heaved her into place. The groan that ripped through him at the effort told her more than she wanted to know about the condition of his ribs.

Zebra sidestepped, almost unseating both riders. Janna spoke reassuringly and sat very still, letting the mare become accustomed to the added weight. When Zebra settled down, Janna nudged her lightly with her heels. The horse moved awkwardly for a few minutes, then settled back into her normal rhythmic walk. Ty slumped forward once more, keeping his seat by instinct, experience and sheer determination.

"Hang on, Ty. We're almost there."

It was a lie, but it was more helpful than the truth, which was that they had a lot of hard going left—and no assurance at all that the slot wouldn't be choked with floodwaters when they finally arrived.

# Chapter Six

Ty awoke with the sun shining right onto his face and the familiar sound of a horse cropping grass nearby. As he turned to check on Blackbird, pain brought back all the memories—his horse's death and his own capture, Cascabel and the gauntlet, pain and running endlessly, and the gray-eyed waif who had patched up his wounds. Vaguely Ty remembered getting on a zebra dun and riding until he was quite certain he had died and gone to hell.

Except that this wasn't hell. True enough, the overhang he lay beneath was hot red stone, but the canyon floor was lush with the kind of vegetation that only came from water. Definitely not a flaming hell. In fact, with the sun's warmth and the lazy humming of insects and the calling of birds, this could only be a slice of heaven.

Automatically Ty sat up to have a better look around. Pain and dizziness struck, chaining him in place, forcing him to revise his opinion of where he was. Eyes closed, his weight braced on his elbows, he decided that the valley might be in heaven, but his body was indeed in hell.

"Lie down, Ty. You've been sick."

He opened his eyes. Gray eyes watched him with concern. Without thinking, Ty shifted his weight until he could raise his hand to touch the cheek that was so close to his.

The skin was smooth and fine grained, as soft as an angel's wing.

"It's all right," he said fuzzily. "I'm fine now."

"Lie down," Janna said, pressing against his bare shoulders.

It did no good. He remained as he was, propped half-upright on his elbow.

"Please, Ty," Janna said, her voice husky with emotion. "Lie down. The fever's broken and you're much better, but you need to rest."

"Thirsty," he mumbled.

Instantly Janna grabbed a canteen, poured a stream of amber, herbal-smelling tea into a tin cup and helped Ty to drink. The taste of the liquid brought back other memories. He had drunk from this cup many times, with slender hands holding him upright and then easing him back down and stroking him until he fell once more into feverish sleep.

Sighing deeply, Ty allowed Janna to help him to lie down again.

"How long?" he asked.

"How long have we been here?"

He nodded slightly.

"Four days."

His eyes opened.

"You've been sick," Janna explained. "You caught a chill riding through the rain. That, plus your injuries from the gauntlet…" Her voice died. Automatically she reached forward and brushed back the slightly curly lock of black hair that had fallen over Ty's forehead.

Ty flinched from the touch and looked Janna over with narrowed green eyes. "You don't look so good yourself. You're skinnier than ever. If you don't take better care of yourself, you'll never get tall and put on muscle."

"Not all men are built like a side of beef," Janna retorted, hurt because Ty had refused her touch. She reached into the herb pouch, brought out a twist of paper and sprinkled the white powder into another cup of the herbal tea. "Here. Drink this."

"What is it?"

"Poison."

"Fresh as paint, aren't you, boy?"

"You're half-right," Janna muttered, but she said it so softly that Ty couldn't hear. She silently vowed that she would make him see which half of the truth he knew—and that he would be crazy with desire before he figured it out.

Ty drank the contents of the cup, grimaced and gave his companion a green-eyed glare. "Tastes like horse piss."

"I'll take your word for it, having never tasted that particular liquid."

Ty laughed, grabbed his left side and groaned. "Damn. Feels like a mule kicked me."

"It won't be so bad in a few minutes," she said, standing up. "Then I'll unwrap the bandages and take another look."

"Where are you going?"

"To check on the soup."

The thought of food made Ty's salivary glands contract in anticipation.

"Hungry?" she asked wryly, recognizing the look.

"I could eat a horse."

"Then I'd better warn Zebra to stay away from you."

"That old pony would be too tough to eat," Ty drawled, smiling slowly as he relaxed against the folded blankets beneath him.

Janna watched from a distance while Ty's eyelids closed and the taut lines around his eyes relaxed as he drifted into sleep. Only then did she return to his side, kneel and pull up the blanket so that his shoulders were covered once more. Even with the overhang of red rock to reflect back the sun's heat, she was afraid of his catching another chill. She didn't know what she would do if he became ill again. She was exhausted from broken sleep or no sleep at all, and from worrying that she had helped Ty to escape from renegades only to kill him by dragging him through a cold rain into the secret valley.

These had been the longest days of Janna's life since her father had died five years before, leaving his fourteen-year-old daughter orphaned and alone at a muddy water hole in southern Arizona. Watching Ty battle injury and fever had drained Janna's very soul. He had been so hot, then drenched in cold sweat, then hot and restless once more, calling out names of people she didn't know, fighting battles she had never heard of, crying out in anguish over dead comrades. She had tried to soothe and comfort him, had held him close in the cold hours before dawn, had bathed his big body in cool water when he was too hot and had warmed him with her own heat when he was too cold.

And now Ty flinched from her touch.

*Don't be foolish,* Janna told herself as she watched Ty sleep for a few moments longer. *He doesn't remember anything. He thinks you're a skinny boy. No wonder he didn't want you petting him.* And then, *How can he be so blasted blind as not to see past these clothes?*

As Janna went to the small campfire to check on the soup, she couldn't help wondering if Ty would have responded differently if he had known she was a girl.

Her intense desire that he see her as a woman caught her on the raw. She knew she was becoming too attached to the stranger whom chance had dropped into her life. As soon as Ty was healed he would leave with as little warning as he had come, going off to pursue his own dreams. He was just one more man hungry for gold or for the glory of being the person to tame the spirit horse known as Lucifer.

And he was too damned thickheaded to see past the skinny boy to the lonely woman.

*Lonely?*

Janna's hand froze in the act of stirring the soup. She had been alone for years but had never thought of herself as lonely. The horses had been her companions, the wind her music, the land her mentor, and her father's books had opened a hundred worlds of the mind to her. If she found herself yearning for another human voice, she had gone into Sweetwater or Hat Rock or Indian Springs. Each time she went into any of the outposts of civilization, she had left after only a few hours, driven out by the greedy eyes of the men who watched her pay for her purchases with tiny pieces of raw gold—men who, unlike Ty, had sometimes seen past Janna's boyish appearance.

Gloomily Janna studied the soup as it bubbled and announced its readiness in the blended fragrances of meat, herbs and vegetables. She poured some soup into her steep-sided tin plate and waited until it cooled somewhat. When she was sure the soup wouldn't burn Ty's mouth, she picked up her spoon and went to the overhang.

He was still asleep, yet there was an indefinable change in his body that told her Ty was healing even as she watched. He was much stronger than her consumptive father had been. Though Ty's bruises were spectacular, they were already smaller than they had been a few days before. The flesh covering his ribs was no longer swollen. Nor was his head where a club had struck.

*Thick muscles and an even thicker skull,* Janna told herself sarcastically.

As though he knew he were being watched, Ty opened his eyes. Their jeweled green clarity both reassured and disturbed Janna. She was glad that he was no longer dazed by fever, yet being the focus of those eyes was a bit unnerving. He might have been just one more gold- and horse-hungry man, but he had the strength, intelligence and determination to succeed where other men never got past the point of daydreaming.

"Are you still hungry?" Janna asked, her voice low and husky.

"Did you cook up poor old Zebra for me?"

The slow smile that followed Ty's words made Janna's nerve endings shimmer. Even covered with beard stubble and lying flat on his back, Ty was one of the most handsome men she had ever seen.

"No," Janna said, smiling in return. "She was too big for my pot." With unconscious grace, Janna sank to her knees next to Ty, balancing the tin plate in her hands without spilling a drop. "A few weeks back I traded a packet of dried herbs, three letters and a reading of *A Midsummer Night's Dream* for thirty pounds of jerked beef."

Ty blinked. "I beg your pardon?"

Janna laughed softly. "I'll tell you while I feed you soup. Can you sit up?"

Cautiously, then with greater assurance, Ty sat up. He started to say that he could feed himself before he realized that he was light-headed. He propped his back against the gently sloping stone cliff that was both wall and, eventually, ceiling to the natural shelter. The blanket covering him slid from his shoulders, down his chest, and finally rumpled across his lap.

Janna's pulse gave an odd little skip at the sight of the dark, masculine patterns of hair curling out from beneath Ty's bandages and down his muscular body. The temptation to trace those patterns with her fingertips was almost overwhelming.

*Don't be a goose,* she told herself firmly. *I've been washing, feeding and caring for Ty like a baby for four days. I've seen him wearing nothing but sunlight and soapy water, so why on earth am I getting all foolish and shivery now?*

*Because he's awake now, that's why.*

Ty looked down at his own body, wondering why he was being stared at. What he saw made him wince. Spreading out from beneath his rib bandage were bruises every color of the rainbow, but the predominant hues were black and blue with garish flourishes of green.

"I'm a sight, aren't I?" Ty asked wryly. "Looks worse than it feels, though. Whatever medicine you've been using works real well."

Janna closed her eyes for an instant, then looked only at the plate of soup in her hands. The surface of the liquid was disturbed by delicate rings, the result of the almost invisible trembling of her hands while she had looked at Ty.

"Don't go all pale on me now, boy. You must have seen worse than me."

*Boy.*

*And thank God for it,* Janna reminded herself instantly. *I have no more sense than a handful of sand when he looks at me and smiles that slow, devil-take-it smile.*

*But, God, I do wish he knew I was a woman!*

She took a deep, secret breath and brought her scattering emotions under control.

"Ready?" she asked, dipping the spoon into the soup.

"I was born ready."

She put the spoon into Ty's mouth, felt the gentle resistance of lips and tongue cleaning the spoon, and nearly dropped the plate of soup. He didn't notice, for the taste of the soup had surprised him.

"That's good."

"You needn't sound so shocked," she muttered.

"After that horse piss you've been feeding me, I didn't know what to expect."

"That was medicine. This is food."

"Food's the best medicine save one for what ails a man."

"Oh? What's the best?"

Ty smiled slowly. "When you're a man you won't have to ask."

The spoon clicked rather forcefully against Ty's teeth.

"Sorry," Janna said with transparent insincerity.

"Don't look so surly, boy. I felt the same way you did when I was your age. You'll grow into manhood with time."

"How old do you think I am?"

"Oh . . . thirteen?"

"Don't try to be kind," she said between her teeth.

"Hell, boy, you look closer to twelve with those soft cheeks and fine bones, and you know it. But that will begin to change about the time your voice cracks. It just takes time."

Janna knew that there would never be enough time in the whole world for her to grow into a man, but she had just enough common sense and self-control to keep that revealing bit of truth to herself. With steady motions she shoveled soup into Ty's mouth.

"You trying to drown me?" he asked, taking the soup from her. "I'll feed myself, thanks." He crunched through a pale root of some kind, started to ask what it was, then decided not to. The first thing a man on the trail learned was that if it tastes good, don't ask what it is. Just be grateful and eat fast. "What's this about herbs and Shakespeare and letters?" he asked between mouthfuls of soup.

"My father and I used to divide up a play and read parts to each other. It helped to pass the time on the trail. I still have a trunk of his books," Janna said, helplessly watching the tip of Ty's tongue lick up stray drops of broth. "When I need supplies, I'll go to the Lazy A or the Circle G and write letters for the cowhands. Most of them can't read anything but brands, so I'll also read whatever letters they've saved up until someone like me happens by."

Ty looked at the thick, dark lashes, crystalline eyes and delicately structured face of the youth who was much too pretty for Ty's comfort. "Where did you go to school?" he asked roughly.

"On the front seat of a buckboard. Papa had a university degree and a case of wanderlust."

"What about your mother?"

"She died when I was three. Papa told me her body just wasn't up to the demands of her spirit."

The spoon hesitated on the way to Ty's mouth. He pinned Janna with an intense glance. "When did your Daddy die?"

Janna paused for an instant, thinking quickly. If she told Ty her father had died five years before, he would ask how a kid under ten had survived on his own. If she told Ty that she was nineteen, he would realize that the only way a nineteen-year-old boy could lack a deep voice and a beard shadow and muscles was if said boy were a girl wearing men's clothing. She wanted Ty to figure that out for himself—the hard way.

"Papa died a few seasons back," she said casually. "You lose track of time living alone."

"You've lived alone since then?" Ty asked, startled. "The whole time?"

Janna nodded.

"Don't you have any kin?"

"No."

"Wouldn't any of the townspeople let you trade room and board for work?"

"I don't like towns."

"Surely one of the ranches would take you on as a cook's helper or fence rider. Hell, if you can tame a mustang, there isn't a ranch anywhere that wouldn't take you on as a mustanger," Ty added, disturbed at the thought of an orphaned child wandering homeless over the land. "You could make a decent living catching and breaking horses for the rough string."

"I don't catch mustangs," Janna said flatly. "Too many of them refuse to eat once they're caught. I've seen them starve to death looking over a corral fence with glazed eyes."

"Most mustangs accept men."

Janna simply shook her head. "I won't take a mustang's freedom. I've gentled a few ranch-bred horses for women's mounts or for kids, but that's all."

"Sometimes a man has to do things he doesn't want to in order to survive," Ty said, his eyes narrowed against painful memories.

"I've been lucky so far," Janna said quietly. "More soup?"

Slowly, as though called back from a distance, Ty focused on Janna. "Thanks, I'd like that," he said, handing over the plate. "While I eat, would you mind reading to me?"

"Not at all. Anything in particular you want to hear?"

"Do you have *Romeo and Juliet*?"

"Yes."

"Then read to me about a woman more beautiful than the dawn." Ty closed his eyes and smiled. "A well-bred lady of silk, softer than a summer breeze, with pale hair and skin whiter than magnolias, and delicate hands that have never done anything more harsh than coax Chopin from a huge grand piano..."

"What's her name?" Janna asked tightly.

"Who?"

"The silk lady you're describing."

"Silver MacKenzie, my brother's wife." Ty's eyes opened, clear and hard. "But there are other women like her in England. I'm going to get one."

Abruptly Janna came to her feet. She returned a few minutes later with a heavy book tucked under her left arm and carrying a bowl of soup with her right hand. She gave Ty the soup, opened the worn book to *Romeo and Juliet*, Act II, Scene II, and began to read:

"'But, soft! What light through yonder window breaks?
It is the East, and Juliet is the sun...'"

# Chapter Seven

That day set the pattern for the next two weeks. When Janna thought Ty had been pushing himself too hard in his efforts to regain full strength, she would bring out the Bible or the Shakespearean plays or the poetry of Dante, Milton or Pope, and she would read aloud. Ty saw through what she was doing, but didn't object. He had too much fun teasing "the boy" over the real meaning of the words in *The Song of Solomon* or Pope's *The Rape of the Lock*.

"Read that verse to me again," Ty said, smiling. "You ran over it so fast I missed most of the words."

Janna tilted her head down to the worn pages of the Bible and muttered, " 'Vanity of vanities . . . all *is* vanity.' "

"That's Ecclesiastes," Ty drawled. "You were reading *The Song of Solomon* and a woman was talking about her sweetheart. 'My beloved is gone down into his garden, to the beds of spices, to feed in the gardens . . .' Now what do you suppose that really means, boy?"

"He was hungry," Janna said succinctly.

"Ah, but for what?" Ty asked, stretching. "When you know the answer, you'll be a man no matter what your size or age."

Janna looked at Ty's long, muscular arms and the smooth give-and-take of his skin over his chest and torso and vowed again that she would go into Sweetwater first thing tomorrow and get Ty some clothes. She wasn't going to be able to look at him running around in a breechcloth much longer without reaching out and running her hands over all that tempting masculine hide.

The thought of Ty's shocked expression if she gave in to temptation restored her humor. It would be worth almost anything to see him shocked. Until that time came, she would have to be satisfied with watching his unease when she leaned too close or casually brushed against him, making him uncomfortable because of "the boy's" closeness.

When Ty saw Janna's full lips curve into a slow, almost hidden smile, he felt a jolt of something uncomfortably close to desire lance through him.

*That boy is too damned feminine for my self-respect, much less for my peace of mind. I think I'd better take another long soak in that hot pool in the head of the valley. Doubt that it will take the starch out of me, though. I haven't been this hungry since I was fourteen. Dammit, but I need a woman.*

Disgusted with himself, Ty came to his feet in a muscular rush. Janna was so surprised by the abrupt movement that she dropped the book she was holding. A sheet of paper that had been held safely between the pages fluttered out. Ty scooped it up before Janna could. He looked at the paper and let out a low whistle of admiration.

"Now there is a real lady," Ty said, gazing at the drawing of a woman in long, formal dress and elaborately coiffed hair. "Elegance like that is damned rare. Where did you get this?"

"Papa drew it when Mother was alive."

"This is your mother?"

Janna nodded.

"I see where you get your fine bones and . . ."

Ty's voice died. There was no point in telling the kid that his mouth would have done credit to a courtesan and his eyes were too big and too expressive to belong to a boy of any age. So Ty kept his mind on the drawing and off the fey creature whose skin and hair smelled like a meadow drenched in sunshine and warmth.

"Your daddy was a lucky man," Ty said after looking at the drawing for a long time. "This is a woman to dream on. All silk and sweet softness. After I catch Lucifer and build my own horse herd, I'm going to Europe and court a fine lady just like this. I'll marry her and bring her home, and we'll raise strong sons and silky daughters."

"Silk doesn't last long on the frontier," Janna said stiffly.

Ty laughed. "That's why I'm going to build my fortune first. I'd never ask a true lady to live in a dirt-floored shack and ruin her soft hands on scrub brushes and the like."

Janna looked at her hands. While not rough, they weren't exactly silky, either. "Soft isn't everything."

Ty shook his head, seeing only his dream. "It is in a woman. I'll have my silken lady or I'll have none at all for longer than it takes to pleasure myself."

The words sliced into Janna like knives, wounding her. The pain she felt shocked her, and the rage, and the sense of ... betrayal.

"What makes you think that a silken woman would have a man like you?" Janna asked coolly.

Ty smiled to himself. "Women kind of take to me, especially when I'm cleaned up a bit."

"Huh," she sniffed. "I don't think there's enough cleaning time between now and Christmas to make any fancy woman look at you twice."

Before Ty could say anything, Zebra whinnied in alarm. Even as he turned toward the sound, Ty yanked Janna to the ground and pulled out the hunting knife he wore at his waist. An instant later his big body half covered hers, pinning her against the earth.

"Don't move," Ty breathed against Janna's ear, his voice a mere thread of sound.

Janna nodded slightly. She felt Ty's weight shift as he rolled aside. There was a flash of tanned skin in the tall grass, a suggestion of movement in the streamside willows, and then nothing more. Ty had vanished. A shiver went over Janna as she realized how very quick Ty was now that he was well, and how powerful. She thought of wiggling backward until she was in better cover, then discarded the idea. Ty would expect her to be where he had left her—and he would attack anything that moved anywhere else. That thought was enough to rivet her in place.

The willows slid soundlessly past Ty's nearly naked body as he eased through the streamside thickets. The creek was no more than a few feet wide and still slightly warm from its birth in a hot springs back at the head of the small valley, a place where lava and red rock and lush greenery entwined in a steamy Eden whose water contained a sulfurous whiff of hell.

Nothing moved in the willows around Ty, nor was there any sound of birds. The silence was a warning in itself. Normally small birds darted and sang in the valley, enjoying the rare presence of water in a dry land. If the wildlife were quiet, it meant that an intruder was nearby.

Fifty yards away, belly-deep in grass, Zebra snorted. The sound was followed by a drumroll of hooves as the mare fled. The mustang's flight told Ty that the intruder was either a cougar or a man. Nothing else would have sent the horse racing away in fear. Without disturbing the thick screen of willow branches, Ty looked out into the valley. Zebra was standing seventy yards away with every muscle quivering and poised for flight. Her head was high and her black ears were pricked forward. She was looking at something that was well downstream from Ty.

*Something just came out of the slot. Which direction is the intruder going, girl? Is he going for the hot springs at the north end or the Indian ruins at the south end?*

Motionless, Ty watched the mare, knowing that she would track the intruder better than he ever would have been able to with mere human senses. Zebra kept her head and ears up, watching something that he couldn't see. Slowly her head turned toward Ty.

*All right. The intruder is coming toward me.*

Mentally Ty reviewed the small, irregularly shaped valley. Barely more than a mile long, never more than a quarter of a mile wide, the valley was walled in by red sandstone on one side and black lava on the other. The hot springs at the north end fed the small stream. Other watercourses joined the stream at various points of the valley, but they held water only after heavy rains, when cliffs wore lacy waterfalls that were as beautiful as they were short-lived.

Ty decided that the best point for an ambush was right where he was. A very faint trail wound between the edge of the willows and the ancient lava flow that all but cut the valley in two. Anything trying to reach the head of the valley would be forced to walk between the willow thicket and the cliff. All Ty had to do was be very still and watch what passed within reach.

Motionless, poised for attack, Ty waited as he had waited too many times before.

*Wish Logan were here. A man's unprotected back gets real itchy at times like this.*

But Logan was in Wyoming with Silver. As for his other brothers, the last Ty had heard, both Case and Duncan were looking for gold with Blue Wolf, trying to repair the MacKenzie family fortunes and make a future for themselves. At least, that's what Duncan was doing. No one but God—more likely, the devil—knew what went on in Case's mind. Fighting in the war had closed Ty's youngest brother up tighter than bark on a tree.

A few minutes later Ty heard the faint sounds of a man's progress through the tall grass. When the sounds passed the willows where Ty hid, he came out in a silent rush. One arm hooked around the intruder's neck from behind as the knife sliced upward in a lethal arc.

At the last instant Ty realized that the man was old and unarmed. He pulled the knife aside.

"Who are you?" Ty asked quietly, holding the blade across the man's throat.

"John Turner. And I'm right glad you ain't an Injun or a bandit. I'd be dead by now."

Ty didn't bother to make welcoming sounds. "Walk ahead of me toward that red cliff. Don't hesitate or turn around. If you make a wrong move I'll kill you."

# Chapter Eight

Ty followed close behind the intruder, but not so close that a sudden turn and lunge would have caught him off guard. A few minutes later they walked up to the edge of Janna's hidden camp.

"All right, kid. Come on out," Ty said.

Janna stood up. "How many times do I have to tell you that my name isn't kid, it's—oh, hello, Jack. Did you run out of stomach medicine already?"

The old man didn't answer, because Ty's knife was resting once more against his throat.

"You told me your name was John Turner," Ty said.

"'Tis, but most folks call me Mad Jack."

Ty looked over at Janna.

She nodded. "It's all right, Ty. Jack was Papa's friend."

Ty lowered the knife. Mad Jack turned and spat a thin stream of brown liquid toward a nearby bush.

"Her pa staked me. We was partners," Mad Jack said, shifting the cud of tobacco to the other side of his mouth. "He cashed in his chips a few years back, but I ain't done with the game yet." He looked at Janna. "Brung you some more gold, but you wasn't in any of the old places."

"It wasn't safe anymore. Cascabel's new camp was too close."

"Yeah, them pony soldiers have made that old rattle-snake's life pure hell this summer." Mad Jack shucked off his backpack, untied a flap and pulled out a fat leather bag that fit in his hand. "Figured you'd need to lay in some winter supplies. From the size of your young buck, I shoulda brung two pokes of gold."

"How has your stomach been?" Janna asked hurriedly, wanting to get off the subject of her "young buck."

"Middlin'," Mad Jack said, shifting the wad of tobacco again. "How 'bout you, Janna? You be all right? You come early to your winter-over place."

"Ty was injured," Janna said. She glanced briefly at him and prayed without much hope that he would ignore the difference between the names Janna and Jan. "He ran Cascabel's gauntlet and got away."

Mad Jack turned and looked at Ty as though for the first time. "So you're the one, huh?" The old man's chuckle was a dry, rustling sound. "Made Cascabel the laughing-stock of the Utes. Black Hawk ever finds you, he'll like as not give you a medal 'fore he lifts your hair. How'd you hitch up with Janna?"

The second time Ty heard the name Janna, he knew it hadn't been a slip of the old prospector's tongue. Ty turned and looked at the "boy" with narrowed green eyes. After an instant the "boy" began to study the ground as though it were alive and likely to start nibbling on toes at any instant.

"Janna, huh?" Ty asked. "Is that your real name, kid?"

She threw him a quick, sideways glance, looked away and nodded very slightly.

Ty's right hand flashed out as he yanked off the floppy old hat Janna always wore. Two long, thick, Indian-style braids fell down her back. The braids were tied with leather thongs. An Indian band went around her forehead and tied in back, keeping any stray locks from escaping the hat's confinement. Her hair was a dark auburn that shimmered with unexpected fire whenever her head moved. In contrast with the darkness of her hair, the pale, crystalline depths of her eyes looked as brilliant as diamonds. The delicacy of her bone structure and the fine-grained texture of her skin seemed to taunt him for his blindness.

"Well, kid," drawled Ty, narrow eyed, furious with himself for having been deceived and with her for having deceived him, "I'll say this—you made a prettier boy than you do a girl."

Mad Jack's rustling chuckle did nothing to make Ty feel better. He flipped the hat over Janna's head and pulled down hard, covering her to her nostrils.

"Fooled ya, did she?" Mad Jack asked, slapping his hands together in pleasure. "Don't feel bad, son. That's a right clever gal. She's got the Indians believing she a *bruja*— a witch—and the mustangs believing she's just a funny kind of two-legged horse."

Ty grunted.

"'Course," Mad Jack continued, looking at Ty's nearly bare, tanned body, "a body what runs around near naked and sneaks up on folks might be accused of tryin' to make folks think he's an Injun. Might also explain why a young lady might want to be taken fer a boy."

"Lady?" Ty asked sardonically, looking up and down Janna's ragged length. "That might indeed be a female, Jack, but it sure as hell isn't a lady. A lady wouldn't be caught dead in that outfit."

Janna ignored the hurt caused by Ty's caustic comments and let her anger bubble forth instead. She turned to Mad Jack and spoke in the cool, cultured voice that her father had taught her was appropriate for reading Shakespeare.

"Of course, you have to understand that Ty is an expert on ladies. You can tell that just by looking at him. Note the fashionably cut pants and the spotless linen shirt. His suit coat is obviously handmade from the finest blend of silk and wool. His boots are fine examples of craftsmanship raised to the level of art. His own skin couldn't fit him better."

Long before Janna had finished her sarcastic summary of Ty's attire, Mad Jack was laughing so hard he nearly swallowed his cud of tobacco. Ty's smile was a bleak warning curve carved out of the blackness of his beard.

"There's more to a man than his clothes," Ty said.

"But not to a woman, hmm?"

"Kid, you don't have enough curves to be a woman." Ty turned away before Janna could say anything more. "I'm going to the Tub," he said, using Janna's nickname for the deep pool in which they both bathed—separately. "Don't worry about hurrying along to scrub my back. I can reach it just fine."

Careful to show no expression at all, Janna watched Ty stalk from the camp. Then she turned and began preparing an herbal tea for Mad Jack.

"Sorry, gal," Mad Jack said, watching her work. "If I'd thunk about it, I wouldn't've opened my trap. You want I should stay with you?"

Janna shook her head. "It's not necessary. I know how restless you get after you've been in camp for a few hours. Ty's mad, but he'll get over it."

"That wasn't what I meant. Now that he knows you're a female, maybe you won't be wanting to be alone with him."

"There won't be any problem," Janna said unhappily. "You heard him. He thinks I'm about as appealing as a fence post." She shrugged, trying to appear casual about her lack of feminine allure.

Mad Jack's faded eyes watched Janna shrewdly. "And you be kinda wishin' it was otherwise," he said after a moment.

She opened her mouth to object forcefully, then realized there was no point in denying the truth, no matter how painful that truth might be.

"Yes, I'd like to be attractive to him. What woman wouldn't? He's all man," Janna said. She added a pinch of herbs to the tiny pot. "And he's a good man. Even when he was half out of his head with pain, his first instinct was still to protect me rather than himself. He'd never force himself on me." She grimaced and added wryly, "Not that he'd ever have the chance. I'd probably say yes so quick it would make his head spin."

Mad Jack hesitated, then sighed. "Gal, I don't know how much your pa told you about babies and such, but more women have spent their lives wishin' they'd said no than otherwise. When the urge is ridin' a man, he'll talk sweet as molasses and promise things he has no damn intention of giving."

"Ty wouldn't lie to me like that."

"You can't rightly call it lyin'. When a man's crotch is aching, he don't know lies from truth," Mad Jack said bluntly. "It's natural. If menfolk stood around wonderin' what was right instead of doin' what come natural like, there wouldn't be enough babies to keep the world goin'."

Janna made a neutral sound and stirred the herbal tea. Despite the faint suggestion of red on his weathered face, Mad Jack forged ahead with his warning about the undependable nature of men.

"What I'm tryin' to say," Mad Jack muttered as he dug around in his stained shirt pocket for a plug of tobacco, "is that's a big stud hoss you found, and he's getting right healthy again. He'll be waking up hard as stone of a mornin' and he'll be lookin' for a soft place to ease what's aching."

Janna ducked her head, grateful for the floppy brim of the hat, which concealed her face. She didn't know whether to throw the steaming tea at Mad Jack or to hug him for trying to do what he was obviously ill-suited to do, which was to be a Dutch uncle to a girl who had no family.

"Now, I know I'm being too blunt," Mad Jack continued doggedly, "but dammit, gal, you ain't got no womenfolk to warn you about a man's ways. Next thing you know, you'll be gettin' fat, and I can tell you flat out it won't be from nothing you et."

"Your tea is ready."

"Gal, you understand what I been sayin'?"

"I know where babies come from and how they get there, if that's what you mean," Janna said succinctly.

"That's what I mean," Mad Jack mumbled.

Janna glanced up and made an irritated sound as she saw Mad Jack sawing away on a plug of tobacco with his pocketknife. "No wonder your stomach is as sour as last month's milk. That stuff would gag a skunk."

Dry laughter denied her words. "I'm at the age when a good chew is my only comfort. That and finding a mite of gold here and there. I done right well for myself since your pa died. I been thinking 'bout it, and I done decided. I want you to take some gold and get shuck of this place."

The immediate objections that came to Janna's lips were overridden by Mad Jack, who didn't stop speaking even while he pushed a chunk of tobacco into his mouth and started chewing with gusto.

"Now you just listen to me, gal. Territory's gettin' too damn crowded. One of these days the wrong man's going to cut your trail, the kind of man what don't care about sweet talkin' or protecting or any damn thing but his own pleasure. And I don't mean just renegades, neither. Some of them pony soldiers is as bad as Injuns, an' the scum selling rifles to Cascabel is no better than him."

Mad Jack looked at Janna as she worked gracefully over the fire, every line of her body proclaiming both her femininity and her unwillingness to listen to his advice.

"It's gettin' too damn dangerous out here for any woman a'tall, even one wearing men's clothes. You be too good a woman to go to waste out here alone."

"I've done fine for five years."

He snorted. "Fine, huh? Look at you, thin as a mare nursing two foals. You want to get a man, you gotta put meat on them bones."

"My mother wasn't built like a butter churn," Janna muttered. "Papa didn't mind one bit."

And neither had Ty, if his reaction to the drawing were any guide.

Mad Jack cursed under his breath and tried another tack. "Don't you get lonesome chasing mustangs and living so small you barely cast a shadow?"

"Do you?" Janna countered.

"Hell, I'm different. I'm a man and you ain't, never mind the clothes you wear. Don't you want a man of your own an' kids to pester you?"

Janna didn't answer, because the answer was too painful. Until she had found Ty, she hadn't really understood what life had to offer. Then she had met him—and now she knew the meaning of the word *lonely*.

"The mustangs are all I have," she said.

"And they're all you'll ever have if'n you don't leave."

"If I leave, I'll have nothing," Janna said matter-of-factly. "I'm not the kind of woman to catch a man's eye. Ty has made that real plain, and he's the 'stud hoss' who should know." She shrugged, concealing her unhappiness. "I'd rather live with mustangs than cook at a boardinghouse where men grab at me when they think nobody's looking."

"But—"

"I'm staying, and that's that."

# Chapter Nine

The Tub's slick-walled pool was far enough from its hot-spring source to have lost the scalding edge of its temperature and nearly all of its sulfurous smell. The water was a clear, pale blue that steamed gently in the cool hours of night and gleamed invitingly all the time. Though safe to drink, the water was too hot for plants to grow in it. Nothing but sand and stone ringed the pool. The high mineral content of the water had decorated the rock it touched with a smooth, creamy-yellow veneer of deposits that had rounded off all the rough edges of the native stone, making a hard but nonetheless comfortable place for Ty to soak out the last legacy of Cascabel's cruel gauntlet.

Usually Ty enjoyed the soothing heat of the pool, but not today. Today he simmered from more than the temperature of the water. Knowing that "the boy" was a girl made him want to turn Janna over his knee and paddle her until she learned some manners. When he thought how she had let him run around wearing nothing more than a few rags of blanket...

A flush spread beneath the dark hair on Ty's chest and face. The realization that he was embarrassed infuriated him. It was hardly a case of his never having been nearly or even completely naked around a woman; of all the Mac-Kenzie brothers, Ty had been the one who had caught women's eye from the time he was old enough to shave. What bothered Ty was that he must have shocked Janna more than once. The thought of a girl of her tender years being subjected repeatedly to a full-grown man's nakedness made Ty very uncomfortable.

*She must have been dying of embarrassment, but she never let on. She just kept on washing me when I was delirious and putting medicine all over me and reading to me while I teased her in a way I never would have teased a girl. A woman, maybe, but not a girl. Why, she can't be much more than...* Abruptly Ty sat up straight on the stone ledge, sending water cascading off his body. *Just how old is she? And how innocent?*

Ty remembered the look of desire he had once seen in Janna's eyes. Instantly he squelched the thought. He was nearly thirty. He had no damned business even looking at a thirteen-year-old, no matter how soft her cheeks were or how her gray eyes warmed while she looked at him when she thought he wouldn't notice. Besides, boy or girl, at thirteen a case of hero worship was still a case of hero worship.

If she was, indeed, thirteen.

*She can't be much older than that. I may be blind but I'm not dead. If she had breasts, I'd have noticed. Or hips, for that matter. Even under those flapping, flopping, ridiculous clothes, I'd have noticed... wouldn't I?*

*Hell, yes, of course I would have.*

The reassuring thought made Ty settle back into the pool. A kid was still a kid, no matter what the sex. As for his own body's urgent woman-hunger, that was just a sign of his returned health. It had nothing to do with a gray-eyed waif whose delicate hands had touched nearly every aching inch of his body.

But it was the aching inches she hadn't touched that were driving him crazy.

"Dammit!" Ty exploded, coming out of the water with a lunge.

He stood dripping on the stone rim of the pool, furious with himself and the world in general, and with one Janna Wayland in particular. Viciously he scrubbed his breechcloth on the rocks, wrung it out and put it on, concealing the rigid evidence of his hunger.

Then he turned around and got right back into the Tub again. This time he remembered the bar of camp soap that Janna always left in a nearby niche. Cursing steadily, he began washing himself from head to newly healed feet. When he was finished he rinsed thoroughly, adjusted the uncomfortably tight breechcloth once more and stalked back to camp.

Janna was calmly tying twists of greenery to branches she had laid between two tall forked sticks. The stems of the plants turned slowly in the sun and wind as the leaves gave up their moisture. In a week or two the herbs would be ready to store whole or to crumble and pound into a powder from which she would make lotions, pastes, potions and other varieties of medicine.

"How do your feet feel?" Janna asked without looking up from her work.

"Like feet. Where's Mad Jack?"

"Gone."

"What?"

"He was worried when he didn't find me in any of the usual places, so—"

"Where are the usual places?" Ty interrupted.

"Wherever Lucifer's herd is. Once Jack found out I was all right, he went back."

"To where?"

"Wherever his mine is."

Ty reached to readjust the breechcloth again, remembered that Janna wasn't a boy and snatched back his hands, cursing.

"Do you think that zebra dun of yours would take me to Sweetwater?"

"I don't know. She likes you well enough, but she doesn't like towns at all."

"You two make a fine pair," Ty muttered, combing through his wet hair with long fingers.

"Catch."

Reflexively Ty's hand flashed out and grabbed the small leather poke Janna had pulled from her baggy pants pocket.

"What's this?" he asked.

"Mad Jack's gold. You'll need it when you get to town. Or were you planning to work off whatever you buy?"

"I can't take gold from a thirteen-year-old girl."

Janna looked up briefly before she went back to arranging herbs for drying. "You aren't."

"What?"

"You aren't taking gold from a thirteen-year-old. I'm nineteen. I only told you I was thirteen so that you wouldn't suspect I was a woman."

"Sugar," drawled Ty, giving Janna a thorough up-and-down look, "you could have walked naked past me and I wouldn't have suspected anything at all. You're the least female female I've ever seen."

Janna's fingers tightened on the herbs as the barb went home, but she was determined not to show that she'd been hurt.

"Thank you," she said huskily. "I just took a leaf from Cascabel's book—hide in plain sight. The pony soldiers caught him way down south last year. He escaped from them. They went looking for him, expecting to run him down easily because there was no cover around. It was flat and with only a scattering of stunted mesquite. No place for a rabbit to hide, much less a man."

Ty listened in spite of his anger at having been deceived. As he listened, he tried to figure out why Janna's voice was so appealing to him. Finally he realized that she no longer was trying to conceal her voice's essentially feminine nature, a faintly husky music that tantalized his senses.

And she was nineteen, not thirteen.

*Stop it,* Ty told himself fiercely. *She's all alone in the world. Any man who would take advantage of that isn't worthy of the name.*

"Because the soldiers knew there was no place to hide, they didn't look," Janna continued. "Cascabel is as shrewd as Satan. He knew that the best place to hide is in plain sight, where no one would ever look. So when he was convinced that he couldn't outrun the soldiers and they would catch him in the open, he rolled in the dust, grabbed some mesquite branches and sat very still. The branches didn't cover him, but they gave the soldiers something familiar to look at—something they would never look at twice. And they didn't," Janna concluded. "They rode right by Cascabel, maybe a hundred feet away, and never saw him."

"Probably because Cascabel looks a hell of a lot more like a mesquite bush than you look like a woman."

"That's your opinion," Janna retorted, "but we both know how trustworthy your eyes are, don't we?"

Ty saw the reaction that Janna tried to hide. He smiled, feeling better than he had since he realized how badly he had been fooled. If his brothers ever found out what had happened, they would ride him until he screamed for mercy. Ty had always been the one the MacKenzie men turned to for advice on the pursuit and pleasuring of the fair sex.

He laughed aloud and felt his temper sweeten with every passing second. He was going to get some of his own back from the gray-eyed chameleon, and he was going to enjoy himself thoroughly in the process. She would rue the day she had fooled him into believing she was an effeminate boy.

"If you'd been any kind of a woman," Ty drawled very slowly, "I'd feel right ashamed of being fooled. But seeing as how you only *say* you're a girl, and I'm too much of a gentleman to ask you to prove it . . . I guess I'll just have to keep my doubts to myself."

"You? A gentleman?" Janna asked in rising tones of disbelief. She looked pointedly at his half-grown beard and soggy breechcloth. "From what I can see—and there's darn little I *can't* see—you look like a savage."

Ty's laugh wasn't quite so heartfelt this time. "Oh, I know I'm a gentleman for a fact, *boy*. And so do a lot of real ladies."

Mentally Janna compared herself to the sketch of her mother—loose, ragged clothes against stylish swirls of silk, Indian braids against carefully coiffed curls. The comparison was simply too painful. So was the fact that Ty had been taken with her mother's image and couldn't have been more blunt about the daughter's lack of feminine allure.

Unshed tears clawed at the back of Janna's eyelids, but the thought that Ty might catch her crying appalled her. Without a word she dusted off her hands and brushed past Ty, refusing even to look at him, knowing that for all her scathing comments to the contrary, his eyes were uncomfortably sharp when it came to assessing her mood.

When Janna was at the edge of the grassy area of the valley, she cupped her hands to her mouth and called out to Zebra, using the keening cry of a hawk. To human ears there was almost no difference in the sounds—to Zebra, it was a call as clear as a trumpet's. Within moments the mare was cantering through the grass towards Janna.

"Hello, pretty girl," Janna murmured. She stroked the mare's neck and pulled weeds from her long mane and tail. "Show me your hooves."

She worked slowly around the horse, touching each fetlock. Zebra presented each of her hooves in turn, standing patiently while Janna used a short, pointed stick to worry loose any mud or debris that had become caught between the hard outer hoof and the softer frog at the center.

"It would be easier with a steel hoof pick," Ty said.

Janna barely controlled a start. On the meadow grass Ty's bare feet had made no more sound than a shadow.

"If I bought a pick, people would wonder what I was planning to use it on. Only one other human being knows that I've tamed..." Janna's voice died when she realized that Ty as well as Mad Jack knew that she mingled with Lucifer's herd. "Could it be our secret?" she asked as she looked at Ty, her voice aching with restraint. "It's bad enough that I turn up from time to time with raw gold. If some of the men around here knew that I could get close to Lucifer, they'd hunt me down like a mad dog and use me to get their hands on him."

Ty looked at the face turned up toward him in silent pleading and felt as though he had been kicked in the stomach. The idea of using Janna to get close to Lucifer had been in the back of his mind since he had realized that Zebra was part of the big black stallion's harem.

*They'd hunt me down like a mad dog and use me...*

Before Ty realized what he was doing, he cupped Janna's chin reassuringly in his hand.

"I won't tell anyone," he said quietly. "I promise you, Janna. And I won't use you. I want that stud and I plan to have him—but not like that, not by making you feel you had betrayed a trust."

The heat of Janna's tears on his hand shocked Ty, but not as much as the butterfly softness of her lips brushing over his skin for an instant before she turned away.

"Thank you," she said huskily, her face hidden while she resumed working over Zebra's hoof. "And I'm sorry about what I said earlier. You're very much a gentleman, no matter what you're wearing."

Ty closed his eyes and fought against the tremor of sensation that was spreading out from the palm of his hand to the pit of his stomach and from there to the soles of his feet. Before he could prevent himself, he had lifted his hand to his lips. The taste of Janna's tears went to his head more quickly than a shot of whiskey, making him draw in a sharp breath.

*You've been without a woman too long,* he told himself as he fought to control a combination of tenderness and raw desire.

*Yes—and the name of the cure is Janna Wayland.*

"No," Ty said aloud harshly.

"What?" Janna said, looking up.

Ty wasn't watching her. He was standing rigid, his face drawn as though in pain. When she spoke, he opened his eyes. She wanted to protest the shadows she saw there, but he was already speaking.

"I'm not what you think," Ty said, his voice rough. "I'm too woman hungry to be a gentleman. Don't trust me, Janna. Don't trust me at all."

# Chapter Ten

Under Janna's watchful eyes, Ty sprang onto Zebra's back with a flowing, catlike motion. The mare flicked her ears backward, then forward, accepting Ty as her rider without a fuss.

"I told you she wouldn't object," Janna said. "You've ridden her before."

"Don't remind me," he said. "I've had nightmares about that ride every night since." He leaned down and offered Janna his left arm. "Grab just above the elbow with your left hand, pretend I'm a piece of mane and swing up behind me."

Janna followed Ty's instructions and found herself whisked aboard Zebra with breathtaking ease. She lifted her hand instantly, too conscious of the heat and power of Ty's bare arm. She found herself confronted by an expanse of naked shoulders that seemed to block out half the world.

"H-how is your back healing?" she asked.

"You tell me," Ty said dryly. "You can see it better than I can."

She bit her lip, irritated by her inane question and his goading response. On the other hand, asking that question had been safer than following her original impulse, which had been to run her hands over his tanned, supple skin. Taking a deep breath, Janna forced herself to concentrate on the shadow bruises and faint, thin lines of red that marked recently healed cuts. She traced the longest line with delicate fingertips. He flinched as though she had used a whip on him.

"Don't do that," he snapped.

"I'm sorry. I didn't know it was still painful. It looks healed."

Ty's lips flattened, but he said nothing to correct Janna's assumption that it had been pain rather than pleasure that had made his body jerk. Her fingertips had been like that single touch from her lips, a brush of warmth and a shivering hint of the feminine sensuality concealed beneath men's clothing.

"When we get back from town, I'll put more salve on," Janna continued.

His mouth opened to object, but he closed it without making a sound. The temptation to feel her soothing hands on his body was simply too great for him to deny himself the opportunity of being cared for by Janna.

Silently Ty nudged Zebra with his left heel. The mare turned obediently and headed toward the cleft in the rocks that surrounded the tiny valley. Each motion of the horse's buttocks, combined with the natural forward slope of Zebra's back, gently moved Janna toward Ty's warm body. He flinched again when the brim of her floppy hat touched his skin.

"Sorry," muttered Janna, pulling her head back.

He grunted.

Zebra kept on walking and Janna kept sliding closer to Ty. Before they came to the cleft that led from the valley, she was flush against his body. Only by leaning back at an awkward angle could she prevent her hat—or her lips—from brushing against his skin.

The fifth time Janna felt compelled to apologize for the contact she could not avoid, she wriggled away from Ty until she could put her hands on the horse's back between their bodies. Cautiously she pushed herself backward a fraction of an inch at a time, not wanting to alarm Zebra.

As Janna's weight settled farther back on the mare's spine, her tail swished in warning, sending a stinging veil of hair across Ty's naked calf.

"Damn, what is her tail made of—nettles?"

Janna didn't answer. Instead, she eased herself backward another inch, then two.

Zebra balked and humped her back in warning.

"What's wrong with her?" Ty asked, turning to look over his shoulder at Janna. "What the hell are you doing way back there? Don't you know a horse's kidneys and flanks are sensitive? Or maybe you're trying to get us both bucked off in the dirt?"

"I was trying not to hurt your back."

"My back? My back is just fi—" Abruptly Ty remembered what he had said about his back being hurt by Janna's light touch. "I'll live," he said grimly. "Scoot on up here where you belong before this mustang bucks us both off."

"I'd rather not," Janna said through stiff lips.

Ty kicked his right leg over Zebra's neck and slid off onto the ground. "Get up there where you belong," he said in a curt voice. "I'll walk."

"No, I'll walk," Janna said, dismounting in a rush, landing very close to Ty. "I'm used to it. Besides, I haven't been hurt and you have."

"I'm all healed up."

"But you said your back—"

"Get on that mustang before I lose my temper," Ty said flatly, cutting across Janna's protest.

"Lose your temper? Impossible. You'd have to find it first."

Ty glared into Janna's gray eyes. She didn't flinch. With a hissed curse he grabbed her and dumped her on her stomach across Zebra's back. He had plenty of time to regret the impulsive act. Janna's scramble to right herself and assume a normal riding position pulled the fabric of her pants tightly across her buttocks, revealing to him for the first time the unmistakable curves of a woman's hips.

At that instant Ty abandoned all thought of climbing on Zebra behind Janna. The feel of those soft curves rubbing between his thighs and against his aching male flesh would quickly drive him crazy.

Cursing steadily beneath his breath, Ty reached up to drag Janna off the mare. He told himself it was an accident that his hands shaped Janna's buttocks on the way to pulling her down, and he knew that it was a lie. He could have pulled on Janna's feet or even her knees. He didn't have to grab her hips and sink his fingers into her resilient flesh, sending a wave of heat through his body.

Even as Ty withdrew his hands, he wondered if he had been as wrong about Janna's breasts as he had been about her hips—she had more than enough curves to fill a man's hungry hands. The realization that the ride into town would probably tell him just how soft and tempting her breasts were was enough to make Ty groan and swear even more. The amount of control he had to exert to drag his hands away from Janna's body shocked him. He had never been the kind of man who grabbed at what a woman wouldn't freely offer to him.

"Stand still," Ty said harshly as Janna twisted against him, trying to regain her balance.

"Now listen, you son of—"

A broad, hard palm covered Janna's mouth. Green eyes stared into furious gray ones.

"No, you listen to me, *boy*," snarled Ty. "We're going to get on that horse and you're going to ride far enough forward that Zebra's spine isn't hurt. She's a good-sized mare, but carrying double is still a lot of weight for her, especially when one of her riders is my size."

Janna stopped fighting. She hadn't thought that her foolish scooting about might have hurt Zebra. With a small cry she turned toward the mare. The horse looked back at her with an equine's patience for crazy humans.

"I'll walk," Janna said.

"Like hell you will. It's too far."

"I've walked a lot farther in a morning."

"And left footprints every step of the way. If you take time to hide your trail, it'll take a week to get to town. If you don't hide your trail, the next man through that gap won't be Mad Jack. It will be Cascabel."

There was a moment of silence while Janna digested the unpleasant truth of what Ty was saying. Signs left by an untrimmed, unshod horse wouldn't attract much attention, particularly after they crossed their trail with that of any of the several wild horse herds in the area. Tracks left by a trimmed, shod horse, or a human, would bring down Cascabel quicker than the strike of his namesake reptile—the rattlesnake.

"It won't hurt Zebra to carry double," Ty said, "especially without a saddle. Just don't ride so far back."

"What about you? I don't want to hurt your back, either."

He closed his eyes so as not to see the unhappiness in Janna's at the thought of hurting anything, even the man who was presently making her life very difficult.

"I'm ticklish, that's all," Ty said grimly. "My back is fine."

"Oh."

Ty swung up onto Zebra, helped Janna swing up behind him and gritted his teeth at the feel of her breath against his naked skin. When Zebra walked once more to the cleft that led out of the valley, the gentle rubbing pressure of Janna's thighs against his own was an even worse distraction than the heat of her breath washing over his spine.

*Think of her as a boy.*

Ty tried. All he could think of was the lush resilience of Janna's hips. The smooth, curving heat of them could never have belonged to a boy.

*Be grateful she doesn't have big breasts to rub against you.*

Ty tried to be grateful. All he could think of was pulling off Janna's tentlike shirt and finding out just how soft her breasts were, and if her nipples were as pink as her tongue, and if they would pout hungrily for his mouth.

The reflexive tightening of Ty's body in response to his thoughts was communicated to Zebra. Sensing his agitation without understanding its source, she began to shy at the breeze stirring through the belly-deep grass as though it were a yellow-eyed cougar stalking her.

Janna talked to the mare in a soothing, husky voice that worked on Ty's aroused senses like repeated, silky caresses. He clenched his teeth when she shifted position and leaned around him in order to stroke Zebra's neck soothingly.

"I don't know what's wrong with her," Janna said, keeping her voice low and reassuring. "She's only like this when there are Indians or cougars around. I haven't seen any sign of cats in the valley. Maybe Mad Jack didn't cover his trail out of here well enough and Cascabel followed it."

"Doubt it," Ty said in a clipped voice. "That old man has been outsmarting trackers for more years than I've been alive. Zebra's probably just nervous about having two riders."

Janna made a sound that had no meaning except to soothe the restive mustang.

By the time they approached the slit in the cliffs that surrounded the valley, Zebra no longer shied at every shadow, Janna had relaxed so that she no longer jerked back from the inevitable contact with Ty's nearly naked body—and Ty's jaw ached from being clenched against the hot sensations radiating through his body from every accidental, brushing contact with Janna.

And it seemed that she touched him everywhere, except in those places where he ached to the point of pain.

## Chapter Eleven

Silently Ty endured the continual brush of Janna's body against his as they went toward the cleft. They rode alongside the stream until it spread out into a small slough and vanished, leaving not even a trickle to enter the stone slot that was the valley's only outlet. There was nothing about the mouth of the cleft to suggest that it was any different from the hundreds of other narrow, barren gouges in the eroded flanks of the huge plateau. That, and the fact that the narrow, twisting passage was both difficult and uninviting for a horse, were why the valley had remained Janna's secret.

The slit in the rocks looked like the entrance to hell, but Ty watched it approach with a feeling of relief. When the opening was thirty yards away, he could bear Janna's unintentional sensual torment no longer. With a feeling of relief, he slid off Zebra and away from the fiery brush of Janna's body.

"Wait here," Ty said curtly. "I'll check out the trail."

He was gone before Janna could put her objections into words.

Inside the cleft it was cool, damp, dusky. A few shallow pools left by recent rain showers reflected the dark red, oddly stained cliffs that towered above the floor of the narrow canyon. Overhead the sky was reduced to a thin blue string thrown carelessly between the cliffs. In the places where black lava replaced sandstone, the cleft darkened until it was both somber and eerie, as though night had condensed and taken a solid form on the face of the land itself.

There were no tracks at all in the dry watercourse, not even those of wildlife. Ty wasn't surprised by the lack of animal signs. He had expected to find nothing. Wild animals had an instinctive abhorrence of small openings, of being trapped somewhere that lacked room to run or places to hide. What did surprise Ty was that Mad Jack had left no more trail than if he had flown from the secret valley.

In fact, Ty found it impossible to believe that Mad Jack had gone through the cleft at all.

The passage itself was familiar to Ty. He had made it a point to familiarize himself with the slit that was the difference between the valley being a haven for them or a trap with no exit. Yet each time he walked the cleft he felt a deepening admiration for Janna, who had found and used a passage whose secret had been lost to the Indians for hundreds of years, perhaps even thousands. He doubted that any Indian had used the cleft at all since the coming of the horse several hundred years before.

Or perhaps the valley hadn't been lost by the Indians but simply avoided as a spirit place where mortal men shouldn't go, a place of the People who Came Before. Within the twilight confines of the slot canyon, it would be very easy to imagine malevolent spirits waiting in ambush for anything foolish enough to stray inside the black stone jaws.

The narrowest point of the cleft was not at the entrance to the valley but about a third of the way toward the open land beyond. At the stricture, both canyon walls were of a dense, black, fine-grained stone that cracked in long parallel columns. Water had polished the stone into a slick, shiny mass that, with the addition of a layer of fine mud, was almost as slippery as ice. Unlike Mad Jack, Janna had never found a way to avoid leaving tracks over that segment of the slot, which was why she had always taken on the passage just before or just after a rain, when any tracks she left would be washed completely away by the runoff stream.

That was another thing Ty admired. Few people who knew the country would have had the courage to test the stone slit when clouds massed over the plateau and water was running down its sides in rushing veils. Fewer people still would have had the skill to read the land and weather correctly enough to survive negotiating the narrow slot. He wondered how many times Janna had waited, eyeing the muddy rush of water and calculating her best chance to pass through without leaving a sign or being drowned.

Warily Ty looked up the uneven walls where debris lodged twenty or thirty feet higher than his head. The thought of the risk Janna had taken to get him into the hidden valley made sweat start on his body. He remembered the black clouds, the pelting rain...and nothing more. He only knew that she had taken an enormous risk while getting him to a safe place to heal. In fact, she had taken one hell of a risk for him, period, since the first moment she had begun wiping out his trail so that Cascabel would lose his prey. If the renegade ever found out how his prisoner had truly escaped, Janna's life wouldn't be worth a handful of cold spit.

Ty half walked, half slid over the cleft's slick bottom. Once he was past the place where black walls pinched in, the cleft opened out slightly again. He moved quickly, leaving very little trace of his passage. There was no other sign of life within the steep canyon. When the gloom brightened, announcing the end of the slot, Ty went to the deepest area of shadow and eased forward until he could look over the fan of debris that washed down from the plateau's edge, creating a sloping skirt that led to the flatlands beyond.

For several minutes Ty remained motionless, studying the landscape for any sign of movement. There was no motion but the ragged race of cloud shadows over the earth. No bird was startled into flight. No raven scolded an intruder in hoarse tones. No shape of man or horse separated from cover to ghost over the land. If there were anyone about, he was even better hidden than Ty.

After ten minutes Ty withdrew from the entrance to the slot and returned to Janna. She was waiting precisely where he had left her, for she knew the importance of keeping the secret of the slit canyon and the hidden valley beyond.

"All clear," Ty said, answering the question in Janna's eyes. "Nothing has been in or out since the last shower."

Even though Janna had expected nothing else, she couldn't conceal her relief. Without the secret valley she would have no place to hide, no sanctuary in which to live during the wild country's cold winters.

Ty saw Janna's relief, guessed at its source and had to restrain himself from telling her not to worry, she wasn't going to have to spend another winter hiding in the valley, she was leaving Indian country and that was that. But he said nothing, because she would have argued with him, and arguing against the inevitable was a waste of time. As far as he was concerned, it was inevitable that Janna would no longer live alone. No white woman should have to exist like a savage, fearful of every shadow and without even the company of other human beings when danger threatened.

Ty had decided that he would take Janna to Sweetwater or Hat Rock or Santa Fe or even all the way to Denver, if it came to that. It was the least he could do for the orphan girl who had saved his life.

To Ty's surprise, Janna slid down from Zebra and walked to the cleft. As always, the mare followed her.

"Aren't you going to ride?" he asked.

"Too dangerous. That narrow stretch must still be slick from the last rain."

"We rode in double that way."

"Someone had to keep you astride Zebra. We'll mount after the canyon widens again."

Ty didn't argue. No matter how important it might be not to leave human footprints, he had dreaded the thought of going over the slippery black rock while mounted bareback and double on an unbroken mustang.

In the end it was the very narrowness of the canyon that kept Ty from falling. He simply levered himself along by acting as though he were trying to push the two sides of the canyon farther apart with his hands. Janna, more accustomed to the tricky stretch, knew where there were handholds and niches to use in maintaining her balance. Zebra had the advantage of four feet—if one slipped, there were three to take its place.

"How did you manage on horseback?" Ty asked as he reached a wider point in the slit and Janna came alongside.

"There was no other choice."

He thought about that for a moment, then nodded slowly, understanding that that was how Janna had managed to survive out here on her own: she believed that there was no other choice.

But there was.

"With all your books, you could be a teacher," Ty said as he swung aboard Zebra once more and scraped his knee against the canyon wall in the process.

Janna grabbed his arm and swung up behind him. "Not enough kids except in towns."

"So?"

"I don't like towns. They seem to bring out the worst in people."

Ty opened his mouth to argue, realized that he agreed with Janna and felt trapped. "Not all the time," he muttered.

She shrugged. "Maybe I just bring out the worst in towns."

"Do you really plan on spending the rest of your life out here?" he demanded.

"Unless you keep your voice down, the rest of my life won't amount to more than a few hours," Janna said dryly. "These walls make a dropped pin echo like a landslide."

Ty turned around and glared at her but said nothing more, except for a muffled word or two when his legs scraped against narrow points in the cleft. Janna's slender legs were in no such danger, and in any case were enveloped by protective folds of cloth. Even so, Ty had an acute appreciation of the warm flesh beneath the folds, especially when she rubbed against him as she adjusted to Zebra's motions.

Cautiously Ty urged Zebra out of the cleft, keeping to shadows and high brush wherever possible, trying to break up the telltale silhouette of horse and rider. They had gone no more than a mile when they cut across tracks left by a group of unshod ponies. The horses had moved in a bunch, not stopping to graze or to drink from the few puddles that remained after the previous thunderstorm. From the distance between sets of prints, Janna guessed that the horses had been cantering.

"That's Cascabel's horse," Janna said in a low voice.

She pointed to a set of larger hoofprints that had been all but obliterated by the rest of the group. Though the horse had once been shod, it had no shoes any longer. All that remained were vague traces of nail holes around the rim of the untrimmed hooves.

"He stole two Kentucky horses from an officer at the fort over by Split-rock Springs," she continued. "One of the horses used to be the fastest horse in Utah Territory."

"Used to be? What happened?"

"Cascabel ran it to death trying to catch Lucifer. He takes better care of the second horse. It won't last much longer, though. It's a paddock horse, bred for grooming and grain. All it has out here is grass and a big renegade with a whip."

"Yeah, and that big renegade is too damn close for comfort."

Janna chewed silently on her lip for a moment before agreeing. "Yes. This is only the third time I've found his tracks on the east side of Black Plateau. I wonder what happened to make him come this far. The ranches he usually raids are in the opposite direction."

"I'll bet the soldiers are closing in. They have a real mission where Cascabel is concerned. They're going to see him hang or know the reason why."

She closed her eyes and shook her head, trying to throw off the uneasy feeling that had been growing in her day by day since the beginning of the summer, when she had discovered that Cascabel had been forced to move his camp. He had chosen to make his new camp on the Raven Creek watershed, a place that was perilously close to Mustang Canyon. Whether Black Hawk had driven Cascabel south, or the soldiers had, or Lucifer had lured him to the red buttes and high plateau and brooding Fire Mountains, it didn't matter. Janna knew that she couldn't remain hidden for long once so many eyes started scrutinizing every shadow.

Yet she couldn't leave, either. She had no place to go. A woman alone among men was the subject of snickers and speculation and blunt offers of sex in exchange for money or safety. The closest thing she had to a home was the wild land itself. She couldn't bear to lose it and her freedom in the same blow.

Unfortunately, it was becoming clear that she had no other choice.

Silently Janna guided Zebra in a circuitous route to Sweetwater. When Ty realized where they were going, he turned questioningly to her.

"Hat Rock is closer," he said.

"I know. I went to Sweetwater last time."

"So?"

"So Joe Troon won't be looking for me there."

"What?"

"I never go to the same town or ranch twice in a row," Janna explained. "Except for the hidden valley, I never go to the same places at the same time of year or in the same order. If you don't have a pattern, no one can guess where you're going to be and lay a trap for you."

Ty sensed the apprehension behind Janna's calm words. "Did this Troon character try to trap you?"

"Once or twice."

"Why?"

"Mad Jack's mine, Lucifer or..." Janna's voice died as she remembered overhearing Troon bragging about how he would break her in right and then sell her south to a Mexican whorehouse after she led him to Lucifer and Mad Jack's gold mine. She cleared her throat. "I didn't wait around to find out."

The surge of anger and adrenaline that went through Ty's body surprised him, but it didn't keep him from demanding roughly, "Did he lay a hand on you?"

"He never even saw me that time," Janna said evasively. "I hung back in the brush and listened long enough to figure out how he had found me, and then I swore never to be predictable again. I haven't been, either."

"You said you follow Lucifer's bunch in the summertime."

"Yes."

"Then you're predictable. Every mustanger knows Lucifer's territory. All any man would have to do is to lie in wait at the water holes his herd uses. Lucifer is fast enough to get away from that kind of ambush. You aren't."

"Cascabel is keeping the mustangers away."

"He didn't keep me away. Nothing will. I'm going to have that stud no matter what. I need him too badly to let a few renegades get in my way."

"You plan to use Lucifer to buy your silken lady?"

"Yes," Ty said, his voice flat, inflexible. "The war took everything but my life and my dreams. I'll have that silken lady or die trying."

Janna held herself tightly, trying not to flinch against the pain she felt.

"Then you understand," she said huskily.

"What?"

"You understand why I can't live in a town as a kitchen maid or a saloon girl. I have my own dream."

There was a surprised silence while Ty digested the idea that the ragged waif had a goal beyond simple survival. "What is it?"

Shaking her head, eyes tightly closed, Janna said nothing. There was no point in telling Ty that she had begun to dream of having him turn to her and discover within her the silken lady he sought. It was a dream that would never come true and she was practical enough to know it.

But it was the most compelling dream Janna had ever had. She could no more turn away from it than she could transform herself into the lady of Ty's dreams.

## Chapter Twelve

A mile outside of town, Ty shifted his weight and spoke softly to the mare. Zebra stopped obediently no more than two feet from a clump of boulders and brush.

"Get down," Ty said, handing Janna the big knife she had given him. "I'll be back as quick as I can."

"I'm going with you."

"No."

"But—"

"No!" Hearing the roughness in his own voice, Ty winced. "Janna, it isn't safe. If you're seen with me on a mustang—"

"We'll tell them you tamed her," Janna interrupted quickly.

"They'd have to be dumb as a stump to believe that," he retorted. "I'm going to have enough trouble making them believe I survived without help as it is. You know damn good and well if Cascabel finds out you were responsible for making him the laughingstock of the Utah Territory, he'll come after you until he gets you and cooks you over a slow fire."

Without another word Janna slid down from Zebra. She vanished into concealment between one breath and the next. For a moment Ty couldn't believe that she had ever been with him at all. An odd feeling shot through him, loneli-

ness and desire combined into a yearning that was like
nothing he had ever known.

"Janna?" he called softly.

Nothing answered but branches stirring beneath a rain-
bearing wind. The scent of moisture reminded Ty of the urgency of the situation. They had to be back at the hidden
valley before the storm broke or they would spend a miserable night out in the open, unable even to have a fire to
warm them for fear of giving away their presence.

Thunder rumbled in the distance, causing Zebra to throw
up her head and snort. Ears pricked, nostrils flared, the
horse sniffed the wind.

"Easy, girl," Ty murmured. "It's just the summer rains."

He slid from Zebra's back, landed lightly and pulled off
his breechcloth. His foot wrappings came off next. After he
poked the scraps of blanket into an opening between two
boulders, he turned east and began working his way over the
rocky surface of the land toward a wagon trail a half mile
beyond. He was very careful not to leave any signs of his
passage, for he had been into Sweetwater once before, riding Blackbird and armed with two pistols, a rifle and a
shotgun. He had been glad for each weapon; the only thing
sweet about the town was the name and the tiny spring that
bubbled to the surface nearby, watering stock and men alike
without regard to their individual natures.

As Ty walked toward town, he wished heartily for one of
the new repeating carbines that loaded as fast as they fired.
Even a pistol would have been nice. Two revolvers and extra cylinders loaded with bullets would have made him feel
a lot better about going in among the canted shacks.

Though Janna seemed not to realize it, Sweetwater was an
outlaw hangout, and the two ranches she bought supplies
from had a reputation for branding "loose" cattle that was
known from the Red River to Logan MacKenzie's ranch in
Wyoming. Some of the Lazy A's and Circle G's cowhands
were doubtless reasonably honest men who had been forced

to make a living any way they could after the Civil War had ruined their farms and homes. Other cowhands on those ranches were men who would have been raiders in heaven itself, because they plain enjoyed riding roughshod over people weaker than themselves.

*How the hell did Janna ever survive out here?* Ty asked himself for the hundredth time as he walked quietly into the collection of ramshackle, weathered shacks that constituted one of the few towns within several hundred miles.

No answer came back to Ty but the obvious one, the uncomfortable memory of women in a war-ravaged land, women selling themselves for bread or a blanket, women who in peacetime wouldn't have dreamed of letting a man touch them outside the boundaries of love and marriage.

*Is that how you survived after your father died, Janna? Did you sell yourself until you had the skill and the strength to survive alone?*

Again there was no answer but the obvious one. She had survived. The thought of Janna's soft body lying beneath rutting men both sickened and angered Ty; for a woman to sell herself like that in order to survive was simply another kind of rape.

In the past, Ty had surprised more than one woman caught within the ruins of war by giving her food or shelter or blankets and taking nothing in return. He would never forget one girl's combined look of shock, relief and gratitude when he had refused her thin, bruised body as payment for a plate of beans. She had eaten quickly and then had vanished into the night as though afraid he would change his mind and take her after all.

And when Ty had finally fought his way home, he had discovered that his sister, Cassie, hadn't been so fortunate in the strange men who had crossed her path. Taken by raiders, she had been a captive until she became too ill to service the men; then she had been abandoned to die. She would have, too, if Logan and Silver hadn't caught up with her and gentled her back into sanity and health.

Ty's grim thoughts were a match for the town that he finally reached. There were no men loitering in front of Sweetwater Mercantile when Ty walked by. There were no horses tied to broken railings. No dogs slept in sun-warmed dust. The first person Ty saw was a boy who was emptying slops out the saloon's back door. The boy took one look at Ty and ducked back inside. Instants later the door creaked open again. The bartender stood with a shotgun cradled in his thick hands. A single glance took in Ty's muscular, naked body covered with healing bruises.

"Well, you be big enough and the right color," the bartender said. "Maybe you be Tyrell MacKenzie."

Ty nodded slowly.

The bartender stepped aside. "Come on in. Name's Ned. A breed by the name of Blue Wolf was looking for you 'bout two weeks back."

When he heard Blue Wolf's name, Ty almost laughed aloud. "Wondered how long it would take him to catch up with me."

"Friend of yours?"

"Yeah."

"Good thing, too. From the look of that buck, he'd make a powerful bad enemy. He's damn near as big as Cascabel and white-man smart into the bargain. Talks English better than me."

"He's a dead shot, too."

Ned grunted, reached behind the door and pulled a ragged shirt off a nail. He threw the cloth to Ty. "Wrap up and sit down."

Within moments Ty had the shirt wrapped around his hips and between his legs in a semblance of a breechcloth. He sat down, enjoying the unfamiliar sensation of a chair after months on the trail. Ned went to a sooty corner of the small room and pulled a pot off a broken-legged stove. He wiped a spoon on his britches, stuck it into the pot and shoved it in front of Ty.

"Reckon you're hungry."

Ty wasn't, but admitting that would raise too many questions, so he dug into the cold beans and ate quickly, trying not to remember how much better Janna's food had been. Cleaner, too. Living in the camp with the hot springs had spoiled him. A bath every day, clean dishes, and clean company. It would take him a long time to get used to the smell of a sty like Ned's saloon.

"Thanks," Ty said, shoving away the empty pot.

"Smoke?"

Ty shook his head. "Gave it up the night I saw a man get killed lighting a pipe when he should have been holding still and looking out for enemies."

Ned grinned, revealing teeth about the color the beans had been. "Yep, war can be hard on a man. Worse 'n robbin' banks or rustlin'."

The oblique question about his past was ignored by Ty.

"Don't mean to jaw your arm off," Ned said quickly, "but it's been nothin' but me and Johnny for two weeks now. Rest of 'em went to the fort. Old Cascabel's got 'em pissin' their britches. Hear tell he killed two white men a week ago."

"I wouldn't know about that. I've been too busy hiding and healing. Did Blue Wolf say when he'd be back here?"

Ned opened a stone jug and thumped it onto the table. "Don't know as he's comin' back. I told him you'd been took by Cascabel. He said you wouldn't stay took. Left a poke of gold for you over to the fort. Said you'd be needful of it when you got shuck of Cascabel. From the look of you, he was right."

"Did he say where he was going?"

"He was meetin' up with your brothers north of here. Looking for gold." Ned grunted. "Probably'll find it, too, if'n Black Hawk don't lift their hair first."

"With Wolf on scout, no one will even know they're around." Ty paused, then added casually, "When my brothers come back here looking for me—and they will—tell them I headed for Mexico. I'm going to finish healing up in some *señorita*'s bed."

Ned's smile was as crooked as a dog's hind leg as he absorbed Ty's gentle message: Ty might be naked and alone, but if he were killed his brothers would come hunting for the killer. So Ned poured cloudy liquid from the jar into a dirty tin cup and put it in front of Ty.

"Drink up."

"If it's all the same, I'd rather have water," Ty said. "My daddy always told me not to mix liquor with an empty stomach or a knot on the head."

Ned chuckled, picked up the cup and drained it. His harshly expelled breath made Ty glad there wasn't an open flame nearby. Sure as hell, the alcohol on Ned's breath would have caught fire and burned down the saloon.

"Damn, but that's good 'shine," Ned said, wiping water from his eyes. "A man couldn't get from dawn to dusk without it."

Ty could have gotten from birth to death without moonshine, but he said nothing. He had known a lot like Ned, men for whom the savage bite of homemade liquor was the sole joy of life. With outward patience, Ty waited while Ned's hands stroked the cold curves of the stone jar, lifted it and shook it to gauge the amount of liquor left within.

"You say you and the boy are the only ones left in Sweetwater?" Ty asked after a few moments.

Ned poured another half cup of pale liquid, belched and sat down opposite Ty. Though it was daytime, the interior of the saloon was gloomy. If there had ever been glass windows in the slanting walls, the panes had long since been replaced by oiled paper.

"Yep. Just me and that useless whelp. He's so scared he's gonna run off first time I turn my back." Ned took another swig of liquor, shuddered deliciously and sighed. "And Joe Troon. That sidewinder ain't never far off. Used to keep a Mex gal stashed somewhere off in the rimrock to the north, but she run off with Cascabel's renegades. Ol' Troon's real lonely these days, less'n he caught that *bruja* again."

"What?"

"That red-haired gal the renegades call Sombra, cuz she leaves no more sign than a shadow. Lives with the mustangs, and she's a wild 'un just like them." Ned took another huge swallow, grimaced and sighed out the fumes. "Troon had her once a few years ago but she got away. Gals don't cotton much to Joe Troon. Mean as a spring bear, and that's gospel. Wish he'd kept her, though. I get right tired of squaws."

When Ty understood that the *bruja* under discussion was Janna, it was all he could do not to hurl himself over the table and hammer the half-drunk bartender into the floor.

"But now Troon's decided to make hisself rich off of that old black stud," Ned continued. "He took his rifle and went to Black Plateau. Gonna crease that stud bastard, break him and take his colts while every white man in the territory is too scared to butt in."

Ty grimaced. "Creasing is a chancy thing. A lot more horses are killed than caught that way."

"One mean stud more or less won't make no never mind in this world. If'n it was me, I'd kill the stud, grab the best colts and light a shuck clean out of the territory before the Army finds Cascabel and the whole shootin' match goes up in smoke."

Ty thought of Lucifer as he had last seen the stallion—ears pricked, neck arched, muscles gleaming and sliding beneath a shiny black hide. The thought of someone killing that much animal just to grab his colts made Ty both disgusted and angry. But he had no doubt that Troon would do just that, if he got to Lucifer first.

"Is the mercantile closed?" Ty asked, interrupting Ned's monologue.

"What? Oh, you mean the Preacher's store. Naw, he didn't close up when he went to the fort. Ain't no man would steal from him. Sooner steal from Satan hisself. Even the renegades leave the Preacher alone. Cunning as a coon and snake-mean into the bargain. Troon gave up on the red-haired gal after the Preacher told him to leave her be. See, she gave him a Bible once. So when you see her again, you tell her it's safe to come into Sweetwater. Troon won't bother her."

A cold breath of caution shivered over Ty's skin. The bartender was no more drunk than Ty was.

"Who?" Ty asked, scratching his beard.

"The red-haired gal."

"Don't know her. She live around here?"

Ned squinted at Ty with pale, watery eyes. "Nobody knows where she lives. 'Cept maybe you. She pulled your tail out of a mighty tight crack."

"Mister, the only crack my tail has been in lately was with Cascabel's renegades, and I got shuck of them by running my feet to the bone, hiding in brush, drinking rainwater and eating snakes. Not a one of them had red hair."

Ned stared at Ty for a long time and then nodded slowly. "If that's the way you want it, mister, that's the way it is."

"Wanting has nothing to do with it," Ty drawled coolly, standing up. "I'm telling you the way it was. Thanks for the beans. I'm going over to the Preacher's store. I'll leave a list of what I take. He can get his payment out of the gold Blue Wolf left at the fort."

"I'll tell Preacher when I see him."

"You do that." Ty started for the door, feeling an acute need for fresh air, then realized he wasn't through with Ned yet. "I need to buy a horse."

"The Circle G has right fine horseflesh. Best in the terri-tory. Course, if'n a man was to ride one out of the territory, he might run into a cowpoke what lost a horse just like it.''

Ty smiled wryly as he got the message. ''I'll settle for a town horse.''

''Ain't none,'' Ned said succinctly. ''Took 'em all to the fort.''

''Where's the closest homestead that might have an animal to sell?''

''Ain't none left for a hundred miles, 'cept renegade camps and wherever that redheaded gal lives. But you don't know nothin' about her, so it don't help you none.''

Ty shrugged. ''I'll find a horse between here and Mexico. Thanks for the beans, Ned.''

The door shut behind Ty, but he still felt Ned's narrow, calculating eyes boring into his naked back. It made Ty's spine itch and his palms ache for the cool feel of an army rifle.

Janna didn't know it, but she wasn't coming back to Sweetwater again. Ever.

# Chapter Thirteen

Janna awoke when a man rose up from the ground in front of her, blocking out the sun with his body. She was grabbing for her knife when Zebra snorted and the man turned and sunlight caught the emerald glint of his eyes.

Hardly recognizing Ty beneath his store-bought clothes, Janna could do no more than stare. The slate-gray shirt and hat, black bandanna, and black pants emphasized Ty's size and masculine grace. He looked as handsome as sin and twice as hard. His beard was shaved off, leaving his face clean but for a midnight slash of mustache that heightened the pronounced planes of his cheekbones and made his teeth gleam whitely. In that instant, with fright still vibrating in her body and her defenses awry, Janna's response to him was so intense that she could scarcely breathe.

"Ty?" she asked huskily. "Is that really you?"

"You better hope it is," Ty snapped. "What the hell were you doing asleep? It could have been Joe Troon who cut your trail rather than me. Or maybe you'd like to be kept by him again?"

Janna's heart was beating too rapidly for her to make sense out of Ty's words. "You scared the life out of me, sneaking up like that!"

"Sneaking up? Hell's bells, Janna, you expect Cascabel to march in here with a band playing 'Onward Christian

Soldiers'?'' Ty demanded. ''You should have been on guard and seen me coming half a mile away!''

''Zebra was on guard,'' Janna said, standing and wiping her palms on her baggy pants. ''Yell at her. She must have recognized your smell and not made a fuss.''

Ty looked over at the mustang. Zebra was cropping at wisps of dry grass, lifting her head to scent the wind, then relaxing once more for a few moments before sniffing the wind again.

''Scented me, huh?'' Ty said, feeling his anger slide away as he realized that Janna had been well guarded after all. ''Are you saying I need some more time in your hot spring?''

''Ask Zebra. Her nose is better than mine,'' Janna retorted, forcing herself to look away from the hard, handsome planes of Ty's face. She closed her eyes, braced her fists in the small of her back and knuckled the tight muscles. ''Lordy, there was a root beneath me the size of my arm. No matter how I lay I couldn't avoid it.''

Whatever Ty had been going to say was forgotten beneath the impact of the supple reach and sway of Janna's body while she worked out the kinks of lying in cover for several hours.

''Here,'' he said gruffly. ''This will help.''

Janna's eyes flew open when she felt Ty's strong hands knead down her spine to her hips and back up again, lingering at the curve of her waist, rubbing the muscles in the small of her back, then caressing her waist once more before probing at the bands of cloth that wrapped her rib cage beneath her shirt. When he discovered the knotted muscle in her shoulder, he pressed down firmly, smoothing away the knot, making her knees loosen with relief.

''Oh, that feels good,'' Janna said huskily, her voice catching with pure pleasure. ''Yes, there. Ahhh ... You're unraveling me like a snagged mitten.''

With a low sigh that was almost a moan of pleasure, Janna let her head slowly drop back until it rested on Ty's chest. His hands hesitated as his heart slammed suddenly, sending blood rushing through his body, making him feel both heavy and powerful. Taking a discreet, deep breath, he resumed the leisurely, gentle massaging of Janna's back. Each murmur of her pleasure was like flames licking over him, tightening every muscle in his big body, flushing him with sensual heat.

The piñon-and-sunshine smell of Janna's hair intoxicated Ty. The curve of her neck above her clothes tantalized him. The sounds she made inflamed him. He wanted to bend over and taste the clean skin rising above her collar; then he wanted to peel her clothes away and taste soft skin that had never seen the sun. Yet she felt so fragile beneath his big hands, almost frail.

*She's just a girl,* Ty reminded himself harshly.

The memory of what Ned had said about Joe Troon and Janna went into Ty like a knife.

*Poor little thing,* Ty thought, moving his hands up to her shoulders and rubbing very gently before he released her with a reluctance he couldn't disguise. *She's known little of kindness from men. I can't take advantage of her just because she comes undone at a gentle touch.*

Janna turned her head, brushing her lips lightly over Ty's fingers as they moved away from her shoulder.

"Thank you," she murmured, her eyes closed and her voice a sigh of pleasure. "That felt as good as sunlight on a cold day."

Head still turned toward Ty, Janna opened her eyes—and felt her breath wedge tightly in her throat. He was so close, his eyes a glittering green that was both beautiful and savage. Tiny shards of black acted to deepen and define the vivid green surrounding the pupils. The dark gleam at the center of his eyes was repeated in the dense midnight of his eyelashes. His pulse beat full and strong at his temple and his lips were a flat line, as though he were angry or in pain.

"Ty? Did . . . did everything go all right in Sweetwater?"

Janna's question sounded very far away to Ty. Slowly he realized that he was staring into the depths of her rain-clear eyes while his fingertips traced and retraced the soft curve of her cheek.

"You're never going back there, Janna. That damned greasy bartender . . ." Ty's voice died. He could think of no delicate way to put into words what he had seen in Ned's eyes when he talked about women.

"Ned?" Janna asked, shrugging. "I stay out of his way. I'm careful never to be in town more than a few minutes at a time. Even if someone sees me, the Preacher makes sure I'm left alone."

"The Preacher pulled up stakes and went to the fort along with everybody else except Ned. Renegades from all over the territory are drifting down to Black Plateau to join Cascabel."

She frowned. "Why would Ned stay in town? Nothing in his dingy old shack is worth dying for."

"Before Cascabel caught me, I spent some time in Hat Rock. The folks there think Ned is the one selling guns to the Indians. If that's true, he wouldn't be too worried about getting his hair cut by a renegade barber."

"Pity," she said. "He could use a trim."

Ty smiled and Janna's stomach did a little dip and curtsy. She looked away hastily.

"Guess we'd better get back to Black Plateau," she said, clearing her throat. "It will be—"

"You're going to the fort," Ty interrupted.

"What?"

"It's too dangerous for a woman out here. On the way in to Sweetwater I cut the trail of three different groups of Indians. Two or three braves to a group. No sign of women or kids."

"Utes?"

Ty shrugged. "If they are, they're renegades. Black Hawk is trying to keep a short rein on his young warriors."

"Where were the tracks headed?"

"Sweetwater," Ty said succinctly. "I'll bet they bought rifles from Ned and then hit the trail for Cascabel's new camp."

Frowning, Janna looked at the sky over toward Black Plateau. The thunderheads were a solid, blue-black mass that trailed dark curtains of rain. The Fire Mountains had been buried in storm clouds when Ty left for town, which meant that several hours of rain had fallen on top of Black Plateau. The finger canyons would be filling with runoff before too long.

"Don't even think about it," Ty said, following Janna's glance. "The crack leading to your camp is probably up to a horse's fetlocks by now. Even if Zebra galloped all the way back, the water would be hock-high for sure. Chest-high, more than likely. But it wouldn't matter."

"It wouldn't?" Janna asked, surprised.

"Hell, no. We'd be dead before we got there, picked off by renegades and staked out for the ants to eat."

"But—"

"Dammit, Janna, don't you see? Cascabel must have passed the word that he's getting ready for one last push. Every renegade Indian west of the Mississippi is jumping reservation, stealing a horse and riding hard for Black Plateau. The only safe place for you is at the fort."

"For me?" she questioned.

Ty nodded tightly.

"What about you?" she asked.

"I'm going after Lucifer."

"What makes you think Cascabel won't get you?"

"If he does, that's my problem."

"Then we agree."

"We do?" asked Ty, surprised.

"We do. We'd better get going. I know a good place to camp on the northeast slope of the plateau."

"The fort is to the west of the plateau. Won't you be taking us the long way around?"

"I'm not going to the fort."

"The hell you aren't."

"That wasn't our agreement," Janna said quickly.

"What?"

"Our agreement was that it's your problem if Cascabel gets you, correct?"

"Yes."

"Then it follows that it's my problem if Cascabel gets me."

Ty opened his mouth, closed it, grabbed Janna in his powerful hands and lifted her until she was at eye level with him.

"You," he said coldly, "are going to the fort if I have to tie you and carry you belly down over my saddle."

"You don't have a saddle."

"Janna—"

"No," she interrupted. "You can tie me up and haul me from one end of the territory to the other, but the second you turn your back or take off the ropes I'll be gone to Black Plateau."

Ty looked into Janna's unflinching gray eyes and knew that she meant every word. Her body might have been slender but her will was fully the equal of his own.

Ty looked from Janna's wide gray eyes to her lips flushed with heat and life. He could think of many, many things he would like to do at that moment, but none would be quite as sweet as sliding his tongue into her mouth until he could taste nothing but her, feel nothing but her, know nothing but her.

Yet he shouldn't even touch her. Even if she didn't have the sense to realize it, she was a nearly helpless girl whose life was at risk every hour she spent running free with her mustangs.

"What am I going to do with you?" he asked huskily.

"Same thing I'm going to do with you," she retorted.

Ty smiled slowly. "What are you going to do with me?" he asked, his voice deep, his mouth frankly sensual.

"Hunt L-Lucifer," Janna said, stammering slightly, wondering what had given Ty's green eyes their sudden heat and intensity.

"I thought you didn't want to help anyone catch Lucifer."

"I said 'hunt,' not 'catch.'"

"Little one, what I hunt, I catch."

Janna tried to breathe, couldn't, and tried again. "Ty..." she said, her voice ragged.

The word sounded more like a sigh than a name. She licked her lips and prepared to try again.

Ty's hands tightened almost painfully around Janna's rib cage as he watched the pink tip of her tongue appear and disappear, leaving behind lips that were moist, soft and inviting. Knowing he shouldn't, unable to help himself, he slowly brought Janna closer to his own mouth.

Just beyond the shelter of the brush, Zebra threw up her head and pricked her ears, staring upwind. Her nostrils flared, fluttered and flared again. Abruptly her ears flattened to her head.

Ty dropped to the ground, taking Janna with him.

Moments later, no more than two hundred feet away, a group of four Indian warriors rode out of a shallow ravine.

# Chapter Fourteen

Stomach on the hard, uneven ground, Janna lay wedged between a boulder on one side and Ty's body on the other. Very slowly she turned her head until she could see beneath Ty's chin. He had a pistol in his left hand and was easing his right hand toward another boulder, where he had propped his new carbine before he woke her up. From the corner of her eye she saw his long fingers wrap around the stock of the weapon. Without making a sound he lifted the carbine and slowly, slowly eased it into firing position at his shoulder.

Screened by brush and rocks, Janna and Ty watched the warriors cross a small rise and angle back toward the cover of another dry wash. For long minutes after the Indians vanished, Ty lay unmoving. The weight of his body ensured that Janna stayed motionless, as well. Not until Zebra snorted, rubbed her muzzle against her knee and then resumed grazing did Ty release Janna. Even so, when he spoke to her, he laid his lips against her ear, and his voice was a mere thread of sound.

"Ready to go to the fort now?"

Janna turned until she could see his eyes, so close they all but filled her world.

"No," she said distinctly.

"You're a fool, Janna Wayland."

"Then so are you."

"I'm a man."

"You support my argument," she shot back in a fierce whisper.

Thunder broke and rumbled over the land.

"We should go as far as we can before the storm breaks," Ty said. "That way our tracks will be washed away before any wandering renegades can find us." He came to his feet, pulling Janna after him. "Get on Zebra. I'll ride behind you."

Janna swung up on the mare and looked back at Ty. He was shrugging on a big, heavy backpack stuffed with clothes, bedding and supplies. The carbine was strapped to the back of the pack, muzzle down, riding in what would have been a saddle holster if Ty had had a saddle; but he didn't. He was his own pack mule for the moment.

Ty handed Janna an oilskin slicker, jerked his new hat into place and swung up behind her, heavy backpack and all.

Fat, cold drops of rain began to fall.

"Put on the slicker," he said.

"What about you?"

"Put on the damned slicker!"

Janna shook out the drab, canvas-colored cloth, saw that it was no more than a tarpaulin with a slit for a man's head, and promptly widened the slit with her knife.

"What are you doing?" Ty demanded.

"Making it big enough for two. Hang on to your hat."

Janna turned around enough to pull the slicker over Ty's head. Facing forward again, she put her own head through the slit and tucked flapping folds beneath her legs. Ty's motions told her that he was doing the same thing, although while he did it, he was muttering a lot of words she preferred not to overhear.

When Janna settled into place to ride, she realized that she was sitting quite close to Ty. In fact, she couldn't have been sitting closer unless she had been on his lap rather than surrounded by it. She felt the rub of his thighs along hers, the small movements of his hips and the supple swaying of his torso as he adjusted his body to Zebra's stride. Janna was doing the same—rocking slightly, rubbing gently, swaying, cocooned in oilcloth and wrapped in warmth.

Once she got used to the novelty of being so close to Ty, she realized that it was deliciously warm and comfortable, except for the shivery sensations that uncurled along her nerve endings at odd moments when his hands brushed her thighs or his breath rushed over her neck. And even those unexpected quivers of heat within her body were—intriguing. With an unconscious sound of pleasure, she settled more deeply into the warmth and muscular resilience of Ty's body.

Ty set his teeth until his jaw ached, barely resisting the impulse to rip off the oilcloth and free himself from the innocent, incendiary rock and sway of Janna's body. The wind gusted, bringing cold splashes of sensation that only made the shared intimacy of the oilcloth more vivid.

After a time it began to rain in earnest, as though the descending sun had somehow freed the water drops from their cloud prisons. The oilcloth turned away much of the rain, but not all. Although it became increasingly damp beneath the poncho, neither Janna nor Ty suggested stopping, for there was no cover nearby worthy of mention. When lightning bolts became closer and more frequent, Janna said something that Ty couldn't catch. He bent forward, bringing his mouth against her ear.

"What?"

She turned toward him, so close that her warm breath washed over his lips. "Hang on."

The belling of thunder drowned out Ty's response, which was just as well. Instinctively his legs clamped around Zebra's barrel as the mare went from a walk to a gallop. The rhythmic rocking motion intensified the friction of Janna's body rubbing against Ty's. The resulting heat was a bittersweet pain. Each time the mare climbed a small rise, Janna's buttocks pressed more snugly into his lap, stroking his aroused flesh. Each time the mare descended, he slid harder against Janna, their bodies separated by only a few folds of cloth, until he wanted nothing more than to imprison her hips in his hands and move with her until he burst.

"How much farther?" asked Ty through gritted teeth.

"Two miles."

Ty wondered if he would survive. He couldn't decide if the stimulation would have been easier to bear at half the pace and twice the time of suffering, or if twice the stimulation and half the time was indeed the easier course.

Oblivious to Ty's masculine discomfort, Janna guided Zebra into what looked like a simple thickening of brush. It turned out to be a narrow trail snaking up the base of a nameless mesa. Soon Ty had to reach around Janna and grab the mare's mane with both hands to keep his slippery seat.

Partway up the mesa, the trail ended in a shallow overhang of red rock stained with streaks of very dark brown. There was no way out and no other trail but the one they had just come up. Obviously this was the shelter Janna had chosen.

Ty didn't wait for an invitation to dismount. He ducked out of the shared slicker and slid from Zebra's back, barely biting off a savage word when the shock of landing jolted through his aroused body. He eyed the narrow shelter with a mixture of relief and anger. There was just enough room for the mustang and two people to stay reasonably dry—if the mustang weren't restless and the two people occupied the same space at the same time.

Bitterly Ty told himself that at least staying warm without a fire wouldn't be a problem. All he had to do was look at Janna, or even think about looking at her, and his new pants fit way too tightly. He told himself that it was because the pants were too small, and he knew he lied. He could count his heartbeats in the hard flesh that had risen between his legs, and every beat made him want to draw up in pain.

*What the hell is the matter with me?* he asked himself savagely. *I've never gotten this hot over a full-grown woman wearing silk and perfume. Why am I getting in a lather over a ragged little waif with no more curves than a fence rail?*

The only answer that came to Ty was the memory of Janna's uninhibited response when he had rubbed her back. If such an impersonal touch made her breath shiver and break, what would happen if he touched her the way he wanted to, no holds barred, nothing between them but the sensual heat of their bodies?

Biting back a curse, Ty fought to subdue the demands of his own flesh. He forced himself to ignore the sexual urgency that grew greater with each of his rapid heartbeats, reminding him that he was very much a man and that Janna, despite her ragged men's clothes and slender body, was way too much woman for his comfort.

Without a word to Janna, Ty began exploring the dimensions of the ledge that would be his prison for the night. From the corner of her eyes, Janna watched Ty prowl while she dismounted and checked Zebra's hooves for stones. There were none. She caressed the mare's curious, nudging nose for a few minutes, tugging from time to time on the horse's soft lips in a gentle kind of teasing that Zebra enjoyed as much as Janna did.

"Go find dinner," Janna said finally, pushing Zebra's velvet muzzle away.

Apparently the mare had grazed enough while waiting for Ty to return. She showed no inclination to go back down the steep trail to look for food.

"Then get out of the way," Janna said, exasperated.

Zebra looked at her.

Janna laced her fingers in the mare's mane and tugged. Obediently Zebra moved forward, allowing herself to be led to the opposite end of the ledge, where it angled down to the nearly invisible trail.

"It's all yours, girl."

Thunder rumbled heavily, making the ground quiver. Zebra flicked her ears and sighed.

"Have you ever hobbled her?" Ty asked, eyeing the narrow space they all had to share.

Janna shook her head.

"Hope to hell she doesn't walk in her sleep," he muttered, unloading his backpack. The burden hit the ground with a *thump* that spoke eloquently of weight.

"We spent three days up here in the spring, when Cascabel was trying to catch Lucifer," Janna said. "Zebra never stepped on me once. I think she has me confused with a foal. When I lie down to sleep, she'll move off to graze, but she always keeps her eye on the place where I'm sleeping. If anything happens, she gives me a warning."

"Are all your mustangs like that?"

She shook her head again. "No, just Zebra. Most of the time she really likes my company."

"Most of the time?"

"When she's in season, she stays close to Lucifer and I stay away."

Ty glanced over at Zebra. "Is she in season now?"

"It's early. But if she isn't pregnant by winter, it won't be Lucifer's fault," Janna said dryly.

Ty's smile gleamed for an instant and he drawled, "I'm sure Lucifer takes good care of his mares. I'm surprised he lets her wander, though."

"He's too busy running from men and driving off other stallions to worry about a stubborn bunch quitter. Besides, he's figured out that Zebra always comes back."

"How long have you been following Lucifer's bunch?"

"Since Pa died."

"Has Lucifer always kept to the same territory?"

"It's bigger than it was in the beginning, but otherwise Lucifer is like all wild animals. He sticks to what he knows is safe unless he's forced to change. When that happens, he goes into hiding with just a few of his wildest mares."

"Do you know where he goes?"

Janna gave Ty an unhappy look and said nothing. He knew that she was protecting the big stud's secrets. He didn't blame her, but he intended to have those secrets just the same.

"You know Joe Troon," Ty said. "How good a shot is he?"

The change of subject surprised Janna. "Pretty good, unless he's been drinking. Then he's only fair."

"Is he a good tracker?"

"Not as good as you or me."

"You're sure?"

"Once he spent a whole afternoon looking for me, and I was only fifteen feet away most of the time."

Ty closed his eyes against the sudden rush of adrenaline that came when he thought of Janna alone, hiding in the brush, and a man like Troon searching for her with tight britches and pure lust in his blood.

"Can Troon get within rifle range of Lucifer?"

Janna froze. "What are you saying?"

"Ned told me that Troon took his rifle and went hunting. He's going to crease Lucifer. Unless Troon is a damn fine shot, he'll end up killing Lucifer by mistake."

A shudder ran through Janna's clenched body. Her greatest fear had been that some greedy mustanger would give up trying to catch the elusive stallion and simply kill him instead, thereby making the job of capturing the herd much easier.

"If Troon catches the mustangs in one of the pocket canyons, he could shoot from the cliffs above. But Lucifer's been chased so much lately that he's stayed away from the east side of Black Plateau. He's pushed north and west, into the slick rock country that only the Indians know."

"Will he stay there?"

Janna wanted to say yes, but she knew Lucifer too well. He had been driven from his preferred range in the past; he had always returned to Black Plateau, often with new mares he had run off from ranches or other wild herds. The stone canyons, year-round seeps and untrammeled space of the land spreading out from the plateau seemed to have an indelible allure for the big stallion. Year after year he returned, no matter how hard man chased him. But this time he would be chased by bullets that even his strong legs couldn't outrun.

The thought was unbearable to Janna. There was only one way she might be able to prevent Lucifer's death—by betraying him to a man who wouldn't use a gun.

Janna looked up into Ty's steady green glance and prayed that she was making the right decision.

"The best grazing and water for a hundred miles in any direction is around Black Plateau," she said, her mouth dry. "I know every seep, every bit of cover, every place where grass grows lush and thick. I'll take you to each secret place until we find Lucifer, but first you have to promise me one thing."

The unhappiness and determination in Janna's face made Ty wish for a moment that he had never heard of the big black stallion. But he had heard of Lucifer, and so had every other man from the Rio Grande to the Snake River. The stallion's time as a free-ranging mustang was rapidly coming to an end, and Janna knew it as well as Ty did. That was why she was blinking back tears and trying to speak.

"I'll be as gentle as possible with him," Ty said in a low voice, taking Janna's hand between his own. "I don't want to break Lucifer's spirit. I just want to breed him with some fine mares. I'll take him to Logan's ranch in Wyoming and let him run with the remuda while I build my own ranch. For

Lucifer, it will be almost as good as running free down here. He'll be safe, Janna. No man will come after him with a rifle or a whip.

"And if he can't accept capture," Ty continued, stroking Janna's hand with his fingertips, "I'll turn Lucifer loose myself. I'd rather that he die free than live in a cage with eyes as dull as stones. Is that what you wanted me to promise?"

She drew a shaking breath. "Thank you, but I already knew those things about you or I'd never have spoken in the first place and offered to help you."

"Then is it money you want? I don't have much, but I'll be glad to—"

"No," she interrupted swiftly. "I'd never take money for Lucifer. I want you to promise that you'll let me try to gentle him first. I couldn't bear to see him brought down by a rope and broken by force."

Ty thought of the stallion's raw power and his hard, flashing hooves. "No. It's much too dangerous."

For a long moment Janna looked at Ty's face. The dying rays of the sun revealed a determination as great as her own. Without a word she eased her hand from his grasp, tossed the rain poncho aside and went about smoothing out a place to sleep for the night. As she worked Ty watched her in silence, wondering what she was thinking.

Finally the lightning barrage ended, leaving only a hard, steady rain. Ty looked over at Janna, who was half-reclining against the stone wall. In the darkness he couldn't be sure whether she was asleep. He thought she was.

"Janna?" he called softly.

No answer came.

Ty pulled on the rain poncho and walked from the protection of the ledge. If he had been camping with one of his brothers, he wouldn't have gone more than ten feet before relieving himself. As it was, he went considerably farther.

When he came back Janna was gone.

# Chapter Fifteen

The cold rain made Janna shiver and long for the bedroll he had left in her winter camp, but no matter how much it rained, she didn't stop to find shelter from the downpour. As long as it rained her tracks would be washed out. Besides, she was less than three miles from one of her Black Plateau caches. By morning she would be warm and dry and sleeping in a place no man would ever find.

Not even Ty MacKenzie.

When the clouds finally dissolved into streamers of mist buffeted by a playful wind, Janna was beginning to wish she hadn't left Zebra behind. But she hadn't been able to bring herself to leave Ty afoot in a land teeming with Indian renegades. Zebra would at least take him as far as the thousand hidden canyons and secret springs of Black Plateau before she trotted off to look for Lucifer's herd once more.

And Janna had no doubt that it would be toward Black Plateau that Ty headed, rather than toward the safety of the fort. He wouldn't leave the territory until he had what he had come for—Lucifer.

The cold light of a new moon gave small illumination and less comfort to Janna as she walked steadily toward the dark bulk of the plateau, which rose from the land until it shut out the stars along the horizon. When she could see the faint notch she called Wind Gap, she turned west. Alternately running and walking, she came closer to the place that was as much a home as she had ever had.

In the darkness before dawn, it took Janna three tries to find the mound of broken boulders where she had stashed a spare canteen, blanket, knife and matches. The blanket was mouse chewed and musty but dry. She wrapped it around her and filled her canteen from a hole that had been worn in solid stone, creating a bowl that held rainwater after a storm.

Canteen and knife on her hip, dry matches in her shirt pocket, Janna climbed farther up the canyon until she came to a place where water from runoff streams had long ago worn out a room-size hole in the canyon wall. Water no longer reached the hollow; even in the highest flood it remained safe and dry. By the time she scrambled up the last steep pitch of rock to the east-facing hollow, Janna was trembling with hunger, cold and exhaustion.

Because the wind was from the north, only the hardest gusts reached her. She thought longingly of the hot spring in her winter camp, and of sunlight and of beds fragrant with piñon. Then she thought of the warmth of Ty's big body, and the sweet friction of his chest against her back, his thighs against her thighs, his arms like warm steel around her as he hung on to Zebra's long mane.

The curious, fluttering warmth returned to the pit of Janna's stomach, making her shiver with something more than cold. She remembered Ty's strength, the feel of his flexed muscle when he had lifted her and she had balanced herself by hanging on to his arms. The memory made her palms tingle as though she had been rubbing them along his sleeves. She thought of the strained, intent look on his face when he had bent down to her in the thicket where he had startled her from a deep sleep; and she wondered what would have happened if Zebra hadn't scented the renegades on the wind, ending the hushed expectancy of the moment.

After a time Janna finally fell asleep. Her dreams were as restless as the wind.

Ty slept until the wind swept the sky free of clouds, allowing the moon's narrow silver smile to illuminate the land.

"How about it, girl?" Ty said very softly. "You afraid of the dark?"

Zebra tugged impatiently against the hand restraining her nose. She wanted to be free to go down the trail.

"Yeah, that's what I thought. Which will you go after, Janna or that big black stud?"

Zebra snorted.

"Well, I'll tell you, girl," Ty said, swinging onto the mare's warm back, "I hope it's Janna. When I find her, I'm going to..."

Ty's voice faded. He didn't know what he was going to do when he found Janna. His dreams had left him restive and aroused, and as surly as a bear with a broken tooth. He was furious that Janna had slipped out into the stormy night without so much as a makeshift poncho to turn away the rain. No matter how many times he told himself that she had earned whatever her stubbornness brought her—or that she was obviously able to take care of herself in any case—the thought of her being wet and cold and hungry haunted him.

"Hell, why didn't she at least ride you?" muttered Ty to the horse. "Did she figure your tracks wouldn't wash out well enough? Or did she figure you would run off and I'd follow and miss her tracks completely?"

Zebra didn't even pause at the sound of her rider's muttered questions. She picked her way down the slope with the swift, clean poise that only a mustang could achieve over the rugged land.

Ty didn't bother trying to guide Zebra. He didn't know where he was going. Besides, in the dark the mare's senses were much more acute than his own. His only advantage over the mustang was his brain.

*Some advantage,* Ty told himself sardonically. *I can't even outwit a slip of a girl.*

The thought didn't improve his disposition. Nor did the fact that every time he closed his eyes, he saw the utter stillness of Janna's face when he had refused to promise that she would be the one to capture Lucifer.

*Hellfire and damnation,* Ty seethed silently. *What kind of a man does she think I am to let her risk her scrawny little ass fighting that stud?*

A vivid memory of Janna's body condensed in Ty's mind, reminding him that her bottom wasn't scrawny at all. It had been smooth and resilient beneath his hands when he had pulled her from the horse. Her hips had curved enticingly below her slender waist, curves that sheltered feminine secrets, curves that invited a man's hands to follow them, then his mouth, his lips, his tongue....

Ty shifted to relieve the pressure on his burgeoning, hardening flesh. He ached with every heartbeat, an ache that had become all too familiar since his mind had discovered what his body had known all along: Janna was a woman, not a boy.

*Did she know how much I wanted her? Is that why she ran out into the storm?*

Uneasiness flattened Ty's mouth into a hard line. Janna had saved his life, risking her own in the process. The thought that he, however unintentionally, had driven her away from the protection he could offer in this troubled land made him disgusted with himself and his unruly body.

Ty's reaction to Janna baffled him. He had never pursued women in the past; he had never had to. They came to him like moths to a naked flame. He took what they offered, gave them pleasure in return and avoided virgins because he was determined not to marry until he could have a fine silk lady for a wife. He had made no secret of his intention to remain free, but the women who came to him either hadn't believed him or hadn't cared.

*But none of them ran from me, by God. Hell, often as not
I was running from them!*

The cold wind swirled down from Black Plateau's rumpled heights, reminding Ty of how miserable Janna must
be—on foot, no real jacket and probably soaking wet, as
well. He glared out at the pale rose dawn as though it were
responsible for all that had gone wrong since he had been
within moments of catching the big black stud, only to find
himself caught by Cascabel instead.

The dawn sky passed from pale pink to a pale, rain-
scrubbed blue. There was little real warmth in the early-
morning sun, but as Zebra trotted toward the crest of a long
rise, the light was strong enough to allow Ty to find out
where he was. He halted Zebra just below the top of the rise,
dug a new spyglass out of his backpack and looked out over
his trail. Nothing moved behind him but a few ravens flying blackly through the hushed air.

Ty shifted position, looking to the right and the left. It
was the same everywhere he could see. Nothing moving. He
couldn't have been more alone if he had been the first man
on earth.

Zebra snorted and shifted her weight, telling Ty that she
wanted to be on her way.

"Easy girl. Let me look around."

No matter where Ty looked, the countryside was daunt-
ing. It was also beautiful to anyone who appreciated the
naked form of mountains and mesas, stone pinnacles and
steep canyons, long crests and ridges of rocks devoid of
gentle greenery. The plants that existed were spread out over
the rugged countryside so thinly that the stone substructure
of the land was visible in many places. Against the deepening blue of the sky, rock ridges and cliffs and gorges gleamed
in every color from white through pink to rusty red and
black. On the lower slopes juniper stood out like deep green
flames burning at random on the fantastic rock formations.

The only familiar-looking part of the landscape to someone who hadn't been born west of the Mississippi was the pile of stone known as Black Plateau; from a distance, it rather resembled a ruined mountain. Other than that, the stark combination of sheer red or white cliffs and rumpled rivers of black lava were like nothing Ty had ever seen. He could still remember the excitement and visceral sense of danger that the land had called forth from him at first look. Harsh, beautiful, beguiling in its secrets and its surprises, the vast country threatened his body even as it compelled his soul.

Frowning, Ty looked out over the land behind him once more, letting his gaze go slightly unfocused. Even using that old hunter's trick to reveal movement in a vast landscape, Ty saw nothing new. If Janna were somewhere behind him, he couldn't see her. Nor could he see any renegades, soldiers, mustangs or rabbits. He put the spyglass away.

"All right, girl. Let's go."

Zebra moved out smartly, hurrying over the crest of the rise as though she understood that to silhouette herself against the sky was to ask for unwanted attention. The mustang had taken a straight line beginning at the place where they had sheltered from the worst of the rain and ending at the long, broken line of cliffs that marked the eastern margin of Black Plateau. Ty knew of no way up onto the plateau from the east side, unless there was a game trail. In any case, he wouldn't want to try such a path riding bareback on a mustang that might take a notion to unload him at any time.

"I can ride you or track you," Ty muttered. "Which would be better?"

If personal safety were the most important consideration, Ty knew he should let the mustang go and track her. But he wasn't worried about his own safety half as much as he was about finding Janna quickly; and for speed, riding beat tracking six ways from Sunday. If Zebra unloaded him, then he could worry about tracking her through the afternoon thunderstorms that occurred as often as not in the canyon country. Until then, he would stay with her like a cactus thorn and hope to get to Janna before she caught lung fever from running around in the rain.

And Ty would also hope that Troon poured enough rotgut down his throat to ruin his aim, so that Lucifer lived to be captured by Tyrell MacKenzie.

## Chapter Sixteen

The track was as perfect and as unexpected as a diamond in a handful of mud.

"Whoa, Zebra."

Ty might as well have saved his breath. Zebra had already stopped and lowered her nose to the footprint. She sucked in air, blew it out and sucked it in again. Unlike the mare, Ty didn't have to rely on his sense of smell; he had no doubt that the line of slender footprints was Janna's. What baffled him was that the tracks appeared from nowhere and vanished within thirty feet.

*Bruja.* Witch.

Skin shifted and prickled on Ty's neck. He wasn't a superstitious man, but it was easier to believe in witches than it was to believe that something as generous and gentle as Janna had survived unaided in this land.

Atop Zebra, Ty quartered the land where the prints had vanished. Beyond them he spotted a narrow tongue of stone coming in from the right. The toe of the last track was more heavily imprinted, as though Janna had dug into the wet ground in the act of leaping toward the stone. Zebra whuffed over the stone tongue for a minute before she looked back at Ty as though to ask, *Well, what now?*

"Good question," Ty muttered.

The runner of rock led to a rugged, narrow ridge that was nothing but wind-smoothed stone. Someone as agile as Janna might have been able to use the ridge as a trail, but it would be rough going for the mustang and her rider.

Like all good hunters, Ty had learned long ago that tracks weren't the only way to follow prey. A better way was to know where the prey was going. He had seen the dismay and fear in Janna's face at the thought of Lucifer being hunted with a rifle. It took no particular prescience on Ty's part to decide that she would head for Lucifer by the shortest possible route. Unfortunately, nothing of the country ahead of him looked passable by man, much less by horse.

Then Ty remembered what Janna had said: *I know every seep, every bit of cover, every place where grass grows lush and thick.*

Sitting motionless, Ty looked at the land ahead of him. It wasn't simply luck that had led him to cut across Janna's trail. In fact, luck had had little to do with it. Despite the vastness of the land itself, there were relatively few places where people and animals could move freely, and fewer still where they could pass from one mesa or canyon to another. The jutting mesas, deep stone ravines, and unfailing ruggedness of the land limited movement to the broad washes between Black Plateau and the mesas or to snaking around the plateau itself. Everything—deer, wild horses, Indians, cattle and cowhands alike—was forced to follow pretty much the same course over the face of the land.

Hiding was another matter entirely. There were literally thousands of places for a person to hide. But eventually every rabbit had to come out into the open to find water or to find food or simply to find a safer place to hide.

Janna was no different.

Janna bit her lip and tugged her hat lower over her auburn hair, concealing any telltale flash of color. The sun's heat had strengthened to the point that cold was no longer a problem for her. Her canteen took care of her thirst. Her stomach, however, was unhappy. It reminded her ceaselessly that it was past time for breakfast and lunch, not to mention that she hadn't had so much as a snack after her midnight walk in the rain.

Yet hunger wasn't Janna's biggest problem. Ty was. Barely a half mile away, he sat on stone outcropping that gave him a commanding view of the countryside. A rugged piñon that grew in the crevices gave concealment to his body; if Janna hadn't caught a glimpse of movement when he had climbed up to his present position, she would never have spotted him in time to go to ground.

Now she was trapped. She had to move across bare rock in order to get to the sole path up Black Plateau's steep eastern side. The instant she broke cover Ty would be on her like a hungry coyote on a rabbit.

*Why didn't you just ride Zebra up onto the plateau when she became restless?* Janna silently demanded of Ty. *Why did you turn her loose? She could lead you to Lucifer as fast as I could, so why are you staked out over there looking for me instead of for that stallion?*

Nothing answered Janna's silent questions. She shifted her weight carefully, rubbing her hip where a loose rock had been digging into tender flesh. With an impatient sound she turned her head just enough to look across the distance separating her from Ty.

He was still there.

Ordinarily Janna would simply have settled deeper into cover and outwaited her hunter. She had done it many times before, when Cascabel's men had come across her tracks and given chase. Always her patience had proven to be greater than that of her pursuers.

But no longer. Janna's patience was evaporating even more quickly than rain puddles beneath the hot sun. Every minute she stayed in hiding was one minute closer to Lucifer for Joe Troon. The thought was agony to Janna, especially when she knew that she wasn't in any real danger from Ty. Even if he caught her, he wouldn't beat or rape or torture her. In fact, Janna couldn't think of anything painful he would be likely to do to her, except to remind her of how far she was from his ideal of a silken lady.

The thought deepened the unhappy downward curve of Janna's mouth. Beyond being certain that she didn't stand out against the rugged landscape, she had never thought much about her appearance one way or another. Now she did. Seeing Ty in his new clothes with his cheeks smooth shaven had driven home to her just how handsome he was, and by how great a margin she missed being the fragile silken lady who could attract and hold him.

Janna looked across the wild land at Ty and admitted to herself how much she wanted to be his dream. And at the same time she admitted to herself how impossible it was for her to be that dream.

If she had been the silken lady of Ty's desire, she would have died at the same lonely water hole her father had, for there had been no one to depend on but herself. If she hadn't died there, she would certainly have starved, because she would not have been able to catch and kill her own food. Instead of feeling wretched because she was self-sufficient, she should be thanking God for her ability to adjust to the harsh demands of surviving in the wild land.

*Do I really want to be all soft and useless just so I can attract Ty?* she asked herself scornfully.

*Yes.*

The prompt, honest reply didn't improve Janna's humor. She glared out across the ground separating Ty from herself.

*If I'd been all simpering and soft in the head, Cascabel would have tracked Ty down and killed him. But did Ty ever think of that? No. He just mooned over a will-o'-the-wisp that would probably faint combing tangles out of her own hair.*

Janna glared across the space separating herself from Ty. *Move, dammit! I've got better things to do even if you don't.*

Ty remained in place.

Another half hour crawled by, marked by no more motion than that of the shadows responding to the slow arc of the sun across the empty sky. Ravens called across empty ravines. Rabbits nibbled on brush. Lizards whisked across hot rock, towing the racing black shape of their shadows behind. A hawk circled overhead, sending its keening cry to the earth like a thrown lance. Janna felt like calling out in return, venting her growing frustration.

Another sound came—a rifle shot rather than the call of a hawk. The sound was distant and wasn't repeated.

Three things occurred to Janna simultaneously. The first was that no white man was crazy enough to call down the attention of Cascabel's renegades by shooting at game. The second was that Joe Troon had taken a shot at Lucifer. The third was that Ty would be looking in the direction of the shot rather than at the open space between herself and the route up the east side of Black Plateau.

No sooner had the thought occurred than Janna acted. She popped out of the crevice in which she had hidden and began running swiftly.

Ty had heard the sound of the rifle shot at the same instant Janna did. Like her, he had thought of several things simultaneously while he strained to hear other shots and heard only the wind. But he didn't look in the direction of the shot. He knew that whatever had happened or was happening over there was too far away for him to affect. His attention never wavered from the broken land between himself and the plateau.

He spotted Janna instantly. He had spent the past few hours memorizing the possible approaches to the vague trail he had spotted up onto Black Plateau, so he didn't even hesitate to choose his own route. He came to his feet and hit top speed within a few strides, running hard and fast and clean, covering ground with a devouring speed, closing in on Janna with a diagonal course.

Janna caught the motion from the corner of her eye, recognized Ty and redoubled her own efforts to reach the plateau trail. It was as though she were standing still. She had seen Ty run once before, but he had been injured then, reeling from the effects of running Cascabel's gauntlet. Ty wasn't injured now. He ran with the speed of a wolf, closing the space between himself and his prey with every leaping stride.

One instant Janna was in full flight—the next instant she was brought down on the hard earth. Only it wasn't the ground she fell upon, it was Ty, who had turned as he grabbed her so that it would be his body that took the impact of the unforgiving land.

Even so, Janna was knocked breathless. By the time she could react, it was too late. She was flat on her back, pinned to the hot earth by the weight of Ty's big body. He caught her wrists and held them above her head, imprisoned in his hands.

"Don't you think it's time that you and I had a little chat?" Ty drawled.

"Let go of me!"

"Promise you won't run?"

Janna twisted abruptly, trying to throw Ty off. He simply settled a bit more heavily onto her body.

"I'm bigger than you are, if you hadn't noticed," Ty said. "A little thing like you doesn't have a chance against a man of any size, much less one as big as I am."

Janna started calling Ty the same names her father had used when the wagon mule wouldn't move. "You misbegotten whelp of a cross-eyed cow and the stupidest stud son of a bitch that God ever—"

A big hand clamped over Janna's mouth, cutting off the flow of her invective.

"Didn't anybody ever tell you a girl shouldn't use such language?"

The muffled sounds from beneath Ty's hand told him that Janna wasn't listening to him. She flailed against his shoulder and chin with the hand he had freed in order to cover her mouth. He lifted that hand and grabbed her wrist again.

"Bastard son of a one-legged whore and a one-eyed, flea-brained—"

Abruptly Ty's hard mouth covered Janna's. Her lips were open, her breath hot, the taste of her as fresh as rain. He shuddered heavily and thrust his tongue deep into her mouth again and again, wanting to devour her.

The fierceness of Ty's mouth and the wild penetration of his tongue shocked Janna into complete stillness. She trembled helplessly, overpowered by his strength and by her awareness of his body moving over hers, rubbing urgently, as though he were trying to push her into the ground.

Janna couldn't move, couldn't breathe, and still the contact went on and on, his big body crushing hers, showing her how futile it was to fight him. She tried to speak and found she couldn't even do that. Twisting, writhing, she tried to fight him but he was too big, his body was everywhere; she was as helpless as a mouse caught in the talons of a hawk.

# *Chapter Seventeen*

When Ty finally tore his mouth away and stared down at Janna, he was breathing in deep, ragged bursts and her pupils were wide, dark, enormous, magnified by tears.

"Don't you ever run from me again," Ty said, his voice hoarse and his eyes almost black from the dilation of his pupils.

Janna felt the violent shudder that shook his body, felt the quick force of his breaths against the tears on her cheeks, felt the savage power of his clenched muscles. She should have been terrified, yet at some deep, subconscious level she knew that Ty wouldn't truly hurt her. Even so, she trembled, not understanding the feelings that were coursing through her body—and through his.

"You can let me g-go," she said shakily. "I w-won't run."

For the space of several breaths there was only silence and the wild glitter of Ty's eyes. Abruptly he let go of Janna and rolled aside into a sitting position, drawing his legs up to his body as though he were in pain.

"Christ," Ty said through clenched teeth. "I'm sorry, little one. I've never forced myself on a woman in my life."

Janna let out one long, ragged breath and then another. "It's all right."

"Like hell it is," he snarled. He turned his head and looked at her with eyes as hard as stone. "You don't be-

long out here, Janna Wayland. You're a walking temptation to every man who sees you all alone and unprotected.
I'm going to take you to the fort and that's final.''

"If you do that, Joe Troon will kill Lucifer, assuming he
hasn't already. That could have been the rifle shot we
heard.''

Ty said something savage beneath his breath, then added,
"You don't understand.''

"No, it's you who doesn't understand,'' Janna said
quickly. "At the fort or in any town or at one of the ranches,
I'm a girl without kin, fit only for washing clothes or dishes
or feeding men or...well, you know.'' Janna shook her head
fiercely. "I don't want that. Out here I'm free of their sly
looks and pawing hands. The only man out here is you, and
you don't think of me that way.''

"I don't? What the hell do you think just happened?'' Ty
demanded, hardly able to believe his ears.

"I made you mad and you got even.'' Janna shrugged.
"So what? I've taken a lot worse from men and survived.''

Ty started to ask what Janna meant, then realized that he
didn't want to know. He had heard his sister's broken cries
when she relived in nightmare the time of her captivity at the
hands of white raiders. The thought of Janna being brutalized like that was unendurable. She was so fierce in her desire for freedom, so terrifyingly fragile beneath the heavy
clothes that muffled her.

"God,'' Ty groaned, putting his head in his hands, hating himself. "Janna...little one...I didn't mean to hurt
you.''

"But you didn't.'' She looked at him anxiously when he
didn't respond. She put her hand on his wrist where the shirt
ended and his warm flesh began. "Ty? Honest. You scared
me a little and confused me a lot, but you didn't hurt me at
all. And I've changed my mind. I'll help you get Lucifer
before Joe Troon does.''

For a long moment Ty stared at the hand resting on his wrist. The fingers were long and delicate, gently browned by the sun, the nails beautifully formed and pink with health, the skin supple and warm. He wanted to pick up that feminine hand and kiss the hollow of her palm, lick the sensitive skin between her fingers, bite gently at the pad of flesh at the base of her thumb until her breath broke and her hand curled around his touch like a sleeping flower....

"Stop looking at me like that," Janna said, snatching her fingers back. "I know my hand isn't lily-white and soft and stinking of perfume, but it's a good hand all the same. It helped to save your stupid masculine hide, remember?"

Ty opened his mouth to tell Janna that she had misunderstood, that he had been thinking how alluring her hand was rather than the opposite. At the last instant common sense held his tongue in check. She refused to leave the country, and he couldn't leave until he had Lucifer. He needed her help with the stallion and she needed him to guard her back; but he was so woman hungry that he barely trusted himself to keep his hands off her. Keeping her irritated with him would go a long way toward maintaining a safe distance between them. Knowing what her experience with men must have been like, he simply couldn't have lived with himself if Janna thought he were demanding sex in return for safety or anything else he could give her.

"And I've been trying to thank you for saving my hide by saving yours in return," Ty drawled, "but to hell with it. You want to run around here risking your scrawny little self, you go right ahead. Me? I'm just thanking God that He made you so damned unappealing to men. Any other woman and I'd be tempted to find out what was beneath all the rough clothes. But you? You're like a baby quail, all eyes and mouth and frizzled features. With you I'm as safe from the temptations of the flesh as any monk in a monastery."

"Why, you—"

Ty's hand shot out, covering Janna's mouth and cutting off her words.

"You should be down on your knees thanking God that I feel that way," Ty said savagely. "If I ever put my hands on you, it wouldn't be violins and roses. I'm too woman hungry to stop short of taking what I need. And that's all it would be. Taking. No promises, no soft words, no wedding vows, nothing but male hunger and a handy female."

Janna heard every word but only cared about Ty's admission that he was woman hungry. It gave her the weapon she needed. It appeared that her efforts at proving she was a woman had been having some effect.

She smiled rather bitterly and decided that she would make him eat every one of his cutting words about her lack of womanly allure. From that moment on she would redouble her efforts to remind him that she was a woman and he was a hungry man. She would bring him to his knees with desire...and then she would laugh in his face and walk away, leaving him as miserable and unhappy as she was now.

"Now that we understand each other," Janna said tightly, "could we possibly get going so that Joe Troon doesn't kill Lucifer before we can stop him?"

Ty told himself that the hurt and anger he saw in Janna's eyes were better than the bigger hurt that would come if he couldn't keep his hands off her. From what he had heard, at best she had been roughly treated by men; at worst she had been brutalized. If he took advantage of her, he would be no better than Joe Troon.

Ty told himself that, but he wasn't sure he believed it. He would be gentle with Janna even if it killed him...wouldn't he? Surely he would. He wasn't an animal to take what a woman wouldn't freely give him.

*Oh, sure. I'm a real Southern gentleman. That's why I was grinding Janna beneath me into the dirt as though I'd never had a woman and never would unless I had her right*

*there. I can't trust myself with her any farther than I can*
*throw myself uphill.*

Ty looked at Janna's gray eyes watching him with too
many shadows, waiting for his answer.

"Hell of an idea," Ty said curtly. "Wait here while I get
my pack."

Janna watched him get up and leave without a backward
look. She didn't move. She knew that he was testing her,
finding out if he could trust her. If she were going to run off
at the first opportunity, better that he discover her untrust-
worthiness now than when it came time for her turn at night
guard while he slept. Approving his pragmatism almost as
much as she approved his lithe, muscular stride, Janna
watched until Ty disappeared. She waited for his return
without moving one inch from her cross-legged position on
the ground.

When Ty returned and saw Janna precisely where he had
left her, he understood her silent message: he could trust her.
He nodded approvingly and held out his hand to help Janna
to her feet.

It was the opportunity she had been waiting for. She allowed herself to be pulled upright, then stumbled and fell
against Ty's body, letting him take her full weight. His arms
closed around her automatically, supporting her.

The impact of Janna's weight was negligible to a man of
Ty's size, but the warmth of her body wasn't. When his
arms tightened around her to keep her upright, he knew a
lightning stroke of pleasure at how perfectly she fit against
him. Supple, slender, smelling of piñon, she was like an
armful of sunlight.

"Janna? What's wrong?"

For a moment longer she savored the delicious warmth
and strength of Ty's body before she slowly began to take
her own weight again. Even then, she held on to his muscular arms, bracing herself against his strength.

"Sorry," Janna said, eyes downcast as she flexed her fingers into the swell of Ty's biceps and very slowly released him. "I guess I'm a little . . . hungry."

Ty was glad Janna wasn't looking at him when she confessed her hunger, because she would have seen the naked statement of his own need in the tension of his face. In the next instant he understood that Janna wasn't talking about the elemental hunger of sex but the equally basic hunger of the stomach. Hers was growling audibly as she rested her cheek against his chest, leaning as though she were too tired to stand entirely by herself. He smiled despite the desire snaking through his loins. He tapped the bridge of Janna's nose gently with his index finger.

"Poor little baby bird," Ty said sympathetically. "Come on. As soon as we get in better cover, I'll feed you."

His voice was a deep rumble beneath Janna's cheek, but the indulgence in his tone was unmistakable. *Baby bird.* Her mouth drew down unhappily. Her attempt to arouse desire in him had resulted in a brotherly pat. The temptation to bite the hard, warm chest that lay beneath her cheek almost overwhelmed her. She sensed that would have been a serious mistake in her campaign of "accidental" seduction, so she contented herself with pushing away from the shelter offered by Ty's arms.

"Thank you," Janna said politely. "I'm fine now."

She turned away and began walking quickly toward the rugged wall of black lava and red sandstone that formed the east face of Black Plateau. Ty stood and watched the almost concealed sway of Janna's hips beneath the men's clothing and prayed that she would find Lucifer and find him very soon; the more he looked at Janna, the harder it became to ignore her unconscious, utterly feminine allure.

Yet he had to ignore it. He had to forget how good it had felt to rock his hips hard against the softness beneath her clothes.

He had to . . . but he couldn't.

# *Chapter Eighteen*

**A**nger helped Janna to hold to a good pace despite her growling stomach. Without looking back to see how Ty was doing with his heavy pack, she attacked the steep, winding trail that led to the top of Black Plateau. As she climbed, she looked for signs of anyone else using the trail.

She found no traces of man and very little of beast. There were no signs that anything had used the trail recently other than herself. There were no hoofprints in the rare patches of dirt, nor scars where hooves had slipped or scraped across stone. She had never seen signs of any hoofed animal on the trail except occasional deer—and once, just once, tracks that indicated that Lucifer had skidded down over the precipitous path in order to shake off mustangers who had gotten too close.

The idea of any horse taking the trail down the plateau's east face made Janna's heart stop. She herself used the route only when she was afoot and wanted to go to Sweetwater by the shortest possible route. There were other, safer routes up onto the plateau. One route was on the north side, one on the south, and there were several on the western side. All of them were far easier than the eastern trail.

Climbing at a rapid rate, Janna worked her way up the trail until it dipped into one of the many runoff ravines that channeled the plateau's east face. Safe from observation

from any angle but directly overhead, Janna sat on a ston
seat and awaited Ty's arrival. She didn't wait long. He ha
walked only far enough behind her to avoid the shower o
pebbles disturbed by her passage.

Ty grunted and shucked off the heavy pack, using it as
seat while his breathing returned to normal.

"Hell of a path," he said after a bit. "I didn't see any sig
of Zebra coming up, but she sure headed straight here lik
she had something in mind."

"She did—avoiding a river of black rock about a quarte
mile south of here," Janna explained. "It's too rough t
climb over. To avoid it, you have to go several miles awa
from the plateau until the rock sinks into the dirt, or yo
have to climb partway up the east face of the plateau to g
around the head of the rock river. That's what Zebra usu
ally does. Then she goes up onto the top by the souther
route, which is easy."

For several minutes there was silence while Ty looked o
over the land from his new perspective, checking his men
ories against Janna's words.

"Does the lava flow—the river of black rock—begi
there?" he asked, pointing to what looked like a dusty blac
creek running out from the base of the plateau.

Janna leaned out to look, taking the opportunity to brus
against Ty's outstretched arm.

"Yes."

Ty grunted. "I can see why Zebra goes around it. A lot o
jagged rock and nothing much else."

He looked for a time longer, waiting for Janna to with
draw the tantalizing brush of her body. She didn't. H
shifted slightly, ending the intimacy, for his blood was sti
running hotly. Even worse, he suspected that it was going t
be a permanent condition around the ragged, too-feminin
waif.

"How deep are those canyons?" Ty asked, pointing toward the shadows that looked rather like a network of black lightning fanning out from the base of the plateau.

For a few moments Janna considered moving closer to Ty in order to brush against him again, but then she decided against it. Next time she would choose her moment better, so that retreat would be impossible. In a place as narrow as this crevice, she shouldn't have to wait long for her opportunity.

"The canyons are deep enough that the wild horses go around them," Janna said. "The countryside is full of ravines and washes and canyons like that. Most of them are dry, but nearly every butte and mesa has at least a tiny seep or rock tanks that hold water almost year-round. Black Plateau is different. It's big enough to have water all year up top as well as seeps and springs at the base. That's why there's so much grass and game."

Saying nothing, Ty smoothed a patch of dirt with his hand, then began drawing on the surface with his fingertip. Knowing that the plateau was Lucifer's preferred range, Ty had spent weeks scouting the area before he had decided on the best way to capture the wild stallion. Unfortunately Ty had ended up captured by Indians before he could try out his plan. Janna, however, had spent years on and around Black Plateau. If there were anything wrong with Ty's plan, she would spot it.

"This outline is Black Plateau," he said, pointing to the very rough rectangle he had drawn in the dirt. He added sides to the rectangle, showing depth as well as area. Only the western side remained untouched, suggesting the relative flatness where the plateau's surface blended into the rumpled front of the Fire Mountains. "From what I've seen, the closer you get to Black Plateau from the east, the steeper and deeper the canyons, gullies and ravines get."

Janna shifted position, brushing against Ty's thigh as she did so. When she leaned forward to look at what he had drawn, she braced her hand on his thigh. Ty's hand, which was drawing lines in the dirt, jerked. He said something beneath his breath and changed position until Janna's hand was no longer resting on his thigh.

"That's right," she said. "The plateau's east face rises very steeply from the flatlands." She leaned forward again and again braced herself on Ty's leg, ignoring his attempts to evade her touch. "Black Plateau is really part of the Fire Mountains," she added, drawing a series of pyramids along the plateau's western flank to represent the mountains. "According to Indian legends, the spirits fought each other until the earth cracked and bled and everything the blood touched became fire. Long after the earth healed, the angry spirits roared and spit fire among the peaks of the Fire range, and sometimes new blood flowed over the plateau and dripped down into the desert, where it turned into black rocks. The angry spirits still live beneath the earth around here, turning water so hot that there are springs that cook food faster than a campfire."

Ty tried to concentrate on Janna's words, but the presence of her hand on his leg was burning hotter than anything in the Indian legend. He would have retreated to the side again if he could have. He couldn't. The crevice in the plateau's side where they had taken shelter was simply too small. He was up against a black boulder right now—and her hand had slipped around to the inside of his thigh. She was so involved in the map he had drawn that she didn't seem to notice.

*Talk about being between a rock and a hard place*... Ty told himself, disgusted because the hard place was in his own lap. He pulled off his hat and dumped it between his legs, hiding the growing evidence of his discomfort in the only way he could.

"There are two good trails up on top of the plateau on its western side," Janna continued, flexing her fingers slightly as she shifted position. Now that she had discovered it, the heat and resilience of Ty's leg fascinated her. "The first trail is here, about two miles from the southern boundary. It's called the Long View Trail." She leaned down and forward until her ribs brushed Ty's leg as she marked the trail on the map he had drawn in the dirt. "That's the easiest way up. The Indians have used it for as long as anyone can remember. The second trail is here." She made another mark. "The trails are about twenty miles apart as the crow flies. Walking it doubles the distance. The second route up is called Raven Creek Trail. It isn't as easy as the Long View Trail, and it doesn't lead immediately to water or good grazing, so Raven Creek Trail isn't used except by Indian hunting parties."

"Or war parties?"

Janna nodded. "Cascabel has his camp at the base of the plateau, where Raven Creek empties into Santos Wash. Mustang Canyon," she added, pointing to the northern edge of the plateau, where a large notch had been cut into the stone foundations of the land, "is here. There's good grazing all year and a trail to the top of the plateau that only deer and mustangs use, and occasional crazy mustangers."

"And you?"

She smiled. "And me. But Zebra grew up on that trail. Sometimes I think her mama was a goat. Zebra is as surefooted as one. Besides, most of the time I get off and walk. There's one slick rock patch that gives me nightmares."

Ty smiled thinly. "You? Nightmares?" he scoffed. "You're too tough to be afraid of anything."

Janna said nothing, though she couldn't help remembering all the nights after her father had died when she had jumped at the smallest sound, biting off screams that would have given away her position rather than summoning the help she needed. Even years later, certain combinations of sounds and smells could set her heart to hammering hard enough to break her ribs.

"Is your keyhole canyon about here?" asked Ty, pointing to a place near the southeast corner of the plateau.

"Yes."

Steadfastly ignoring the gentle crowding pressure of Janna's body, Ty looked at the map and mentally began turning the plateau's neat edges into a fringe of varying lengths, for that was closer to the truth of the landscape. The plateau's north, east and south edges were fringed with sheersided stone promontories and cliffs, as well as canyons and ravines of varying sizes and depths; and the larger canyons had side canyons, which in turn branched into finger canyons, which branched into runoff crevices.

The result was a maze in which a person could stand on one canyon edge and look at the opposite edge only a few thousand feet away—and it would take a day of circling around to get to the other side. Most of the hundreds of nameless canyons that fringed the plateau were blind; ultimately they had only one outlet, and that was down onto the flatlands rather than up onto the top of Black Plateau itself.

"Do you know of any other trails up to the top?" Ty asked, marking the ones Janna had already mentioned. "What about all these fringe canyons? Could a man on foot climb out of some of them and up onto the plateau itself?"

Janna shrugged. "Ask Mad Jack the next time you see him. He knows things about Black Plateau that even the Indians don't. But the canyons I've seen end in sheer cliffs, the kind you'd have to be crazy or running for your life to try to climb."

"Does Lucifer graze in blind canyons?"

"The biggest ones, yes. The narrow ones, never. Some mustangers must have trapped him once. He won't even go near the entrance of any canyon that isn't at least a quarter mile across. He's smart and wild as they come."

"No wonder he's still running loose," Ty said, admiration and disgust mixed equally in his voice. "I was lucky to get as close as I did before Cascabel nailed me. What are the chances of startling Lucifer and getting him to run headlong into a small blind canyon before he knows what's happening?''

"It's been tried by every mustanger who ever came here."

Ty didn't ask what the result had been. He didn't need to. The stallion still ran free.

"No wonder Troon decided to try creasing that black devil," Ty muttered.

Janna thought of the rifle shot they had heard and bit her lip.

Ty saw and had to look away. The idea of gently biting Janna's lip himself was too tempting. In fact, everything about her was too tempting. Though she was no longer leaning over to add marks to his rough map, her hand was still resting on his leg, sending heat spreading out in all directions through his body, tantalizing him with how close those slender fingers were to the very part of him that ached for her touch.

Cursing silently, viciously, Ty tried to ease away from the intimate contact. Half an inch away he came flat up against the crevice's stony limits. Close beside him, Janna's stomach growled audibly in the taut silence, reminding Ty that she hadn't eaten since they had left Keyhole Canyon yesterday morning.

"Scoot over so I can reach my pack," Ty muttered.

Even if Janna didn't move, the pack was within a long arm's length of Ty—if he were willing to press against her in order to increase his reach. She gave him a sideways look and decided not to point out how close the pack was. Without a word she eased backward and to the side an inch or two.

"More."

Ty's curt command irritated Janna. "Haven't you noticed? There's not much room in this crack."

"Yeah, and you're taking up at least three-quarters of it," he retorted. "Quit crowding me."

"Crowding you? My God, you'd think I had fleas or something," Janna muttered beneath her breath. "Seeing as how you're the one who's been to Ned's saloon recently, you're more likely to have fleas than—"

"Janna," Ty interrupted, his voice threatening. "Move!"

"All right, all right, I'm moving." She pushed herself to the far side of the crevice and hugged the wall as though there were a cliff inches away from her feet. "This better?"

Ty snarled something Janna chose not to hear. A pocketknife appeared in his hand. He grabbed his pack and began rummaging through it. A few moments later he pulled out a tin can. He punched the point of the blade twice into the top of the can. The second time he rotated the knife, making a wider opening. He handed the can to Janna.

"Here. Drink this."

Janna lifted the can, tilted, sipped and made a sound of disbelief as the thick, sweet, peach-flavored liquid trickled across her tongue. She took two long, slow swallows before she reluctantly handed the can back to Ty. He refused to take it with a shake of his head.

"Finish it," he said.

"I can't do that. Preacher charges a dollar a can for his peaches."

A look at Janna's clear eyes told Ty that arguing over the peaches would be futile. He took the can, drank two small sips and handed it back over.

"Your turn," he said flatly.

She said nothing, but she took the can and drank slowly, savoring each drop. Her undisguised pleasure made Ty smile with the knowledge that he had given her a real treat. He had spent more than enough time on the trail to know how much a person began craving something sweet and succulent after weeks or months of dried meat and biscuits and beans.

The can was passed back and forth several times, and each time Ty swore that the metal became warmer to his touch. He tried not to think about the lips that had been pressed against the rim before his own lips drank. In fact, he was doing fine at controlling the direction of his thoughts until Janna tipped the can up and waited for several seconds for the last sweet drop to fall from the rim onto the tip of her outstretched tongue. The temptation to suck that drop from her tongue with his own lips was so great that he had to turn away.

"Now what?" she asked, holding the can under Ty's nose.

*Hell of a question,* he thought savagely. *Wish I had an answer I could live with.*

Using swift, vicious strokes of the pocketknife, Ty cut the lid from the rim, speared a peach half and held it out to Janna. She took the lush golden fruit with her fingertips, ate with delicate greed and waited her turn for another. They traded turns eating until only one piece of fruit was left, a piece that stubbornly eluded Ty's knife. Finally he speared it and held it out to Janna. As she slid the fruit from the knife blade she sensed Ty's intense interest. She looked up to find him watching her mouth. His eyes were a smoky green that made frissons of heat race over her skin. Without thinking she took a bite of the succulent fruit and held out the remainder to him with her fingertips.

"Your turn," she said huskily.

For a long, aching moment Ty looked at the sweetness dripping from Janna's slender fingers. Then he stood up in a controlled surge of power, grabbed his pack and strode out of the crevice without a word.

# Chapter Nineteen

A late-afternoon storm had swept across Black Plateau, making the rocks and trees shine as though freshly polished. The slanting golden light transformed the winding meadow into a river of glistening gold. Once Janna would have felt the beauty of the land like a balm over her hungry soul; today she only saw what was absent rather than what was present. Lying on her stomach, using a row of evergreen seedlings for cover, she scanned the length of the long meadow in front of her once more, staring through the spyglass until her arms trembled with fatigue.

Ty didn't bother to go over the land again with his own glass. He knew he would see what he and Janna had seen for the past five days—grass and water and wind in abundance, but no Lucifer standing guard over his herd. Cascabel's renegades had been present, however. They were the reason that Ty and Janna had had to tiptoe around the plateau like thieves, able to get only as close to the mustangs as the tracks they had made yesterday or even the day before.

"I don't understand it," Janna said, finally lowering the spyglass and wiggling backward deeper beneath the cover of the pines that grew right to the meadow's edge. "Even if Lucifer had been caught, wouldn't we at least see some of his herd wandering around? No mustanger is going to want the older mares or the spring foals. Besides, we haven't seen or heard any sign of Troon or any other mustanger since we came up the east trail."

"Except for that flurry of rifle shots yesterday," Ty said. "That didn't sound like the hunting parties we've been hearing. Troon could have run afoul of Cascabel."

Janna frowned and said reluctantly, "I suppose I should scout Cascabel's camp."

"What?" Ty asked, astonished.

"That's how I found you," she explained. "I heard gunfire, ran over, saw where the tracks of two shod horses were crossed by a bunch of unshod Indian ponies. The ponies turned to follow your horses and so did I. Eventually the tracks led to Cascabel's camp. I couldn't get to you right away to free you, so I hid and waited for a chance to help. It finally came when you got through the gauntlet and were still able to run."

Ty thought of the danger Janna had risked to save a total stranger and shook his head in wonder. That deceptively slender body hid a lot of plain old courage, but there was no need to spend it on a swamp Yankee like Joe Troon.

"Is Troon a friend of yours?" Ty asked.

Janna gave Ty a startled look. "Joe Troon? I wouldn't cry one tear at his funeral," she said in a low, flat voice. "In fact, he..."

Her voice died. She didn't like to remember the time Troon had trapped her and started stripping off her clothes before she managed to break free and run. He had spent hours searching for her. The whole time he had yelled just what he would do when he caught her.

The combination of fear and dislike on Janna's face told Ty more than he wanted to know about Janna and Joe Troon.

"Janna," Ty said softly, pulling her out of her unhappy memories, "from what I've heard in towns where I bought my supplies, Troon is a drunk, a thief, a coward, a woman beater and a back shooter. He deserves whatever Cascabel feels like giving to him. Besides, you don't even know if Troon has been captured. He could be back in Sweetwater right now, getting drunk on Ned's rotgut. There's no point in either of us risking our butt to scout a renegade camp for a no-good bit of swamp gas like Joe Troon."

"I know," Janna said. "I just hate to think of anyone caught by Cascabel. He's so cruel."

Ty shrugged. "Cascabel doesn't see it that way. He's a warrior who has stood up to the worst the country, the pony soldiers and his fellow Indians can offer in the way of punishment. He's never given quarter and he's never asked for it. And he never will."

"You sound like you admire him."

There was a long silence before Ty shrugged again. "I don't like him, but I do respect him. He's one hell of a fighter, no matter what the weapon or situation. He has knowledge of how to use the land and his limited arms to his own advantage that many a general would envy."

"Do you have any idea what he does to the captives who don't escape?"

"Yes," Ty said succinctly. "I didn't say I admired him, Janna. But I learned in the war that honor and good table manners don't have a damned thing to do with survival. Cascabel is a survivor. Black Hawk knows it. He hasn't pressed a confrontation because he hopes that the U.S. Army will take care of the renegades for him."

"Black Hawk is lucky that Cascabel hasn't lured the whole tribe away from him," Janna grumbled. "Cascabel must have half of Black Hawk's warriors down here by now, and they're still coming in by twos and threes every day."

"Cascabel is half-Apache. The elders in the Ute tribe would never let him be a headman. As for the younger men, they still believe that they're invincible. They haven't had time to learn that the same army that flattened the South sure as hell won't have too tough a time ironing out a few renegade wrinkles in the Utah Territory.''

Janna started to speak, then caught a flash of movement at the far edge of the meadow. Ty had seen the movement, too. As one they flattened completely to the earth, taking advantage of every bit of cover offered by the slight depression in which they had lain to watch the meadow.

Four hundred feet away, five Indians rode out into the wide river of meadow grass that wound between the two evergreen forests. The men rode boldly, without bothering about cover or the possibility of ambush, because they knew that Cascabel ruled Black Plateau. The only reason they weren't laughing and talking among themselves was that human voices carried a long way in the plateau's primal silence, and the deer they were hunting had excellent hearing.

Peering cautiously through the dense screen of evergreen boughs, spyglass shielded so that it wouldn't give away their position by reflecting a flash of light, Ty watched the hunting party ride along the margin of forest and meadow. Usually in any group of Indians, barely half the men were armed with carbines, rifles or pistols, and there were rarely more than a few rounds of ammunition for each weapon. Part of the problem for the Indians in getting arms was simply that it was illegal to sell weapons or ammunition to Indians. What they couldn't take as the spoils of war they had to buy from crooked white traders.

But most of the problem the Indians had in staying well armed was that none of the tribes had any experience in the care and repair of machines or in the art of making reliable bullets. The weapons they acquired through war or bribery quickly became useless either because of lack of ammunition or because of mechanical failure.

Cascabel's men were well outfitted. As well as the traditional bow and arrows, each man had a carbine and a leather pouch bulging with ammunition. Ty was relieved to see that the carbines were single-shot weapons of the type that had lost the Civil War for the South. None of the five Indians had a weapon that could compete with the new Winchester carbine he had discovered in an otherwise empty box at the store Preacher had rather hastily abandoned. Ty's new carbine was the type of weapon Johnny Rebs had enviously insisted that a Yank "loaded on Sunday and fired all week long." With his new Winchester, Ty could reload as fast as he could fire, an advantage the Indians didn't have unless they used their bows and arrows.

Ty went over the details of the Indians' gear with the experienced eye of a man to whom such knowledge had meant the difference between continued life and premature death. The presence of good weapons explained some of Cascabel's allure for young warriors—on a reservation, these men would have barely enough to eat, no weapons beyond what they could make with their own hands, and no freedom to roam in search of game. With Cascabel, the young men would have a chance to gain personal fame as warriors, they would be well fed and well armed, and they could live the roving life celebrated in tribal legends.

The fact that the young men would also find themselves the target of every white man with a gun simply added spice to the Indians' lives. After all, there weren't that many white men.

Ty knew that the situation would change, even if the Indians didn't. Since the end of the Civil War, footloose and disenfranchised white men had pressed west in greater and greater numbers. Most of them had already been in shooting battles, so the prospect of occasional skirmishes with Indians wasn't much of a deterrent. Ty himself was one of those men, as were his brothers. There were hundreds and thousands more men like the MacKenzies, drawn by the West's wild horizons and seductive promises of a better life for anyone who had the courage and stamina to withstand the hardships. Not all the promises of the new land would be kept, but each man was certain that, for him, the dreams would indeed come true.

And a lot of those men would be armed with repeating rifles and carbines and as many bullets as they could wear without dragging their belts down to their boot tops. The Indians would take some of those weapons and put them to deadly use, but more white men would come west, and then more and more, and their superior arms would always be enough to offset the Indians' superior knowledge of the land.

Ty had no doubt about the eventual outcome of the battle between Indian and white; he just wasn't sure he would be alive to share in the celebration when the renegades were defeated.

Abruptly the five Indians stopped their mounts. One of the warriors leaped from his horse, landed lightly and sat on his heels while he examined something on the ground. After a time he stood again, walked a few steps and then bent over the ground once more, looking at everything from a different angle.

Ty lay without moving, going over in his mind once more what he would do if he and Janna were discovered. With his new carbine he could cause as much damage in one minute as ten men with single-shot guns. Even allowing for the fact that he hadn't had time to accustom himself to the Winchester's action, he should be able to put two warriors out of the fight before the others took cover. That would give Janna plenty of time to slip away while he played cat and mouse with the remaining warriors. With a little luck, he might even get away himself.

With a lot of luck, he and Janna wouldn't be discovered in the first place.

When the warrior finally remounted and the five continued along the far edge of the meadow without looking in the direction where Janna and Ty lay concealed, he breathed a quiet sigh of relief. He had known some men who loved fighting and killing. He wasn't one of them. He was quite pleased to see the Indians disappear into the trees without a single shot having been fired from his shiny new carbine.

Neither Ty nor Janna stirred from their prone position. Something had piqued the Indians' curiosity enough to deflect them from their original course of hunting. If the curiosity were quickly satisfied, the Indians would come back to the meadow and resume hunting deer.

Besides, Janna was lying quite close to Ty, able to feel him all along her right side, able to move subtly against him, reminding him of her presence. She had done a lot of that in the past five days, leaning over him by the campfire, brushing his hand when she gave him a plate of food, tripping and falling against him when the trail permitted it.

She had seen the green intensity of his glance and had known that her presence was felt, but she was no longer certain that she would laugh and walk away if she brought him to his knees with desire. The thought of being close to him, truly close, brought her to her own knees with an answering desire that burned just beneath her skin, silently reaching out to him even as his own male heat radiated out to her, caressing and calling to her.

The bronze light of very late afternoon burnished the meadow. Soon deer would be emerging from cover to feed. At first they would graze only along the western margin of the meadow, where the descending sun pushed thick shadows out of the dense pines. As the shadows stretched across the grassy clearing, the deer would follow until finally the meadow would be dotted by graceful shapes grazing upon moon-silvered grass.

That was when it would be safest for Ty and Janna to move, when the much more acute senses of the deer would give warning of other men roaming around in the night. Not that Ty expected to run across any Indians on the move in full darkness, but he had learned that allowing for the unexpected was the best way to survive life's lethal little surprises.

Besides, it was very pleasant to lie in the warm aftermath of day on a thick bed of pine needles and listen to birds settling into cover for the night, calling and singing to one another as though they had a lifetime of information to pass on and only a few minutes until the last golden sunlight faded, bringing with it darkness and night.

It was also pleasant to feel Janna's warm body pressed against his left side.

After a moment's thought, Ty conceded to himself that perhaps pleasant wasn't the right word to describe the combination of sensuous heat and mental torture she had inflicted on him in the past days. He couldn't turn around but he was there, touching him in the most casual ways, never forward or aggressive, just... *there*. Always. A smile or a fleeting brush of her body over his, a look from gray eyes as clear as springwater, a soft laugh that made his loins tighten. He sensed that she was getting even with him for belittling her feminine allure, but he couldn't prove it. There was always a logical reason for her touches.

And her touches were driving him crazy, sending fire licking over his skin, heat whispering to him, telling him that beneath those flapping clothes was a woman. With each second that passed, the chance of the Indians returning became less likely, and the fragrance of her body became more compelling. He sensed each of her breaths, knew that she felt him as well, and he wanted nothing more than to turn toward her and mold her along the aching length of his body.

Ty kept remembering that single, penetrating kiss he had given to Janna. He could recall the feeling of her body beneath his with a vividness that sent blood rushing hotly, hardening his male flesh until it ached.

But she hadn't enjoyed that kiss. She had taken it as a punishment.

Yet it was Ty who was being punished. He owed Janna hi
life. He had sworn to himself that he wouldn't repay tha
debt by frightening or hurting her as other men had. The
only way he could keep his promise to himself was to keep
his hungry hands off her. And his hungry mouth. And mos
of all, his hungry—

"Ty?" Janna whispered softly.

Her body was shaking. So was her voice. Though she
made no more noise than a sigh, Ty heard her. He hear
every breath she took, saw every time she licked her lips
tasted her in his memory. He didn't know how much longe
he would be able to admire her without touching the easy
sway of her hips as she led him along the plateau's secre
byways.

"Ty?" she said, a bit more loudly.

"What?" he groaned, wondering how much longer h
could lie next to her without grabbing her.

"There's a snake crawling along my leg."

# Chapter Twenty

"Don't move."

Ty knew as soon as he whispered the urgent words that his command was unnecessary—Janna knew better than to make a sudden move around a snake. She also must know that all she had to do was lie quietly until the snake slithered off into the late afternoon and she would be all right.

"Can you see the snake?" he whispered.

Janna's answer was more a whimper than a "no."

"Just stay quiet," he repeated. "The snake isn't interested in you and he won't be as long as you don't move."

But Janna couldn't remain still. Tremors of sheer terror were rippling through her. She could face almost anything without losing her head, but not a snake. She remembered all too well the nightmare of awakening to her father's shouts and frantic flailing about as he tried to shake off the rattlesnake that had crawled into his bedroll. He had been bitten on his feet and his calf, his wrist and his cheek.

At the time they had been deep in Indian country, chasing one of her father's dreams of gold. There had been no one to help. None of the herbs or balms or potions her father knew had managed to pull the poison out of his body. Nor had lancing the oozing wounds helped.

She would never forget the endless death throes of the big snake after she had cut off its triangular head with her sheath knife. Nor would she forget the long days of her father's agony and delirium before he finally died.

Without realizing it, Janna began whimpering softly with every shallow breath she took. Ty heard and realized that she wouldn't be able to lie still until the snake moved on in search of its normal evening meal of mice or young rabbit. She was terrified. In the grip of such mindless fear she might scream, and then the snake would be the least of their worries.

"Janna," Ty whispered urgently. "You'll be all right. Just lie still. I'll take care of it. Whatever happens, *don' move*."

The increasingly violent trembling of Janna's body was her only answer.

Slowly Ty eased onto his right side, lifted himself on his elbow and reached to his waist for his sheath knife. The way he and Janna were lying, he had no choice except to use his left hand, but that fact didn't slow him down. The first thing the elder MacKenzie had taught his boys was that a left-handed knife fighter had an advantage in a brawl, and two-handed fighter would win every time.

Ty's movements and Janna's trembling had made the snake freeze in place as it tried to decide whether the movement represented food or danger or simply a neutral presence such as the wind. In the dying light the motionless snake blended so well with its surroundings that Ty had hard time seeing it. When he did, he swore silently.

It was a timber rattlesnake, and it was as thick around as his forearm. There would be enough venom stored up in that big mouth to kill a man, much less a girl the size of Janna.

When nothing came of Janna's quaking movements, the rattler lowered its head and continued on its evening hunt. The snake was so close that Ty could easily make out the flickering tongue and the triangular head darting from side to side with the forward motion of the coils. He could even distinguish the third "eye" that identified the deadly pit viper.

The rattlesnake's body made an odd rubbing-rustling sound as it progressed slowly along the length of Janna's pant leg. Ty watched with the poised patience of a predator, knowing that he had no choice but to wait for an opening. Until the snake's head was drawn away from Janna's body by the sinuous movements of reptilian coils, there was nothing Ty could do that the snake couldn't do quicker—and it would be Janna rather than Ty who suffered from any miscalculation on his part.

Speaking softly and reassuringly to Janna, telling her that there was nothing to fear, Ty waited until the snake's undulating forward motion finally pulled its head to the left, away from Janna's leg. Ty struck swiftly, cleanly, severing the rattlesnake's head from its body. Then he struck again with savage speed, using the knife point to pick up the deadly head and fling it far away from Janna. He grabbed the writhing coils and threw them away, as well. Then he went down beside Janna and pulled her into his arms.

"It's all right, little one," Ty whispered, holding her shaking body. "It's all right. The rattlesnake is dead."

The soothing rumble of Ty's voice and the gentle stroking of his hands over Janna's back calmed her more than his words. Unable to control the trembling of her own body, she clung to him, whispering incoherently about a water hole and a rattlesnake that had struck again and again, and the long days and nights before her father had finally died.

When Ty finally understood what Janna was saying, emotion went through him like a burst of dark lightning. He couldn't bear the thought of Janna alone with her dying father, watching him swell and blacken as the poison slowly destroyed his flesh. It could so easily have been her bedroll the snake had chosen, her tender skin pierced by fangs, her life draining away between labored breaths; and then Ty never would have known Janna, never held her, never breathed kisses over her tear-streaked face.

The realization of how close he had come to losing Janna caused a surge of emotion that was both tender and fierce. The thought of almost having been deprived of her presence made it impossible to deny himself the sweet luxury of holding her now.

The warmth and comfort of Ty's big hands rubbing slowly down Janna's back gradually penetrated her panic. His gentle, brushing kisses brought heat back to skin that had been chilled by fear. Turning her face up to his lips, she gave a long, shaky sigh and snuggled even closer to him, needing the reassurance of his body in a way that she couldn't put into words. Nor did she have to. He needed her physical proximity in the same way, the warm pressure of her body against his telling him that they both were alive and safe.

When Ty's arms tightened around Janna and he whispered her name, her hands crept up his chest to his stubble-roughened cheeks and beyond. Her fingers sought the thick black hair she longed to caress as she had in the days when he had been too ill to object to her touch. She slid her hands beneath his hat, dislodging it, and she shivered with pleasure when her fingers knew again the silky textures and fullness of his hair. She moved her hands slowly, flexing them gently, caressing him and the sensitive skin between her fingers at the same time.

The intimate, changing pressure of Janna's hands on Ty's scalp made his breath catch, break and emerge as an almost silent groan. He moved his head slowly, increasing the pressure of her caressing hands, and the sound he made seemed to Janna more like a purr from a very large cat than any noise a man might make. Smiling, she closed her eyes and concentrated on the delicious sensations radiating out from her hands to envelop her whole body.

Janna's small, almost secret smile was irresistible to Ty. Knowing he shouldn't, unable to help himself and no longer caring, he bent his head until he could trace the curve of her mouth with the tip of his tongue. The unexpected caress startled a soft cry from her.

"Hush," Ty breathed against her lips, moving his head slowly from side to side, gentling her with soft kisses. "You're all right, little one. You're safe with me. I won't let anything hurt you."

Janna parted her lips to explain that she wasn't frightened any longer, but the gentle glide of Ty's tongue into her mouth stole from her both the ability and the desire to speak. This was totally unlike the kiss he had given her before. His mouth was seductive rather than demanding, his tongue tempting rather than overwhelming. The sliding, hot, almost secret touches were unbearably sweet. Without realizing it, she began to return his caresses. At first the movements of her tongue were tentative, but when his arms tightened, bringing her even closer to his body, she knew that he was enjoying the kiss as much as she was.

Ty felt the hesitant touch of Janna's tongue as though it were a soft flame. The knowledge that she wasn't frightened of him both reassured Ty and tightened every muscle in his body with the anticipation and hunger that had been growing in him since he had first looked through a haze of pain into her clear, compassionate eyes. Even though he had been beaten, bloodied, half-dead with exhaustion, some elemental male level of awareness within himself had seen past her clothes and recognized the essential female presence beneath.

"Janna," Ty sighed. He nuzzled her lips, trying to part them again, knowing he shouldn't. He was too hungry, blood rushing too hotly, the aftermath of danger and adrenaline mixed wildly with his need of her. "Let me kiss you, really kiss you. It won't be like the other time. I won't hurt you," he whispered, licking her lips gently, feeling her tremble. "Do you trust me not to hurt you?"

The sweet glide of Ty's tongue over Janna's sensitized lips made her shiver again. She knew that her moment had finally arrived, the moment when she could get even with him for making fun of her lack of allure. He wanted her now. He couldn't deny it. It was there in the tension of his body, in his ragged breath, in the heat of his flesh hard against her hip.

Trembling, she breathed her answer into his mouth, tasting him. "I trust you."

With gentle, inevitable movements of his head, Ty fitted his mouth more deeply to Janna's. She felt herself tasted and enjoyed in the sensuous rhythm of penetration and retreat, advance and withdrawal, the cycle repeated endlessly, like flames dancing up from a campfire. Each caressing movement of their joined mouths brought more and more pleasure until her whole body trembled in anticipation of the next touch, the next intimate tasting, the next languid tangling of warm tongues.

Heat stole beneath Janna's skin, flushing her face, shortening her breath. Bubbles of sensation grew slowly inside her, expanding with each warm movement of Ty's tongue until she shivered and a bubble burst, drenching her with golden heat; and then pleasure gathered again, burst sweetly, made her shiver and moan Ty's name. The slender hands buried in Ty's hair flexed and relaxed in the same rhythms of Janna's tongue—seeking, stroking, finding, mating with the slow, deep motions he had taught her.

The sensuous, searching caresses brought a violent hardening of Ty's flesh that both shocked and dismayed him, telling him that he was very close to the edge of his self-control. With an effort he turned aside from Janna's mouth.

"Little one," he whispered, grabbing her hands, stilling them. "Don't."

When Janna felt Ty's withdrawal, she was unable to control a soft cry of protest. "I thought—I thought you wanted—"

Her voice broke. She didn't try to speak again; the loss of his warmth was devastating to her. Even the hushed light of dusk couldn't conceal the hurt twisting through her at his abrupt rejection. Just as she gathered herself to turn away from him, he shifted his hands and pinned her in place.

"Hell yes, I want you!" Ty whispered fiercely, looming over Janna. "I want your hands all over me. I want to take off your clothes and put my hands all over you, and then I want to open your legs and slide into that soft body of yours and feel you take every bit of me. I want it so much I couldn't stand up straight right now to save my soul."

The look of stunned disbelief on Janna's face made Ty want to laugh and swear at the same time.

"Can't you feel me shaking?" he demanded, barely remembering to keep his voice low. "Do you think it's because of that fool snake? Hell, I've eaten bigger snakes than that and looked around for seconds. It's you that's making me shake. You've been driving me crazy since I first came to after hiding from Cascabel and saw your beautiful gray eyes watching me."

"You th-thought I was a boy," Janna accused in a low voice.

"I thought you were too damned sexy, girl *or* boy, because my britches had a better grip on the truth than my eyes did. My eyes kept telling me that you were a boy and I was some kind of crazy to get all hot and bothered when you touched me. My britches kept telling me that you were as female as they come and I was some kind of moron not to peel off your clothes and get better acquainted."

The hands that had been tightly gripping Janna eased and began rubbing her shoulders with gentle, circular motions.

"I know you've been hurt in the past," Ty said, his voice low, carrying no farther than her ears. "And I want you so bad that I can't even think, but I would cut off my fingers rather than hurt you. And the way you were kissing me..." He closed his eyes as a sensual echo resonated through his body, tightening his loins until he had to clench his teeth against the bittersweet ache. "Do you want me, little one?"

Janna tried to speak but she had no breath. Her heart was wedged in her throat, blocking the passage of air. Seeing Ty's need turned her inside out. She wanted to hold his head against her body and comb her fingers soothingly through his hair; and she wanted to kiss and be kissed again, teasing his tongue with her own and tasting him in a slow, secret kind of dance that made pleasure expand and softly burst deep within her body. Her need to experience that again was so great it was pain.

Was that what was drawing Ty's face into taut lines? Did he feel the same aching need?

"Ty?" she whispered.

His eyes opened. In the fading light they were a green as deep as the forest itself.

"I..." Janna's voice died. She licked her lips and felt the sudden tension in Ty's body as his glance followed her tongue. "Did you like kissing me?"

Ty almost laughed in the instant before he remembered that any knowledge Janna had of men was brief and brutal.

"Yes," Ty murmured, brushing his open mouth over hers. "I liked it. Did you?"

He felt her breath hesitate, catch, then flow over his face in a sweet sigh of agreement. Smiling, he gently caught her lower lip between his teeth, testing the warmth and resilience of her flesh. She went very still in the instant before she trembled and made a small sound.

"I'm sorry," Ty said, releasing her. "I didn't mean to frighten you."

"You didn't," Janna said quickly. "I don't know what's wrong. It just felt so good it made something burst inside me and I went all shivery. I'm sorry."

Ty's breath caught and his eyes narrowed in sensual response to her words. Whatever might have happened to Janna in the past, she was a total innocent when it came to the pleasure a woman could find in the arms of a loving man. The thought of teaching Janna the secrets hidden within her body made Ty feel hot, heavy, thoroughly masculine.

"Don't be sorry," he said huskily. "I like knowing that I've pleased you."

"You do?" she whispered, looking at his lips, wanting to taste him again, to feel his tongue moving within her mouth.

"Yes." Ty smiled and nuzzled the slanting line of Janna's cheekbones until he came to the silky edge of her hair. He stripped off her hat and headband, untied the rawhide thongs holding her braids and unraveled them until his hands were full of the cool fire of her hair. He made an inarticulate sound of pleasure as he searched blindly with his mouth for the tempting curves of her ear. "I want to please you, little one. Will you tell me if I do?"

"Y-yes."

"Yes," Ty breathed as he found Janna's ear with the tip of his tongue, teased the rim and then penetrated the hidden, sensitive core.

Frissons of pleasure tightened Janna's skin, sending telltale parades of goose bumps up and down her arms. She made a startled sound and her hands tightened on Ty's shirt in sensual reflex. When his tongue repeated the penetration again and then again, she felt a sensation like wires tightening deep within her body, making her feel languid and restless at the same time.

"More?" Ty whispered, biting Janna's ear delicately.

He felt her helpless shiver of response and his lips shifted into a very masculine smile of approval and triumph. Before she could speak he softly devoured her ear, his tongue pressing into its core with the same rhythmic movements that had made pleasure swell and burst within her before. Her husky, barely audible moan made him feel as though he were being bathed in golden fire.

With a swift movement of his head Ty captured Janna's mouth. There was no surprise this time when his tongue slid between her teeth, filling her mouth with the taste and feel and textures of his hungry kiss. She answered him by spearing her fingers into his hair and holding his mouth hard upon her own, moaning softly at the sensual heat of him, wanting to take that heat within her own body. The rhythmic caress of tongue against tongue was reinforced by the unconscious movements of her body against his as she tried to ease the heaviness and aching that had condensed in her tightly bound breasts and between her restless legs.

Making a sound halfway between a curse and a prayer, Ty gently disengaged from Janna's hot embrace.

"Before you ask," he said, breathing quickly, audibly, keeping his voice low, "I liked having your body rubbing over mine. I liked it too damn much. I don't want to hurt you, little one. That means we have to take it slow for a bit longer, until you're ready." He closed his eyes and wondered how the hell he would manage it. "Which means that you'll have to give me a minute or two to catch my breath."

"Can I talk while you breathe?" she asked hesitantly, keeping her voice as low as his.

Ty laughed softly despite the savage ache between his legs. Leaning down, he brushed his lips over Janna's mouth, tasting her with a single quick stroke of his tongue before straightening and smiling down at her.

"What do you want to talk about?" he murmured.

"I wish it were darker. Then you wouldn't see me blush when I ask you."

"I'm glad it isn't darker," Ty whispered, nibbling on her chin. "I want to see you, blushes and all. Especially the 'all.' What's your question?"

"Will it—will you hurt me?"

"Oh, God," Ty whispered, gathering Janna into his arms and rocking her gently against his body. "No, little one," he said, kissing her hair, her ear, her flushed cheek, her eyelids, her lips, butterfly brushes that reassured her as no words could have. "If I go slow and you try to relax and not be afraid, it won't hurt you at all. And I'll go slow, Janna. I'll go slow if it kills me."

Slowly her arms came up and around his neck. She pressed her face against the hot skin at the opening of Ty's shirt.

"Will going slow spoil it for you?" Janna whispered. "I don't want to make it bad for you. I want to please you, Ty. I want that so much I ache."

"Going slow won't spoil it. In fact, it can make it so good you feel like dying."

"It can?"

Janna's voice was husky with the conflicting emotions racing through her, passion and nervousness and a hunger to touch and be touched that was completely new to her.

"It can," Ty said. "At least, that's what I'm told. I've never known that kind of pleasure myself."

Janna tried to speak but had no voice. She licked her lips and tilted her head back until she could look into the darkly luminous green of Ty's eyes.

"I want to pleasure you like that," she whispered. "Will you teach me how?"

# Chapter Twenty-One

The husky intensity of Janna's voice and her honesty made Ty want to ravish and cherish her in the same instant. The thought of teaching her how to tease and ease and pleasure him was more heady than any liquor he had ever drunk. He traced the lines of her face with his fingertips before caressing the taut curve of her neck and the warm flesh inside her collar. Inevitably his fingers found and undid the first button of her shirt. He bent and pressed his lips against the pulse beating rapidly just beneath her skin.

"Janna," Ty said, breathing her name as much as saying it, "I hope to God I can set fire to you half as hot as you set fire to me. If I can, we'll burn down the whole damn plateau."

"Is that—is that good?"

"Ask me tomorrow," he said, barely stifling a groan as he felt the leap and quickening of her pulse at the touch of his tongue.

Then Ty could deny himself no longer the minor consummation of Janna's mouth. He kissed her slowly, deeply, hungrily, as he finished unbuttoning her shirt. When the cloth parted he expected to find the warmth of her flesh beneath. Instead he found thick layers of fabric and no buttons at all. Even after he took Janna's arms out of the

sleeves of her shirt, he could see no way of removing the
layers of cloth that bound her.

"What the hell?" muttered Ty.

Belatedly Janna realized that her shirt was unbuttoned
and Ty was looking at the wrapping she used to flatten her
breasts, disguising her feminine outline.

"Do you sew yourself into that thing?" Ty asked, giving
her a crooked smile that made her toes curl.

Janna laughed helplessly, torn between embarrassment
and the delicious feeling of having Ty's hands caressing her
bare arms. His palms stroked her from her wrists to her
shoulders, caressing her inner arms with his long fingers. As
he softly probed, he discovered the place beneath her left
arm where she tucked in the tail of the cloth, securing the
wrapping.

"So that's how you do it."

Pulling the end of the cloth free, Ty turned it back upon
itself several times, rolling it loosely. When he had unrolled
the fabric across her chest and under her other arm, he put
his hand just below Janna's shoulder blades and arched her
back enough that he could reach beneath, continuing the
slow unwrapping.

With each complete circuit of her body, an inch of pre-
viously hidden skin was revealed. Both the cloth and her
skin had an elusive fragrance that was a compound of herbs
and wildflowers and warm femininity that made his head
spin. When he could bear it no longer, he bent and kissed
the smooth band of flesh he had just unwrapped.

The feel of Ty's lips skimming below her collarbone made
Janna tremble. She slid her hands into his thick hair and
rubbed his scalp, smiling when she felt the answering
movement of his response. After a few moments the temptation of her still-covered breasts overcame Ty and he resumed unwrapping the long length of cloth.

Gradually the pressure of Janna's bindings eased as more
and more layers of fabric were removed. As always, the re-

lief was exquisite. She arched her back, trying to make the unwrapping go more quickly, eager to be able to breathe easily once more, to be free of the cloth restraints.

Ty refused to be rushed, for he was finding an unexpected, intensely sensual pleasure in the slow revelation of Janna's body. As the turns of fabric moved down her chest, the first curves of her breasts were unveiled. There were long lines of red pressed into her skin, legacy of the tight bindings. He smoothed his thumb over the lines as though to erase them, then brushed his lips over the marks and traced them with the tip of his tongue.

Eyes closed, Janna made soft sounds of pleasure as Ty soothed her skin. She was still breathless from the unexpected caress of his tongue when he arched her back, lifting her so that the cloth could unwind beneath her. He circled her body once and then twice, three times; and then the unwrapping stopped again. But instead of gently lowering her to the ground as he had before, he held her suspended over his powerful forearm, the graceful line of her back like a drawn bow. Slowly Janna opened her eyes and saw Ty staring at her as though what he saw was totally unexpected.

And it was. He never would have guessed at the presence of full, firm curves and lush pink tips hidden beneath turn after turn of tight cloth.

"Ty?" Janna whispered, not understanding why he was so still, so intent. "What's wrong?"

He looked up and her eyes widened at the harsh lines of his face.

"Don't ever," Ty said distinctly, "punish yourself like that again."

Before Janna could speak he bent over her breasts and soothed each mark that had been left by the cloth, working from the first smooth swell of flesh toward the deep pink crowns. The feel of his tongue laving the small marks the bindings had left was indescribable. She wanted to twist slowly in his arms like a flame, offering every bit of her

reasts to his mouth. When he came to the margin between
ne satin of her skin and the velvet of her nipple, he circled
er with exquisite care, ignoring her startled cry and her
roken breath and the fingers tightening reflexively in his
air.

And then Ty could bear the temptation no longer. He
ook Janna's offering into his mouth, sucking on the velvet
ipple until it was tight and hard, and still he tugged on her
ith slow, sensual rhythms that made small cries ripple from
er.

When the nipple could be drawn out no more, he slowly
eleased it, admiring the taut, glistening peak. He cupped
ne breast in his hand and made tight circles with his palm,
ubbing the hard nipple as he bent and caressed her other
reast with lips and tongue, drawing her out, shaping her,
ulling sensuously until her breath was quick and broken
ith the lightning strokes of sensation streaking through her
ody.

Dizzy, breathless, lost in a hushed, shimmering world she
ad never known existed, Janna felt pleasure expand and
urst and radiate through her. Ty felt it too, the flush of
nsual heat spreading beneath her skin, the small move-
ents of her hips as she sought the pressure of his body, the
ny cries when his teeth and tongue brought new heat to her.

Finally Ty lifted his head, releasing the nipple he had so
vingly shaped. Janna whimpered very softly, wanting
ore of the pleasure that had grown in her with each move-
ent of his mouth. She opened her gray eyes and looked at
m with silent pleading.

"More?" Ty asked, smiling, his voice as heavy as the
ood beating in his veins.

Janna shivered helplessly as Ty's hand closed over one of
r breasts and slowly pleasured her.

"Yes," she whispered.

He smiled, enjoying her open pleasure and the growin
flush of arousal beneath her skin. "Where else would yo
like to be kissed?"

The shocked look that came to Janna's face told Ty tha
she had never thought about such things.

"Never mind, little one," Ty said. He circled the erect ti
of each breast with his tongue and whispered, "I'll think o
something."

With a speed and power that surprised Janna, Ty turne
and lay on his back and in the same movement lifted he
pulling her over his body like a living blanket. When he
hips pressed against the hard ridge of flesh that waited in
patiently beneath the thick cloth of his pants, he made a lo
sound of pleasure-pain.

Not understanding, Janna pulled away. Ty's legs parte
and her own legs sank between his. He moved quickly, lif
ing his legs just enough to trap hers beneath, twining his leg
with hers at the ankles, forcing their bodies into an int
mate match, hard against soft, consummation no more tha
a few layers of cloth away.

"Unbutton my shirt," Ty said in a thick voice. "You'
like the feel of my bare skin against your breasts. And so w
I."

The slight movement of Janna's body when she reache
for Ty's collar button made her hips rock against the h
cradle he had made for her between his legs. He groaned
a kind of exquisite agony, for he had never needed a woma
so much as he needed Janna at that instant.

"Again," he whispered. "Move against me just on
more. Just once."

Hesitantly Janna moved her hips against Ty again, fee
ing the hard bulge of his erection like a brand against h
abdomen. The sound he made deep in his throat could ha
come from agony or undiluted pleasure. His hand came b
tween their bodies. Unerringly he found the most sensiti
part of her and pressed, rocking his hips slowly beneath he

The sudden heat that radiated out from his hand made her gasp. His name came from her lips in a husky, urgent, questioning cry.

"Yes," Ty said, his voice low and thick. "You can feel it, too, can't you?" Gently he released Janna's ankles and lifted her into a sitting position astride his waist. Her breath caught and her hips moved helplessly as he teased her nipples again with his fingertips. "It's going to be good. It's going to be so damn good. Unbutton my shirt, sugar. I want to feel your hands on my bare skin."

With fingers that trembled, Janna undid the buttons on Ty's shirt. She had seen him naked before, but it hadn't affected her one-tenth as much as watching his powerful body emerge from the shirt. In the dusk, the curling pelt of black hair was very distinct, as was the dark center line of his body where the hair narrowed to pencil width and vanished behind his belt. The heat and resilience of him were as alluring as his dark smile. With catlike pleasure Janna kneaded the muscular flesh she had so often bathed or medicated but had never caressed.

And she had wanted to. She realized that now. She understood that her hands had quivered to know every texture of Ty, the satin smoothness where skin stretched over muscle, the power inherent in him, the thick silk of his chest hair, the finer silk of the hair beneath his arms, the flat disk and hard nubbin of his nipples. Just as she had become lost in the discovery of her own body beneath his mouth, she became lost in the discovery of his body beneath her hands.

Ty watched Janna through eyes narrowed with passion. Her transparent pleasure in exploring his body was violently exciting to him. It was unlike anything he had ever known. It put him on an exquisite rack, which pulled him in two conflicting directions. Part of him wanted to grab Janna and thrust into her and end the pulsing ache of his body.

And part of him wanted to keep his hands off her and learn more about himself and her and the sweet torment of being suspended between anticipation and ecstasy.

Again and again Janna's fingers combed through the hair covering Ty's chest, tracing his nipples and then following the quickly narrowing pelt down to the cold of his belt buckle. She knew that slim line of hair would continue down his body for a hand span and then radiate out into a thick curling thatch. She wanted to see that too, to run her hand over him without any boundaries on the touching. She wanted that so much she couldn't breathe.

Not stopping to think or to question, Janna reached for Ty's belt buckle.

"Not yet," he said huskily, grabbing Janna's hands and pulling them back up to the safer territory of his chest. "I will be too quick that way. I want to enjoy you first."

"I thought you had enjoyed me," she whispered, bending to kiss his hands.

His smile made her heart turn over. "Just part of you sugar. There's some very sweet territory I haven't unwrapped yet, much less enjoyed."

Ty reversed their positions with one of the swift, powerful movements that always caught Janna off guard but no longer frightened her. Whatever came next, she was certain Ty would be careful with her. She lay quietly, watching him as he knelt at her feet and removed her knee-high moccasins and his own boots with quick motions. He tugged open his belt but left his pants untouched. When he unfastened Janna's belt she trembled.

"It's all right," Ty said, kissing Janna's lips. "I won't hurt you."

Janna took a shaky breath and nodded. "I know. It just..."

Before she could explain that she had never been naked in front of anyone, it was too late. Her ability to speak deserted her as leather slipped from the buckle with an easy movement of Ty's hand. Without the belt, her oversize men's pants slid easily from her body, and with them her underpants.

When Janna lay completely nude before Ty, his breath came out in a slow, unraveling groan.

"It's like seeing a satin butterfly emerge from a mud cocoon," Ty whispered, running his fingertips over the pale curves and velvet shadows of Janna's body.

When he reached the dark delta at the base of her torso, she made a surprised sound and moved as though to evade his hand, pressing her legs together reflexively.

"Hush, little one," Ty murmured, kissing her lips. "I know you've been hurt there but I won't hurt you. I know how delicate you are, how soft, how warm. Even you don't know how soft you can be or how warm. Let me show you."

"What d-do you want me to do?" Janna's voice broke as she shivered in a combination of nervousness and surprise at the presence of Ty's fingers searching gently through the dense triangle of hair that shielded her most sensitive flesh.

"Don't be so stiff. I won't hurt you," Ty murmured. He kissed Janna coaxingly until her lips parted and he could love her with slow, deep strokes of his tongue. He lifted his mouth and whispered against her lips. "Open your legs just a little, sugar, just a little. I'll be very gentle."

His voice became a husky sigh of triumph and discovery when Janna relaxed enough to allow his fingertip to skim over the soft, hot folds between her legs.

"Just a little more," Ty whispered, caressing her, seeking the heated well of her femininity, finding just its soft, burning edges. But it was enough. It told him that her blood was running as hotly and hungrily as his own. He probed lightly and was rewarded by a hint of the smooth, sultry sheath that awaited him. "My beautiful satin butterfly," he said huskily. "So hot, so sleek. Open a little more for me, butterfly. I won't force you. I just want to love all of you. Let me..."

Janna tried to speak but her voice broke over Ty's name. The gliding, skimming caress of his finger had changed into a gentle penetration that took her breath away. He bent to her mouth and his tongue echoed the tender movements of his hand between her legs. The heat and tension that had been gathering deep within her body flared suddenly, wildly, claiming her in a gentle convulsion that took her wholly by surprise.

But not Ty. He had been coaxing Janna toward just such a minor peak of ecstasy since he had first discovered the sensuality hidden within her body. He repeated the twin, gentle assaults on her body, his tongue gliding over hers in a deep kiss as his finger slid between her legs in a slow, teasing dance of penetration and withdrawal that brought soft whimpers from her throat. Passion shimmered and burst within her again, heat and pleasure overflowing.

Janna moaned softly as Ty withdrew from her sultry center and caressed the bud of her passion with fingertips still slick from her own response. Heat speared through her, tightening her body. She cried out into his mouth and her hips moved beneath his hand, asking for something she had never known. She sensed his hesitation, felt as much as heard him groan, and bit back a cry of protest when he withdrew his caressing hand.

"Hush, little one," Ty murmured, freeing himself of his clothes in a few swift movements. "It won't be long."

"Ty?"

"I'm right here," he said, gently pressing Janna's legs farther apart, making room for himself.

Delicately he teased the nub he had coaxed from her soft, humid folds. She trembled and her knees flexed instinctively, allowing him greater access to her body. Her passionate response spilled over him as he probed her softness with his own aching flesh. The moist, welcoming heat of her body was unmistakable, a silent command that he come deeply within her; but she was so tight that he was afraid of hurting her.

Shivering with the harshness of his self-imposed restraint, Ty began taking Janna as gradually as evening took the day. Her eyes opened in sensual surprise and she looked up into the face of the man who was slowly, so slowly, becoming part of her. Each time the pressure of him within her became almost painful, he sensed it, withdrew and gradually came to her again.

The exquisitely gentle penetration made waves of heat gather and burst within her, showering him with her pleasure. She heard him groan and push more deeply inside and then felt the harsh tension shaking his body as he forced himself to stop.

"You're a virgin!"

# Chapter Twenty-Two

Ty's accusing voice was hoarse as he fought against his deepest needs and tried to force himself to retreat from Janna's moist, clinging heat. But he couldn't. He wanted only to continue taking her a bit at a time; and when he caressed her to ecstasy once more he wanted to thrust past the frail barrier separating their bodies from total unity. She would feel no pain at the instant he took her because she would be too deeply enmeshed in her climax to know or care that for the first time in her life a man would be fully sheathed within her.

*Virgin.*

"Christ," Ty groaned, "if I'd known, I never would have touched you."

"Then I'm glad you didn't know," Janna said huskily. She shivered and melted over him again, moving her hips helplessly, in the grip of a passion she had never expected and had no idea how to control. All she wanted was more of him, more of the sweet friction as she stretched around him. "I want this, Ty. Please. You're not hurting me. I love . . . feeling you." She moved her hips slowly, caressing him and herself in the same motion. "Oh, that's so good," she whispered raggedly, rocking, moving as much as he would allow, "but it's not enough . . . not . . . enough."

"Stop it!" Ty said roughly as he felt the last shreds of his self-control slipping away. "You're a virgin!"

Janna's nails dug into the flexed power of Ty's buttocks and her body twisted wildly beneath his as she whispered again and again that what he had given her was good but not enough. With each movement she became more seductive, more demanding, more welcoming, so hot and sleek that he found himself pressing again and yet again at the fragile flesh that barred total consummation.

Ty groaned and forced himself to move just slightly while his fingers sought and claimed the slick, delicate nub of Janna's passion. He controlled the instinctive rocking of her hips by settling more of his weight between her legs, pinning her in place while he caressed her, bringing her closer and closer to ecstasy.

When he felt the sudden mist of passion flush her skin and her breath broke and her cries came quickly, rising urgently, he covered her mouth with his own and began to move again within her, trying to hold back from the elemental consummation that awaited him in the depths of her virginal body. A groan racked him as he thought what it would be like to sheathe every bit of his need in her, to pierce her virginity and feel her pleasure flow over him in a hot, ecstatic rain.

And then it was happening, the hot rain and the sheathing, ecstasy bursting with each movement of Ty's hips; and Janna wept at the perfection as he let go of control and locked himself so deeply within her that she felt the certainty of his climax as the most intimate kind of caress, a pulsing presence that sent her spinning into ecstasy once again, her body caressing him rhythmically in the quivering aftermath of his own release.

Janna's tiny, ecstatic cries pierced Ty like golden needles, reaching past the flesh to the soul beneath. Violent pleasure racked him until his muscles stood out like iron. The endless, shuddering release that followed overwhelmed him.

Unable to see, unable to think, unable to speak, he spent himself again and again in the virgin who had touched a part of him no other woman ever had.

When Ty was at last quiet once more, Janna clung to his powerful, sweat-slicked body, savoring the intimacy of lying beneath him and feeling him inside her as evening condensed soundlessly into night around them. She hadn't known what to expect from the act of love, but she hadn't anticipated anything so hot, so sweet, so violently complete.

"I love you," Janna whispered, kissing Ty's shoulder.

The words were very soft, barely a whisper, but Ty heard them. A combination of guilt and anger raced through him when he remembered the irrevocable instant when he had taken Janna's virginity. Silently he raged at himself and his baffling lack of control where she was concerned. He had been able to keep himself tightly reined while he seduced her, yet he hadn't been able to pull back after he had discovered she was a virgin.

He didn't understand that. He should have been able to turn away from her; she wasn't the first woman to try that particular marital trap. He had eluded the others in the past, and those girls had been much more accomplished in their snares and lures.

But Janna had been a handful of fire and beauty, and her ecstatic cries as he pierced her virginity would haunt Ty until he died.

"I never should have taken you," he said in a low, bitter voice.

Janna's gently stroking hands became still. "Why?"

"Because I discovered that you were a virgin and I had no intention of marrying you, that's why. But I had a lot of help getting past your innocence, didn't I? First you tell me you're not a virgin—"

"I never said that," Janna interrupted in a fierce whisper.

"What about when you ran and I brought you down and kissed you too hard, and you said you'd taken a lot worse from men and survived?"

"I only meant that you hadn't really hurt me. And you hadn't."

"What about Joe Troon?"

"What about him?"

"Ned said that Troon 'kept' you for a while."

"Ned is a drunk and a liar. Troon caught me but he never kept me."

"Well, sugar, you sure as hell didn't act like any virgin I'd ever met. Ever since I came to after Cascabel's gauntlet you've been rubbing up against me and sighing and smiling and looking at me out of those smoky gray eyes like I'd spilled honey in my lap and you couldn't wait to lick off every bit of it," Ty said in a low, angry voice. "It would have served you right if I'd backed you up against a tree, opened my pants and had you standing up like the lowest kind of camp follower."

Janna thought of the ways she had tormented Ty without truly understanding the elemental force of his need . . . and her own. The thought of how often she had smiled when he had turned away to hide the evidence of his arousal made her ashamed now.

"I'm so sorry," Janna said, touching Ty's face tentatively. "I didn't know what I was doing to you. I didn't know the power of what you were fighting, how much you needed me."

"It was a woman I needed, not you," snarled Ty, jerking away from Janna's gentle touch.

All the movement accomplished was to remind him that he was still held within the satin sheath of her body; and she felt even better now than in his hottest memories. He told himself to roll aside, to separate himself from her, but his body refused to respond. He was drinking her heat, growing inside her, and his blood was beating heavily, urging his hips to move in primal rhythms.

"*Virgin,*" Ty said, and it was a curse. "But you wanted it as much as I did, didn't you? Hell, you damn near burned me alive with your cries and your hips sliding, pushing me deeper and deeper..."

Ty shuddered unexpectedly, memories bursting inside him, sensuality lancing through his body, tightening him, making him feel every bit of the hot perfection of being locked inside Janna.

The knowledge of his own helpless response to her shocked Ty. He shouldn't feel this way. The sweat wasn't dry on his body from the first time he had taken her. He shouldn't want her again the way he did right now—need knotting his guts, his body hard and heavy and hot, filled to bursting once more.

He fought to remain still, not to respond, not to move, but the knowledge of the ecstatic consummation he would find within Janna's body was too new, too overwhelming for him to deny or control it. With a low, raw cry, he fought against the lure of her, but even as he cried out he was moving slowly, surrendering himself to her one hard inch at a time.

Janna's breath caught as Ty deliberately measured himself within her once, then twice, then three times. She didn't understand his rejection of her apology or his anger with her, but she understood the need that was making him tremble; it was her own need, doubling and redoubling with each heartbeat, a flame burning up from their joined bodies, heat delicately melting and ravenously devouring her at the same time. She shivered and arched beneath him in sensual abandon.

Ty groaned and felt fire eat ever more deeply into him, burning away thought, burning away reluctance, leaving only the elemental union of male and female, a joining that was deeper than flesh, hotter than desire, two living flames leaping higher as they touched, overlapped, entwined. He swore in a mingling of awe and savage triumph as he felt his lover's fluid grace rise to match his own savage need.

"Satin...butterfly," Ty said hoarsely, more accusation than affection in his voice. "Did you think that I'd marry you once I found what it was like to have you?"

He thrust his tongue into Janna's mouth, muffling whatever her answer might have been. Before the kiss ended she was moaning softly and moving in languid counterpart to the slow, circular dance of his hips.

"It won't work," he said, his breath coming quickly, heavily. "I'll take every bit of your body. I'll give you every bit of my body in return. But that's all. Just two bodies giving and taking. Do you hear me?"

Janna moaned brokenly and closed herself around him in a deep, instinctive caress.

"Do you hear me?" Ty demanded, clenching himself against the unbearable seduction of her body.

"Yes," she whispered. Her hips lifted slightly, then circled, seducing him, loving him. "I heard you the first time you told me in the valley."

"What?"

Ty's past words echoed cruelly within Janna's mind: *I'll have my silken lady or I'll have none at all for longer than it takes to pleasure myself.*

"I know that I'm not the silken lady of your dreams," Janna said, her voice a whisper of unquenchable hope and a foretaste of despair. "You're pleasuring yourself. That's all."

Ty didn't argue or protest her words.

Janna had expected no more, yet she had to bite her lip not to protest aloud the emotions tearing through her, passion and grief and the shivering precursors of wild ecstasy. When Ty moved within her again, she wept silently, grateful that it was too dark for him to see her tears, feeling his breath as cool, quickening gusts over her wet cheeks.

"But you still want me?" Ty persisted. "No games, no secret plans, no regrets?" He locked their bodies together suddenly, a joining so deep and hot and complete that it tore a low cry from his throat, a cry that was her name. He rocked against her with tiny, intense motions, burning up, buried in fire and wanting it, all of it, *burning*. "Do you still want this?"

"I want..." Janna whispered, but could say no more because tears drowned her voice and the truth was too bitter to speak aloud. She wanted to be loved by him in all ways, not just one.

"Janna?" Ty asked, holding himself motionless but for the helpless shuddering of his aroused body. "Answer me!"

She tried to move, to take from him what he was withholding. It was impossible. He was too strong, too skilled, and she loved him.

"Yes, damn you," she whispered achingly. "Yes!"

Ty heard only the agreement, not the pain. He let out his pent breath in a ragged groan.

"I need you," he said in a low voice. His hips began to move in quickening rhythms as shudder after shudder of tension went through his powerful body. "God help me, I've never needed any woman like this."

Janna heard the bafflement and strain in Ty's voice and felt herself swept up in his overwhelming need. Crying silently, loving him and knowing that he would love no one but the silken lady of his dreams, Janna took all that Ty could give to her of himself and in return gave all of herself that he would take.

The sensual generosity of Janna's response washed over Ty, bathing both of them in fire. She heard his broken groan, felt the power of him within her redouble, felt the hungry, rhythmic penetration as his body drove against hers again and again and again. His urgency excited her, overwhelmed her, shattered her, and still he moved hard within her, drinking her rippling cries, rocking, rocking, rocking…burning, she was burning and there was no end to the wild, consuming flames.

Janna's breath broke and a low cry was torn from her throat as she surrendered to savage ecstasy. Ty drank that cry and silently asked more of her, fierce in his demands of her body, wanting something he couldn't name, driving into her as though she were the last woman he would ever have, wanting at some deep, inarticulate level of his consciousness to leave his imprint upon her very soul.

Her legs twisted around his waist and her body shivered, her mouth bit into his, her nails scored his back; and he smiled and spoke dark words to her as he slipped his arms beneath her knees and slowly pulled her legs up his body, over his shoulders, opening her to him fully.

With deep, shuddering pleasure Ty drove again and again into the satin heat of Janna's body, smothering her abandoned cries with his mouth, penetrating her completely, repeatedly, powerfully, until she was racked by ecstasy; and still his potent movements continued, as though he would become a part of her or die in the effort. She thought she could know no greater pleasure without dying, and she tried to tell him but suddenly she had no voice, no will, for she was transfixed by a savage rapture.

Janna would have screamed her pleasure then, heedless of the danger, but Ty's mouth was consuming hers. He took the ecstatic scream into himself as passionate convulsions swept his body, burning him to his soul, ecstasy racking him with every heartbeat.

And he thought he was dying as he poured himself into her wildly shivering, welcoming body.

## Chapter Twenty-Three

Utterly spent, Ty groaned softly and laid his head next to Janna's. He kissed her very gently, feeling an almost overwhelming tenderness toward the woman who had accepted him without restraint or regret or promises, bringing him the most intense, consuming union he had ever known.

When his lips brushed her cheek he tasted tears. The thought that his ecstasy had caused Janna hurt made pain lance harshly through Ty, an agony as surprising to him as the endless, hot, violent upwelling of his need for her had been.

"I'm sorry," Ty said, kissing Janna's face blindly, gently, finding everywhere the taste of tears. "Little one, I'm sorry. I didn't mean to hurt you."

Janna tried to answer but could not, for emotion had closed her throat.

Ty held her, rocking her in his arms, hating himself for hurting the girl who had saved his life at such great risk to her own.

"I owe you so much more than this..." he whispered, and he was haunted by the silken lady of whom he had dreamed so long, the wife who would be the greatest adornment of the life he would build to replace what war had taken away. "Oh God, what have I done to you, to myself?"

Janna shook her head silently, fighting for control of
erself, not understanding what had caused the pain in Ty's
oice. After a few moments she was able to speak.

"You didn't hurt me."

"Like hell I didn't."

"Ty, you didn't. I felt nothing but pleasure."

He heard Janna's words, felt her hands stroking his hair,
oothing him, and felt a cold rush of self-contempt. He had
anted her, he had taken her despite her innocence, and in
oing so he had left her suited only for the life of a prosti-
ute or a nun.

"You're so innocent. My God, you don't even under-
and what has happened, do you?"

"I understand that you didn't hurt me."

"I didn't hurt..." Ty's laughter was low and as harsh as
e guilt clawing at him. His hands tightened on Janna as he
ealized the extent of his folly. "You little fool, I ruined you!
ou have no family, no profession, no wealth. All you had
f value for a husband was your virginity, and now that's
one. I've left you suited to be nothing except a man's mis-
ess, but you lack the social graces for even that profes-
on. You'll end up locked in a nun's cage or you'll be the
y of many men, not one."

Janna flinched and tried to draw away from Ty's cruel
ummation of her value as a woman, a mate, but she was
o securely held to retreat. He drew her closer, not even
oticing her futile attempts to free herself from his em-
race.

"Never mind, little one," Ty said, his voice low and
npty, echoing with despair at the death of his personal
eam, the silken lady who now would forever be beyond his
ach. "It was my fault, not yours. I'll marry you as soon
we get to the fort."

It took Janna a minute to absorb what he had said, what
had implied—and when she understood, she was wild
ith hurt.

"Like burning hell you'll marry me," Janna said in a low savage voice.

"What?"

"I may be suited only to be a saloon girl, but I keep m word."

"Janna, I didn't mean—" Ty began, only to be cut off.

"No! I said that I wouldn't ask for any promises or hav any regrets or any secret plans," she whispered angrily, tell ing herself that hopes weren't the same as plans.

Not that it mattered. Ty had taken care of the hopes, a well. *No family. No profession. No wealth. No socia graces.* And no emotion in his voice but guilt and despai and anger at being trapped into marrying such a poor spec imen of femininity.

"I've never trapped a living thing in my life," she sai fiercely, "and I'll be damned to hell for eternity if I tak your freedom now. Do you hear me, Tyrell MacKenzie? D you?"

"You didn't take my freedom. I gave it away the sam way men always have, thinking with my crotch instead of m brain."

"You can have it right back—freedom, brain, crotch, a of it! I want nothing that isn't freely given."

"The world doesn't work that way, sugar," Ty sai wearily, releasing Janna and rolling over onto his back "The only virgin a decent man takes is the girl who be comes his wife. We'll be married as soon as—"

"They'll be picking cotton in hell before I marry you, Janna interrupted, her voice shaking, her body cold an empty without him.

It was as though Ty hadn't heard. "I'm responsible fo you. I live up to my responsibilities."

"I'm responsible for myself. I've lived on my own for fiv years. I can do it for another—"

"Christ!" hissed Ty, cutting Janna off. "Are you so na ive that you don't know you could get pregnant after this

low would you take care of yourself, much less a baby,
oo?" He waited, but there was no answer except the small
ounds Janna made as she searched for her clothes in the
arkness. "We'll be married at the fort and you'll stay there
hile I hunt for Lucifer."

"No."

"Janna—oh, the hell with it," Ty whispered harshly.
We'll be married at the fort and then we'll hunt Lucifer
ogether. Does that satisfy you?"

"No."

Janna thrust an arm through a shirtsleeve and fished
round for the other opening. Even if it hadn't been dark,
ie tears streaming down her face would have blinded her.
one of her emotions showed in her constrained whisper,
or which she was grateful. Having marriage offered to her
ut of guilt was bad enough; having it offered to her out of
ity would be unbearable.

"Janna, be reasonable. I'll need Lucifer to build a good
orse herd," Ty said as patiently as he could manage.
Otherwise I'll have no way to take care of my family."

"I said I'd help you catch Lucifer and I will. Marriage
as no part of the bargain."

Ty's patience evaporated. With uncanny speed he grabbed
anna, flattened her beneath him once more and began
hispering furiously.

"Listen to me, you little fool. You have no idea how the
orld works."

"Then teach me," she whispered defiantly. "Teach me
ow to please a man, how to be good enough to be a mis-
ess rather than a whore. That's all I ask of you. Educa-
on, not marriage."

"But if you're preg—" he began.

"I stopped bleeding two days ago," she interrupted.
There's little chance you've made me pregnant."

Ty should have been relieved, but the scent and feel of
nna beneath him was driving everything else from his

mind. Even as he told himself he must be crazy, he realize
that he wanted her again.

"This time, yes," he agreed huskily, "but what about th
next time I take you, and the next, and the times after tha
Because if I'm around you, I'll take you every damne
chance I get." His hand slid down her body until he coul
feel once more her intimate heat. "Satin butterfly," h
whispered, unable to control the faint trembling of his fir
gers as he skimmed the edges of her softness. "Don't yc
understand yet? When I see you, hear you, smell you, touc
you, taste you . . ."

A threadlike groan vibrated through Ty. "You're killi
me. I can't leave you alone if I'm around you. I can't liv
with myself if I get you pregnant. And I need you around :
that I can track down Lucifer before he gets killed or th
whole damned territory blows up in our faces. We have ·
get married, Janna. There's no other way."

"No."

Janna clamped her legs together, trying to deny Ty th
softness only he had ever touched.

It was futile. All she succeeded in doing was imprisonir
his hand between her thighs. He made a sound of pleasu
and despair as one finger slid gently into her and he felt h·
sleek, humid warmth surrounding him once more.

"I won't marry you," Janna whispered, her breat
breaking. "Do you hear me? I won't spend my life havir
you look at me and long for a silken lady."

Ty hesitated, then slowly probed Janna's sensuo
warmth. "I hear you. But what are we going to do abo
this? I meant what I said, little one. Having had you, I car
leave you alone."

She tried not to give voice to her pleasure, but a husl
sound escaped her lips. "Teach me. That's all I ask of yo
A mistress, not a whore."

The words went into Ty like knives, twisting even as the
sliced into him. "I can't live with that. It's not enough. Yc

deserve much more. Come back to Wyoming with me," he said in a low voice, caressing Janna because he was helpless to stop. "Silver and Cassie can teach you how to sit and speak and smile like a lady. They'll teach you how to dress and I'll see that you have enough dowry to attract a good man, a man who won't berate you for what I took from you. Then you'll be a married woman, Janna, not any man's mistress or every man's whore."

"I'll marry no man," she whispered. "Ever."

"Janna..."

Her only answer was a husky cry and her warmth reaching out to Ty, silently promising oblivion within her body. The heat and scent of her filled his nostrils, sending a wave of desire through him. Suddenly he wanted to bend down and immerse himself in Janna, tasting her essence, drinking the very secrets of her body. The thought shocked him, for he had never wanted that kind of intimacy with a woman before.

"You're so sweet to touch," Ty whispered, stroking Janna with slow, hidden motions. "I never knew a woman could be so responsive, so perfect. Satin butterfly, more beautiful to me each time I touch you."

"Ty..." Janna said, moaning his name softly, feeling her tumultuous emotions condense into pure burning desire.

She knew she should tell him to stop but she was unable to form the words. She wanted his touch too much. She had never known such ravishing closeness with anyone, had never even dreamed it was possible. The knowledge that he, too, found something special in her made it impossible to turn away from his need.

Ty heard the telltale break and quickening of Janna's breath and didn't know whether to curse or laugh as he felt himself hardening, succumbing to her sleek satin trap once more. She was a handful of fire, a sensuous dream, so recently a virgin and yet so generous and unafraid as a lover.

Janna's small hands found his in the darkness and she held them motionless, trying to still the secret movement within her body.

"Stop," she whispered, yet even as she spoke she felt her own heat overflowing in silent contradiction.

"Why?" Ty murmured, slowly penetrating and withdrawing from her body despite her clinging fingers. "Am I hurting you?"

"N-no."

To Ty the sensual break and shiver of Janna's voice was as arousing as her heat welling up at his touch.

"You're too innocent to understand how rare you are, how extraordinary this is," he whispered, feeling the vital hardening of his flesh as he bent down to her. "But I'm no innocent. I know. I'd agree to anything in order to keep on touching you. I've never been like this with any woman, *Bruja*, sweet fire witch. You burn me alive and I tremble and spend myself within you... and then you renew me with a breath, a kiss, a touch."

Janna whispered Ty's name helplessly, moved beyond words that she could affect him so deeply.

"Renew me," Ty whispered, lifting her hand and kissing it before placing it over his swelling male flesh.

She felt the helpless, sensuous jerk of his body as her fingers curled around him in answer to the pressure of his own hands.

"Teach me?" she whispered.

"Yes," he said. "Every chance I get. All the way from here to Wyoming. And then—"

"No," she interrupted, arching up to meet him. "No tomorrows. Just teach me. Teach me now."

He started to speak, then forgot what he was going to say when her hands moved.

"Like this?" Janna whispered, measuring and caressing him with the same slow, sensuous motion.

"Sweet...God...yes," Ty said. His whole body tight-ened and moved with her hands in a sinuous dance that made him tremble. He lowered his head until he could feel her breath against his lips. "And like this," he whispered, fitting first his body and then his mouth to hers, thrusting deeply into her generous warmth. "And this...and *this*..."

Even as Janna shivered and softly cried out, Ty bent and drank ecstasy from her lips, sinking wholly into her, won-dering who was the teacher and who the student in the hushed intimacy of the meadow night.

## Chapter Twenty-Four

The brutal crack of rifle fire at the northwest end of Raven Creek's meadow jerked Janna and Ty awake in a heart-pounding instant.

Neither one moved.

No more sounds came. After a few minutes Ty eased away from Janna, grabbed his carbine and crawled to a vantage point where he could look out across the meadow. There was nothing in sight. A moment later he sensed Janna coming up behind him. He turned and shook his head. She retreated as silently as she had come. So did he.

Without talking, they withdrew to the place where they had slept. Ty reached for his backpack at the same instant that Janna reached for the cloth she had used to bind her breasts. Although she and Ty had been forced by the cold to put on their clothes in the hours before dawn, he hadn't allowed her to wrap up in the cloth again. Instead, he had curled spoon fashion along her back, slid his hands up beneath her loose shirt and caressed her gently until they both fell asleep.

As soon as Janna's fingers closed on the binding, she realized that she wasn't going to be allowed to use it this morning, either. Ty snatched the cloth from her fingers, rolled it tightly and jammed it into his backpack. Then he pulled her to her feet.

"I'd kiss you," he said very softly, looking hungrily at her mouth, "but if I did, I'd undress you and lie between your legs again. That wouldn't be a very smart thing to do right now."

Janna's mind agreed, but her body swayed hungrily toward Ty. He let go of her as though he had grabbed something too hot to hold. Saying nothing, Janna turned and began threading through the forest, circling toward the northeast corner of the meadow. After a few minutes she looked at Ty and gestured toward the meadow. He nodded. Together they walked, then crawled and finally wiggled snake fashion toward the edge of the meadow.

In the clear yellow light of morning, the signs were unmistakable—a group of unshod horses had grazed the meadow within the past few days. The presence of small hoofprints and diminutive manure piles told Ty and Janna that the horses were wild, for hunting or raiding parties didn't use mares whose foals were unweaned. Overlaid on the random tracks of grazing animals were those of a shod horse walking across the meadow and into the dense pine forest beyond. It was those prints that had attracted the Indian hunting party the previous night.

"Troon," Janna whispered, looking at the prints.

"How can you tell?"

"See how worn the shoe is on the left front hoof? Troon's too cheap to get his horse shod regularly."

"Wasn't bothering to hide his trail, was he?" Ty muttered.

"He was probably drunk."

"Then he's probably dead. Was it Lucifer's bunch he was following?"

"I can't tell from the tracks around here. I'd have to go to the center and check the muddy spots along Raven Creek. Besides, Lucifer never mixes with his herd when the mares graze. If this is his bunch, his tracks will be off to the side somewhere."

Both Janna and Ty looked out over the empty, inviting meadow that Troon had crossed sometime yesterday. The ground beneath their bodies was still slightly damp with dew, but they were in no hurry to stand up and expose themselves to any watchers who might have been posted by the meadow. Raven Creek's watershed had become all but overrun by Cascabel and his growing band of renegades.

Ty's hard green eyes searched the boundary between forest and meadow, seeking any sign that Indians were about. Birds called and flew naturally, landed in low branches or on the meadow itself. No bird flew up with a startled outcry, indicating that danger lay hidden somewhere around Raven Creek's meadow itself.

Janna watched the area as carefully as Ty. She saw nothing that should disturb her, yet she was reluctant to cross the meadow in pursuit of either Lucifer's tracks or those of Joe Troon. She looked at Ty and gestured toward the meadow in silent question. He shook his head in a slow negative. She didn't disagree. Together they eased backward deeper into the small trees and sun-hungry bushes that ringed the meadow. When both of them were within the cover of the forest once more, Ty gestured for Janna to choose the best route around to the opposite side of the meadow.

Moving quickly and quietly, Janna set off into the forest. Within the fragrant, hushed cover beneath the trees, the going became easier. The tall pines screened out much of the sunlight, making it impossible for plants to thrive on the forest floor. Even so, fallen trees and branches forced Janna to make many small detours. Every few minutes she stopped and stood motionless, watching and listening to the forest with the consummate grace and stillness of a wild deer.

Ty never became impatient with Janna's detours or her seemingly random stops. Watching her blend with the land was a pleasure for him. Though he took second to few people in his ability to track or to hunt, Ty knew that here on

Black Plateau, Janna was at home in a way that only a wild animal could equal.

*It's a good thing she didn't get up here before I found her,* Ty thought as he watched Janna merge with the shadows beneath the trees. *I never would have caught her.*

Part of Ty wondered if that wouldn't have been better for both of them, but even as the question occurred to him he denied it. The thought of never having known such intense, consuming pleasure was unbearable to him. Memories of the night before licked like scented fire over his body. For an instant he savored the sensuous rush of images, tasted again in memory Janna's mouth and breasts, felt again the tightness of her body as she accepted him into her satin heat. Then he put memories aside with a skill he had learned during the war, dividing his mind into compartments like a dresser; and like a man dressing, he had learned to open only the drawer that contained what he needed at the moment.

Making no sound, Janna walked forward once more, a gray-eyed shadow among shadows. With an unconscious movement Ty shifted his carbine into carrying position again, holding his right hand around the stock in such a way that it would take only an instant to pull the trigger and keeping the muzzle pointed so that an accidental firing wouldn't hit anyone in front of him. The buttoned pocket of his wool shirt bulged with a box of bullets. Similar boxes made his backpack heavier than its size would have indicated.

He didn't notice the extra weight, much less complain of it. There had been too many times in the past when he would have sold his soul for extra ammunition. He felt the same way about the beef jerky that he was chewing on at the moment—it might have been tougher than leather, unsalted and stone dry, but it was food and he had been hungry too many times in the past to be fussy about what he ate now.

The wind breathed softly over Janna and Ty, bringing with it the smell of pine resin and sun. Off in the distance a raven jeered at something concealed within pine boughs. Janna and Ty froze as one. The raven's harsh cries rang in the silence, then faded as the bird flew farther away. Both of them remained motionless, wondering if it had been another bird or a man that had disturbed the crow.

The breeze sighed over Janna's face, stirring wisps of auburn hair. The delicate brushing movement reminded her of Ty's gentleness when he had first taken her into his arms to calm her after her encounter with the snake. An odd frisson of sensation raced through Janna's body from her breasts to her thighs as she remembered what had followed the first soft kisses.

And on the heels of hot memories came the icy knowledge that Ty was hers for only a short time, just long enough to find and tame Lucifer. Then Ty would go in search of the silken lady he was determined to have. A yearning to be that lady twisted through Janna with such painful intensity that she couldn't breathe.

*Don't be a fool,* she told herself harshly. *I know all about silk purses and sows' ears. A man like Ty does, too. He was raised in a grand house with servants and tutors and people to tell him how to speak and eat and dress and write a fine hand. I had my father and a wagon seat and a trunk full of old books. I can read and write . . . and that's all. If I ever wore a dress, I've forgotten what it feels like. The only shoes I remember having are the moccasins I make for myself. The only perfume I know is what I make from crushed flowers. The only salves I have are for healing, not for making me beautiful. The only thing my hands are good for is surviving, not for playing grand songs on a piano.*

Then Janna remembered one other thing her hands had proven to be good for—arousing Ty until he was as hot and hard as sun-warmed stone. If she closed her eyes she could still feel him changing within her grasp, becoming full and tight and heavy, moving blindly between her hands, seeking more of her.

*Will he want me like that again tonight, nothing but the two of us locked together and pleasure like a fire burning between us?*

Without thinking, Janna turned and looked over her shoulder where she knew Ty would be. He was standing as motionless as she was, and he was watching her with eyes that glittered like green gems. She sensed in that moment that he knew her thoughts, her memories, for they were his thoughts, his memories.

The breeze blew softly, caressing Janna's face. Ty could see the stirring of soft auburn hair. He knew what those silky wisps felt like on his lips, knew what her skin tasted like along her hairline, knew that she trembled when the tip of his tongue traced her ear or found the pulse beating in her neck. And he knew from the sudden, slight parting of her lips that she was remembering what it had felt like to have his tongue slide between her teeth to probe and caress the passionate softness of her mouth.

Janna made no sound as she turned away from Ty, but he knew why she had retreated. If they had looked at each other for even one more second, he would have pulled her down to the ground and taken her and to hell with the risk. It would have been worth it to die of ecstasy and then to be reborn and die again, sheathed so perfectly within her body.

The small, normal sounds of the forest surrounded Janna as she moved from shadow to shadow, all senses alert. A squirrel scolded a trespassing cousin, two ravens called as they flew overhead, and needles whispered secretively as they combed through the erratic breeze. Through the massed, dark trunks and dead lower branches of the pines, Janna caught occasional views of the sunny meadow.

There were game trails crisscrossing the forest and the meadow itself. Whenever Janna came to such a path, she stopped and read the signs left by passing animals. The damp earth held tracks for a long time, telling of the passage of deer and coyote, cougar and bear, men and horses. The first few game trails were little more than faint threads winding around deadfalls and between trees. The fourth path she discovered was much more obvious, for it was frequently used by wild horses. The trail began at the west end of the meadow and took a reasonably straight line toward the northwest corner of the plateau, where Raven Creek cut through the land on its way to joining the warm, shallow waters of Santos Wash—and Cascabel's sprawling renegade camp guarding the northwest approach to the plateau.

Suddenly Janna went to her knees, her heart pounding. There, alongside the main trail, was a partial track left by a large, unshod horse.

"Lucifer," she said, spreading her fingers, measuring the huge print.

"Are you sure?" Ty asked, quickly kneeling beside her. "There's not much of a track to go on."

"No other horse but Cascabel's is so big. But there's no sign that this horse has ever been shod, and Cascabel's has."

Silently Ty began casting for a sign on either side of the trail. He wasn't long in finding it.

"Janna."

She came to her feet instantly and ran to his side.

"He was coming out of the meadow and something spooked him," Ty said softly, pointing to the place where Lucifer's hooves had dug abruptly into the trail, gouging out clots of dirt and debris as he sprang to one side. "He took off running through the trees."

Janna looked from the churned earth to the forest beyond. A faint trail of disturbed pine needles showed as lighter marks against the forest floor. She bent and studied the damp, undisturbed ground and the tracks themselves.

And then she saw the blood.

*Joe Troon took off with his rifle. Swore he was going to crease or kill Lucifer.*

With a trembling hand she touched the blood spoor. It was neither fresh nor old.

"The tracks were left within the past few hours," Ty said. "So was the blood."

Janna sensed rather than saw Ty's head jerk toward her. Within seconds he was squatting on his heels next to her, rubbing a bit of the dark, thumbnail-size spot between his fingers. He stared at the results and cursed the man who hadn't drunk enough to miss entirely.

"I'll bet it happened just after dawn," Ty said.

"We heard more than one shot."

Ty grunted. "There's more than one renegade riding around here looking for trouble. Maybe one of them found Joe Troon."

Ty rubbed his hand clean on his pants and stood. The idea of the magnificent stallion slowly bleeding to death made him sick. But before they followed Lucifer's trail, they had to know if it were Joe Troon or a renegade party they were likely to run into.

"I'm going to cast around back toward the meadow and see if I can find what spooked Lucifer," Ty said. "You follow his tracks. I'll follow you. If you lose the trail, stay put until I catch up." He looked into her clear eyes. "Do you want the carbine?"

She shook her head. "Keep it. I haven't shot a long gun in years. Snares or a bow and arrow are much more quiet for hunting game."

"At least take my pistol."

Janna hesitated, then gave in. She wouldn't do either Ty or herself much good if she stumbled across renegades and all she had to throw at them was a handful of pine needles.

Frowning uneasily, Ty watched Janna push his big revolver behind her belt. He knew it was irrational of him not to want to leave her alone—after all, she had survived for years on her own in this very country—but he still didn't like it.

"You're coming with me," he said without warning.

Startled, she looked up. "Why?"

"My backbone is itchy as all hell, that's why, and I'm a man who listens to my instincts."

"Lucifer's bleeding. If I hurry—"

"A few minutes more or less won't make much difference," Ty interrupted. "Besides, there's no way we can be sure that it was a bullet that hurt him. Could have been a sharp branch he shied into. Could have been another horse. I've seen him fight more than one eager stud and they both walked away dripping blood." Ty turned back toward the meadow. "Hurry up. We're wasting time talking when we could be tracking."

Mouth open, Janna watched Ty trot off along the game trail, covering ground at a good clip while looking for signs of other horses or other men. If he noticed that she wasn't following, he gave no indication of it.

Without a word Janna turned and began running in a different direction, following the trail Lucifer had left during his panicked flight away from the meadow.

## Chapter Twenty-Five

Head down, his attention focused on the wild horse trail, Ty trotted rapidly through the forest toward the meadow. Tracks and signs abounded, but he could see without slowing that nothing was less than a few days old. He was looking for much fresher marks.

He found them less than two hundred feet from the meadow itself.

The empty rye bottle glittered on top of the pine needles. The bottle hadn't been there long, for when Ty picked it up and sniffed, the smell of alcohol was strong in his nostrils. Nearby was a tree stained with urine from chest high to the ground. There were hoof tracks left by a shod horse next to the tree.

From that point the trail was easy to reconstruct. Troon—for Ty was certain that the empty bottle had belonged to Joe Troon rather than to a solitary Indian—had been relieving himself from the saddle when something had surprised him.

"I'll bet he was hot on Lucifer's trail and had to piss so bad that his back teeth were floating," Ty said very softly, believing that Janna was right behind. "So there he was, still in the saddle and pissing up a storm when he saw Lucifer through the trees, dropped everything and grabbed for his rifle. Lord, what a mess that must have been."

When Janna made no comment, Ty turned and looked at his own trail. Janna was nowhere in sight.

The uneasiness that had been riding Ty crystallized in an instant of stabbing fear. He ignored his first impulse, which was to backtrack along his own trail until he found Janna. That would take too long, for he had come nearly half a mile. Obviously Troon's trail and Lucifer's crossed somewhere ahead. If Ty followed one and Janna followed the other, they would meet much quicker than if he retraced his own tracks and then hers, as well.

If both of them were really lucky, none of Cascabel's renegades would ride over to find the cause of the single rifle shot. But Ty really didn't expect that kind of luck.

Swearing savagely to himself, he began trotting along the trail left by the shod horse. Within ten yards he spotted the brass from a spent cartridge gleaming among pine needles. The shine of the metal told Ty that the cartridge hadn't been long out of a rifle barrel. He had no doubt that it was the debris of the shot that had awakened Janna and himself less than half an hour ago. He also had no doubt what the intended target had been.

*You drunken, greedy swine. If you've murdered that stallion I'll roast you over a slow fire and serve you to Cascabel with an apple in your mouth.*

Rifle shots split the silence, followed by the wild cries of Indian renegades hot on a human trail. Fear splintered through Ty like black lightning, for the sounds were coming from ahead and off to his right, where Troon's trail was going, where Lucifer would have gone if he had followed a straight course through the forest—and where Janna would be if she had been able to follow Lucifer's trail.

Ty had no doubt that Janna could track Lucifer anywhere the stallion could go.

Running swiftly and silently, Ty traced the twisting progress of Troon's horse through the forest. The animal had been moving at a hard gallop, a pace that was foolhardy under the conditions. Stirrups left gashes across tree trunks where the horse had zigzagged between pines. Farther down the trail low-growing limbs showed signs of recent damage. Bruised clusters of needles were scattered everywhere. A man's battered hat was tangled among the branches.

Ty had no doubt that he would find blood if he wanted to stop and check the bark on the limb that was wearing Troon's hat, but at the moment it wasn't Troon's blood that interested Ty. It was the palm-sized splotches that had suddenly appeared along with the hoofprints of a huge, unshod horse.

Lucifer.

Like the rifle cartridge, the blood hadn't been exposed to air for more than a half hour. The spots glistened darkly in the shade and were near-crimson markers in the occasional patches of sun. From their position, they could only have come from the stallion.

Breathing easily, running quietly, Ty followed the bloody trail. He knew that he should be sneaking from tree to tree in the thinning forest. He knew that at the very least he should be hunting cover in case he literally ran up on the heels of the renegades. He also knew that Janna was somewhere up ahead alone, armed with a pistol good for six shots and no spare cylinders or ammunition within reach. He didn't know how many renegades there were, but he doubted that six shots would get the job done.

*Janna's too clever to be spotted by renegades. She'll go to ground and pull the hole in after her. They'll never find her.*

The reassuring thought was interrupted by a flurry of rifle fire. The sounds came from ahead, but much farther to the right than Ty would have expected from the trail he was following. Either Lucifer or Troon—or both—must be hoping to escape by making a break for the steep northern edge of the plateau.

There were a few more sporadic shots and eager cries, then silence. Ty ran harder and told himself it was good that he hadn't heard any pistol shots, for that meant Janna hadn't been spotted. He refused to consider that it could also mean she had fallen in the first outbreak of shooting before she even had a chance to defend herself. He simply ran harder, carrying his carbine as though it were a pistol, finger on the trigger, ready to shoot and fire on the instant.

The hoofprints, which had been a mixture of shod and unshod, abruptly diverged. The unshod prints continued without interruption. The shod hoofprints veered starkly to the right. Ty had no doubt that he was seeing traces of the instant when the renegades had spotted Troon; the prints of Troon's horse were inches deep in the ground at the point where the horse had dug in and spun away from the renegades. Troon had chosen to flee along the rumpled, downward sloping land that led to the plateau's northern edge. There the land was rocky, broken, full of clefts and hollows and sheer-sided ravines where a man could hope to hide.

If Troon were lucky, he might even survive. Ty hoped he didn't. Any man who would shoot at a horse like Lucifer out of greed deserved to die. Without a further thought, Ty veered off after the stallion, leaving Troon to whatever fate luck and the renegades would visit upon him.

The stallion's tracks showed no sudden gouges or changes in direction as Troon's had. When the renegades had spotted Troon, apparently Lucifer hadn't been within sight. The wild horse had cannily chosen a route that looped back toward the eastern end of Raven Creek's long, winding meadow. From there Lucifer could head for the northeast edge of the plateau and slide on his black hocks down into Mustang Canyon or he could run southeast and then straight south, using the entire surface of the plateau, losing himself among the pines, meadows, ridges and ravines that covered the land's rugged surface.

Assuming, of course, that Lucifer was in any shape for a long, hard run. It was an assumption Ty wasn't prepared to make. The stallion's tracks were becoming closer together.

His strides were shortening as though he were winded, and the blood splotches were bigger and more frequent. Part of the horse's slowed progress might have been simply that the land was broken and rolling here, with more uphill than down as Lucifer headed straight toward the eastern lip of the plateau. And the shortening strides might also have been the result of injury.

Ty remembered Janna saying that she had once seen signs that Lucifer had skidded down the steep trail on the plateau's east edge in order to evade mustangers. He wondered if the stallion had remembered his past success and was laboring toward the east trail in hope of another such escape.

But Ty didn't think Lucifer would make it. The path on the east face was too far, too steep, and the blood sign along the stallion's trail was almost continuous now. The land here was steep, rising sharply into one of the many low ridges that marked the plateau's rumpled surface.

*I hope they catch you, Troon. I hope they cut off your—*

Ty's bitter thoughts of vengeance were wiped from his mind the instant he saw over the crest of the ridge to the land below. Less than a quarter mile away, Janna was running flat out down the slope. Her course paralleled a narrow, steep ravine that cut into the body of the ridge. Lucifer was forty feet ahead of her, veering toward the ravine as though he were planning to jump it, but it was too wide a leap for an injured horse. A half mile off to the right, all but concealed in another fold of land, a dust cloud of renegades was in wild pursuit of Joe Troon, who apparently had abandoned the idea of making a run to the northwest and Raven Creek Trail. Instead he was spurring his horse toward the east, leading the renegades toward Janna, who couldn't see them yet but almost certainly could hear their chilling cries.

*Turn around and hide, Janna! Go to ground,* Ty commanded silently. *Don't get yourself caught trying to help Lucifer.*

The stallion reached the edge of the ravine and threw himself toward the far side. His forelegs found purchase on the opposite bank of the ravine, but his left rear leg gave way when it should have provided support. He was too weak to struggle over the lip to safety. Kicking and screaming in a mixture of fear, pain and rage, the black horse skidded and rolled into the narrow, brush-choked bottom of the ravine twenty feet below. There he lay on his side, thrashing wildly in a futile attempt to regain his feet and scramble to safety.

Without pausing, Janna threw herself over the edge of the ravine, hurtling down into the tangle of brush and flailing hooves.

There was only one way Ty could save Janna from being injured or killed by the trapped stallion. Even as he whipped the carbine to his shoulder and took aim at Lucifer's beautiful black head, he saw hooves glance off Janna's body. At the precise instant he let out his breath and took the last of the slack from the trigger, Janna's back appeared in the gun sight. She had thrown herself over the stallion's head, pinning it to the earth, ensuring that the horse wouldn't be able to struggle to his feet.

*Get out of there, you little fool!* Ty screamed silently. *You can't hold him. He'll beat you to death with those big hooves.*

The ravine Lucifer was trapped in was a long crease running down the side of the ridge at whose top Ty waited. It would be an easy shot, no more than three hundred feet. He had made more difficult shots with a pistol. A savage fusillade of shots and triumphant shouts came from the direction of Troon and the renegades. Ty's attention never wavered from the bottom of the ravine, nor did the tension of his finger lift on the trigger.

A man's screams told Ty that either Troon or a renegade had just been wounded. Ty's glance remained fixed on the ravine bottom where Janna struggled to master the big horse. Ty knew that sooner or later Lucifer's struggles to free his head would throw Janna aside. When that happened, Ty's finger would tighten on the trigger and the stallion would die.

*What the hell...?*

Janna had one knee pinning the stallion's muzzle to the ground and the other knee just behind his ears. She was literally kneeling on the horse and ripping her shirt off at the same time.

A crescendo of triumphant whoops and shots told Ty that the chase was over for Joe Troon. Ty still didn't look up from the ravine; he wouldn't have walked across a street to aid the man who had captured Janna once and bragged to a bartender about what he would do when he caught her again. As far as Ty was concerned, Troon had gone looking for trouble and he had found more than he wanted. It often happened that way to a man who drank too much and thought too little. Ty's only regret was that Troon hadn't bought it sooner, before he had led the renegades back to within a quarter mile of Janna.

Over the carbine's steel barrel, Ty watched while Janna turned her torn shirt into a makeshift blindfold and struggled to secure it around Lucifer's eyes. Abruptly the stallion stopped thrashing around. With rapid movements Janna whipped a few turns of cloth around the horse's muzzle. When she was finished, Lucifer could open his mouth no more than an inch. She bent over him once more, holding him down while she stroked his lathered neck.

Ty could see the shudders of fear that rippled over the stallion with each stroke of Janna's hand. Ty could also see that the horse was no longer a danger to her; blindfolded, muzzled, pinned in place by Janna's weight, Lucifer was all but helpless.

Very slowly Ty eased his finger off the trigger and sank down behind the cover of a piñon tree that clung to the rocky ridge top. Screened by dark green branches, Ty pulled out his spyglass and looked off to the right. A single glance confirmed what his ears had already told him: Joe Troon had made his last mistake.

Ty looked around carefully and decided that he had the best position from which to protect the ravine. Pulling his hat down firmly, he chose a comfortable shooting position, shrugged out of his pack and put two open boxes of ammunition within easy reach. Stomach against the hard earth, green eyes sighting down the carbine's metal barrel, Ty settled in to wait and see if the renegades were going to come toward the ravine when they were finished looting and mutilating Troon's body.

# Chapter Twenty-Six

Easy now, boy. Easy...easy."

The ceaseless murmur of Janna's soft voice and the gentle pressure of her hands finally penetrated the stallion's pain and panic. With a long, groaning sigh, Lucifer stopped fighting. Janna rewarded him by shifting her knee from his muzzle to the ground, praising him with a flow of sentences and nonsense sounds, knowing that it was her voice rather than the meaning of her words that reached past the horse's fear.

Very slowly Janna slid her other knee from Lucifer's neck, leaving him able to lift his head, which was the first thing a horse did before it came to its feet. Lucifer made no attempt to take advantage of his freedom in order to stand up. As Janna had hoped, the blindfold held him more quietly and more surely than any rope could have. Even so, she reluctantly bound his left hind foot to his right foreleg. When she began cleaning and treating the bullet wound on his left rear leg, she didn't want him to lash out at the pain. She was already bruised enough as it was. A broken bone wouldn't do either of them any good.

Ignoring her own pain, Janna kept one hand constantly on Lucifer's head, talking incessantly and softly, letting him know where she was. When his ears were no longer flattened against his head, Janna leaned over and snaked her own makeshift backpack to a place within easy reach. While she sorted one-handed through her herbs and salves, she told herself that Ty was all right, that the shots had been from Troon or the renegades, not from Ty's carbine, that he and she were safe even though they were separate....

"God, please let him be safe," Janna prayed softly, stroking the powerful, lathered neck of the stallion.

Though Lucifer was no longer fighting her, he groaned with each heaving breath he took, for the cloth muzzle restricted his breathing. In the silence, the sound of the horse's labored breaths were like thunder. After a few minutes Janna opened her pocketknife and cut the cloth free, allowing the stallion to open his mouth and nostrils fully. Immediately his breathing eased.

"You weren't going to bite me anyway, were you?" Janna murmured, stroking Lucifer's nose.

The stallion's ears flicked but didn't flatten against his head. He was too tired, too weak or simply not fearful enough to attack Janna.

Wondering if anyone had been attracted by the stallion's labored breathing, Janna glanced anxiously up and down the crease in the earth that was their only hiding place. She heard no one approaching. Nor did she see any movement along the ravine's rim.

It was just as well, for there was no way to hide from anyone. The brush through which Lucifer had fallen had been bruised and broken beyond all hope of concealment from any trackers. Nor was there any real cover within the ravine itself. Janna had no illusions about what her chances of escape would be if the renegades found her in the bottom of the ravine with the wounded, blindfolded stallion.

After a last look at the rim of the ravine, Janna pulled out Ty's big pistol, rotated the cylinder off the empty chamber and cocked the hammer so that all it would take was a quick pull on the trigger to fire the gun. Very carefully she laid the weapon out of the way yet within easy reach. Then she turned back to Lucifer.

"This is going to hurt," Janna said in a low, calm voice, "but you're going to be a gentleman about it, aren't you?"

She wet the last torn piece of her shirt with water from her canteen and went to work cleaning the long furrow Troon's bullet had left on Lucifer's haunch. The blindfolded stallion shuddered and his ears flattened, but he made no attempt to turn and bite Janna while she worked over him. She praised the horse in soothing tones that revealed neither her own pain from her bruises nor her growing fear that Ty hadn't been able to evade the renegades.

Lucifer flinched and made a high, involuntary sound as Janna cleaned a part of the wound that had picked up dirt in his slide down into the ravine.

"Easy, boy, easy...yes, I know it hurts, but you won't heal right without help. That's it...that's it...gently...just lie still and let me help you."

The low, husky voice and endless ripple of words mesmerized Lucifer. His ears flicked and swiveled, following Janna's voice when she turned from her backpack to the wound on his haunch.

"I think it looks a lot worse than it is," Janna murmured as she rinsed out her rag and poured more water into its folds. "It's deep and it bled a lot, but the bullet didn't sever any tendons or muscles. You're going to be sore and grouchy as a boiled cat for a while, and you'll limp for a time and you'll have a scar on your pretty black hide for—er, but you'll heal clean and sound. In a few weeks you'll be up and running after your mares.

"And you'll have a lot of running to do, won't you? Those mares will be scattered from hell to breakfast, as Papa would have said. I'll bet that chestnut stud you ran off last year is stealing your mares as fast as he finds them."

Lucifer flicked his ears, sucked in a long breath through his flaring nostrils and blew out, then took in another great breath.

"Easy now, boy. Easy...easy... I know it hurts but there's no help for it."

Janna reached for her backpack again and winced. Her left arm was beginning to stiffen. By the time she was finished doctoring Lucifer, she'd have to start in on herself. With only one hand, it was going to be difficult.

*Ty, where are you? Are you all right? Did you get away? Are you lying wounded and—*

"Don't think about it!" Janna said aloud, her voice so savage that Lucifer, startled, tossed his head.

"Easy, boy," she murmured, immediately adjusting her voice to be soothing once more. "There's nothing to worry about. Ty is quick and strong and smart. If he got away from Cascabel he can get away from a bunch of hurrahing renegades who were looking for a man on horseback, not one on foot. Besides, I'll never get a better chance to tame you," she said, stroking the mustang's barrel, where lather was slowly drying. "If you accept me, you'll accept Ty, and then he'll have a start on his dream, a fine stallion to found a herd that will bring money enough to buy a lady of silk and softness."

Janna's mouth turned down in an unhappy line, but her hand continued its gentle motions and her voice remained soothing.

"Anyway, boy, if I leave you and go looking for a man who is probably quite safe, who will take care of you in three days or four, when your wound gets infected and you get so weak you can hardly stand?"

Lucifer's head came up suddenly and his ears pricked forward so tightly that they almost touched at the tips. His nostrils flared widely as he took in quantities of air and sifted it for the scent of danger.

Watching him closely, Janna reached for the pistol. Being blindfolded was no particular handicap for the stallion when it came to recognizing danger—a horse's ears and sense of smell were far superior to his eyes. But when it came to dealing with danger, a blind horse was all but helpless.

Janna looked in the direction that Lucifer's ears were pointing. All she saw was the steep side of the gully and the brushy slope rising to the ridge top beyond. She hesitated, trying to decide whether it would be less dangerous to crawl up out of the ravine and look around or to simply lie low and hope that whatever Lucifer sensed wouldn't sense them in return.

Before she could make up her mind, Janna heard what was attracting the horse's attention. There was a faint chorus of yips and howls and cries followed by the distant thunder of galloping horses and the crack of rifle fire. The sounds became louder as the renegades galloped closer to the ravine. For a few horrible minutes Janna was certain that the renegades were going to race straight up the slope above the ravine—and then she and Lucifer would be utterly exposed, with no place to hide and no way to flee.

The sounds peaked and slowly died as the Indians galloped off to the northwest, where Cascabel had his camp.

Heart pounding, Janna set aside the pistol she had grabbed and went back to tending Lucifer with hands that insisted on trembling at the very instant she most needed them to be still. She watched Lucifer's ears as she worked on his wound, for she knew that his hearing was superior to hers.

"I hope they're not coming back," she said softly, stroking the horse's hot flank as she examined the long furrow left by the bullet. "Well, Lucifer, if you were a man I'd pour some witch hazel in that wound to keep it clean. But witch hazel stings like the very devil and I don't have any way of telling you to hold still and not make any noise, so—"

Janna froze and stopped speaking as Lucifer's ears flicked forward again. Concentrating intently, she heard the faintest of scraping sounds, as though a boot or a moccasin had rubbed over loose rock, or perhaps it was no more than the friction of a low branch against the ground. Then came silence. A few moments later there was another sound, but this time that of cloth sliding over brush. Or was it simply wind bending the spring brush and releasing it again?

The silence continued with no more interruptions. Very slowly Janna reached for the pistol again, listening so intently that she ached. She didn't breathe, she didn't think, she simply bent every bit of her will toward hearing as much as possible. The stallion remained motionless as well, his ears pricked, his nostrils flared, waiting for the wind to tell him whether to fight or freeze or flee whatever danger existed beyond the ravine.

"Janna?"

At first the whisper was so soft that she thought she had imagined it.

"Janna? Are you all right?"

"Ty? Is that you?"

"Hell, no," Ty said in disgust. "It's Joe Troon's ghost come to haunt you. Stand back. I'm coming down."

A pebble rolled down the side of the ravine, then another and another as Ty chose speed over caution in his descent. Crossing the open spots from the top of the ridge to the gully's edge had taken years off his life span, even though there was no reason for him to think that the renegade would come back right away. Nor was there any reason to think that they would *not*. The sooner he was under even the minimal cover of the gully, the better he would feel.

Janna watched Ty skid down the last steep pitch into the ravine. He braced himself on a dead piñon trunk, looked toward her and smiled in a way that made her heart turn over.

"Sugar," Ty drawled, "you are a sight for sore eyes."

His glance moved over her like hands, reminding her that she was naked from the waist up. Blushing, she crossed her arms over her breasts but couldn't conceal the pink tide rising beneath her skin.

Ty's breath caught and then stayed in his throat at the picture Janna made, the pale perfection of her body rising from the loose masculine pants. Her arms were too slender to hide the full curves of her breasts. The hint of deep rose nipples nestled shyly in the bend of her elbows.

"Ty...don't."

"Don't what?"

"Look at me like that."

"Like what?" he said huskily. "Like I spent most of the night licking and love biting and kissing those beautiful white breasts?"

Janna couldn't conceal the shiver of sensual response that went through her at Ty's words.

"Put your arms down, sugar. Let me see if you remember, too."

Very slowly Janna's arms dropped away, revealing breasts whose rosy tips had drawn and hardened at his look, his words, her memories.

"God," breathed Ty, shutting his eyes, knowing that it didn't matter, the vision was already burned into his memory. Blindly he dug into his backpack, found the roll of cloth he had refused to let her wear, and dropped the cloth on her lap. "Here. Wrap up before you make me forget where we are. Do it fast, little one. A man never wants a woman so much as when he's come close to dying."

"Does it work that way for a woman, too?" Janna asked as she snatched the cloth and began wrapping it over her breasts.

"I don't know. How do you feel right now?"

"Shivery. Feverish. Restless. And then you looked at me and I felt hot and full where you had touched me...and yet empty at the same time."

"Then it works the same for a woman, if the woman is like you," Ty said, trying to control the heavy beat of his blood. "Satin butterfly. God, you don't know how much I want to love you right now. I saw Lucifer jump and fall into the ravine and then you threw yourself after him and I couldn't get a clean shot at his head and—"

"What?" Janna interrupted, appalled. "Why did you want to shoot Lucifer? He isn't that badly injured."

"I know. That's why I was afraid he'd beat you to death with those big hooves."

"You would have killed him to save me?"

Ty's eyelids snapped open. "Hell, yes! What kind of a man do you think I am?"

Janna tried to speak, couldn't find the words and concentrated on wrapping herself tightly.

"For the love of God," Ty said in a low voice. "Just because I seduced you doesn't mean that I'm the kind of bastard who would leave you to be killed when I could have saved you!"

"That isn't what I meant. It's just that . . . that . . ."

"What?" Ty demanded angrily.

"I'm surprised you would have killed Lucifer without hesitation, that's all," Janna said, her voice shaking. "Lucifer is your best chance of building a fine horse herd. He's your best hope of getting enough money to buy your silken lady. He's the beginning of your dreams. He's . . . everything. And I'm . . ." She drew in a deep breath, looked away from Ty's harsh, closed expression and continued quietly. "I'm not your blood or your fiancée or anything but a . . . a temporary convenience. Why should you kill your dream for me?" She glanced quickly at him. "But thank you, Ty. It's the nicest thing anyone has ever done for me."

## Chapter Twenty-Seven

How bad is he hurt?" Ty asked.

Janna jumped in surprise. It was the first thing Ty had said to her in the hour since she had thanked him for being prepared to sacrifice his dream in order to save her life.

After that, Ty had gone to Lucifer's head, knelt and put himself between the horse's teeth and Janna. He had spoken gently to the stallion, stroking Lucifer's powerful neck with slow sweeps of his hand until the horse relaxed and accepted the strange voice and touch. Except for those murmured reassurances to the big horse, Ty had said nothing as he watched Janna tend Lucifer. Ty moved only to stroke the stallion or to hand her a packet from her leather pouch or to rinse the rag she was using to clean Lucifer's cuts and abrasions.

"He's strong. He'll be fine," Janna said, smiling tentatively at Ty.

"That's not what I asked. I've treated horses for sprains and stones in their shoes and colic and such, but bullet wounds are new to me. It's not a deep wound, but I've seen men die of shock with wounds not much worse than that. Do you think Lucifer can walk?"

Janna turned and reached for the stallion's muzzle, only to have Ty quickly intervene.

"I can't answer your question until I've looked at Lucifer's mouth," she explained.

Ty gave Janna an odd look and reluctantly moved aside. She bent over the stallion's muzzle and spoke in low, even tones as her fingers lifted his upper lip. His ears flattened warningly and he jerked his head away. Patiently Janna worked over him until he tolerated her fingers around his mouth without laying back his ears.

"What the hell are you doing?" Ty asked quietly.

"Papa said you can tell a lot about men or animals by the color of their gums. Lucifer was real pale when I first checked him, but he's nice and pink now. He'll be able to walk as soon as I untie his feet, but it would be better if he didn't move around much. That wound will start to bleed all over again at the first bit of strain."

Ty looked at the long gash on Lucifer's haunch and muttered something beneath his breath.

"What?" asked Janna.

"We can't stay here. Those renegades could come back or some of their friends could come prowling to see if anything was missed the first time around. Lucifer left a trail a blind man could follow." Ty glanced at the sky overhead. "No rain today and probably not any tonight, either. And if there was enough rain to wash out the trail, we'd be washed right out of this gully, too. There's no food, no water and no cover worth mentioning. The sooner we get out of here the longer we'll all live."

Janna looked unhappily at the stallion but didn't argue with Ty. What he had said was true and she knew it as well as he did. She just didn't want to have to force the wounded stallion to walk.

"I wish he were human," Janna said. "It would be so much easier if we could explain to him."

"How far do you think he can go?"

"As far as he wants to, I guess."

"He moved fast enough getting here," Ty said dryly.

"He was running scared then. I've seen frightened mustangs gallop on sprained ankles and pulled hamstrings, but as soon as they stop running, they're finished. They can barely hobble until they heal."

Ty said nothing. He had seen men in the heat of battle run on a foot that had been shot off; after the battle, those same men couldn't even crawl.

"The sooner we get going the better our chances are," Ty said finally. "At the very least we've got to get to decent cover and wipe out as much of our trail as we can. Do you know any place near the meadow?"

Janna shook her head. "Not where a horse could hide long enough to heal. The only place Lucifer would be safe is my keyhole canyon, and I don't know if he'd make it that far. By the time we got over to the Mustang Canyon trail and down into the canyon and then clear out away from the plateau to the Santos Wash trail..." She shook her head again. "It's a long way from there to my winter camp."

"And the renegades are real thick in Santos Wash," Ty added. "We've got no choice, Janna. We'll have to take Lucifer down the east face of the plateau. From there it's only a few hours to your hidden canyon."

Janna's objections died before they were spoken. She had come to the same conclusion Ty had; she just hadn't wanted to believe it was their best chance. The thought of taking the injured stallion down the precipitous eastern edge of the plateau, and from there through the tortuous slot canyon, made her want to cry out in protest.

But it was their best hope of keeping Lucifer—and themselves—safe while his bullet wound healed.

"I know how you feel about restraining a horse, so I won't ask you to do it," Ty said firmly. "I don't think Lucifer's going to take too kindly to it, either, but there's no damn choice." He looked at Janna. "Get your medicine bag packed and stand lookout up on the ridge."

"I'll help you with Lucifer."

"There's not room enough for two of us."

"But I'm used to mustangs."

"You're used to coaxing mares into gentleness when they have all the room in the world to run. Lucifer is a stud and trapped and hurting and probably of no mind to be meek about wearing his first hackamore. I don't blame him a bit. I'll be as gentle with him as I can, but I want you a long way away when I pull off that blindfold. Besides, someone has to stand watch. That someone is going to be you."

Janna looked into the crystalline green of Ty's eyes and knew that arguing would get her nowhere. "I'll bet you were an officer in the war between the North and the South."

Ty looked surprised, then smiled. "You bet right, sugar. Now shag your lovely butt up onto that ridge. If you see something you don't like, give me that hawk cry you use to call Zebra. And don't forget my pistol."

Without a word Janna tucked Ty's pistol in place behind her belt and began climbing out of the ravine. When she was safely up on the rim, Ty turned to Lucifer once more.

"Well, boy, it's time to find out if all your piss and vinegar is combined with common sense, or if you're outlaw through and through."

Speaking gently and reassuringly, Ty reached into his backpack and pulled out a pair of sheepskin-lined leather hobbles that he had taken from the Preacher's store in hope of just such an opportunity to use them. When the hobbles were in place on Lucifer's front legs, Ty cut through the cloth that joined the stallion's hind and foreleg. Lucifer quivered but made no attempt to lash out with his newly unbound feet. Ty stroked the horse's barrel and talked soothingly until the stallion's black hide no longer twitched and trembled with each touch.

"You did real well, boy. I'm beginning to think you're as smart as you are handsome."

Ty went to the backpack for the length of braided rawhide and the steel ring he had also bought. A few quick loops, turns and knots transformed the ring and rawhide into a workable hackamore.

"You're not going to like this, but you'll get used to it. Easy, son. Easy now." As Ty spoke, he slipped the make-shift hackamore onto the stallion's head.

Lucifer snorted and began trembling again as soon as he felt the rawhide against his skin. Patiently Ty rubbed the horse's head and neck and ears, accustoming him to the pressure of human hands and hackamore on his head. Lucifer calmed quickly this time, as though he were losing the ability to become alarmed—or questioned the necessity for alarm—at each new thing that happened. Ty hoped that it was common sense rather than weakness that was calming the stallion, but he wouldn't know until he got Lucifer up on his feet how much strength the wound had cost the horse.

"Well, son, this is the test. Now you just lie still and show me what a gentleman you are underneath all that bone and muscle and wildness."

With slow, smooth motions, Ty eased the blindfold down Lucifer's nose until the horse could see again. For a moment the stallion made no movement, then his ears flat-tened and he tried to lunge to his feet. Instantly Ty pinned the horse's muzzle to the ground and held it there, all the while talking soothingly and petting the rigid muscles of the stallion's neck as he struggled to get to his feet and flee.

Ty never knew how long it took to get through Lucifer's fear to the rational animal beneath. He only knew that he was sweating as hard as the stallion before Lucifer finally stopped struggling and allowed himself to be calmed by the voice and hands whose gentleness had never varied throughout the pitched, silent struggle.

"How the hell did she ever hold you long enough to get the blindfold on?" Ty wondered aloud as he and Lucifer eyed each other warily. "Or were you just used to her smell?"

The stallion's dark, dark eyes regarded Ty with an intelligence that was almost tangible. There was no malevolence, no sense of a feral eagerness to find an opening and strike. There was simply an alertness that had been bred into the horse's very bones and had been honed by living in the wild.

"Wonder who your mammy was, and your daddy, too. They sure as hell weren't bangtail ridge runners. You've a lot of the great barb in you, and maybe some Tennessee walking horse thrown in. My daddy would have traded every stud he ever owned to get his hands on you, and he would have considered it a bargain at twice the price. You're all horse, Lucifer. And you're mine now."

Lucifer's ears flicked and his eyes followed each motion Ty made.

"Well, you're half mine," Ty amended. "There's a certain stubborn girl who owns a piece of you whether she admits it or not. But don't worry, son. If you can't take the tame life, I'll set you free just like I promised. I don't mind telling you, though, I hope I don't have to. I left some fine mares with Logan. I'd love to take you up to Wyoming and keep you long enough to have at least one crop of foals from you."

While Ty talked he began to shift his weight off the stallion's muzzle a bit at a time until very little was left to hold the horse down.

"Ready to try getting up again? Slowly, son, slowly. Real nice and gentle. You lunge around this little gully and you're going to hurt both of us."

Once Lucifer realized that his head was free, he rolled off his side and got his feet underneath him. He quickly learned that the same man who could pin his muzzle to the ground could also help getting him to his feet with a few judicious pulls on the halter rope. Very shortly the stallion was standing again, unblindfolded and trembling all over at the strangeness of being close to a man.

"I was right. You're as smart as you are handsome. It's a shame you ran loose so long. You would have been a fine partner for a man, but after all these years I doubt you'd accept a rider. But that's all right, son," Ty said, slowly coiling the rawhide lead rope until he was right next to Lucifer's head. "I don't need to strut and show off how grand I am by breaking you. There are a thousand horses I can ride, but you're the only one I want covering my mares."

The words meant nothing to the stallion, but Ty's calm voice and gentle, confident hands did. Lucifer gave a long snort and stopped rolling his eyes and flinching at every touch. Slowly he was accepting the fact that although man in general had been his enemy in the past, this particular man was different. Lucifer had been pinned and blinded and helpless, but the man hadn't attacked him. Obviously he wasn't going to, either.

As the stallion slowly relaxed, Ty let out a long, quiet breath. "You're going to make it easy on both of us, aren't you? I'm sure glad that bullet and a few miles of running took the starch out of you. I've got a feeling you wouldn't have been nearly so civilized about this if I'd caught you fresh. But then, if you'd been fresh, we'd never have caught you, would we? The Lord works in strange ways, Lucifer. I'm glad He saw fit to give you to us, if only for long enough to heal you and set you free."

Ty stood and praised the stallion for a long time, until at last the horse let wariness slide away and weariness claim his big body. With a huge sigh, Lucifer allowed his head to drop until it all but rested against Ty's chest. Standing three-legged, favoring his injured hip, the stallion took no more notice of Ty than if he had been a foal.

Slowly Ty bent until he could release the hobbles on Lucifer's front legs. The stallion's shoulder muscles flinched and rippled as though shaking off flies, but that was all the notice he took of being free.

"That's real good, son," Ty murmured, stroking the stallion's black hide. "Now let's see if you're going to try to kill me the first time I tug on that hackamore."

# Chapter Twenty-Eight

As Ty slowly tightened the lead rope, Janna watched with breath held and her hands so tightly clenched around the spyglass that her fingers ached.

"Be good, Lucifer," she prayed. "Don't go crazy and hurt Ty when that hackamore gets tight."

Lucifer's head came up sharply when the hackamore began to exert pressure behind his ears and across his upper neck. He snorted and shook his head, but the gradually increasing pressure didn't diminish. Trembling, sweating nervously, ears swiveling forward and then away from the man's gentle voice, the stallion tried to understand what was happening, how to meet the new threat. When he attempted to back away from the pressure, it got sharply worse. When he stood still, it got slowly worse.

But when he limped forward, the pressure lifted.

"That's it," Ty murmured, slacking off on the lead rope immediately. He petted Lucifer, praising the horse with voice and hands. "Let's try a few more steps, son. We've got a long way to go before we're safe."

It didn't take Lucifer more than a few minutes to understand that a pressure urging him forward meant walk forward and a pressure across the bridge of his nose meant stop.

"You're not an outlaw at all, are you?" Ty asked softly, stroking the horse's powerful, sweaty neck. "Men have chased you, but thank God no man ever had a chance to ruin you with rough handling."

Lucifer flicked his ears as he followed the calm sounds of Ty's voice while the man backed up, paying out lead rope as he went.

"All right, son. It's time to get you out of this hole." Slowly Ty tightened the lead rope. "Come on. That's it...that's it. One step at a time, that's all." His mouth flattened as he saw the stallion's painful progress. "That hip sure is sore, isn't it?" Ty said in a low voice. "Well, son, it's going to get worse before it gets better, I'm afraid. But you'll live, God willing."

Ty coaxed the limping stallion along the bottom of the ravine until they came to a place he had spotted from the ridge above, a place where the sides of the gully were less steep. Ty climbed halfway out, turned and began applying a steady pressure on the lead rope once more.

"Up you go. It will be easier to walk once you're on sort of level land again. Come on...come on...don't go all mulish on me now, son. It's not as steep as it looks."

Lucifer disliked the idea of climbing the gully, but he disliked the slowly tightening vise of the hackamore even more. Suddenly he lunged forward, taking the side of the ravine in a hurtling rush. Ty leaped aside just in time to avoid being trampled and scrambled up the slope after the stallion. Once on top, Lucifer came to a stop and stood three-legged, trembling from nervousness and pain.

Janna left her lookout place on the ridge and ran down to meet Ty, slowing to a walk for the last few yards so as not to frighten Lucifer.

"No one in sight," she said quietly.

"All right." Ty lifted his hat, wiped his forehead and re-settled the hat with a hard tug. "How's your arm?"

Surprised that Ty had noticed, Janna hesitated and then shrugged. "Better than Lucifer's haunch."

"Hand over your pack."

She tried not to wince as he helped her out of the rawhide straps, but she couldn't conceal her left arm's growing soreness. With gentle fingertips he traced the dark bruise where one of Lucifer's hooves had struck a glancing blow.

"Any numbness?" Ty asked.

She shook her head.

"All your fingers work?"

Silently she wiggled each of them in turn.

"Can you scout for us?" Ty asked, releasing her arm, caressing her all the way to her fingertips.

Suddenly breathless, Janna nodded.

"Cat got your tongue?"

She smiled and stuck her tongue out at Ty.

"Is that a promise?" he drawled. He smiled and touched her lips with his fingertip. "Stick it out again, sugar."

"I don't think—"

That was as far as Janna got before Ty bent and took what she had promised to him a moment before. Surprise stiffened Janna for an instant before she sighed and invited Ty into the softness and warmth of her mouth. Almost shyly she touched his tongue with her own, retreated, then returned to touch fleetingly again and again, until there was no more retreat, just two mouths in a seething, seamless mating.

When Ty finally lifted his head he was breathing too hard, but he was smiling.

"It occurred to me when that stallion was doing his best to trample me into the dirt," Ty said, "that a man shouldn't die without tasting a woman on his lips. You taste good, like Christmas and Thanksgiving and my birthday all rolled into one. And if you don't turn around and get busy scouting, I'm going to be walking bent over double and in damn near as much pain as Lucifer."

Janna smiled up at Ty, showing him the same near shyness with which she had begun their kiss. His eyelids lowered and desire changed his expression, making it both harder and more sensual. For an instant she thought that he was going to kiss her again, and she longed for it. Then he reached out, turned her around and swatted her lightly on the rear. She would have said something about the trail she was going to take to the east, but the swat had ended with Ty's hand tracing the curve of her buttocks with loving care and suddenly she found herself breathless and aching.

"I'll head east and a little bit south unless you come and tell me otherwise," Ty said. Quickly he removed a handful of bullets from his pistol belt. "Take these."

The bullets felt smooth, cool and heavy in Janna's hand. She put them in her pocket and prayed she wouldn't need them. While she could shoot a pistol, she couldn't hit much at any range greater than a few hundred feet. If she were forced to use the weapon at all, its greatest benefit would probably be as a warning to Ty that he had better take cover.

And he would need that warning. Unable to hide his tracks, forced by Lucifer's injury to go slowly and to take the easiest—and therefore most open—way available, Ty would be a sitting duck in a pond surrounded by hunters. Both he and Janna knew it.

Janna set off to the southeast at a steady trot. Her knee-high moccasins made almost no sound over pine needles and grasses, and she left few marks of her passage. She ran without pausing except to listen for any wind-carried conversations or for the sound of distant gunfire. She heard nothing but the normal calling of birds, the scolding of squirrels, and the restless murmuring of the wind as it tried to herd together enough clouds for a storm.

Behind her, Ty talked to the black stallion, praising him as he limped over the land. For his part, Lucifer moved as quickly as he could. A lifetime of running from man had given the stallion a relentless wariness that worked to Ty's benefit; the horse was as intent upon reaching a safe place as Ty was. And like Ty, the stallion knew instinctively that safety wasn't to be had in the wide-open spaces of the plateau. Space was useful only if you could outrun your enemies. At the moment, Lucifer couldn't outrun anything that was worth fleeing from in the first place.

Initially Ty walked ahead of Lucifer, encouraging him with a steady pressure on the hackamore. After the first hour, the horse no longer needed to be reminded that he was supposed to keep walking. When Ty moved, so did Lucifer. When Ty stood, Lucifer stood. When Ty walked, Lucifer walked with his head even with Ty's left shoulder. The hackamore's lead rope remained slack.

"You're some kind of special," Ty said, talking to Lucifer as they walked. "You're as gentle as a lady's hack. Makes me wonder if maybe you weren't paddock raised and then got free somehow. Of course, it simply could be that we both want the same thing right now—a safe place to hide. You might be a lot harder to get along with if you wanted one thing and I wanted another."

Lucifer's only answer was a brisk swish of his long black tail as he drove off flies attracted to his wound. Ty checked the gash, saw that it was bleeding again and knew that nothing could be done for it.

"Better a wound that bleeds than one that festers," Ty reminded himself, drawing on his battlefield experience. "As long as it doesn't bleed too much."

He kept an eye on the stallion's injury. After a few miles it became apparent that the bleeding was more of a steady oozing than a serious flow.

Janna, using her spyglass, had reassured herself on the same subject; Lucifer was bleeding, but it wasn't a problem yet. Despite his limp he was moving at a good walking pace. With luck they would reach the edge of the plateau before dark. Otherwise they would have to find a place to sleep, because nothing short of the most extreme emergency would force Janna to take on the east trail in full darkness while leading an unbroken, injured mustang.

Ignoring the steady throbbing of her arm, Janna trotted across the plateau's wild surface, scouting both for enemies and for the easiest, quickest way to reach the trail down the east face. She used what cover she could find but didn't waste time trying to be invisible. It was more important that Lucifer and Ty reach the east edge of the plateau before dark than that she leave no trail.

As the day wore on, Janna ranged farther and farther ahead, checking on Ty and Lucifer less and less often. They had agreed that if she didn't check back before Ty reached the east rim, he would take Lucifer down the trail and keep on going toward the keyhole canyon. He was reluctant to stop for a rest, much less for a whole night, because he knew that Lucifer would stiffen up badly once he stopped moving.

By the time Janna reached the last, long fold of land that lay between her and the eastern edge of the plateau, it was late afternoon. She climbed the long ridge at a diagonal heading for two tall pines. From the top she knew she would be able to see out across several hundred square miles of plateau, including the eastern edge and a bit of the low country beyond. She hoped that she would see only the usual things—pines, grass, sky, rivers of black rock spilling down ragged slopes, wild horses grazing, perhaps even an antelope or two. What she hoped *not* to see was any sign of man.

Just below the crest, Janna dropped to her stomach and wormed her way up until she could see over without giving away her own presence to anyone who might be on the other side. The first thing she saw was a hawk patrolling just below the ridge top. The second thing she saw was Zebra grazing with a scattering of Lucifer's mares.

Immediately Janna put her hands to her mouth. A hawk's wild cry floated from her lips. Zebra's head came up, he ears pricked and her nostrils flared. A soaring hawk cried in fierce answer to Janna's call, but Zebra didn't even turn her head toward the bird. Janna's high, keening cry came again. Zebra spun and cantered eagerly toward the ridge, whinnying her welcome.

"Hello, girl," Janna said, standing up, as pleased as the mare was. "Did you know that you're the answer to a prayer? Now I'll be able to cover three times the ground and not have to worry about tracks."

Zebra nickered and whuffled and pushed her head against Janna's body, nearly knocking her off her feet.

"I hope you're as eager for a run as you look, because you're going to get one. Hold still, girl. My arm is as stiff as an old man's knees."

Janna's mount wasn't very elegant, but she managed to finish right side up on the mare, which was all that counted.

"Come on, girl, let's check on your lord and master."

Eagerly Zebra responded to the pressure of Janna's heels. Cantering swiftly, the horse ate up the distance between Janna and Ty. Janna guided the horse in a long, looping curve, wanting to check more of the land on the way back to Ty. The mare sped quickly through the open country, going from tree shadow to full sun and back again, a kaleidoscope of light and darkness flowing over horse and rider, and always the earth flying beneath the mare's hooves.

Janna was only a few minutes away from where she had left Ty when she saw the renegades.

# Chapter Twenty-Nine

Zebra spun aside and leaped into a full gallop in the same motion. Janna didn't try to slow or turn the horse back toward the place where Ty was. She simply grabbed a double handful of flying black mane and bent over the mare's neck, urging her on to greater speed. Behind her the Indians shouted and fired a few shots as they gave chase.

Janna had ridden Zebra at a gallop before, but nothing like this frantic pace. The mare's speed would have been frightening to Janna if it hadn't been for the fact that she was fleeing an even greater danger. As it was, Janna flattened down against Zebra's sleek, driving body, urging greater speed and trying to make herself as light a burden as possible.

Zebra stretched out her neck and ran as though fleeing hell. The force of the wind raking over Janna's eyes made tears stream down her face. Her hat was ripped from her head. One of the chin strings snapped and the hat sailed away. Soon her braids had unraveled and her long hair was streaming out behind her like darkly burning, wind-whipped flames.

The sudden appearance of Janna's distinctive hair cooled the urgency of the chase for the Indians. There was little sport and even less glory or booty in capturing a homeless girl. There were also the uncomfortable whispers about the true nature of that girl. *Bruja*. Witch. Shadow of Flame. That was what she looked like as she bent over the wild horse she rode with neither bridle nor saddle, her body all but lost in the flying mane and her own unbound hair streaming behind her in the wind like a warning flag.

And surely only a spirit horse ridden by a spirit woman could be so fleet.

Janna didn't try to guide Zebra, for the mare knew the plateau's twists and turns and traps as well as Janna did. All that she cared about was that the horse was racing away from the eastern trail and therefore away from Ty and the injured stallion. She made no attempt to use the revolver that was digging into her body as she rode the wildly galloping horse. Drawing the weapon would have been difficult enough; shooting accurately would have been impossible.

With every passing minute it became more obvious that Zebra was outrunning the renegades. Well fed, well rested, carrying only Janna's insignificant weight, Zebra not only had more speed than the renegades' horses, she had more stamina, as well. After a few miles the renegades became certain that they were spending their horses in a losing cause. First two warriors dropped out of the chase, then a third, then a fourth, until finally only one man still pursued the bright banner of Janna's hair. Finally he, too, gave up and stopped whipping his laboring horse.

Zebra knew before Janna did that the chase was over. Even so, the mare kept galloping for a time, putting more distance between herself and her pursuers. Janna sensed the difference in Zebra's pace and knew that the immediate danger had passed. Cautiously she shifted her grip on the mane, wiped her eyes and looked over her shoulder. There was nothing behind her but Zebra's tracks across an empty land.

When Zebra breasted a ridge, Janna urged the mare into the cover of some trees and then checked her trail very carefully, using the spyglass. The renegades weren't anywhere to be seen. What she could see of the land ahead of her looked equally empty.

For a few minutes Janna considered the various ways and means of hiding Zebra's tracks in order to confuse any followers. Every way she thought of, including dismounting and letting the mare go free once more, would make it impossible for Janna to get to the east rim of the plateau before dark. She would have to keep Zebra with her and count on the mare's speed to thwart any more pursuit.

"All right, girl," Janna said, "let's go back and see if Ty and Lucifer are all right."

At a touch from her rider, the mustang turned and began cantering at an angle to her old trail. Though Janna watched warily, she saw no sign that any human had been along recently. Wild horses grazed undisturbed until Zebra appeared, and then the horses spun and raced away. Janna urged Zebra to detour into the three groups of horses she found, mixing the mare's tracks with those of her mustang kin, making it all but impossible for anyone to follow Janna from that point on.

By the time Janna spotted Ty and Lucifer, it was midafternoon and she was only a mile from the eastern trail. Clouds that had been frail and white earlier in the day had matured into towering, seething billows, which were creamy on their curving tops and blue-black on their flat bottoms. The Fire Mountains were already obscured beneath dense clouds. Distant thunder rumbled down from the invisible peaks. Soon the plateau would be engulfed by sound and fury and tiny, icy hammer blows of rain. Lightning would strike the plateau's promontories and lone trees would run the risk of being transformed into torches.

It would be no different for a man caught in the open on the exposed, eastern face of the plateau. If they hoped to get down the east trail today, they would have to move quickly.

As though sensing her rider's urgency, Zebra cantered to the edge of the plateau. There, wind and rain had unraveled the land into countless crevices, gullies, ravines and canyons. There, at the head of an insignificant ravine, began the sole path down the plateau's rugged east face. There, too, were Ty and Lucifer.

Ty didn't wait for Janna to dismount. Before Zebra had come to a full stop, he plucked Janna off and held her close while the two horses nickered and nuzzled each other in friendly greeting.

"What the hell happened to you?" Ty demanded harshly, but the hands stroking her unbound hair were gentle.

"I found Zebra and we were coming back to check on you and we popped up over a rise and found a bunch of renegades." Janna felt Ty's arms tighten abruptly.

"I knew it," he said, his voice rough. "I heard those damned shots and I just *knew*."

"The renegades were as surprised as I was," Janna said, trying to reassure Ty. "They only got off a few shots before I was out of range. None of the bullets even came close."

"Then how did you lose your hat?"

"Wind," Janna said succinctly. "Zebra ran like hell let out for a holiday. I couldn't see for the tears in my eyes."

Ty thought of the rugged land and the wild mustang and Janna riding her with no stirrups to support and balance her, no bridle to help her control her mount, nothing to help her stay in place if the horse should stumble; and injury or death awaiting her if she fell.

"Dammit, Janna...!"

Ty's voice trailed off. He knew that it was unreasonable of him to be angry with her for having been in danger. She could no more help her position in the wild land than he could.

"This can't go on," Ty said beneath his breath. "I've got to get you to a place where you'll be safe."

Thunder muttered across the plateau, reminding Ty that danger wore many faces, and another one was looking at them right now. Reluctantly he turned and measured the hair-raising trail that awaited the injured stallion.

The path began at the head of a narrow ravine that rapidly branched sideways and downward, threading a tortuous zigzag route across the crumbling east face of the plateau. After the first quarter mile the path became less steep. After a mile the trail merged with the sloping outwash plain that began several thousand feet below the plateau itself. At that point the path became no worse than any other game trail in the rugged land.

But that first quarter mile was a nightmare, and the last three quarters were little better. It had been difficult enough to scramble up onto the plateau via that trail. Climbing down was always more dangerous. Ty didn't see how they were going to negotiate the steep path without losing the tug-of-war with gravity and falling a long, long way down.

"The first part is the hardest," Janna said.

"Is that supposed to make me feel better?"

"Well, it shouldn't make you feel worse."

For an instant Ty's smile flashed whitely beneath his black mustache. He brushed his lips over Janna's answering smile before he released her.

"Keep Zebra back until Lucifer is through with the worst of it," Ty said. "I'm going to have enough trouble staying out from under the stallion's hooves. I sure don't need to be looking over my shoulder for the mare, too." He turned to Lucifer and pulled gently on the hackamore's lead rope. "Come on, son. Might as well get it over with. As my daddy used to say, 'We can't dance and it's too wet to plow.'"

Lucifer walked to the beginning of the path, looked down the slope and refused to take another step.

"Don't blame you a bit," Ty said soothingly, "but it has to be done." He increased the pressure on the lead rope. "Come on, you big black stud. Show Janna what a well-behaved gentleman you've become during our walk to-day."

The stallion's head came up sharply, counteracting the pressure that tended to pull him toward the steep, danger-ous path. Thunder rolled and muttered. A freshening wind brought with it the scent of rain, warning that the possibil-ity of a storm grew greater with every passing minute.

"Come on," Ty said, increasing the pressure on the lead rope until he could pull no harder. "If you think that little bit of a path looks rough now, wait until it's raining fit to put out the fires of hell. When that happens we want to be long gone from here."

Lucifer's ears went back as he set himself more firmly, pulling hard against the pressure on the hackamore.

"Your daddy must have been Satan's own black mule," Ty said, but his tone was still mild and reassuring. "Come on, son. You heard the lady. The first part is the hardest. After that it's as easy as licking honey off a spoon."

Lucifer's ears flattened against his head.

Ty had several choices. He could keep pulling and hope the stallion would give up. He could keep pulling and have Janna make a loud noise, stampeding the stallion over the rim—and right onto Ty. Or he could lure the stallion onto the trail using the oldest bait of all.

"Janna, do you think that cat-footed mare of yours will go down this trail?"

"I don't know. It's worth a try."

"Easy, son," Ty said as he went up to Lucifer and put pressure on the horse's black nose to make him back up. "If you don't want to be first you'll just have to get out of the way and let your lady show you how easy it is."

Lucifer willingly backed away from the trail. Wind gusted suddenly, bringing with it a foretaste of the chilly storm. The stallion pricked his ears and snorted, feeling an instinctive urge to seek shelter.

Ty wrapped the lead rope and secured it around Lucifer's neck, freeing his own hands and at the same time making sure that the stallion didn't get all tangled up in loose rope. When Ty was finished he led the stallion aside, making room for Janna and Zebra to approach the rough path. When Zebra was pointed in the right direction—straight down—Janna smacked the mare on her warm haunch.

"Down you go," she said hopefully.

Zebra turned and looked at Janna.

"Shoo, girl! Go on, get on down that trail. Get!"

The mustang shook her head as though ridding herself of persistent flies. Deliberately she backed away from the trail.

"Dammit," Ty said. "Maybe if we—Janna, don't!"

It was too late. Janna had already darted around in front of Zebra and started down the trail herself. She picked her way down the first steep pitch, found a relatively secure place to stand and turned to call to Zebra.

"No," Ty said urgently. "Don't take the trail in front of Zebra. If she slips she'll roll right on over you and leave you flatter than a shadow!"

"I'll stay out of her way," Janna said, but her voice was tight. She knew even better than Ty the danger of being on the downhill side of a horse on a precipitous slope. "Come on, girl. Point those black hooves in this direction. Come to me, Zebra. Come on."

As always, Janna's coaxing murmur and her outstretched hands intrigued the mare. She edged as far forward as she could without committing herself to the trail. Neck outstretched, nostrils flaring, ears pricked forward Zebra leaned toward Janna. Her hooves, however, remained firmly planted.

Without hesitation, Janna retreated farther down the trail. When she reached another relatively level patch of ground, she was fifty feet away. She put her hands to her mouth and a hawk's wild cry floated up. Zebra nickered nervously and shifted her feet. The hawk cry came again reminding the mare of all the times she had answered the call and found Janna waiting with her backpack full of treats.

One of the mare's black hooves lifted, then set down barely a few inches away. Another hoof lifted. Another few inches gained. Ears pricked, skin flinching nervously, Zebra literally inched her way down the trail. Janna melted away in front of the mustang, calling softly, praising Zebra with every breath.

As Ty watched, his body ran with sweat. A single hesitation, a loose stone, any miscalculation on the mare's part and Janna quickly would be engulfed in a flailing, lethal windmill of horse and human flesh. There was no place for her to leap aside, no place to hide. If Zebra fell, Janna would be killed.

Unknowingly Ty prayed in low tones, never lifting his glance from Zebra's mincing progress, feeling as though his soul were being drawn on a rack.

*If you get out of this alive, Janna,* Ty vowed silently, *I'll make sure you stay out of danger if I have to tie you up and stuff you in my backpack and never let you out.*

Lucifer whickered nervously, calling to Zebra. The mare ignored him, intent on the trail and on the girl who kept retreating down the dangerously steep slope. The stallion's next call was louder and more urgent but it had no more effect than the first. He whinnied imperiously. Zebra's ears swiveled and her tail swished. She lifted her head to look, began slipping and sat down on her haunches. For the space of several breaths the mare simply remained motionless, then she slowly gathered herself and resumed her inching progress down the trail.

The stallion's barrel swelled as he took in air for another whinny.

"Shut up, son," Ty said.

Long, powerful fingers closed gently and completely over the stallion's nostrils, making it impossible for the horse to whinny. Lucifer threw up his head but Ty hung on, talking calmly the whole time.

"Yelling at her won't do any good right now," Ty assured the stallion. "That little mare no more listens to you than Janna listens to me. Later I'll be glad to let you give your woman a royal chewing out—and I plan to do the same to mine—but first let's get them to a safe place."

The firm hands and reassuring voice held Lucifer quiet, though his half-flattened ears told anyone who cared to look that the stallion wasn't very happy about the situation.

Ty didn't notice. The farther the mare got down the trail, the more impossible it seemed that a horse had descended it at all. But Zebra had. The evidence was everywhere, in clumps of dirt gouged out by hooves and in hoofprints elongated by skids. Beneath his breath Ty counted out the steps remaining on the last steep pitch before the trail leveled out to the point where Zebra didn't have to go down half-sitting and braced on her stiffened forelegs.

"Seven, six, fi—"

Zebra skidded the last fifteen feet and then stood quietly, absorbing Janna's praise. Ty let out a long breath as he released his grip on Lucifer's muzzle.

"All right, son. It's our turn. And this time I'm not taking no for an answer."

# Chapter Thirty

Lucifer went to the edge of the plateau, whinnied loudly and was answered by Zebra. He whinnied again. Zebra looked up the steep path but didn't move one step in the stallion's direction.

"She's not about to scramble up to you," Ty said calmly. He stood to the side of Lucifer's head and pulled steadily forward on the hackamore. "If you want her, you're going to have to do it the hard way."

The stallion stood at the trailhead, laid back his ears... and began climbing down.

Janna found it more unnerving to watch Ty descend alongside the stallion's big hooves than it had been for her to climb down the plateau's face in front of Zebra. The first quarter mile was especially dangerous, for there really wasn't enough room for Ty to stand alongside the horse on the path without being under Lucifer's feet half the time.

*Let go, Ty. Let Lucifer do it alone,* Janna urged silently. *He won't back out now. He can't. The only thing he can do is keep coming down and he knows it.*

Snorting, mincing, sliding, sweating, the muscles in his injured leg trembling at the strain, the stallion negotiated the first quarter mile with surprising speed. More than once it was Ty's timely jerk on the hackamore that saved Lucifer from a fall by levering his head up, which helped the horse to regain control when his feet started sliding. Under normal conditions the mustang's own agility would have been sufficient to get him down the trail, but his injury made the difficult footing all but impossible had it not been for Ty's help.

Without warning the stallion's injured leg gave way and he lost his footing. Ty threw all his muscle behind the hackamore, forcing Lucifer back onto his haunches. Front legs braced, hooves digging into the path, the horse slid about twenty feet before he came to a stop. Sitting up like a big black hound, the stallion sweated nervously while displaced pebbles bounced and rattled down the slope. Right beside him, Ty sweated just as hard. It had been much too close to disaster. Someone with less strength than Ty wouldn't have been able to prevent the horse from falling.

Janna held her fist against her teeth as she forced back a scream. Ty had taken a terrible gamble, for if his weight and leverage hadn't been enough to counteract gravity, he would have been swept away with Lucifer in a long, lethal fall.

"That's it, son," Ty said, his voice soothing despite the hammer blows of his own heart. "You rest and get your wind back. That old leg just keeps fooling you. You expect it to be there for you and it isn't, not the way you need it to be. That's the problem with strength. You get to counting on it and then it lets you down. So use your head instead. You can't just rush the path and scramble and slide and get it over with the way you would if you had your usual muscle and coordination. You have to take it nice and slow."

When Lucifer's skin no longer rippled with nervous reaction, Ty gradually released his pressure on the hackamore. Gingerly the stallion shifted his weight forward and began descending once more. As though he had understood Ty's words, the mustang moved more slowly now, demanding less of his injured leg.

Even so, by the time Lucifer reached the end of the steepest portion of the path, Janna was trembling with a fear she had never known for herself. When both man and horse were on safe ground, she let out a shaky breath and ran to Ty, throwing herself at him, holding on to him with fierce strength despite her bruised arm.

"I was so frightened," Janna said against Ty's neck. "All I could think of was what would happen if Lucifer got to sliding too fast or lost his footing completely and you couldn't get out of the way in time."

Ty's arms closed around Janna, lifting her off her feet. "The same thought occurred to me about every other step," he said roughly, "but worst of all was watching you stand in front of Zebra and knowing there wasn't a damn thing I could do if things went to hell." He held Janna hard and close, savoring the feel of her in his arms, her living warmth and resilience and the sweet rush of her breath against his neck. "God, little one, it's good to be alive and holding you."

A cool wind swirled down the plateau's face, trailing the sound of thunder behind. Reluctantly Ty released Janna and set her back on her feet. A moment later he fished the crumpled rain poncho from his backpack. Without a word he tugged the waterproof folds over Janna.

"That should do it," he said. "Now let's get off this exposed slope before lightning has better luck at killing us than that damn trail did."

With the casual strength that kept surprising Janna, Ty tossed her onto Zebra's back.

"Don't wait for me. Just get off the slope," Ty said to Janna. He stepped back and smacked Zebra lightly on her haunch. "Get to it, horse. And you keep your rider hair side up or I'll skin you for a sofa covering."

Zebra took to the path again with an eagerness that said more plainly than words that the mustang understood the danger of being caught out in the open during a storm. Lucifer was just as eager to see the last of the exposed trail leading from the foot of the plateau to the lowlands beyond, but his injury forced a slower pace. Limping heavily, the stallion started off down the rocky decline.

Out in the distance to the east, blue-black buttes and localized thunderstorms were intermixed with golden cataracts of light where sunshine poured through gaps between squall lines. Overhead, lightning played through the massed clouds and the wind increased in power.

By the time Lucifer and Ty reached the place where the plateau merged with the lower canyon lands beyond, the last luminous shafts of sunlight had slowly merged with the thunderstorm gathering overhead, leaving behind an odd, sourceless gloaming that made every feature of the land stand forth as though outlined in pale gold. The effect lasted for only a few minutes, until the first sweeping veils of rain came down, blending sky and land into one seamless whole. Lightning danced across the land on incandescent feet, while thunder rumbled behind its shimmering, elusive mistress.

"Well, son," Ty said, pulling his hat down tighter against the wind and pelting rain, "this cloud's silver lining is that no self-respecting renegade is going to be out chasing around in the rain."

If that fact cheered Lucifer, the horse didn't show it. He limped along with his ears half-laid-back in warning of his surly temper. Ty felt the same way himself. With luck the storm would turn out to be a small, fast-moving squall line. Without luck, the rain would last for hours. With bad luck, the slot leading into Janna's hidden canyon would be too deep with runoff water from the thunderstorm for them to enter and they would have to spend another night in the open.

Janna was worrying about the same thing. If she were alone, she would have hurried Zebra toward the miles-distant slot. But she wasn't alone, and despite Lucifer's best efforts, his shuffling, painful walk meant that it would be several hours before they reached the haven of her hidden canyon.

The rain quickly limited visibility to a few hundred yards, making scouting both impossible and unnecessary. Janna turned Zebra and retraced her steps until she saw Lucifer and Ty. She slid off Zebra and fell into step beside Ty.

"Go ahead on to the canyon," he said. "No sense in you catching your death out in the rain."

"It will be dark an hour before you get to the slot. You'll miss it. Besides, you know how it is with misery. I was feeling like a little company."

Ty thought of objecting more forcefully to Janna's presence but didn't. Part of him agreed with her that he would have trouble finding the narrow slot in the dark in the rain, because the only other time he had been through it from this direction he had been more dead than alive. But the real reason he didn't object was that he enjoyed having Janna beside him, her fingers laced through his, their hands slowly warming with shared body heat.

"Janna?" Ty asked after a long time of rain and silence, voicing a thought that had been nagging at him for hours.

"Yes?"

"Why did you risk your life holding on to Lucifer in that ravine?"

"I didn't want Troon to get him again."

"But you heard the renegades. You had to figure that Troon was as good as dead. You could have let Lucifer go, but you didn't. You hung on despite the danger to yourself."

Janna said nothing.

"Sugar? Why?"

"I promised you a chance to gentle Lucifer," Janna said simply. "There would never be a better chance than in that small ravine."

Ty swore very softly. "I thought it was something crazy like that. Listen to me. You're free of that promise you made. Do you hear me? If Lucifer decides to take off in twelve different directions, that's my problem, not yours.

You just get the hell out of the way where you won't ge
hurt." Ty waited but she said nothing. "Janna?"

"I heard you."

"Do I have your word that if Lucifer bolts or goes loco
you'll get out of the way instead of trying to help?"

"Ty—"

"Give me your word," he interrupted, "or so help me
God I'll turn around right now and walk back to Wyoming
and to hell with that damned black stud."

"But he's your future, the only way you'll get a chance to
buy your silken—"

Ty interrupted with a burst of language that was both
savage and obscene. It was a mile before Janna had the
courage to break the silence that had followed.

"I promise," she said finally. "I don't understand why
you won't let me help you, but—"

"You don't understand?" Ty demanded fiercely, cutting
off Janna's words once more. "You must have a damned
poor opinion of me if you think I'd build my dream on top
of your dead body!"

"I never meant anything like that!" Janna said instantly, shocked that Ty had misunderstood her words. "I
know you'd never do something that awful. You're much
too kind and gentle and generous."

Ty's laughter was as harsh as his swearing had been, for
he knew that a man who was kind or gentle or generous
wouldn't have eased his violent hunger at the cost of Janna's
innocence. But Ty had done just that and now she was no
longer innocent . . . and worst of all, he couldn't bring himself to truly repent his action. The ecstasy he had known
within Janna's body was too great, too consuming, to ever
be repudiated.

If he had it to do all over again, he would no more be able
to preserve Janna's virginity than he had been the first time.
She was wildness and grace and elemental fire, and he was
a man who had hungered a lifetime for all three without

knowing it. She had sensed his needs, given herself to him and had required nothing of him in return. Not one damn thing.

And he felt the silken strands of her innocence and generosity twining more tightly around him with each moment, binding him.

"Do you do it on purpose?" Ty demanded angrily.

"What?"

"Give everything and ask nothing and thereby chain me to you tighter than any steel manacles could."

Janna felt as though she had been struck. The cold rain that had been making her miserable became her friend, for it hid the tears and disappointment she was too tired to conceal. When Ty had swept her up in his arms and held her as fiercely as she had held him, she had begun to hope that he cared more for her than simply as a sexual convenience. When he had held her hand and walked in companionable silence with her through the storm, she had been certain that he cared for her.

What she hadn't realized was that he would resent that caring, and her.

"Well, you're by God going to take something from me," Ty continued. "Lucifer is half yours."

"I don't want him."

"I didn't want you to risk your neck, either," Ty shot back, "and a lot of good my wanting did me."

Janna jerked her hand free of his. "Did you ever think that the reason I didn't ask for anything from you was that there was nothing you had that I wanted?"

"Nothing?" Ty asked sardonically. "You could have fooled me."

The tone of his voice told Janna that he was remembering her hands caressing him, her lips clinging, her hips lifting in silent pleading that his body join with hers. Shame coursed through her.

"Don't worry," she said, her voice strained. "You won't have to lose any sleep on my account tonight. I won't seduce you again."

"Seduce me? Is that what you think happened? You seduced me?" Ty laughed. "Sugar, you don't have the least idea how to seduce a man. A woman seduces a man with rustling silks and secret smiles and accidental touches of her soft, perfumed hands. She seduces a man with her conversation and the sweet music of her voice when she greets her guests for a fancy ball. She seduces a man by knowing fine wines and elegant food, and by her special grace when she enters a room knowing he'll be there." Ty shook his head and added, "You well and truly bedded me, but you sure as hell didn't seduce me."

Janna remembered what Ty had said about her last night...*suited to be nothing except a man's mistress, but you lack the social graces for even that profession.*

Without a word Janna turned away from Ty and swung onto Zebra's warm back, ignoring the pain that mounting the horse without aid gave to her bruised arm.

"Janna? What the hell ... ?"

She didn't answer. Her heels urged Zebra forward until Janna could see and hear only the rain.

## Chapter Thirty-One

"Come on, it's just a little bit farther," Ty said to the stallion, hoping he wasn't lying. Neither Ty's voice nor the steady pressure he put on the hackamore revealed the weariness that had settled into the marrow of his bones, turning his muscles to sand.

For a moment Ty was afraid that the stallion wouldn't respond, but the pressure on the hackamore eased abruptly as the horse resumed his awkward walking gait.

"That's it, son," Ty said encouragingly. "She said the slot was at the top of a little rise."

And that was all Janna had said through the long hours of intermittent rain and wind. When it wasn't raining she rode far ahead of Ty and Lucifer. When it rained she rode in close enough that her tracks were always clear for Ty to follow. When it became dark she rode closer still, ensuring that Lucifer wouldn't get lost.

Ty was certain that it was the stallion's welfare rather than his own that concerned Janna. Not once since she had mounted Zebra had she said anything to Ty. He missed her conversation. In the past weeks he had become accustomed to her insights into the land and its animals, her uninhibited response to the wind and sun, and her shy smile when he touched her. He missed her laughter when she talked about hiding from Cascabel in the same way the renegade had once hidden from the soldiers—out in plain sight. Ty missed the snippets of plays and poetry and essays she liked to talk about with him, drawing from him the missing parts of her education. Most of all he missed the warm, companionable silence they had shared while they walked hand in hand in the cold rain.

The silence Ty and Janna had shared since she had ridden off was anything but companionable. It was as chill and empty as the night.

"Maybe you can tell me," Ty said to Lucifer. "Why would a woman get all upset because I told her it isn't her fault that she's not a virgin anymore? Because it sure as hell isn't her fault. Janna didn't have the faintest idea of what waited for her at the end of that primrose path. She could no more have known when to say no to me than she could have walked down the plateau trail carrying Zebra on her back.

"But I knew where we were going. I knew the first time I kissed Janna that I should stop myself right there or I wouldn't be able to quit short of burying myself in that sweet young body. But I didn't stop. I wanted her the way a river in flood wants the sea. Just plain unstoppable. And God help me, I still want her just like that.

"I knew what I was doing every inch of the way... and it was every inch the best I've ever had. I'll die remembering the beautiful sounds she made while I was inside her, pleasuring her with my whole body."

Ty's voice thickened as memories poured through him in an incandescent tide. Despite his exhaustion, his blood beat heavily at the thought of being sheathed within Janna's fire and softness once more.

"She didn't have a chance to refuse me," Ty continued, his voice rough. "Not a single damned chance in hell. It should have made her feel better to know that what happened was my fault, not hers.

"So why won't she speak to me?"

Lucifer didn't have any answer for Ty. Not that he had expected one. If the stallion had known how to handle the supposedly weaker sex, Zebra wouldn't have been racing around the plateau with Janna for the past few years. Muttering to himself, Ty walked up the rise, urging the limping stallion along with a steady pressure on the hackamore.

At last a low nicker came floating out of the darkness in front of them. Lucifer nickered in return. No verbal welcome came to Ty, however. Nor did Janna say anything when she dismounted and walked around the stallion. Frowning, peering into the coldly brilliant moonlight that had replaced the wind-frayed clouds, she tried to gauge Lucifer's condition.

"Is there too much water in the slot for us to get through?" Ty asked.

"No."

He waited, but Janna had nothing more to say on that subject—or any other, apparently. At least, not to him. But it seemed she had nothing against talking to the stallion.

"You poor, brave creature. You've really been put through it today, haven't you?" Janna said in a gentle voice as she reached out to pet Lucifer.

Ty opened his mouth to warn Janna that the stallion was feeling surly as hell, but the words died on his tongue when Lucifer whickered softly and stretched his muzzle out to Janna's hands. Slender fingers stroked his muzzle and cheeks, then searched through the stallion's thick, shaggy forelock until she found the bony knob between his ears. She slid her fingers beneath the hackamore and rubbed away the unaccustomed feel of the leather.

Lucifer let out a breath that was almost a groan and put his forehead against Janna's chest, offering himself to her touch with a trust that first shocked Ty, then moved him, making his throat close around all the emotions he had no words to describe. Seeing the stallion's gentle surrender reminded Ty of the ancient myth of the unicorn and virgin.

But as Ty watched Janna, he wondered if it weren't some elemental feminine quality that had attracted the unicorn to the girl, rather than her supposedly virginal state.

*That poor unicorn never had a chance,* Ty told himself silently. *He was born to lay his head in that one maiden's lap and be captive to her gentle hands.*

The insight made Ty very restless. Though Janna had done nothing to hold him, he felt himself somehow confined, caught in an invisible net, tied with silken threads; and each thread was a shared caress, a shared smile, a shared word, until one thread became thousands woven into an unbreakable bond, and the silken snare was complete.

"Ready, boy?" Janna asked quietly. "It's going to be hard on your poor leg, but it's the last thing I'll ask of you until you're healed."

Janna turned and walked toward Zebra. Lucifer followed, silently urging Ty forward with a pressure on the lead rope he still held. The reversal in their roles gave Ty a moment of sardonic amusement. He wondered what would happen if he tied the rope around the stallion's neck and then turned and walked away, leaving everything behind.

*I'll tell you what would happen,* Ty thought to himself. *You'd spend the night hungry and freezing your butt off in the cold and Lucifer would spend it belly-deep in food with Janna's warm hands petting him. So who do you think is smarter—you or that stallion?*

With a muttered curse Ty followed Lucifer over the wet, rocky ground to the invisible opening in the plateau's wall. The face of the plateau at this point was made of broken ranks of sheer rocky cliffs punctuated by dark mounds of black lava. As though to make up for the precipitous nature of the land, the cliffs were only a tenth of the height of the heavily eroded wall Janna and Ty had descended earlier.

Even so, Janna had discovered no trail up onto the plateau itself from this area. If she wanted to go back up on top, she had to walk much farther south, following the ragged edge of the plateau as it rose and fell until she reached the gentle southern ascent. That would have been a full day's ride on a good horse. The east path, while steep, was only a few hours by foot.

Ahead of Ty both horses stopped abruptly. Zebra snorted nervously when Janna waded into the water gushing from the slot, but the mare didn't balk. She followed Janna into the ankle-deep runoff stream, for she had done this before and not been hurt by the experience. Lucifer hesitated, lowered his head and smelled the water, then limped into the stream in the manner of an animal who was too exhausted at the moment to do more than go where he was led.

Inside the slot, moonlight was reduced to a pale glimmering over the surface of the water. The horses were better off than the humans, both by reason of four legs and the superior night vision of equines. Even with those advantages, the horses didn't have an easy time of it. Janna, with her greater experience in negotiating the slot, managed not to slip and fall more than twice. Ty fell four times and considered himself fortunate that it wasn't a lot worse.

When they emerged into the valley, humans and animals alike were soaked by a combination of rain, runoff water and sweat.

"That's it, girl," Janna said tiredly, slapping the mare on her muscular haunch. "We're home."

Zebra trotted off into the moonlight, heading for the sweet grass and clover she had discovered on her previous visit. Ty considered hobbling Lucifer, then rejected the idea. Even if the stallion wanted to leave Zebra, Lucifer was too tired to take on the slot again. With a few smooth motions Ty removed the hackamore. When it was off, he rubbed away all the marks the leather had left on the horse's head. Lucifer leaned into the touch, obviously enjoying it.

"Yeah, I know. It doesn't take long to get spoiled, does it?" murmured Ty, thinking of Janna and the night before.

"Tomorrow I'll give you a good rubdown, but right now you need food more than you need petting. Go follow Zebra, son. She knows where all the sweet things are in this place."

After Ty removed his hand, it took a moment for the stallion to realize that he was free. When he did, he snorted, shook his head and limped off after Zebra. Ty looked away just in time to see Janna vanish into the willows that grew alongside the stream.

By the time Ty got to the cliff overhang Janna called home, a small glow of flame was expanding into the darkness. Sitting on her heels next to the fire, Janna fed in fuel from the supply she kept dry in one corner of the overhang. Once the fire took hold she added wet wood from the pile that was stacked beyond the protection of the rock.

Only when water was warming over the fire did Janna turn away and go to the small trunk she had laboriously tugged through the slot three years before, when she had discovered the secret canyon. Most of the trunk was filled with books. A small part of it was taken up with the last of her father's clothes. Only one ragged shirt remained, one pair of Sunday pants, three socks and the moccasins she had traded medicines for last spring.

"I took three shirts from Preacher's store. Do you want one of them?"

The sound of Ty's voice startled Janna. She hadn't realized that he was in camp. But there he was, standing on the other side of the fire, stretching muscles that were tired from carrying the heavy backpack that now rested against the stone cliff. Ty peeled off his hat and slapped it against his thigh, driving water from the hat rim in a fine spray.

"No," Janna said, turning away from Ty again, refusing more than his offer of a shirt.

She unlaced her soggy moccasins and set them aside to dry. With cold hands she worked beneath the poncho, unwinding the cloth that bound her breasts. The motions sent stabbing pains through her bruised arm. She set her teeth and continued. She had suffered worse injuries in the past; she would probably suffer more in the future.

Ty didn't bother to ask if Janna wanted any help, for he knew she would refuse him. Without a word he lifted the cumbersome poncho from Janna's shoulders and threw it aside. The sight of the bruise on her arm made his breath come in with an audible hiss. Even though experience told Ty that the bruise looked much worse than it actually was, he hated seeing the dark shadow of pain on her skin.

"Don't you have something for that?" he asked.

"Yes."

Janna tried to step away. Ty's hands closed around her lower arms in a grip that was gentle but unshakable.

"Hold still, sugar. Let me help you."

Afraid to trust her voice, Janna shook her head in a negative.

"Yes," Ty countered instantly. "You've patched me up often enough. Now it's your turn to be patched."

Janna looked up into Ty's glance. His eyes were very dark yet alive with flames reflected from the campfire. The warmth of his hands on her chilled skin was shocking, but not as shocking as the heat that uncurled in her loins at the thought of being cared for by him. She shivered in a combination of cold and remembered desire.

And she hated it, both the memory and the desire, hated wanting a man whose feelings for her teetered between pity and contempt, lust and indifference.

"You're chilled through and through," Ty said, frowning as he saw Janna shiver violently. With quick motions he began unwrapping the cloth that bound her chest. "Where's the medicine you need?"

She shook her head, refusing him, refusing her memories, refusing everything.

"Janna, what in hell is the matter with you?"

Ty didn't wait for an answer. Janna felt cloth being stripped from her body by his big hands. Suddenly she couldn't bear the thought of her naked breasts being revealed to Ty again. He would touch them, kiss them, and the heat that was spreading from the pit of her stomach would flare up, burning away everything, even the knowledge that she loved a man who loved only his own dream . . . and she was not that dream.

With an inarticulate cry Janna tried to push away Ty's hands. It was like pushing on warm stone.

"It's too late to be shy," he said flatly, ignoring her attempts to stop him from unwrapping her breasts. "Hold still while I get this wet stuff off you."

"*Let go of me.*"

The quality of Janna's voice was chilling. Ty's hands froze in the act of unwrapping her.

"Janna, what's wrong?"

His voice was gentle but Janna didn't hear that, or the emotions churning just beneath his control. She heard only her own memories, Ty's voice echoing and reechoing in her mind as he listed all her shortcomings as a woman—nothing to offer a husband, too unskilled to be a mistress, good only for the male need that built up inexorably when no other woman was around.

"Little one?" Ty asked, tipping Janna's chin up and brushing a kiss over her lips. They were as cold as her voice had been. "What did I do to make you so angry with me?"

When he would have kissed her again, she jerked her head away. "Don't touch me. I don't feel like being your whore tonight."

# Chapter Thirty-Two

Ty's tightly held emotions exploded into a fury that was unlike any he had ever felt. He stopped trying to peel off layers of wet cloth and grabbed Janna's shoulders instead.

"Don't say something like that about yourself! Do you hear me, Janna Wayland? *You are not a whore!*"

Angry, ashamed, defiant, Janna stood shivering within Ty's grasp. "Just what would you call it?"

"We're . . . lovers."

"I don't think so," she said distinctly. "To be someone's lover suggests a certain affection mixed in with the lust. I'm not your lover. I'm a convenience until you take Lucifer and go off to buy your silk—"

"Don't say it," Ty interrupted savagely. "I'm sick to death of having those words flung in my face."

"Then stop flinging them in mine."

"I've never—"

"The hell you haven't!" Janna interrupted, her voice as savage as his. " 'I'll have my silken lady or I'll have none at all for longer than it takes to pleasure myself,' " Janna quoted, each word clipped. " 'You're the least female female I've ever seen.' Then you said that Cascabel looked more like a mesquite bush than I looked like a woman, and the comparisons didn't stop after you had me, either. You couldn't wait to tell me that it was a woman you'd needed, not me."

Janna's voice broke, then steadied as words rushed out. "And then you told me that my virginity was all I had to offer to a husband because I had no family, no profession, no money. You said that you had ruined me, because now I wasn't good enough to be a wife and wasn't educated enough to be a mistress and that meant that I wasn't good enough to be anything but a 'toy of many men, not one.' That's a whore in any man's language."

"Janna—my God, I never meant—"

"I'm not finished," she said, cutting across Ty's shocked words. "Or maybe I should say *you're* not finished. You've had a lot to say about my shortcomings as a woman. As woman hungry as you were, I couldn't even seduce you. You said, 'Sugar, you don't have the least idea how to seduce a man. A woman seduces a man with rustling silks and—'"

Ty's hand clamped across Janna's mouth, cutting off her bitter recitation of his words.

"You don't understand," Ty said urgently. "I didn't mean any of that to belittle you. Especially after we made love."

The mute defiance of Janna's eyes and the hot rain of her tears said that she had understood him all too well.

"Janna," he whispered, kissing her eyelashes, tasting her tears, "please believe me. I never meant the words as an insult to you. You're a young girl alone in the world and I seduced you, knowing I shouldn't. That's all the words meant. My shortcomings, Janna, not yours."

She trembled as she felt Ty's caresses and soft words stripping away her anger, revealing the despair that was the other side of her fury. Nothing he had said or could say would change the heartbreaking reality: she was not the silken lady of her lover's dreams.

"Do you believe me?" Ty asked, the words as soft as the repeated brush of his lips over Janna's eyelids, her cheeks.

her mouth. "I never meant to belittle you. Satin butterfly...believe me...I never meant..."

Gentle words became tender kisses, which lingered and deepened until Ty's tongue touched Janna's for just an instant. Then he withdrew.

"You're so cold you're shivering," he said huskily.

With a volatile mixture of despair and tenderness and desire, Janna waited for Ty to suggest the obvious way to warm her.

Ty looked from Janna's clear, fathomless eyes to the fire whose flames were licking against a huge wall of stone. "And that fire has a lot of rock to warm before it will do us any good." Suddenly he smiled. "But there's a better way."

Janna's answering smile was bittersweet as Ty's hands went to the soggy material that was still wrapped around her breasts. She could refuse him when she was in the grip of anger, but she could never refuse the man who had kissed her so gently just moments before.

When Ty saw the sad acceptance of Janna's smile, he felt as though a knife were turning within his body. He knew that he could have her now, that she would give herself to him once more with all the sensual generosity that had been such a marvel each time he had experienced it; but this time, after the shattering ecstasy had passed, she would believe herself a whore once again.

Nothing he could say would change her mind, for he had said too much already, heedlessly, not knowing that his words were wounding her. He had never meant to strip her pride away. But he had, and he finally knew it.

Too late.

Janna felt the world tilt as Ty picked her up and carried her away from the fire. She made a startled sound and threw her arms around his neck.

"It's all right, Janna. I won't drop you."

Although Ty's voice was as gentle as his kisses had been, in the moonlight his face was a portrait composed of harsh planes and angles, and the line of his mouth was as sad as Janna's had been. At first the clammy fabric of his shirt made Janna shiver with renewed chill. Caught between two bodies, the cloth quickly warmed, and so did she.

Neither of them spoke while Ty walked down the path that led to the hot spring. As the stone ramparts closed in and the valley narrowed, the temperature rose due to the heat radiated by the hottest pool. Ty stopped well short of the first pool, choosing instead the one they called the Tub. There he knelt and lowered Janna into the water without bothering to remove the rest of her clothes. She made a long sound of pleasure as the water's heat penetrated the chill that had come from hours of riding through the storm with only the haphazard protection of the poncho to turn aside the cold rain.

"That feels wonderful," Janna murmured.

With a sigh she sank up to her chin in the water, all but disappearing beneath the veils of steam lifting from the pool's surface. Automatically she searched out the water-smoothed ledge that she usually half floated and half lay on while she soaked in the pool's heated water. Closing her eyes, she eased down the ledge to make room for Ty to join her. When minutes passed and there was no splash or displacement of water from his entry into the pool, she opened her eyes.

She was alone.

"Ty?" she called softly.

No one answered.

"Ty?" This time Janna's call was louder. "There's room here for both of us. You don't have to wait to get warm."

Words that Janna couldn't distinguish came from the direction of camp. She listened intently but no other sounds came. She started to get out of the pool, only to begin shivering immediately. Experience told her if she stayed in the pool for a long enough time her body would absorb so much heat that the walk back to the campfire wouldn't chill her, even in the middle of winter.

Janna took off her remaining clothes, slid back into the pool and let the hot water claim her body once more. Eyes closed, half-floating in the gently flowing water, she wondered why Ty hadn't gotten into the pool with her. Surely he had to be as cold as she was, for he hadn't even had the protection of the makeshift poncho against the rain and wind.

Gradually Janna realized that she was no longer alone. She opened her eyes and saw Ty sitting cross-legged at the edge of the pool, fully clothed, smiling as he watched her. She didn't know that her answering, half-shy smile was another knife of regret turning within him; she only knew that for an instant he looked so sad that tears burned behind her eyes.

"Ty?"

"I'm here, little one."

Janna didn't hesitate or withdraw when Ty bent over the pool. She turned her face toward him, expecting to be pulled into his arms for a kiss that was as steamy and deep as the hot spring itself.

"Close your eyes and hold your breath," he said huskily.

She blinked in surprise, then did as he asked.

"Now go under the water."

Saying nothing, Janna moved down the ledge until she slipped beneath the veils of mist and water. When she surfaced again Ty was waiting for her with a mound of soft, fragrant soap in his palm. The haunting scent of summer roses expanded through the steamy air.

"No wonder your backpack was so heavy I could hardly drag it," Janna said. "You must have cleaned Preacher out."

The white curve of Ty's smile gleamed in the moonlight. "It had been a long time since I'd been in a store with a poke of gold to spend."

Soon Ty's strong fingers were working the soap through Janna's hair until soft mounds of lather gathered and dropped to the water, only to float away downstream like tiny ghost ships in the moonlight. Janna closed her eyes and luxuriated in the unprecedented pleasure of having someone wash her hair.

"Ready to hold your breath again?"

She nodded even as she sank beneath the gently steaming water once more. When she emerged he was waiting with more fragrant soap. He lathered her hair again, working slowly, enjoying the feel and scent of the soap, savoring the pleased curve he had brought to her lips, a smile that was untinged by sadness. It was many minutes before his fingers reluctantly released her soft, rose-scented hair.

"Hold your breath."

Smiling, Janna held her breath and slipped into the pool's seamless embrace. When she came up again her hair was free of soap, yet the fragrance of roses lingered. Ty inhaled deeply, letting the scent caress his senses. He dipped into the pot of soft soap once more before he began washing the rest of Janna as gently as though she were a child. The hard rise of her nipples beneath his palms told Ty that she was a woman, not a child, but he forced himself to continue bathing her without lingering over the breasts that were silently begging for his caresses.

Ty's hands didn't hesitate in their slippery travel from her ribs to her hips. He tried to bathe her sleek legs with the same, almost impersonal touch he had used on her shoulders. He succeeded until he came to the triangle of hair that was glittering midnight now but had been brushed by fire in the hushed twilight when he had first undressed her.

As Ty's long fingers began washing the warm mound at the apex of Janna's thighs, she trembled and made a broken sound.

"Hush, little one," he murmured, ignoring the doubled beating of his own heart. "At least you won't have to hold your breath to rinse off. I'll be able to do it for you."

Janna's answering smile lasted only an instant before the intimacy of Ty's touch called another small cry from her lips. He made the same kind of meaningless, reassuring, almost purring sound he had so often used on Lucifer.

"It's all right," he said softly. "I'm not going to take you again. I'm just bathing you. Do you mind that so very much?"

"It's ... no one has ever ..."

Janna's words fragmented into an involuntary sound of pleasure as Ty's fingers moved between her legs, washing and setting fire to her in the same sliding motions.

Despite his fierce desire, Ty's smile was gentle. "I'm glad. I've never bathed a woman before." He started to add that he had never wanted to, but Janna cried out and he remembered the past night, her innocence ripped away, and his repeated, urgent penetrations of her untouched body. "Are you sore, darling? Am I hurting you now?"

Janna tried to speak, couldn't and shook her head instead, sending wavelets lapping against the sandy rim of the pool.

"Are you sure?"

She nodded, making more tiny waves.

"Cat got your tongue?"

The lazy, sensual humor in Ty's voice made Janna smile just before she stuck out her tongue. As she had hoped, he pulled her halfway from the pool even as he bent to kiss her; and the kiss was what she had longed for, a sharing as hot and deep as the pool itself.

"I'm getting you wet," Janna said when Ty finally released her, letting her slide back into the heated water.

"The rain already took care of that. Open your legs, sati butterfly. I don't want to leave any soap on that soft, sof skin."

The swirling motions of the water as Ty rinsed Janna made heat shimmer up through her body. She smelled th haunting fragrance of roses again when Ty scooped a bi more soap onto his palm.

"Wash your hair once for cleanliness, twice for beauty Isn't that what mothers tell their daughters?" Ty asked.

"Is that what mothers tell daughters?"

"Yes."

"Yes," Janna whispered, shivering in anticipation.

Again Ty's hand slid and pleasured, skimming ove Janna, sensitizing her until her breath was a husky sigh When he pressed apart her thighs, she gave herself will ingly, shivering with each hot swirl of water rinsing her crying out helplessly when his finger began to ease into he warmth. Instantly he stopped.

"Was that a cry of pain?" Ty asked huskily.

"No."

The word became a moan as he stole tenderly into Janna The satin flutter of her response tore a barely throttled groa from him. He didn't know how he had borne being withou her all the long hours of the day—or how he would be abl to bear not having her again day and night without end.

"Satin butterfly," Ty whispered, withdrawing fror Janna, his hand trembling.

He lifted her from the water and laid her in the center c the blanket he had brought back to the pool. Steam ros from her body even as it did from the water itself, veiling he in silver mist. He folded over the sides of the blanket unt she was covered snugly. With long, leisurely sweeps of h hands over the blanket, he dried her. When she would hav helped, he captured her hands, kissed them and tucked ther along her sides beneath the blanket once more.

"Let me," he said huskily, peeling back the edges of the blanket until her nipples were just barely uncovered.

"Yes," Janna whispered, feeling herself tighten as she remembered the pleasure of Ty's mouth loving her.

But it was his hands that came to her breasts, caressed them, plucked at their rosy tips until her back arched in response to the currents of pleasure pouring through her. She closed her eyes and gave herself to the shimmering sensations her lover's hands called from her body. Her teeth sank into her lower lip, biting back the cries that came when his mouth caught one nipple and suckled until a bubble of pleasure burst within her. When his hands skimmed down her body and pressed between her legs, she shifted, allowing him the freedom of her body.

Janna's reward was a love bite that made pleasure expand through her until she could hold no more and sultry heat overflowed, merging her scent with that of roses. Ty groaned beneath the redoubled violence of his own arousal. He would have given his soul to take her while she melted around him, but he knew it wasn't his soul that would be forfeited. It would be hers.

Janna trembled as Ty kissed and licked and nuzzled the length of her torso, smoothing her legs apart as he had in the pool. This time there were no hot swirls of water to caress her, only the heat and textures of her lover teasing the humid softness that his fingertips had first discovered.

The first gliding touch of Ty's tongue brought a startled cry from Janna. It was answered by a reassuring murmur and a kiss both tender and hotly intimate. She tried to say his name, but all that came out was a whimper of shock and pleasure. She started to sit up, only to be impaled by a shaft of ecstasy when her lover captured and teased the violently sensitive nub that had been hidden between soft folds of skin. A sound came from deep in her throat, protest and extraordinary pleasure combined.

Ty's hands flexed, holding Janna captive and sensuously kneading her thighs at the same time.

"Don't pull away," he said in a low voice. "I won't hurt you. I just want to . . . love you." Slowly he turned his head from side to side, caressing Janna with his breath, his stubble-roughened cheeks, his mouth. "You're so sweet, so soft, so warm. I'll be gentle with you. Let me . . ."

Janna didn't answer, for the hunger and passionate intimacy of Ty's caresses had taken from her the ability to think, to form words, to speak. Her breathing disintegrated into ragged gasps as she felt her body begin a slow, sensual unraveling that had no end, no beginning, just a timeless, ravishing moment in which pleasure burst and grew and burst again, incandescent sensations rippling through her body until she moaned and moved helplessly, totally captive to the man and the ultimate instant of pleasure.

And still the moment and the unraveling and the sweet ravishment continued. Ty's name burst from Janna's lips in a cry of protest and pleasure, for she hadn't known that ecstasy was the mythic phoenix, rising newborn from the steamy ashes of sensual completion. She rose with the phoenix, spiraling higher and higher until she screamed at the violent currents of pleasure searing through her, burning through flesh and her mind, leaving her soul as naked as her body.

And then he touched her so perfectly, so gently, so hotly that she wept his name and died.

For a long time Ty held Janna's trembling body against his own, ignoring the violent demands of his own hunger stroking her slowly until she could take a breath that didn't fragment with the aftershocks of ecstasy. When she stirred and sighed and began sliding from ecstasy into sleep, he tilted her face up and brushed her lips with his own.

"You're not a whore, Janna Wayland."

# Chapter Thirty-Three

Lucifer cantered across the valley toward Ty and Janna. His ears were pricked alertly, his tail was held up like a black banner and his stride was both muscular and effortless. It was only in the chill of morning that he walked stiffly, revealing the injury that was almost, but not quite, healed.

"Hard to believe he's the same horse that stumbled into this valley three weeks ago," Janna said.

"More like a month," Ty corrected.

She said nothing, although she knew that it had been precisely twenty-four days since Ty had carried her to the steamy pool and then had brought such intense, exquisite pleasure to her. Twenty-four days, each one longer than the one before, because he hadn't touched her since then. Not once. Not even in the most casual way. It was as though she stood behind an invisible wall too thick and too high for him to reach across.

Lucifer came to a stop a few feet away from Janna and Ty, tossed his elegant black head and watched both of them. Then he nickered a soft welcome and stretched his neck toward Ty's hands. Janna smiled to see the big stallion's trust. Although he often looked to her to be petted, it was to Ty the stallion came first. An unusual, deep bond had been forged between man and horse on the painful trip from the plateau to the keyhole valley. The bond had been reinforced in the weeks that followed, weeks when Janna had deliberately stayed away from Lucifer much of the time, wanting it to be Ty whose touch and voice and medicines both healed and tamed the stallion.

With a hunger Janna couldn't conceal, she watched Ty's long-fingered hands smooth over Lucifer's black coat. She didn't realize how much her stare revealed until she sensed Ty's attention and looked up to find him watching her in the same way that she had watched him. Hastily she looked away, not knowing what else to do, unable to slow the sudden hammering of her heart.

Each time she had begun to think Ty didn't want her anymore, she would turn around suddenly and see him watching her with hunger blazing in his green eyes. Yet he never moved toward her, always away. He would not touch her.

*You're not a whore, Janna Wayland.*

The words Ty had spoken that first night in the valley echoed in Janna's soul every hour of every day. She believed Ty, but it was the way he had made love to her that had instilled that belief; without his healing touch, the words would have been but a thin balm over a deep wound.

When a week had gone by and Ty had made no move to touch Janna in any way, she had tried to tell him that she understood why he couldn't love her, that she had accepted not being his dream, that it was all right if he touched her, that she wanted to be his lover; but he had turned away and walked out into the meadow, leaving her alone, ignoring the words she called after him in her futile attempt to make him understand that she wanted him without vows or pledges or guarantees of anything beyond a sharing of selves within the hushed stone boundaries of the secret valley.

He still would not touch her.

Janna would have tried to seduce Ty, but she didn't know how. She had no silks to wear, no grand home in which to throw parties, no room to enter gracefully knowing that he waited within to see her. She knew nothing about such civilized rituals of seduction. She only knew that she awoke in the middle of the night with her hands clenched into fists and her body on fire and her heart beating so harshly that her head felt as though it would split with the pain and force of her rushing blood.

But that wasn't the worst.

The worst was the emptiness growing inside Janna, the feeling of having lost something unspeakably rare and beautiful. It was the certainty that where she had once gone through life alone and content, now she would go through life alone and lonely. She was doomed to remember a time when she had touched love and had had it slide like sunlight through her outstretched fingers, leaving bleak night behind to pool in her palms until it overflowed and kept on overflowing, consuming the remaining light, consuming her.

A velvety muzzle nudged Janna gently, then more insistently. She started and realized that she had been staring at Ty once more, her breath held in anticipation of . . . something. Yet there was nothing to anticipate now but one more day, one day worse than yesterday, more light sliding through her outstretched fingers, more darkness pooling in her empty soul.

With a stifled cry Janna looked away from Ty again. She tried to make herself breathe deeply. It was impossible. Her body was so taut that she vibrated like a bow being drawn by too powerful an archer, the wood bent so harshly that breakage was only a breath away . . . so she refused to breathe.

*I can't be with Ty like this. I can't bear it. It's worse than being alone. It's like watching Papa die all over again, all the life, all the possibilities, all the laughter, all the love, everything sliding away beyond my reach.*

Something thumped soundly against Janna's chest. She made a startled noise and looked down. The thump had come from Zebra's muzzle. The mare was getting impatient for her mistress's attention.

"H-hello, girl," Janna said, stammering slightly, unable to prevent the telltale trembling.

The catch in Janna's voice made Ty feel as though a knife had flicked over an open wound. Like her body, her voice said that she wanted him until she shook with it. He wanted her in the same way, wanted her until he felt as if his guts were being drawn through the eye of a red-hot needle.

And he wouldn't take her.

"Easy, son," Ty said, making his voice as gentle as he could under the circumstances.

Lucifer eyed Ty warily, telling the man that his attempt to be reassuring hadn't been very convincing.

"Let's take a look at that wound," Ty murmured, smoothing his hands over the stallion's warm hide. "Easy, son, easy. I'm not going to hurt you."

The echo of Ty's reassurances to Janna by the pool pierced the silence between the two of them with uneasiness. He refused to look at her, knowing that if he did he would see in her eyes the sweet, consuming wildfire of her passion. He had never touched a woman as he had Janna that night; even the memory of it brought an almost shocked disbelief...and a searing hunger to know her that way again, to bathe in her like a warm pool, washing away the impurities of the years in which he hadn't known that he could touch his own soul by soaring deep within Janna's sensual generosity.

"You'll have a scar," Ty said tightly, looking at Lucifer's haunch, "but that's little enough for a bullet wound to leave as a calling card."

Silently Ty wondered what wound would be left on his own life by the much softer, much more agonizing brush of a satin butterfly's wings.

"Soon Lucifer will be strong enough to go to Wyoming," Janna said, speaking her worst fear aloud.

"Yes." Ty's tone was curt. "You won't be able to take much except clothes, but your books should be safe enough here. When things settle down in the territory, you can..." His voice died. "I'll see that you get your books. I'll see that you get everything you need for the kind of life you deserve."

Janna turned away from Ty, hiding her face, not letting him see in her expression the decision she had made not to go to Wyoming. She really had no choice but to stay. Instinctively she knew it would be easier to live alone in the valley than anywhere on earth with Ty always within reach, never touching her.

"Janna?" he asked roughly.

After a few seconds she said calmly, "I'll do what has to be done."

It sounded like agreement, yet...

Ty stared at the back of Janna's head and wished that he could read her mind as easily as she seemed to read the animals and the clouds. And himself.

"The sooner we start, the better," he said.

Janna said nothing.

"We should get out of here before the Army decides to move against Cascabel."

She nodded as though they were discussing nothing more important than the shape of distant clouds.

"We'll have to take it slow until I can find a horse to ride. Even if Lucifer would accept me as a rider—which I doubt—he should have another week or so without any strain." Ty waited. Janna said nothing. "Janna?"

Auburn hair flashed in the sun as she turned to face him. Her eyes were as clear as rain—and haunted by elusive shadows.

"Yes, it would be better for Lucifer not to have to take the strain of a rider for a few more days."

"That's not what I meant and you know it."

Janna hesitated, then shrugged. "The first days will be slow and dangerous. Walking is always slower than riding."

"You're coming with me," Ty said bluntly.

"Of course. Lucifer would never leave the valley without Zebra," Janna said, turning away again, stroking the mare's dust-colored hide with loving hands.

"And Zebra won't leave the valley without you," Ty said.

"She never has before."

Ty's scalp prickled. Every instinct he had told him that Janna was sliding away from him, eluding his attempts to hold her nearby. She was vanishing as he watched.

"Say it," he demanded.

"Say what?"

"Say that you're coming to Wyoming with me."

Janna closed her eyes. Hidden beneath Zebra's mane, her hands clenched into fists. "I'm leaving the valley with you."

"And you're coming to Wyoming with me."

"Don't."

"Don't what?"

"Force me to lie to you."

"What does that mean? You can't stay here forever and you know it!"

"I can't stay on your brother's ranch in Wyoming, either."

"You won't have to stay there forever."

"Just long enough to set a marriage snare for some man who's too stupid to know the difference between true silk and an ordinary sow's ear?" Janna offered bitterly.

"Dammit, that's not what I said!"

"You don't have to say it. I did." She swung onto Zebra's back with a quick motion that was eloquent of wild emotions barely restrained. "I promised to help you get your stallion. You promised to teach me how to please a man. Those promises were made and kept on Black Plateau. Wyoming was no part of it."

Abruptly Zebra exploded into a gallop.

In seething silence Ty watched while the mare swept toward the far end of the valley where Indian ruins slowly eroded back into the stony land from which they had come. Janna had spent a lot of time in the ancient place since they had brought the stallion into the valley. Ty had thought Janna's sudden interest in the ruins was an attempt to remove Zebra's distracting presence while he spent hours with Lucifer, accustoming the wild stallion to a man's voice and touch.

But now Ty suspected that Janna had been trying to wean Lucifer of Zebra's company so that the stallion wouldn't balk at being separated when the time came for Ty to head for Wyoming—without Janna.

"It won't work!" Ty called savagely. "You're coming to Wyoming with me if I have to tie you over Zebra's back like a sack of grain!"

Nothing answered Ty but the drumroll of thunder from the mare's speedy, fleeing hooves.

Ty's words echoed mockingly in his own ears. He knew that all Janna had to do was ride off while he slept or worked with Lucifer. On foot he couldn't catch her. Even if she didn't ride Zebra, Ty wasn't much better off. Black Plateau was an open book to Janna; she could hide among its countless ravines the way a shadow could hide among the thousand shades of night.

He would find her eventually, of course. Assuming Cascabel didn't find them first.

# Chapter Thirty-Four

The stallion's clarion call resonated through the valley, echoing and reechoing from stone walls, telling anything with ears that an enemy had appeared in the tiny, concealed Eden.

Ty dropped his dinner plate, grabbed his carbine and sprinted for the willows. Within seconds he was under cover, but he didn't slow his speed. Running, twisting around slender limbs, leaping roots and rocks, heedless of noise, Ty raced toward the entrance of the valley.

When he arrived at the edge of the willows' dense cover, he stopped and watched the meadow for signs of man. Nothing moved near the cleft, which was the valley's only access to the outer world. Carbine at his shoulder, Ty stared down the metal barrel at the expanse of grass. Nothing moved in the emptiness but the wind.

Lucifer's wild, savage call to arms came again, making the skin of Ty's scalp ripple in primal response. The stallion was far up the valley, out of sight in the narrow bend where the Indian ruins were hidden. Neither Zebra nor Janna was in sight.

Desperately Ty wanted to call out to Janna and reassure himself that she was safe. He kept silent. He didn't want her to give away her position to a skulking renegade.

Ty had no doubt that the stallion's savage cry had been triggered by the presence of a strange human being. In the weeks since he had come to the valley, Ty had never seen signs of anything larger than a rabbit within the valley itself. Of all the animals in the vast land, only man had the curiosity—or the need—to follow the narrow, winding slot through stone-lined darkness into the canyon's sunlight.

*Stay down in the ruins, Janna,* Ty prayed silently. *You'll be safe there. The Indians avoid the spirit places.*

The birds that usually wheeled and darted over the meadow were silent and hidden. Ty's narrowed glance raked the valley again, looking for any sign of the intruder.

Suddenly Lucifer burst out from the area of the ruins into the larger meadow. Zebra was running at his side. When the stallion dug in and stopped, the mare kept galloping, stopping only when she was several hundred feet beyond. Lucifer reared and screamed again, hooves slashing the air, putting himself between the mare and whatever danger threatened.

As the stallion's feral challenge faded, the cry of a hawk soared above the silence, followed by Janna's voice calling what could have been Ty's name. He turned toward the sound. Over the metal barrel of the carbine, he saw Janna coming from the area of the ruins. A man was walking behind her. Reflexively Ty took slack from the trigger, let out his breath and waited for the trail to turn, giving him a view of the stranger.

It was Mad Jack.

Gently Ty's finger eased from the trigger as he lowered the carbine from his shoulder. When he emerged from the cover of the willows and trotted out into the open and across the meadow, Lucifer neighed shrilly, as though to warn him of danger. Ty turned aside long enough to reassure the stallion.

"Thanks for the warning, but it's just a crazy old prospector," Ty said, talking soothingly to the stallion.

Lucifer snorted and stamped nervously but permitted Ty to stroke his neck. Even then the stallion never stopped watching the two figures that were coming out of the ruins. When the people began walking toward him, Lucifer spun and ran away, sweeping Zebra before him. Ty turned and waited for Janna and Mad Jack.

"Right fine lookout you have there," Mad Jack said, holding out his hand for Ty to shake.

Smiling, Ty took the old man's hand. He was surprised at how fine Mad Jack's bones were beneath his scarred, leathery skin. The prospector's grip was a quick, light pressure, as though any more would be painful.

"Run out of stomach medicine again?" Ty asked, although he suspected that medicine was the last thing on the other man's mind.

Mad Jack laughed. He knew what Ty was thinking—that he had come to check up on Janna, not to replenish his supply of medicine.

"You be half-right, son. I come to check on my gal."

"Well, you can see that she's bright eyed and bushy tailed," Ty said dryly.

Mad Jack's faded eyes appraised Janna with a frankness that made her flush.

"You be right," he said, fishing in his pocket for his chewing tobacco. "'Course, mares in foal look right sassy for the first few months, too."

"Don't beat around the bush," Janna said in a combination of embarrassment and exasperation. "Just say anything that's on what passes for your mind."

"I make it a habit to do just that. So are you?"

"Am I . . . ?"

"Pregnant."

Red flags burned on Janna's cheeks. "Jack!"

"Well, are you?"

"No."

"You sure?"

"Yes," she said succinctly. "As sure as I am that water runs downhill."

Jack rubbed his face and sighed. "Well, durn it all anyway. That's gonna fuss things up considerable."

"Have you been drinking?" Janna demanded.

"No." He sliced off a big hunk of tobacco, stuffed it in his mouth and said, "I been thinkin', which is a horse of another color entirely. Both of 'em make my head hurt, I'll give you that."

"What," Ty asked, "is going on?"

"Mad Jack has been thinking," Janna said. "That's a serious matter."

"Damn straight it is," Jack agreed. "Last time I got to thinkin', I took old Jimbo—he was my mule—out of the traces, hiked my leg across his back and headed west. Nary a word to my wife since then, nor my kids, neither. Thinkin' is right hard on a man."

"Sounds like it wasn't real easy on your wife, either," Ty said dryly.

"That's what I got to thinkin' about," Mad Jack agreed. "I been pokin' in rocks for years, tryin' to find the one glory hole what's got my name on it. Well, I don't rightly think I'm gonna find it this side of heaven and more 'n likely I'm a-headed straight for hell." Jack spit, wiped his mouth and continued. "Now, ol' Charity—that's my wife—probably died of some woman's complaint or another by now, but my kids was right healthy grasshoppers. Some of 'em are bound to be alive, or their kids. An' that's why I'm unhappy that you ain't pregnant," he added, pointing at Janna.

Ty looked sideways at Janna. She was watching Mad Jack as though he had just sprouted horns or wings or both.

"I don't understand," she said flatly.

"Hell, gal, it's as plain as the color of the sky. I got gold to give to my kids, an' I ain't gonna leave this here country and you can't get out the gold alone, an' if you ain't pregnant, you ain't got no stud hoss to protect you, an' my gold won't get delivered an' my kids won't know their pappy ever thought about 'em."

Janna opened her mouth. Nothing came out. She swallowed and tried again, but it was too late. Ty was already speaking.

"Let me be sure I understand," Ty said smoothly, seizing the opportunity with both hands. "You have gold you want taken to your children. You thought if Janna were pregnant, we'd be leaving the valley and we could deliver the gold to the fort for you."

Mad Jack frowned. "I had in mind something more... friendly like than the fort. See, I ain't sure where my kin are no more. Now, if'n I go hire some man at the fort I don't know from Adam's off ox, how can I be sure my gold gets to my kin once I turn my back?"

Ty tried to say something. It was impossible. Mad Jack had been thinking, and the result of that unusual exercise had made the future clear to him.

"I can't be sure," Mad Jack said forcefully, answering his own question. "But if'n I give the gold to a friend, I can rest easy. You get my drift, son? Now, you ain't my friend. No offense, just the God's truth. Janna here, she's my friend. If'n she told me she'd get the gold to my kids, I know she would or die trying.

"And that's the crux of the matter. She's game but she ain't real big. Ain't mean, neither. Carryin' gold needs someone who's mountain big and snake mean."

"Like me?" Ty suggested.

"Yep."

"But I'm not your friend. No offense."

"None taken, son. It's the God's truth. But if'n you was Janna's man, an' she took the gold, you'd go along to protect her. Then she'd be safe and the gold, too. But she ain't pregnant so you ain't her man an' that means my gold ain't got no man protectin' it once it leaves here."

"The fact that I'm *not* pregnant should reassure you that Ty is an honorable man," Janna pointed out quickly. "If he agreed to take your gold, you could be sure that he wouldn't keep it for himself."

Mad Jack made a sound that was a cross between a mutter and a snort. "Hell's bells, gal, if you ain't pregnant, it ain't because you was sayin' no, it's because he weren't askin'. That may say somethin' about his honor right enough, but it sure as hellfire don't reassure me none about his manly, er, notions."

A wave of scarlet humiliation went up Janna's face as she realized that Mad Jack knew how much she had wanted Ty to notice her as a woman. When the blood ebbed Janna was very pale. All that kept her from turning and walking away was the need she sensed in Mad Jack, a need that was driving the old man far beyond the boundaries of even his customary bluntness. She looked at the prospector's face and saw the yellowish pallor underlying the weathered skin. Although he had always been wiry, now he seemed almost frail. He looked . . . desperate.

Thinking could be hard on a man, especially when he was old and ill and had only one chance to right past wrongs.

Janna gathered her courage, ignored her own raw feelings and touched Mad Jack's arm reassuringly. "There's nothing wrong with Ty's sense of honor or his 'notions' or anything else," she said with a fierce kind of calm. "He took what I was offering and decided it wasn't for him, that's all."

"Janna—" Ty began.

"What?" she demanded, interrupting without looking away from the old man. "I didn't say it as fancy or as long-winded as Ty did, but that doesn't change what happened, does it? I wanted him. He took me. He doesn't want me anymore. It's an old story. From the books I've read, I'd say it's the oldest story on earth. But that doesn't mean one single thing against Ty's honor, Jack. He didn't lie to me, not even the way you said a woman-hungry man would. No pretty words, no fancy promises, nothing but Ty and me and the night.''

Mad Jack was quiet for a long moment before he sighed and patted Janna's hand. ''I'm sorry, gal.''

''Don't be. I'm not. When I go back and read that trunk full of books again this winter, I'll understand them better. That's nothing to be sorry over. It will make spring come faster for me. Then Zebra will have a foal for me to fuss over and by the end of summer I'll be riding Zebra again and we'll fly over the plateau like a hawk's shadow and then autumn lighting will come again and thunder and the mustangs' breath will be like earthbound clouds and snow will turn the night silver and I'll make up stories about the shadows my campfire throws against the stone cliff, people and places and memories coming to life . . .'' Janna's voice faded into a whisper. ''Don't be sorry.''

Ty tried to speak and found he had no voice. Janna's words were in his own throat, crowding out speech, filling him until he ached. He clenched his teeth against a sadness as piercing as it was unexpected.

''You can't stay,'' Ty said hoarsely.

It was as though he hadn't spoken. Janna didn't look away from the old prospector, who was watching her and shaking his head slowly.

''He's speakin' God's truth,'' Mad Jack said. ''You can't stay here, gal. Not no more. I been thinkin' about that, too. Spent a lot of time on it. A lot of my gold belongs to you.''

''Don't be ridic—'' began Janna.

''No, young'un,'' Mad Jack said, cutting across her objections. ''You jest button up and listen to an old man what's seen more of this here world's good an' bad than you have. Your pappy gave me money more times than either of us counted.''

''And you've given us gold as long as I can remember,'' Janna said quickly.

Mad Jack grunted. "What about the time you found me all broke up at the bottom of a gulch and you set my bones and patched me up and you were no more than a kid in men's britches? You saved my life, you keep my stomach from eatin' a hole in itself, and you listen to my stories no matter how often I tell 'em. Half my gold is yours and that's flat. Should of give it to you years ago so you could get out and get a life for yourself, but I liked knowin' there was one soul in this godforsaken land that wouldn't kill me for my gold."

"Thank you, but I enjoyed your company as much as you enjoyed mine," Janna said. "Any gold you have is yours."

"You ain't been listening, gal. It ain't safe for you here no more." Mad Jack turned to Ty. "Beggars can't be choosers, son. I got a proposition. You be willin' to listen?"

"I'm willing."

"This here gal is game, but game ain't gonna get the job done. Injuns been comin' into the country like rain. Soldiers' scouts been comin', too. Everybody's sayin' that the Army is gonna clean out that rattlesnake's nest once an' for all. Cascabel's been fastin' an' prayin' up a storm. A few days back a vision come to him. He's gonna lead his renegades to a big victory—but not until Janna's hair hangs from his war lance."

Ty's whole body changed subtly, as though Cascabel himself had just appeared at the slot entrance to the valley. Mad Jack measured the change and smiled beneath his ragged beard; Ty might not be Janna's man, but he wasn't about to go off and leave her to fend for herself against the likes of Cascabel.

"Well, she was right about the honor," Mad Jack said. "An' I'll take her word about the rest of you bein' man enough. Here's the deal, son. You get her out of here and to a safe place, and my gold with her, and a quarter of my gold is yours."

"Keep your money, old man," Ty said savagely. "I'll get Janna out of here and to a safe place. You've got my word on it."

Mad Jack chewed for a few moments, turned aside and spat a brown stream into the grass. Turning back, he wiped his beard on his frayed shirtsleeves.

"Suit yerself. Just so's you get her shuck of this place, and my gold with her. She'll need her quarter so's she won't have to marry no mean lard-butt town widower nor sell her company to strangers just to put beans on the table."

"I'm not going to leave just because you—" Janna began hotly.

"Shut yer mouth, gal," Mad Jack said, giving her a fierce glare. "You ain't dumb so don't get to actin' like it. Only reason Cascabel ain't caught you is he ain't took a hard notion before now. Well, he done been took somethin' fierce. Long as that evil son of a rattlesnake is alive, this country ain't safe for chick nor child."

Janna closed her eyes and fought against the ice condensing in her stomach. "Are you sure that Cascabel is after my hair?"

"Dead sure. Sound carries right good in some of these canyons. He bragged on his intentions to Ned."

"The saloon keeper?" Ty asked. "What was he doing with Cascabel?"

"Sellin' rifles, same as always. But don't worry, son. He won't be doin' it no more. He upped the ante once too often. Cascabel took Ned's rifles, then he took his liver, lights and hair."

Janna shuddered.

Mad Jack turned aside, spat and straightened, pinning Ty with a shrewd glance. "You break that stud hoss yet?"

"No."

"Better get to it, son. Man on foot carryin' gold ain' gonna do nothin' out there but die."

# Chapter Thirty-Five

My God." Ty knelt in the dirt and gritty dust of the ruins and looked up at Janna for a long moment. With hands that were none too steady, he refastened the old saddlebags. "It's gold. All of it. Sweet Jesus. When Mad Jack talked about gold, I thought he meant a few pokes, not two big saddlebags jammed full to overflowing." Ty looked at his hands as though hardly able to believe the wealth that they had held. "Pure. Gold."

Ty lifted the bags and stood with a grunt of effort. Janna watched him with wide gray eyes. His words had meant little to her. Even the sight of the gold hadn't made it seem real to her; but watching the saddlebags make Ty's muscular arms bunch and quiver made the gold's weight all too real. She had tested that male strength, seen Ty's power and stamina and determination; and she knew that it wouldn't be enough.

*Man on foot carryin' gold ain't gonna do nothin' out here but die.*

"You can't take it all," Janna said.

"Doesn't weigh much more than you," Ty said, "but lead weight is the hardest kind to carry." He shook his head in continuing disbelief. "When I get back to camp and get my hands on that crazy old man, I'm going to ask him how the hell he got these saddlebags into the valley."

"Maybe he's been bringing the gold in a poke at a time."

Ty grunted. "If so, he didn't leave any more tracks between here and the slot than the wind. Anyhow, it doesn't matter. I'm not taking a quarter of his gold and he's not staying behind to get spitted and roasted by Cascabel. Like it or not, that old man's coming out with us."

Janna didn't argue or point out the difficulties in taking a third person when there was only one horse to ride. She felt as Ty did about leaving Mad Jack behind.

Finally Janna had realized that staying in the valley was the equivalent of a death sentence. Mad Jack was correct: the only reason she had been safe during the past years was that she had been more trouble to track down than she was worth to Cascabel. That was no longer true. Cascabel now believed that she was all that was standing between himself and the conquest of the Utah Territory.

Unhappily Janna followed Ty as he picked his way out of the crumbling ruins that filled the small side canyon. Once out in the meadow again, the walking was easier. Lucifer and Zebra waited out in the middle of the grass. The stallion was restive. He kept watching the willows that fringed the valley as though he expected a predator to leap out. Zebra was calmly grazing, not nearly as upset by Mad Jack's presence as Lucifer was.

"We could rig a surcingle for Zebra," Janna said, spotting the mare. "That way she could carry the saddlebags and your pack while we walked."

Ty gave her a sideways look that was little more than a flash of green.

"Zebra can't carry both of us and the gold, too," Janna pointed out.

"She can carry you and the gold if it comes to that. All you have to do is get her used to a hackamore and a surcingle."

"But what about you?"

"That's my problem."

White teeth sank into Janna's lower lip as she bit off her retort. She closed her eyes and silently asked for Lucifer's forgiveness. But there was really no choice. If he could be broken to ride, it had to be done.

"Be as gentle with Lucifer as you can," she said in a low voice, "but don't hurt yourself in the process, Ty. Promise me that you'll be careful. He's so strong and so quick." She looked at the stallion standing poised in the meadow, his big body rippling with strength, his ears erect, his head up, sniffing the wind. "And he's so wild. Much wilder than Zebra."

"Not with you. He comes up and puts his head in your hands like a big hound."

"Then why won't you let me be the one to break him?" Janna's voice was tightened by fear and exasperation. She and Ty had argued about just this thing since the moment Mad Jack had pointed out that a man on foot didn't have much chance of surviving.

"God save me from stubborn women," muttered Ty. "I've spent the last half hour telling you why. That stud's big enough to buck you into next week and you know it. I sure as hell know it! You're quick and determined as they come, but that's no substitute for sheer strength if Lucifer goes crazy the first time he feels a rider's weight."

Impatiently Ty shifted the slippery leather connecting the saddlebags. When the bags were in a more secure position over his shoulder he continued his argument. "Besides, you'll have your hands full talking Zebra into a hackamore and surcingle. She's not going to like that belly strap worth a damn. I'm going to rig stirrups for you, too. She won't like those, either, but it's the only way you and that old man stand a chance of staying on if we have to run for it. One of you has to be stuck on tight enough so the other has something to hang on to."

Janna opened her mouth to object but didn't. She had lost this argument, too, and she knew it. She hadn't wanted to put restraints on Zebra, yet there was little rational choice. If their lives were going to depend on their mounts, the riders had to have more than intangible communication with their horses. Particularly if she and Mad Jack were going to be riding double.

"Once we get to Wyoming, you can go back to riding Zebra any way you want," Ty said. "Hell, you can let her run wild again for all of me. But not until then, Janna. Not until you're safe."

Closing her eyes, she nodded in defeat. "I know."

Ty gave Janna a surprised look. He had expected a fierce battle over the necessity of introducing any real control over Zebra. Janna's unhappy expression told him just how much the concession cost her. Without thinking about his vow not to touch her again, he took Janna's hand and squeezed it gently.

"It's all right, sugar. Even with a hackamore and surcingle, you aren't forcing Zebra to obey you. You aren't strong enough to force an animal her size. Anytime Zebra lets you up on her back, it's because she wants you there. All the hackamore will do is make sure Zebra knows where you want her to go. After that, it's up to her. It's always that way, no matter what kind of tack the horse wears. Cooperation, not coercion."

The feel of Ty's palm sliding over her own as they walked was like being brushed by gentle lightning. Janna's whole body tingled with the simple pleasure of his touch.

"Thank you," she said, blinking back sudden tears.

"For what?"

"For making me feel better about putting a hackamore on Zebra. And—" Janna squeezed his hand in return "—for understanding. It's frightening having to give up the only home I've ever known."

Knowing he shouldn't, unable to prevent himself, Ty lifted Janna's hand to his face. The long weeks during which he hadn't shaved had softened his beard to the texture of coarse silk. He rubbed his cheek against her palm, inhaled her scent and called himself twelve kinds of fool for not touching her in the past four weeks—and fifty kinds of fool for touching her now.

She wasn't a whore or a convenience. She was a woman who appealed to him more with every moment he spent in her company. Her sensuality was like quicksand, luring him deeper and deeper until he was trapped beyond hope of escape. But she didn't mean to be a trap any more than he meant to be trapped. He was sure of it. That was what made her feminine allure all the more irresistible.

With aching tenderness Ty kissed Janna's palm before he forced himself to let go of her hand. The loss of her touch was a physical pain. The realization appalled him.

*God in heaven. I'm as stupid as that damned unicorn being drawn to his captivity and not able to pull away to save his life, much less his freedom.*

Abruptly Ty shifted the heavy gold to his other shoulder, using the saddlebags as a barrier between himself and Janna. She barely noticed. She was still caught in the instant when his hand had been sharply withdrawn. It had been like having her sense of balance betray her on a steep trail, leaving her floundering. She looked at Ty questioningly, only to see a forbidding expression that promised unhappiness for anyone asking questions of a personal nature, especially questions such as *Why haven't you touched me? Why did you touch me just now? Why did you stop as though you could no longer bear my touch?*

"Will you take the gold on Lucifer?" Janna asked after silence. She forced her voice to be almost normal, although her palm still felt his caresses as though Ty's beard had been black flames burning through her flesh to the bone beneath.

"He's strong enough to take the gold and me both and will run rings around any other horse."

"Then you'll have to use a surcingle on him, too, either for stirrups or to hold the saddlebags in place or both."

"The thought had occurred to me," Ty said dryly. "First time he feels that strap bite into his barrel should be real interesting."

Ty shifted the gold on his shoulder again and said no more. In silence they continued toward the camp beneath the red stone overhang. Janna felt no need to speak, for the simple reason that there was little more to say. Either Lucifer would accept a rider or he wouldn't. If he didn't, the odds for survival against Cascabel were too small to be called even a long shot.

"We have to talk Mad Jack into leaving the gold behind," Janna said finally.

Ty had been thinking the same thing. He also had been thinking about how he would feel in Mad Jack's shoes—old, ill, eaten up with guilt for past mistakes, seeing one chance to make it all right and die with a clean conscience.

"It's his shot at heaven," Ty said.

"It's our ticket straight to hell."

"Try convincing him."

"I'm going to do just that."

Janna's chin came up and she quickened her pace, leaving Ty behind. But when she strode into camp, all that was there of Mad Jack was a piece of paper held down by a stone. On the paper he had painfully written the closest town to the farm he had abandoned so many years ago. Beneath that were the names of his five children.

"Jack!" Janna called. "Wait! Come back!"

No voice answered her. She turned and sprinted toward the meadow.

"What's wrong?" Ty demanded.

"He's gone!"

"That crafty old son of a bitch." Ty swore and dropped the heavy saddlebags with a thump. "He knew what would happen when we found out how much gold there was to ha out of here. He took our promise to get his gold to his children and then he ran like the hounds of hell were after him."

Janna raised her hands to her mouth. A hawk's wild cry keened across the meadow. Zebra's head came up and she began trotting toward them.

"What are you going to do?" Ty asked.

"Find him. He's too old to have gotten far in this short a time."

Ty all but threw Janna up on top of Zebra. Instants later the mare was galloping on a long diagonal that would end at the narrow entrance to the valley.

By the time they arrived at the slot, Zebra was beginning to sweat both from the pace and from the urgency she sensed in her rider. Janna flung herself off the mare and ran to the twilight shadow of the slot canyon.

Heedless of the uncertain footing, she plunged forward. She didn't call Mad Jack's name, however; she didn't want the call to echo where it might be overheard by passing renegades.

No more than fifty feet into the slot, Janna sensed that something was wrong. She froze in place, wondering what her instincts were trying to tell her.

There was no unexpected sound. No unexpected scent. No moving shadows. No sign that she wasn't alone.

"That's what's wrong," Janna whispered. "There's no sign at all!"

She went onto her hands and knees, but no matter how hard she examined the ground, the only traces of any passage over the dry stream course were those she herself had just left.

Zebra's head flew up in surprise when Janna hurtled back into the valley from the slot.

"Easy, girl. Easy," Janna said breathlessly.

She swung onto the mare. Within moments a rhythmic thunder was again rolling from beneath Zebra's hooves. When she galloped past Lucifer, he lifted his head for an instant, then resumed biting off succulent mouthfuls of grass, undisturbed by the pair racing by. In past summers, Zebra and Janna often had galloped around while he grazed.

"Well?" Ty demanded when the mare galloped into the campsite.

"He's still in the valley. You take the left side and I'll take the right."

Ty looked out over the meadow. "Waste of time. He's not here."

"That's impossible. There's not one mark in that little slot canyon that I didn't put there myself. He's still here."

"Then he's between us and Lucifer."

Janna looked to the place where the stallion grazed no more than a hundred feet away. There wasn't enough cover to hide a rabbit, much less a man.

"Why do you say that?" she asked.

"Wind is from that direction. Lucifer stopped testing the wind and settled down to graze about ten minutes ago."

Janna's urgency drained from her, leaving her deflated. If the stallion didn't scent Mad Jack it was because Mad Jack wasn't around to be scented.

Grimly Janna looked at the heavy saddlebags, an old man's legacy to a life he had abandoned years before. It was too heavy a burden—but it was theirs to bear. Her only consolation was that Ty's share, plus her own, should be enough to buy his dream. She didn't know how much silken ladies cost on the open market, but surely sixty pounds of gold would be enough.

Ty's expression as he looked at the saddlebags was every bit as grim as Janna's. His consolation, however, was different. He figured that Janna's thirty pounds of gold, plus his thirty, would be more than enough to ensure that she would never have to submit her soft body to any man in order to survive.

# Chapter Thirty-Six

Lucifer's ears flattened and he screamed his displeasure, lashing out with his hind feet. Ty made no attempt to hold the mustang. He just ducked and ran for cover. The stallion exploded into wicked bucking as he tried to dislodge the surcingle Ty had cut from the buffalo robe in Janna's trunk. When bucking didn't work, the stallion tried outrunning the strap and the flapping rope stirrups.

By the time Lucifer realized that he couldn't outrun the contraption clinging to his back—and that he wasn't being attacked by whatever was on him—the stallion's neck and flanks were white with lather and he was breathing hard. Janna wasn't surprised at the horse's signs of exertion; Lucifer had been racing flat out around the valley for nearly half an hour.

"Lord, but that's one strong horse," she said.

Ty grunted. He wasn't looking forward to the next part of the stallion's education, the part when he felt a man's weight on his back for the first time. Ty approached the big mustang slowly, speaking in a low voice.

"Yeah, I know, it's a hell of a world when you can't outrun all of life's traps and entanglements. But it isn't as bad as it seems to you right now," Ty murmured, stroking the stallion. "Ask Zebra. She took to the surcingle and stirrups like the good-hearted lady she is."

Lucifer snorted and butted his head against Ty as though to draw the man's attention to the irritation caused by the unwanted straps.

"Sorry, son. I'll rub away the itches but I'm not taking off that surcingle. I had enough trouble getting the damned thing on you in the first place."

Janna had a hard time not saying a heartfelt "amen." Watching Ty risk his life under Lucifer's hooves in the process of getting the surcingle in place had been the most difficult thing she had ever done. She had both admired Ty's gentle persistence and regretted ever asking him not to use restraints on the powerful stallion.

Ty continued petting and talking to Lucifer until the horse calmed down. Gradually Ty's strokes became different. He leaned hard on his hands as he moved them over the horse, concentrating mainly on the portion of Lucifer's back just behind the withers, where a man would ride. At first the stallion moved away from the pressure. Ty followed, talking patiently, leaning gently and then with more force, trying to accustom the mustang to his weight.

Again, Janna watched the process with a combination of anxiety and admiration. Most of the men she had known would have snubbed Lucifer's nose to a post, twisted his ear in one hand and then climbed aboard in a rush. Once the rider was in the saddle, the horse would have been released and spurs would have begun raking tender hide. The bucking that would have followed was inevitable. So was the fact that some horses broken that way weren't trustworthy. They tended to wait until the rider was relaxed and then unload him with a few wicked twists of their body.

Yet Ty had to be able to trust Lucifer with his life, and he had promised Janna to treat the stallion as gently as possible and still get the job done.

Breath came in sharply and then stuck in Janna's throat while she watched Ty shift his weight until his boots no longer touched the ground. Lucifer moved nervously, turned around in a circle rapidly several times, then accepted the fact that Ty's soothing voice was coming from a new direction. After a few minutes the stallion began grazing rather irritably, ignoring the fact that Ty was draped belly down over his back.

By the time two more hours passed, Ty had gotten Lucifer to the point of not flinching or even particularly noticing when Ty's weight shifted from the ground to the horse's back. Janna had seen Ty creep into position, moving so slowly that every muscle stood out as he balanced against gravity and the mustang's wary, mincing steps. When Ty finally eased from his stomach to a rider's normal seat, Janna wanted to shout a cheer. All that kept her quiet was an even bigger desire not to spook the mustang.

For the stallion's part, Lucifer simply twitched his ears and kept grazing when Ty sat upright. The horse's whole stance proclaimed that the bizarre actions of his human companion no longer disturbed him.

Elation spread through Ty when he felt the calm strength of the stallion beneath him. More than ever, Ty was certain that Lucifer had been gently bred, raised by humans, and then had escaped from his owners to run free before any brand of ownership had been put on his shiny black hide.

"You're a beauty," Ty murmured, praising the stallion with voice and hands. "Does part of you know that you were born and bred to be a man's friend?"

Lucifer lipped grass casually, stopping every few minutes to sniff the wind. Ty made no attempt to guide the stallion with the hackamore. He simply sat and let the mustang graze in a normal manner. When Lucifer moved in the course of grazing, he walked a bit awkwardly at first, unaccustomed to the weight settled just behind his withers. But by the time the sun was tracing the last part of its downward arc in the west, Lucifer was moving with his former confidence, adjusting automatically to the presence of a rider. Occasionally he would turn and sniff Ty's boot as though to say, "What, are you still here? Well, never mind. You're not in the way."

Ty's answer was always the same, praise and a hand stroking sleek muscles. When Lucifer responded to a firm, steady pull on the hackamore by turning in that direction, the praise and the pats were redoubled. When the pulls were accompanied by gentle nudges with Ty's heels, Lucifer learned to move forward. When the pressure on the hackamore was a steady pull backward, the stallion learned to stop.

"That's it for now, son," Ty said, sliding carefully from Lucifer's back. "You get the rest of the day off."

The stallion snorted and sidestepped at the release of the pressure from his back, but that was all. When Ty raised his hands and tied the hackamore lead rope securely around the black neck, Lucifer didn't even flinch.

"You're a shining wonder," Ty murmured.

Lucifer promptly put his head against Ty's chest and rubbed hard, trying to dislodge the hackamore. Laughing softly, Ty began soothing away the itches that came from wearing leather against hot, sweaty hide.

"Sorry, son. I'm going to leave all this gear in place. It won't hurt you and it will save me a hell of a lot of trouble come tomorrow, when the lessons resume. But right now you've earned a good graze and I've earned some time in the Tub. Get along, son. Go over and berate Zebra about the crazy humans she sicced on you."

A few minutes later Janna looked up from sorting herbs and saw that Lucifer was riderless. For a moment her heart turned over in fear. Then she realized that Ty had probably dismounted of his own accord, giving both himself and Lucifer a rest. Janna turned back to her herbs, testing the leaves' dryness. Fragrances both pungent and mild rose from the rustling herbs as she set some aside to be taken from the valley and designated others to be made into tinctures or lotions or balms. She knew that she wouldn't have

time to properly prepare more than a fraction of the herbs
and seeds she had collected, but that didn't stop her. Working with them gave her hands something to do besides remember how it had felt to touch Ty and her mind something
to do besides think about leaving the valley behind . . . and
then leaving Ty behind, as well.

*Stop thinking about it,* Janna told herself urgently. *And
don't think about Mad Jack probably being sick or Cascabel probably waiting to kill me. Don't think about anything but these herbs. I can't affect Mad Jack or Ty or that
cruel renegade. I can make lotions, though. I can make a
batch of stomach medicine and leave it behind. I can do the
same with the other medicines. I can do anything I want
while I'm still here.*

*Except seduce Ty.*

Herbs and seeds tangled and fell to the ground as Janna's
hands jerked at the thought of seducing Ty. She bit back
unhappy words and picked up the mess. The second time
she thought of making love with Ty the same thing happened. Her fingers were just too shaky to deal with anything as finicky as preparing medicines.

"Well, I can at least get some of that sulfur water from
the high spring," she muttered to herself. "Surely that
shouldn't be too difficult for my clumsy hands."

Janna grabbed a small metal pot and set off toward the
Tub. In the past weeks the trail had become rather well
beaten. Both she and Ty loved to float in the warm water
and watch the clouds change shape overhead. They did their
floating alone, but the thought of what had happened the
one time she and Ty had been together in the Tub nearly
made Janna drop the small pot. She would have given a
great deal to be allowed again to touch Ty so tenderly, so
intimately, so wildly. Just once more.

Just once before they left the valley and never saw each
other again.

When Janna entered the narrowest part of the valley, the hot springs' steamy silence brought an onslaught of memories. The lush profusion of soft-leaved plants, the sparkling condensation of water on black rock, the vague sulfur odor underlying that of earth and sun and greenery, everything combined in her mind to create a dizzying mixture of memory and desire.

And then she saw Ty rise out of the nearest pool and stand naked on the sandy shore. Silver streamers of mist lifted from his hot skin, moving as he moved, their fragile grace in sharp contrast to the bunch and ripple of his powerful muscles. Unable to move, Janna simply stared at Ty, transfixed by the pagan beauty of the man, memorizing every pattern of water curling down through the dark hair of his chest and torso and thighs.

Janna didn't have to look at Ty's face to know that he had seen her. The visible evidence of his maleness stirred into life, growing rapidly, insistently, rising from its dark nest of hair as inevitably as Ty had risen from the steaming pool.

The pot Janna carried made a sharp sound as she dropped it onto a rock. She didn't even hear the noise. She had attention for nothing but the man who stood naked before her. Without knowing it she began walking to him.

The expression on Janna's face was the most potent aphrodisiac Ty had ever known. A savage, elemental need twisted through him, black lightning tightening his body until he could barely speak; and with the lightning came an even blacker despair. He had fought so hard to keep from touching Janna, from taking her, from making her feel like a convenience with no value beyond the passionate moment. He had lain awake night after night in the willows, his body on fire, his mind determined not to allow himself the surcease he knew waited within her generous, sensuous body. But he had also known that whatever private hell o deprivation he suffered would be worth it if he never again had to listen to Janna describe herself as a whore.

Yet there she was, inches from him, and her gray eyes blazed with reflections of the need that burned within him.

"Janna," Ty said hoarsely. "No."

# Chapter Thirty-Seven

Janna's slim fingers covered Ty's lips, preventing him from
saying any more.

"It's all right," she murmured. "I just want to..."
Whatever Janna was attempting to say was lost temporarily
when she bent her head and kissed the hard swell of Ty's
biceps. "Yes," she breathed, shivering with the exquisite
pleasure of brushing her lips over his naked arm. "Let
me..."

When the tip of Janna's tongue traced the shadow line
between Ty's arm and the flexed muscles of his chest, he
made a sound as though he were in pain; yet she knew that
it was need, not pain, that had dragged the sound from his
body. The cry sent piercing needles of pleasure through
Janna, making her tremble with the intensity of her response. She turned her head and found the dark, flat disk
of Ty's nipple with her tongue and lightly raked the erect
nub with her teeth.

Ty's hands closed suddenly around Janna's upper arms
as though to push her away, but the attempt never was
made. His hands refused to take the commands of his mind.
He simply couldn't force himself to push her away. He had
wanted her too much for too long. He held her closer and
shuddered as though each gliding caress from her tongue

was a harsh blow rather than the most tender kind of caress.

"Yes," Janna whispered, feeling the lightning strokes of desire racking the man she loved. "Yes, you need this. You need . . ." She shivered and her teeth pressing into the hard muscles of his torso became less gentle. "You need to . . . be tasted. And I need to taste you. Please, Ty. Let me. Please."

Janna didn't wait for an answer before she flowed down his body. The flesh beneath her caressing mouth was hot, misted with sweat, tasting of salt and passion and the indefinable flavor of masculinity. Touching Ty was a pleasure so great it was nearly pain. A shivering ripple of sound came from her lips, for she had dreamed of being given the gift of his body once more.

Ty's clenched thigh muscles barely gave beneath the testing of Janna's teeth. Feeling the intense strokes of desire that shook him with each of her moist caresses was intensely arousing to her, but she was too consumed by her sensual explorations to realize that her own body was as hot as his. She only knew that bursts of pleasure went through her when she rubbed her breasts over his hard thighs and brushed her cheeks over the rigid evidence of his desire.

"Janna," Ty said raggedly. His voice when she turned her head and her lips brushed over him in a caress that nearly undid him. "Sweet God, you're killing me. Love, don't, I've never . . . you'll make me . . ."

The intimate touch of Janna's tongue was a liquid fire that burned away Ty's words, burned away his thoughts, burned away everything but the incandescent instant when she first tasted him.

Speech unraveled into a cry that was torn from deep in Ty's throat. The harsh sound made Janna stop. She looked up. The green blaze of his eyes made her tremble.

"Did I hurt you?"

"No."

"But you . . . cried out," she said hesitantly.

"So did you when I touched you that way."

Janna's eyes half clouded as sensual memories burst inside her, drenching her with heat. She looked at Ty and remembered what it had been like to feel his mouth loving her, enthralling her, devouring her in steamy intimacy. She looked again at the potent male flesh that had felt so hard and smooth and intriguing to her tongue just a moment ago.

"Don't," Ty said huskily, biting back a raw sound of need. "You'll make me lose control."

"But I'm not even touching you," she whispered.

"You are in your mind. And in mine. Satin butterfly, hot and sleek and perfect. When you took me into your body it was like being taken into a fiery paradise. You burned me to my soul. You're still burning in my soul, burning in my body, everything burning. You don't know what you do to me."

Ty saw Janna's shivering response to his words and thought he would lose what little control remained to him.

"You burned me the same way," she said, touching him with the tip of her tongue. "I'm still burning."

Restlessly Janna stroked her hands over Ty's clenched leg muscles, trying to tell him something for which she had no words, seeking something she couldn't name. One of her hands caressed the inside of his thigh until she could go no higher. She felt him shudder, heard his ripping intake of breath and knew she had found another way to touch him with fiery paradise. Fascinated by the tangible variation between his body and her own, she caressed the very different flesh suspended so tightly between his thighs.

Ty watched Janna with eyes that were no more than green slits set against the stark tension of his face. He had thought he could want her no more without losing control. He had been wrong. He wanted her more now than he ever had; yet he made no move to take her, for he was learning more about himself and her with every instant, every caress, each sweet glide of her tongue as she discovered the changing textures of his masculinity.

The sight of Janna loving him, enjoying him, pleasuring him and herself at the same time was unlike anything Ty had ever known. Slowly his legs gave way, unable to bear the weight of his passion any longer. He sank to his knees, then onto the grass; and she moved with him, loving him in silence, displaying that love with every caress.

When her mouth circled him, accepting and cherishing him with a shattering intimacy, a cry was ripped from him once again. This time she didn't stop loving his hot flesh, for she knew that he had but given voice to the savage, overwhelming pleasure that was shaking his body.

"*Janna . . .*"

Her answer was silent, a changing pressure of her mouth that dragged a hoarse sound of ecstasy from his throat. He tried to tell her what she was doing to him, consuming and renewing him with each clinging movement of her lips and tongue. Despite his efforts no words came, for he had none to describe the shattering beauty of being loved without inhibition, without bonds, without expectations, nothing but the sultry heat of her mouth cherishing him.

"Janna," he said hoarsely. "Don't. I'm going to . . ." Words became a groan of ecstasy dragged from Ty as his hips moved in helpless need. "For the love of God . . . stop."

"Am I hurting you?" Janna asked, knowing the answer, wanting to hear it anyway.

Ty laughed brokenly, then made a low sound when her hands and mouth slid over him once more, caressing him, burning through his control, burning him alive.

"Love . . . stop. I can't take any more without losing control."

He felt the shiver that overtook Janna in the instant before she stroked him and whispered, "Yes, I'd like that."

Ty clenched against the pulses of ecstasy that were bursting through his body, not knowing how to give himself in that elemental way.

"Please," Janna whispered. She touched the tip of her tongue to the blunt masculine flesh that was no longer a mystery to her. "You taste like life itself."

Watching her, Ty made an anguished sound as he fought the tide of ecstasy that was surging through him. Deep within his soul he realized that he would never forget the picture she made as she loved him with a generosity that was a kind of ecstasy in itself, a giving and a taking that became a profound sharing he had never imagined possible. She accepted and cherished him without restraint, teaching him that he had known nothing of true intimacy before he had known Janna.

Ty felt his control being stripped away with each loving instant, each sweet and wild caress. Pleasure convulsed him, shaking his body and soul with each primal pulse of rapture; and the word he cried out at the shattering peak of ecstasy was Janna's name. The cry pierced her soul, bringing tears that were both hot and sweet, an overflowing of her joy in the certainty that she had given the man she loved such intense pleasure.

When Ty could again control his own body, he caught Janna between his hands and pulled her into his arms, needing the feel of her close to him. She closed her eyes and held him as strongly as he was holding her, savoring the closeness and the sound of her name repeated over and over by her lover as the aftermath of ecstasy shuddered through his powerful body. When he finally tilted her face up to his own, she smiled and nuzzled against the masculine lips, which were resilient and soft and...insistent.

"Ty?"

Her husky voice was like a caress on his hot skin.

"I need to be part of you," he said simply. His hand slid from Janna's cheek, skimmed down her shirtfront, below her waist, seeking and finding the soft mound at the apex of her thighs. He made a deep sound of discovery and satisfaction when he felt the sultry heat of her. "And you need me, too. I can feel it even through all the clothes you use to conceal your beauty. My own satin butterfly, waiting to be freed of your cocoon."

The pressure of Ty's strong hand cupping her so deliberately made a shimmering tension gather in the pit of Janna's stomach.

"You need me, butterfly," Ty said, flexing his hand, feeling Janna's alluring heat calling to him. He bent to take her lips, then stopped just short of that goal. "You need me, but do you want me, too?"

Janna tried to answer. All that came out was a breathless sound when Ty's tongue touched her lips and she realized how hungry she was for his kiss. Vaguely she felt a shifting pressure at her waist, but she barely noticed, for Ty's teeth had caught her lower lip and were holding it captive for the slow probing of his tongue. He released her soft lip by tiny increments.

"Do you want me?" he asked huskily while his hand flicked open buttons, pushed aside cloth, slid beneath fabric, seeking her feminine core. "Will you let me undress you, touch you, tease you until you're hot and wild and you can't breathe without calling my name?"

Janna couldn't answer, for his hand had claimed her and the blind searching of his fingertip was making her tremble in anticipation of the ecstasy she would know again at her lover's hands.

"Janna," Ty said in a low voice. "Tell me what you want."

"Touch me," she said raggedly.

"I'm already touching you."

She shivered and shifted her legs unconsciously, silently telling him what she wanted.

"Say it," he whispered. "I want to hear it. I need to know that I'm giving you something as sweet and powerful as you gave to me."

"I . . . I . . ."

Janna turned her face against Ty's chest in a gesture of trust and shyness that made him smile despite the need clenching fiercely within him. She had been so abandoned in her seduction of him a few moments before that he had forgotten she was new to sensuous play.

"Then I'll tell you what pleases me," Ty said, and as he spoke, his fingertip barely brushed the dark auburn triangle that both defined and concealed Janna's softness. "I love seeing you this way, with your clothes opened and your breasts bare and my hand between your beautiful thighs. I love watching your nipples rise and tighten even though nothing of me is touching you but my words. I love watching your breath shorten and your legs move restlessly until you open for me, asking that I touch what no other man has."

Smiling with frank sensuality, Ty watched the effect of his words on Janna. He encouraged her movements with teasing hesitations and tiny touches on her breasts, her navel, the heavy auburn silk at the apex of her thighs; and she moved beneath his touch, response and plea at once.

"Yes, like that. Just like that," Ty said, his voice thickening. His hands moved, caressing and revealing her in the same motions. "I love parting your soft lips and sliding into you. So warm . . ."

A ragged cry came from Janna as she felt a bubble of sensation expand wildly within her and then burst, heat spilling over at her lover's words, his touch, his clear enjoyment of her body.

"Yes, I love that, too," Ty said.

He advanced then withdrew his touch from her, teasing her and pleasuring her in the same motions, feeling the increase in her heat and softness with each caress. His voice changed with the heavy running of his own blood, becoming dark, deep, as elemental as the endless hunger he felt for the woman whose body became his at a touch.

"The way you respond to me makes me feel like a god. Hot satin butterfly..." Ty's voice broke as he felt the sudden constriction in Janna's satin depths, heard her breath hesitate and then come out in a low moan. "Love," he whispered, bending down to her, "tell me what you need. I'll give it to you, all of it, and then I'll begin all over once more, touching you, pleasuring you again and again until neither one of us has the strength to speak...if that's what you want. Tell me what you want."

Ty's name came from Janna's lips in a ripple of small cries marking the rings of pleasure expanding and bursting sweetly within her body. Blindly her hands moved over his hot skin until she found the flesh that she had come to know so intimately. He was hard and smooth to her touch, as tight as though it had been weeks rather than minutes since he had known release. Having tangible proof of her ability to affect Ty was like another kind of caress, deep and hot and unbearably sweet.

"I want you," Janna said, her voice breaking beneath an unexpected, wild burst of pleasure at feeling him so thick and heavy in her hands. "I want to be joined so closely with you that I can feel each heartbeat, each pulse of life..."

Her words shattered into rippling sounds, tiny cries called from her very core as Ty swept her loose pants from her body and merged their bodies with a single powerful motion, giving her all that she had asked for and more, for he had wanted the joining as intensely as she had.

The swift fulfillment was like lightning searching through Janna's flesh, creating an incandescent network of fire, burning through to her soul. She didn't know that she called Ty's name even as ecstasy transfixed her, but he knew. He heard his own name, felt the satin convulsions deep within her body, and he smiled in a mixture of triumph and passionate restraint as he bent to drink from her lips the taste of ecstasy.

Only when the last of Janna's cries had faded and the final echoes of passionate release had stilled in her body did Ty begin the slow dance of love, penetration and withdrawal, sliding deeply, retreating, sheathing himself within her once more, retreating, sheathing.

Janna's body gave no warning; suddenly she was in the grip of something unknown, something hot and vital coiling relentlessly within her, tighter with each movement, tension dragging breath from her lungs and strength from her limbs.

"*Ty.*"

His answer was an even more complete sheathing followed by husky laughter when he felt Janna's back arch in helpless reflex to his presence deep within her body. Her cries unraveled into a moan as she joined with Ty in the sinuous dance of love, her body driven by the pressure coiling within her. He encouraged her with dark words whispered into her ear and the strength of his arm circling beneath her hips, sealing their bodies tightly together. He felt the tension vibrating within her satin depths as surely as she did; the realization that she was poised on the brink of violent rapture slammed through him, nearly wrenching away his own control.

Ty fought against his own climax, dragging himself back from the brink. He didn't want release yet. Not before he had drunk the wine of Janna's passion to the last glorious drop.

The feel of her nails against his buttocks was like being burned by sensual fire. He groaned and gave her what she was demanding, what she needed, the elemental joining of his body to hers, no barriers, no calculation, nothing but heat and sweet friction and the driving rhythms of life.

The tightness within Janna increased until she would have screamed, but her voice was paralyzed. Her body twisted and her legs wrapped around Ty's lean hips as she strained toward something she both feared and needed, something so powerful that having it might destroy her; but not having it would certainly destroy her. She began to call Ty's name with each breath, broken sounds; she was being pulled apart by the tension that had no end, no release, nothing but a need that drove her relentlessly higher.

And then the tension doubled and redoubled with each heartbeat. She screamed his name and burst into a thousand blazing pieces, each one of them a separate ecstasy consuming her all the way to her soul.

Ty held Janna and himself, drinking her passion, feeling her climax to the marrow of his bones and beyond, kissing her with both gentleness and hunger, holding himself still despite the tension still hammering in his body with each breath, each heartbeat; and he didn't move because he wanted it to last forever.

There had never been a woman for him like Janna. He had learned in a twilight meadow on Black Plateau Janna's rare gift for ecstasy. Now he was driven to learn the boundaries of that gift. He began to move again, caressing and probing and filling her once more, each motion inciting flesh still quivering from the height of sensual stimulation and wild release.

"Ty?" she asked, opening dazed eyes.

"Yes," he said, bending down to Janna's mouth. "To the last drop of passion. Until we can't breathe. Until we die."

# Chapter Thirty-Eight

Janna looked at the stone overhang that had been the only home she had ever had. Only scattered ashes remained of the campfire that had always been carefully tended. The pots and pans had been washed, upended and set aside. The trunk had been filled with herbs that would discourage insects or mice from settling in. All that she had kept out was a small pack consisting of her bedroll, herb pouch and canteen ... and the sketch of her mother, a silken lady who hadn't survived the rigors of frontier life.

"We'll be able to get the books once the Army takes care of Cascabel," Ty said, putting his arm around Janna.

For an instant Janna leaned against Ty, savoring his strength and the knowledge that for once she didn't have to stand alone. Then she straightened and smiled up at him, but she said nothing about their coming back to the secret valley. If she kept her portion of Mad Jack's gold, she could build a home anywhere she wished, save one—wherever Ty was. That she would not do. She had been lucky enough to have her dream of a home made possible. The fact that she now wished for Ty to share that dream was unfortunate, but it was her misfortune, not his. She had taken advantage of his natural woman-hunger by teasing him until he was beside himself with need. She hadn't realized the power of the weapon she had turned on him. He had tried to resist, but he hadn't been able to, not entirely. That was her fault, not his.

Especially yesterday, when she had thrown herself at him with utter abandon, touching him in ways that made it impossible for him to turn away. Even now the memories made her tremble with the aftershocks of what he and she had shared.

But to Janna, her wantonness was no reason for Ty to give up his own dream. Requiring him to give up his deepest desire just because he had been the first man to show her ecstasy; that would be an act of hatred, not of love...and she loved Ty so much it felt as though she were being pulled apart by claws of ice and fire and night.

*Silken lady, wherever you are, whoever you are, be kind to the man I love. Give him the dream he has wanted for so many years.*

"Janna?" Ty asked, his throat aching with the sadness he felt twisting through her, the bleak shadow of night just beneath her sunny smile. "We'll come back. I prom—"

She put her fingers over his lips, sealing in the unwanted promise before it could be spoken. "It's all right," she said. "I knew I would have to leave someday. Someday...is today."

Ty lifted Janna's hand and pressed a kiss into her palm. "Wyoming is beautiful, too. If you don't like it there we can go anywhere."

Tears Janna couldn't conceal came to her eyes. Ty's words were agony to her, for they weren't the words she had longed so much to hear, the words he only spoke to her in her dreams, the words his silken lady would someday hear from his lips.

*I love you.*

But Ty didn't love Janna. He was amused by her, he liked her, and he was enthralled by her sensuality without realizing that passion's wellspring was her own deep love for him. He talked about their future together, but it was a future

decreed by his unbending sense of honor and duty, not his
desire to make Janna his mate, his lifetime companion, the
mother of his children.

Honor and duty weren't love. Neither was kindness.
Janna would rather live the rest of her life in the wild than
watch Ty become bitter and ground down by regrets for the
freedom and the dream he had lost.

And Janna would rather die than live to see the day when
Ty stood like a captive mustang, his head down and his eyes
as dead as stones.

"Go ahead and cry," Ty said, folding Janna into his
arms, rocking her. "It's all right, sugar. It's all right. You'll
have the home you've dreamed of if it's the last thing I do.
It's the very least that I owe you."

Janna closed her eyes to conceal the wave of pain his
words had caused. Very gently she brushed her lips over his
shirtfront, savoring for the last time his heat, his scent,
his strength, the male vitality that radiated from him.

"You owe me nothing at all."

Ty's laugh was harsh and humorless. "Like hell I don't.
You saved my life, and all I've done since then is take from
you. When I think of you throwing yourself under Lucifer's
hooves just to catch him for me, I..."

Ty's words faded into a hoarse sound. Strong arms tightened almost painfully around Janna, as though Ty were
trying to convince himself that she was all right despite all
the dangers she had endured for him.

"I didn't catch Lucifer to make you feel obligated to me,"
Janna said quietly. "I did it so Lucifer wouldn't be killed by
some greedy mustanger or be caught by a man too cruel to
do anything but make Lucifer into a killer. You were the one
who gentled Lucifer. You were the one who taught him to
trust a man. Without that, what I did would have been
worse than useless. Thank yourself for Lucifer, not me."

Ty tilted up Janna's chin and stared at her translucent
gray eyes. "You really believe that, don't you?"

"I know it. *You don't owe me anything.* Not for your life, not for Lucifer, and not for the pleasure we shared. Not one damn thing. Once we get to the fort we're quits. You're as free as Lucifer once was. And so am I."

A chill came over Ty, making his skin tighten and move in primitive reflex. Janna's voice was calm and precise, lacking in emotion, as bleak as the darkness underlying her smile. She was systematically pulling away from him, cutting the ties that had grown silently, powerfully between them during the time they had spent in the hidden valley.

"No."

Ty said nothing more, just the single word denying what Janna had said. Before she could say anything in argument, Ty turned away and whistled shrilly.

Moments later Lucifer came trotting over and began lipping at Ty's shirt in search of the pinch of salt Ty often had hidden in a twist of paper. There was no salt today, simply the voice and hands Lucifer had come to enjoy.

Ty petted the stallion for a few moments before he picked up the heavy saddlebags Mad Jack had left behind. Ty had cut slits in the leather that joined the saddlebags. Through the slits he had threaded the surcingle. Once the strap had been tightened, the saddlebags would stay in place on the stallion's back.

Lucifer didn't care for the surcingle around his barrel, but he had become accustomed to it. He did nothing more than briefly lay back his ears when the strap tightened just behind his front legs. Ty praised the stallion, shrugged his own backpack into place and vaulted onto the mustang's back. It was a heavy load Lucifer was carrying, but Ty wasn't worried. Lucifer was an unusually powerful horse. Even if Ty had added a saddle to the load, the stallion wouldn't have been overburdened for normal travel.

"I'll scout the area beyond the slot," Ty said. "Get Zebra over there and wait for my signal."

"Ty, I won't let you—"

"Let me? *Let* me!" he interrupted, furious. "To hell with 'letting'! You listen to me and you listen good. You might be pregnant. If you think I'll run off and leave an orphaned girl who could be carrying my child to fend for herself in Indian country, there's no damned point in even talking to you! I'll try hammering my message through that thick skull of yours after we get to the fort. Maybe by then I'll have cooled down or you'll have grown up. Until then, shut up and stop distracting me or neither one of us will live to see tomorrow."

Lucifer leaped into a canter before Janna had a chance to speak, even if she had been able to think of something to say.

By the time the stallion reached the exit to the valley, Ty had gotten his temper under control. He didn't permit himself to think about Janna and the immediate past, only about Cascabel and the immediate future.

Ty dismounted and looked at the area right in front of the cleft. No new tracks marked the meadow. A vague, telltale trail had been worn through the grass despite his and Janna's efforts never to take the same way twice into the cleft.

*It doesn't matter now. By the time we come back the grass will have regrown. And when we do come back, we won't have to try to live so small we don't even cast shadows.*

Beyond the ghostly paths there were no signs that anything had ever passed through the cleft to the outer world. Ty picked his way over the narrow watercourse and through the shadowed slot between rock walls. The afternoon light glowed overhead, telling him that the sky was nearly cloudless. Until the sun went down they would be vulnerable to discovery, for there would be no rain to conceal their presence while they crossed the wild land.

Yet they had no choice but to move in daylight. There was simply too much risk that one of the horses would injure itself scrambling over the cleft's treacherous watercourse in the dark. Besides, even if they got through the slot safely at night and then traveled until dawn, they would still be deep within Cascabel's preferred range when the sun once more rose, exposing them to discovery.

Their best chance was to sneak out of the slot and take a long, looping approach to the fort, hoping that Cascabel would have been driven to the southern edges of his territory while the two of them traversed the northern part. The fort itself was a hard three-day ride, and there was no haven short of the stockade walls.

Standing well back from the sunlit exit to the cleft, Ty pulled out his spyglass and examined as much of the land as he could see beyond the stone walls. A quick look showed nothing. A long look showed no more. A point-by-point survey revealed no sign of renegades.

*Wish my backbone didn't itch.*

But it did, and Ty wasn't going to ignore his instincts. There was danger out there. His job was to find out where and how much. Unconsciously he fingered the hilt of the big knife he always carried at his belt. He waited for fifteen minutes, then lifted the spyglass and studied the land again. Again he saw nothing to alarm him. He took off his backpack, checked the load in his carbine, grabbed a box of bullets and went out to have a closer look at the land.

He was no more than thirty feet from the cleft when he cut the trail of three unshod ponies. The hoofprints stayed together and marked a purposeful course, telling Ty that the horses had been ridden; they had not been grazing at random as wild horses would. The horses had come out of Cascabel's usual territory.

As Ty followed the traces he hoped that the Army had been successful in driving the renegades away. That hope died when he saw other tracks meet those that he was following. The two sets of tracks mingled, then split once more, heading in all directions, as though the riders had ex-

changed information and had then separated and gone to
search for something.

Ty had a terrible suspicion that what the renegades were
searching for was a *bruja* called Janna Wayland.

Keeping to cover as much as possible, crawling when he
had to, walking when he could, Ty followed the tracks that
crisscrossed the flatlands in front of the cleft. Everything he
saw brought him to the same conclusion: the renegades were
going to beat the bushes and ravines until their auburn-
haired quarry burst from cover. Then they would run her
down and bring her back to Cascabel. There would be
medicine chants and dances, celebrations of past victories
and future coups; and then Cascabel would lead his renegades into war with Janna's long hair hanging from his lance
like a flag, proving to the world that his spirit was the
greatest one moving over the wild face of the land.

For a moment Ty considered simply sneaking back to the
cleft and waiting until Cascabel got tired of searching for his
elusive quarry. That was what Janna had done in the past—
hide. But in the past, Cascabel hadn't been so determined
to catch her. If Ty and Janna retreated to the valley and then
were found, they would be trapped in a stone bottle with no
chance of escape. Better that they take their chances in the
open.

Retreating silently back toward the cleft, Ty made a brief
side trip to the top of a rise. From there he hoped to get a
better view of the rugged land they had to cross. Just before he reached the edge of the rise, he took off his hat and
went down on his stomach, presenting as little human silhouette as possible.

An instant later Ty was glad he had taken the trouble to
be very cautious. On the far side of the rise, four warriors
sat on their heels, arguing and gesticulating abruptly as they
divided up the area to be searched for the Shadow of Flame,
the witch who had been stealing Cascabel's spirit. Just be-

yond the warriors, seven horses grazed on whatever was within reach.

*Four renegades. Seven horses. And my backbone is on fire.*

The only warning Ty had was a slight whisper of sound behind him. He rolled onto his back and lashed out with his booted feet as the renegade attacked.

# Chapter Thirty-Nine

Ty's kick knocked the air from the Indian's lungs, preventing him from crying out and alerting the others. Even so, Ty had no sooner put his hand on his knife hilt than the renegade was on his knees and trying to bring his rifle to bear. Ty threw himself forward, pinning the Indian to the ground with a hard forearm across his throat. A knife flashed and blood burst silently into sunlight. The renegade jerked once, twice, and then lay motionless.

For a few instants it was all Ty could do to breathe despite the screaming of his instincts that the danger had just begun, not ended, and he should be running rather than lying half-stunned. He rolled off the dead renegade and began collecting himself, relying on the survival reflexes he had learned in war. He cleaned his knife blade and put it back in its sheath. He picked up the carbine, checked it for dirt or mechanical damage, found none and made sure the weapon was ready for instant use.

Only then did Ty retreat silently, pausing long enough to close the dead warrior's eyes.

*Ashes to ashes, dust to dust... And may God have mercy on both our souls.*

Three hundred feet away Janna sank slowly to her knees, feeling as though her own heart had burst. The barrel of the pistol she was holding clanked softly against stone. She took a deep breath, then another, trying to quiet her body's trembling as she watched Ty glide from brush to boulder, retreating toward the cleft's uncertain shelter.

It had been nerve stretching for Janna to stay within the slot's narrow shadow, knowing as she did from Ty's actions that he must have cut the trail of renegades. She had been watching him for the past half hour while he reconnoitered. Her eyes ached from staring out and trying to guess what Ty was reading from various signs crisscrossing the earth.

Then an Indian had risen up out of the very ground and launched himself at Ty, choosing the greater glory of personal combat to the sure kill offered by picking off Ty with a rifle. Even though the range had been too far for Janna to use the pistol with real accuracy, she had reached for the gun. The fight had ended before she could even lift the weapon above her waist to take aim. She had never seen a man so quick as Ty, or so deadly in that quickness. She realized at that instant just how much of his strength he held in check when he was with her.

And Ty could have died despite all his power and speed, his blood a crimson stain bursting from his body to be drunk by the thirsty earth. All that was Ty, the passion and the laughter, the anger and the sensual teasing, the silence and the silken dream, all of it gone between one breath and the next.

Janna watched each of Ty's movements hungrily, needing the reassurance that he was alive. She scanned the land behind him as well, and she did it from over the barrel of the pistol, wanting to be able to shoot quickly at anything she saw.

Despite Janna's alertness, she didn't see the second renegade until the sun glinted off a rifle barrel as the warrior shifted position to shoot at Ty. Not even bothering to aim, Janna triggered a shot in the direction of the Indian.

At the sound of the shot, Ty dived for cover in a shallow ditch left behind by storm water fanning out from the cleft's narrow mouth. A few instants later he had his hat off and his carbine barrel resting on the lip of the ditch as he searched for the source of the attack. He didn't have to search long. The Indian shifted his aim again, sending more sunlight off his rifle barrel and drawing another shot from the cleft.

Janna's second bullet came much closer than the first had. The renegade's answering shot sent rock chips flying not four feet from her.

Despite the heavy pack Ty wore, he was up and sprinting for the next bit of cover while the renegade reloaded. Ty halfway expected to draw more fire from the other Indians, but none came. He hit the dirt a second before Janna fired at the rifle barrel that was once more poking out from a low mound of rocks and brush. The sharper *crack* of a rifle shot occurred a split second after Janna triggered her pistol.

Ty scrambled up and began running again, counting off the seconds he had before he must throw himself to the ground again. As intently as a hawk, Janna watched the cover that concealed the renegade. Steadying the heavy pistol with both hands, she waited for the renegade to reload and poke the rifle barrel out again, giving her a target.

Suddenly a flash of human movement off to the side caught Janna's eye. She screamed at Ty to take cover as she spun to the left and fired. Two rifle shots rang out, kicking dirt just in front of Ty. He flattened out into another shallow runoff ditch while Janna fired a shot at the orginal attacker.

*Five,* Ty counted silently to himself. *That's it. She has to reload.*

The pistol in Janna's hand clicked loudly twice before she realized that she was out of ammunition.

"Reload!" yelled Ty without looking away from his right, where the new attacker was hidden. *Come on, come on,* he silently urged the second renegade. *Show yourself.*

Reloading was much easier said than done for Janna. White lipped, she worked to eject the spent casings, fumble bullets from her pocket and shove them one by one into the six waiting chambers. This time she wouldn't leave one chamber empty as a precaution against accidentally discharging the revolver; she wanted all six shots and she wanted them right now.

But first she had to get the bullets into the chambers.

Four hundred feet away and to the right of Ty, a thrown pebble bounced harshly on the hard ground. Knowing it was a fcint, Ty fired in that direction anyway, then turned quickly toward the position of the first attacker.

*Come and get it,* he urged silently.

As Ty had hoped, the first renegade assumed he was facing an enemy armed with a single-shot rifle. The Indian broke cover and stood up, striving for a clean shot before his prey could reload or find better cover. Smoke puffed from Ty's carbine and the renegade died before he could even realize what had gone wrong. Ty levered another bullet into the firing chamber even as he whipped around to confront the second renegade, who had had time to reload and was taking aim.

Ty threw himself to the side, spoiling both his own shot and the renegade's. Ty's second and third shots were dead on target. He rolled to a new position of cover and waited. No more shots came. Either the other renegades hadn't had time to take position yet or the speed with which Ty could "reload" and fire his carbine had made them cautious.

"Janna," called Ty. "Are you all right?"

"Yes." Her voice was oddly thinned but strong.

"Tell me when you've reloaded."

Swearing shockingly, Janna worked at the unfamiliar task of putting cold, slippery bullets into the warm cylinder. She dropped two bullets before she managed to get all six chambers full. Cocking the revolver, she looked out over the land once more.

"Ready," she called.

"I'm coming in from your right."

"Go!"

An instant later Ty was on his feet and running toward the slot, dodging and turning every few seconds, doing everything he could to spoil a hunter's aim. Janna's gray eyes scanned the countryside to the left of the slot, alert for any sign of movement. At the edge of her side vision she watched Ty's long-legged stride eat up the distance between himself and safety.

Only twenty yards to cover. Then ten, then—

There was no time to warn Ty, no time to aim, no time to do anything but fire at almost point-blank range as a renegade sprang from cover just outside the cleft and came at Janna with a knife. Her first shot was wild. Her second shot hit the renegade's shoulder a glancing blow, knocking him backward. The third and fourth shots were Ty's. No more were needed.

"Get back," Ty said harshly, dragging Janna farther inside the cleft. "There are three more out there and God knows how many will come in at the sound of the shots."

Breathing hard, Ty shrugged out of his backpack and took up a position just inside the slot. He began refilling the carbine with quick, sure motions. As he worked he looked up every few instants to scan the landscape. What he saw made him swear tonelessly. There was a distant swirl of dust, which was probably a rider going off for reinforcements. One of the remaining renegades was taking up a position that would cover the mouth of the cleft.

The second Indian wasn't in sight, but he was within rifle range, as a screaming, whining, ricocheting bullet proved. Rock chips exploded, showering Ty with dust and stinging shards.

"Get farther back," he yelled as he blinked his eyes and took aim.

Ty fired several times at the most likely patches of cover from which the renegade might be shooting. Then he lowered his carbine and waited. A few moments later another shot whined past. This time he saw where it had come from. He answered instantly with closely spaced shots, sending bullets raking through the cover. There was a startled yell, then silence. Methodically Ty shoved bullets into the carbine's magazine, replacing those he had spent.

No more shots came.

"Janna?"

"I'm back here," she said.

The odd acoustics of the canyon made her sound close, though she was thirty feet away.

"We're going to have to get out on foot and try to steal horses from the Indians," Ty said.

Janna had arrived at the same conclusion. Getting Lucifer and Zebra out without being spotted by the Indians would be impossible.

"There's no moon tonight," Ty continued without looking away from the bit of cover where the Indian had hidden. "We'll go out an hour after full dark. Try to get some sleep until then."

"What about you?"

"I'll guard the entrance."

"But the ricochets—"

"If I get out of range of a ricochet," Ty interrupted impatiently, "I won't be able to see the mouth of the slot to guard it." Ty's expression softened for a moment when he looked at Janna. "Don't look so worried, sugar. He doesn't have a very good angle from where he is. I'll be all right."

Turning back to the slot, Ty fired six times in rapid succession, stitching bullets on either side of the place where the renegade had taken cover, forcing anyone who might still be in range to get down and stay down. Janna hesitated, then went quickly to Ty. She threw her arms around him and hugged him fiercely. He returned the embrace with a strength and a yearning that made tears burn against Janna's eyelids. In tones too soft for him to hear, she whispered her love against his neck before she turned away and retreated toward the meadow.

But Ty had heard Janna's words. For an instant he closed his eyes and felt the exquisite pain of having been given a gift he didn't deserve.

With automatic motions Ty propped his backpack against a stone, sat on his heels and loaded the carbine to full capacity once more. The angle of the shadows on the canyon walls told him that he had several hours to wait until sunset came, much less full dark.

Leaning against the wall, carbine at the ready, Ty tried to convince himself that when dawn came he and Janna would still be alive.

# Chapter Forty

The meadow's sunlight seemed blinding after the cool, dim passage into the secret valley. Janna stood on the edge of the opening and sent a hawk's wild cry into the still air. A second call brought Zebra at a trot, her head high, her ears pricked. Lucifer followed after the mare, for the two horses had become inseparable during the weeks when the stallion was healing.

Janna mounted Zebra quickly and turned the mare toward the ancient ruins where Mad Jack had hidden his gold. She had never pried into the old prospector's secrets before—but then, she had never been trapped in a stone bottle before, either.

"Jack must have had a way in and out of this valley without coming through the slot," Janna said aloud to Zebra, "because I never saw a mark in that creek bed. If he had been coming and going from my end of the valley, I'd have heard him or you would have or Lucifer would have."

Zebra flicked her ears back and forth, enjoying the sound of Janna's voice.

"But you didn't hear Jack, and that old man was too weak to carry more than a few pounds of gold at a time, which means there was a lot of coming and going before those saddlebags were full. He had to have left some kind of trail, somewhere. He just had to."

And Janna had until dark to find it.

She urged Zebra into a canter, watching the rocky walls and lava flows, probing light and shadow for any sign of a faint trail. The valley narrowed in at the south end, where the ruins were. Beyond ascertaining that there was a clear spring welling up at the base of the ramparts that were just before the ruins, Janna had never really explored this part of the valley. The ruins were eerie by daylight and unsettling by night. She much preferred the clean reach of the stone overhang at the opposite end of the valley to the cramped and broken rooms of a people long dead.

But Janna wasn't looking for a campsite now, or even for temporary shelter. She was looking for the ancient trails that the vanished Indians must have left if they came and went from their home by any route other than the dark cleft. It was possible that the Indians might have built their fortress in a blind valley with only one exit, but Janna doubted it. A tribe that took so much trouble to hide its home was a cautious people, and cautious people knew that the only difference between a fortress and a trap was a bolt hole.

In the country outside the valley, Janna had spotted ancient trails in the past simply by standing on a ridge and allowing her eyes to go slightly unfocused. When she lost the finest edge of visual acuity, other patterns came to light, vague lines and odd shadows. Most often they were simply random lines in a wild land, but sometimes they were ghost trails no longer used by man.

Crisscrossing the area around the ruins, Janna searched for any trail, new or old. She found nothing on the ground but grass, brush, rocks, sunlight and signs of her own passage. She urged Zebra farther into the ruins. The angle of the sun made shadows spill out from crumbling stone rooms, as though darkness had breached stone dams and was welling up to fill the valley beyond.

A frisson of uneasiness ran through Janna. She had always avoided the ruins in the hours beyond midafternoon, when the descending sun played odd tricks with light and shadow and stone. All that drove her farther into the ruins now was the certainty that nothing a ghostly Indian had to offer could be worse than what waited beyond the cleft in the form of flesh-and-blood renegades.

No matter how Janna focused her eyes or didn't, tilted her head or held it straight, narrowed her eyelids or widened them until her eyes ached, she saw nothing on the ground to suggest an ancient, forgotten trail. Working out from the room in which Mad Jack had stored his gold, she quartered the open space. She found nothing she could be sure was Mad Jack's sign rather than her own or a random displacement of pebbles.

The farther back into the ruins Janna went, the narrower the canyon became. Stone rubble covered the ground. At first she assumed the rocky debris was the result of stones falling from the surrounding cliffs, but the farther back into the narrow throat of the canyon she went, the more she was struck by an odd thing—in some places the rubble looked as though it once had been level, as though broad steps or narrow terraces had once climbed up the throat of the valley.

With growing excitement Janna followed the frayed remnants of what might once have been a well-built path snaking back and up the broken ramparts of stone that surrounded the hidden valley. Behind Zebra a pebble rolled under Lucifer's feet. The mare snorted and shied at the sound, giving vent to her nervousness at being asked to take a trail that showed every evidence of getting more and more narrow while going nowhere at all.

"Easy, girl," Janna said soothingly, stroking the mare. "There's nothing around but you, me, Lucifer and a lot of rock. The shadows just look scary, that's all. There's nothing in them but air."

Under Janna's urging Zebra climbed the steepening path. The farther along she went, the more Janna's hopes sank.

What had once looked like a wide path was rapidly degenerating into a jumble of stone that resembled nothing so much as the debris that always built up at the foot of stone cliffs.

Janna's hopes sank when Zebra scrambled around a tight corner and was confronted by a rock wall. Nothing that in any way resembled a trail broke the sheer rise of stone. Apparently Janna had been following a random chute paved with fallen rocks rather than a ghost path left by an ancient people.

For a long time she simply sat, staring at the end of her carefully constructed and entirely false logic of hope. However Mad Jack might have come into the valley, it wasn't this way; and this had been by far the best hope of finding his path. The other possibilities—the random ravines and slender runoff gullies and crevices that opened into the narrowest end of the valley where Janna was—were much less likely to lead to the top of the plateau than the ground she had just covered.

But Janna had no choice except to try the other possibilities. No matter how small they were, they were better than the chance of sneaking past Cascabel and his renegades while they were camped outside the valley's only exit like a horde of hungry cats waiting at a mouse hole.

There was barely enough room for Zebra to turn around in order to head back where she had come from. Lucifer saw Zebra turning and followed suit. He led the retreat over the rough ground at a brisk trot, relieved to be free of the narrow passage between broken walls of stone. Zebra was equally relieved. She followed after the stallion eagerly.

They had retreated no more than a hundred feet when Janna noticed a small ravine that she hadn't seen before, for it joined at an oblique angle to the main passage and was walled off by a pediment of stone. Immediately she turned Zebra toward the side ravine. The mare tossed her head, not wanting to leave Lucifer and enter the narrow gulch.

"Come on, girl. There's nothing up this trail but stone
nd shadows and maybe, just maybe, a way out of here."

Zebra didn't budge.

Janna stopped using pressures of her hand to guide the
are. Instead, she pulled on the knotted hackamore reins Ty
ad insisted that Zebra be trained to wear. Reluctantly the
are turned away from Lucifer and walked into the gulch.
nce past the rocky outcropping that guarded the ravine's
arrow mouth, the passage opened out again, becoming
ider than the slot where Ty waited for a renegade who was
rave or foolish enough to show himself.

Janna didn't know if it were wishful thinking or truth, but
seemed to her that the new path had once been made more
vel by a series of broad steps composed of stony rubble,
hich followed the steep rise of the ravine farther and far-
er back into the body of the plateau. The steps, or ramps,
d since largely crumbled and been washed away beneath
rrential rains, but enough remained to give a mustang ad-
uate footing.

To Janna's surprise, Lucifer followed, as though deter-
ined not to lose sight of Zebra in the midst of echoing
ne ravines. The path snaked higher and higher, some-
nes scrambling over stony ridges to follow a different
noff course up the broken walls that constituted the
:stern side of the valley.

There were places where Janna was certain that rock must
ve been hammered away to make passage possible. In
her places she was just as certain that nothing had touched
e trail but wind and water, sun and storm. Then she would
: gouge marks on the stone and wonder if they weren't the
:ult of intelligence rather than past landslides.

The trail came to yet another narrowing of the branching
twork of runoff channels that covered the eroding face of
e western ramparts of the valley. Without being urged,
bra scrambled and lunged over the small rise, for there

had been many such changes of direction in the past ha
mile.

There was sun shining on the rise, for they had climbe
far enough to be beyond the reach of lengthening shadow
Janna shaded her eyes and looked ahead, confidently e
pecting to find an obvious way to proceed. She saw nothi
except a lateral crack in the stone cliff, but the crack was to
small to be called a passage. Turning slowly, she looked ov
her trail. Her breath came in with a sharp sound. She w
nearly to the top of the stone ramparts that surrounded h
hidden valley.

"There has to be a way to get out from here," Janna sa
aloud as she stroked Zebra absently.

For several minutes Janna looked at the dubious later
crevice that angled up and across the remaining cliff. T
narrow ledge she saw might or might not lead to the top
the plateau. If the ledge ended short of the top, she wou
be stuck; there was no place for a horse to turn around.
the mustangs entered the crack they would be committed
going up, not down.

Janna slid off Zebra, then pressed the mare's nose ir
signal for her to stay behind. Ears pricked, nostrils flare
the mustang watched her mistress take the narrow tra
Janna looked back only once to assure herself that Zet
wasn't going to stray.

After Janna had gone fifteen feet, she was certain that s
was going the right way. The crack became a very narr
ledge, too narrow for a horse to pass safely. Marks tl
could have been left by a chisel or hammer showed in
stone. Apparently the ancient tribe had widened and l
eled a natural split in the rock face until it became a le
just wide enough to take a man on foot. With overhangi
rock on her left, a path no more than twenty inches wide
her feet—and sometimes less, if the rock had crumb
away—and a sheer drop to the valley floor on her right,
scrambled the length of the crack.

When Janna vanished around a column of rock on the far end of the ledge Zebra nickered as though to call a foal back to her side. When that didn't work, the mustang neighed loudly. Lucifer added a ringing, imperious command that carried from one end of the hidden valley to the other.

Janna popped back into view, sliding and skidding down to the ledge, desperate to calm the stallion before he alerted half of Utah Territory. Despite the need for haste, Janna slowed to a very careful walk while she negotiated the dangerous ledge. Zebra whickered softly in encouragement or warning, then nuzzled Janna when she was within reach once more. Having achieved his purpose in calling back a straying member of his band, Lucifer made no further noise.

"Lord, what a bugle you have," Janna said to Lucifer, who ignored her irritation. She looked back at the ledge and shook her head. "I know, that's a scary path even for humans. I can imagine what it must look like to you. But you didn't give me a chance to find out if the rest of the trail—if it really is a trail—goes all the way to the top."

After a few moments spent reassuring the horses, Janna started toward the ledge again. She had taken no more than two steps when she heard a barrage of rifle fire.

She froze, listening intently, trying to decide where the shots were coming from. The lighter, rhythmic barks of Ty's Winchester resolved the issue beyond a doubt. The sounds were coming from the cleft that Ty had remained behind to guard. The Indians must have decided to try rushing the cleft's entrance, or perhaps it was only a feint.

Either way, Janna wasn't comforted. The number of shots that were being fired told her that renegade reinforcements must have arrived. If they timed their attack carefully, they could provide cover for one another while they reloaded their rifles. But Ty was alone in the rocky cleft with no one to cover him while he reloaded.

# Chapter Forty-One

The trip back down the ancient trail took much less time than the trip up had, but it seemed like an eternity to Janna. The instant it was safe to demand speed from Zebra, she kicked the mare into a hard gallop that ended only at the shadowed entrance to the cleft. Heart hammering, Janna leaped from Zebra and ran into the dark opening just as there was a renewed fusillade of rifle fire. The cleft distorted sounds, making them seem to come from nearby and far away all at once. She kept hoping to hear the carbine's lighter sound but heard only her own breath and the erratic bark of renegade rifles.

Just as Janna rounded the last bend before the exit, Ty's carbine resumed its rhythmic, rapid firing. She slowed slightly, almost dizzy with relief.

Ty heard her footsteps and looked over his shoulder. "You're supposed to be sleeping."

"Not likely with all the racket you're making," she said breathlessly.

His smile was rather grim as he turned his attention back to the land beyond the cleft. He fired quickly three times and was answered by a scattering of shots.

"I'm having a little help making noise, as you can see."

"How many?" Janna asked.

"I saw enough dust for an army, but I don't think there are more than ten rifles out there right now, and all of them are single shot."

"For these small blessings, Lord, we are thankful," Janna said beneath her breath. "I think."

Ty's smile was little more than a hard line of white beneath his black mustache. He wasn't sure that it made a difference what kind of rifles the renegades were shooting. The chance of Janna and himself slipping past the Indians—much less of stealing a horse or two on the way by—had dropped to the point that it would be frankly suicidal rather than probably suicidal to try escaping through the cleft.

But there was no other way out.

"I think I found a way out," Janna said.

Her words echoed his thought so closely that for a moment Ty wasn't sure that she really had spoken. His head snapped around.

"What did you say?"

"I think I found how Mad Jack got his gold into the ruins without our seeing him."

A movement beyond the cleft commanded Ty's attention. He turned, got off two quick shots and had the satisfaction of knowing that at least one of them had struck home. There was a flurry of return fire, then silence. As he watched the area beyond the cleft he began reloading methodically.

"How did he do it?" Ty asked.

"You know how the valley narrows out behind the ruins?"

"Yes."

"I followed it," Janna said.

"So did I about two weeks ago. It ends in a stone cliff."

"There's a ravine coming in before that."

"There are at least ten ravines 'before that,' and those ravines branch into others, which branch into others. And they all end against a stone cliff," Ty concluded flatly.

"Even the one with the ledge?" Janna asked, trying to keep the disappointment from her voice.

"What ledge?"

"The one that goes along the western lip of the valley almost to the rim."

"Are you certain?"

"I was on it until I heard rifle fire."

Slowly Ty lowered his carbine and turned toward Janna. "You said 'almost to the rim.' How close is 'almost'?"

"I don't know. Zebra started whinnying when I got out of sight and then Lucifer set up such a ruckus that I came back to calm him down. Then I heard rifle fire and was afraid they were rushing you and you didn't have anyone to cover you while you reloaded." Janna closed her eyes briefly. "I got back here as quick as I could."

"How close is almost?" Ty repeated calmly.

"A hundred feet. Maybe a hundred yards. Maybe a quarter mile. I couldn't see."

"Would you bet your life on that path going through?"

"Do we have a choice?"

"Probably not. If Cascabel isn't out there soon, he will be when word gets to him. Until then, there are at least eight able-bodied warriors and two wounded renegades under cover out there, just waiting for something to show at the cleft."

"What if we wait until dark?"

"We can try it."

"But?" Janna prodded.

"Our chances of getting out alive through that cleft are so slim they aren't worth counting," Ty said bluntly. "The same darkness that would cover our movements also covers theirs. Even now the renegades are moving in closer, finding cover, covering each other, closing in on the cleft. By dark they'll have the cork well and truly in the bottle. After that, it's just a matter of time until I run out of ammunition and they rush me."

Ty said nothing more. He didn't have to. Janna could finish his bleak line of thought as well as he could.

"There's something else to consider," Ty said. "If you can find that trail from this end, sure as God made little green apples, a renegade can find it from the other end if he has a good enough reason to go looking—and your hair is a good enough reason, thanks to Cascabel's vision."

Janna nodded unhappily. The same thought had occurred to her. "We can take the horses most of the way."

"But not all?"

"The ledge was made for men, not horses."

Ty had expected nothing more. He bent, put his arms through the straps of his heavy pack and shrugged it into place. "Let's go. We only have a few hours of light left."

Janna turned to leave, then was struck by a thought. "What happens if the Indians rush the cleft while we're still in the valley?"

"I've made the renegades real wary of showing themselves. But if they do—" Ty shrugged "—I can hold them off in the ruins almost as well as in the cleft. You'll have plenty of time to follow the path."

"If you think I'd leave you to—"

"If I tell you to take that trail," Ty interrupted flatly, "*you damn well will take that trail.*"

Without another word Janna turned and began working her way rapidly back through the cleft. Ty was right on her heels. When they came out into the little valley, Zebra and Lucifer were standing nearby, watching the opening attentively. Janna mounted and waited while Ty pulled the saddlebags full of gold out of a hiding place and secured them on Lucifer's muscular back. As soon as Ty had mounted, Janna urged Zebra into a gallop.

The mustangs quickly covered the distance to the ruins. Janna didn't slow the pace until the valley narrowed and the rubble underfoot made the going too rough for any speed greater than a trot. The sounds of stones rolling beneath the horses' hooves echoed between the narrowing walls of the valley. Walking, trotting, scrambling, always pushing ahead as quickly as possible, Zebra climbed up steeper and steeper byways, urged by Janna through the twisting web of natural and man-made passages. Lucifer kept up easily despite the double load of Ty and the gold. The stallion was powerful, agile and fully recovered from his brush with Joe Troon's rifle.

More than once Ty thought that Janna had lost her way, but each time she found a path past the crumbling head of a ravine or through places where huge sheets of rock had peeled away from the ramparts and smashed to pieces against stone outcroppings farther down the cliff. When Zebra scrambled over a ridge of stone and came to a stop, Ty wondered if Janna had finally lost her way. He hoped not; he had begun to believe there was a way out of the hidden valley that had been first a haven and then a deadly trap.

Janna turned and looked back at Ty. "This is as far as the horses can go."

Before Ty could answer, Janna slid from Zebra's back, adjusted the small pack she wore and set off to traverse the narrow ledge. Ty dismounted, scrambled up the last few feet of trail and saw the ledge—and the sheer drop to the valley below.

"Sweet Jesus," he whispered.

Ty fought against an urge to call out to Janna to come back. All that made him succeed was the fear of distracting her from the trail's demands.

The sound of rifle fire drifted up from the direction of the cleft, telling Ty that the renegades were on the move once more. He turned and looked toward the east. He couldn't see the spot where the cleft opened into the meadow. He could, however, see that once the renegades spread through the valley looking for their prey, it would be just a matter of time until a warrior looked up and saw Janna poised like a fly on the wall of the valley's western ramparts.

Zebra called nervously when Janna vanished around a bulge of stone. The stallion's ringing whinny split the air, reverberating off rocky walls. Ty went back to Lucifer and clamped his hand over the horse's nostrils. The stallion shook his head but Ty only hung on harder. He spoke softly, reassuring the mustang, hoping the horse's neigh hadn't carried over the sound of rifle fire.

"Easy, boy, easy. You and Zebra are going to be on your own again in just a little bit. Until then, shut up and hold still and let me get this surcingle undone."

Lucifer snorted and backed away, tossing his head even as his nostrils flared. Ty threw himself at the stallion's head, just managing to cut off Lucifer's air before he could whinny again.

"What's wrong with you?" Ty asked soothingly. "You've never been this jumpy. Now hold still and let me get this strap off you."

Without warning Lucifer lurched forward, shouldering Ty roughly aside.

"What the hell?"

Ty regained his balance and followed Lucifer up the last few feet of trail. Ty was fast, but not fast enough. Lucifer's demanding bugle rang out. Reflexively Ty lunged for the stallion's nose. The horse shouldered him aside once more. Cursing, Ty scrambled to his feet, wondering what had gotten into Lucifer.

"Dammit, horse, where the hell do you think you're going?"

The stallion kept walking.

Then Ty looked past the stallion and realized what had happened. "God in heaven," Ty whispered.

Zebra had followed Janna out onto the ledge—and the stallion was going out right after her, determined not to be left behind.

# Chapter Forty-Two

Afraid even to breathe, Ty watched Zebra and Lucifer picking their way over the narrow ledge with the delicacy of cats walking on the edge of a roof. The worst part of the trail was halfway along the ledge, where rock had crumbled away to make an already thin path even more skeletal. All that made passage possible was that the cliff at that point angled back from the vertical, rather than overhanging as it did along much of the ledge.

When Zebra reached the narrow place where rock had crumbled away, she stopped. After a moment or two her hooves shifted restively. Small pieces of rock fell away, rolling and bouncing until there was no more stone, only air. The mare froze in place, having gone forward no more than an inch or two.

"Go on," Ty said under his breath. "You can't turn around and you can't back up and you can't stay there forever. There's only one way out and that's to keep on going."

Zebra snorted. Ears pricked, she eyed the ledge ahead. Her skin rippled nervously. Sweat sprang up, darkening her pale hide around her shoulders and flanks. Trembling, she stood on the narrow ledge.

And then she tried to back up.

A hawk's wild cry keened across the rocks. The sound came once, twice, three times, coaxing and demanding in one; Janna had returned to the far side of the ledge to see what was taking Ty so long. A single glance had told her what the problem was, and how close it was coming to a disastrous solution. She began speaking to Zebra in low tones, calming the mare, praising her, promising her every treat known to man or mustang if Zebra would only take the few steps between herself and Janna.

Slowly Zebra began to move forward once more. Holding out her hands, Janna backed away, calling to the mustang, talking to her, urging her forward. Zebra followed slowly, placing each hoof precisely—and on her right side, part of each hoof rested on nothing but air.

Gradually the ledge became wider once more, allowing Zebra to move more quickly. She completed the far end of the trail in a subdued rush, barely giving Janna a chance to get out of the way.

Ty had little time to be relieved that Zebra was safe, for now it was Lucifer's turn on the crumbling stone. The stallion liked it even less than the mare, for he was bigger and the saddlebags tended to rub hard against the overhang along the first part of the ledge, pushing the horse outward and toward the sheer drop to the valley floor. Unlike Zebra, Lucifer didn't stop on the narrow section of the trail. He simply laid back his ears and placed each hoof with excruciating care, sweating nervously until his black coat shone like polished jet.

Just as he reached the far end of the ledge, a piece of stone crumbled away beneath his great weight. His right rear hoof lost purchase entirely, throwing him off balance.

Janna bit back a scream as she watched Lucifer scramble frantically to regain his balance and forward momentum. For long seconds the stallion hung poised on the brink of falling. Without stopping to think of the danger, Janna darted past Zebra, grabbed Lucifer's hackamore and pulled forward as hard as she could, hoping to tip the balance.

"*Janna.*"

Ty's horrified whisper was barely past his lips when Lucifer clawed his way over the last of the ledge and lunged onto the wider trail, knocking Janna down and aside in his haste to reach safe footing. The stallion crowded against Zebra, nipping at her haunches, demanding that she keep going up the trail.

Ty barely noticed the narrowness of the ledge or the rub of his left shoulder against the overhang. He covered the stone pathway with reckless speed, wanting only to get to Janna. With fear like a fist in his throat, he knelt next to her and touched her cheek.

"Janna?"

She tried to speak, couldn't and fought for air.

"Take it easy, sugar," Ty said. "That fool stud knocked the breath out of you."

After a few more moments air returned to Janna in an aching rush. She breathed raggedly, then more evenly.

"Do you hurt anywhere?" Ty asked.

Janna shook her head.

"Have enough air now?"

She nodded.

"Good."

Ty bent and pulled Janna into his arms, hugging her hard, then taking her mouth in a kiss that was both savage and tender. After a long time he lifted his head.

"Don't ever do anything like that again," Ty said roughly. "Nothing's worth your life. Not the stallion. Not the gold. Not *anything*. Do you hear me, Janna Wayland?"

She nodded, more breathless from Ty's searching, hungry and gentle kiss than from her skirmish with Lucifer.

Ty looked at Janna's eyes. They were clear and warm as summer rain, radiant with emotion, and he felt his heart turn over in his chest. He closed his own eyes, unable to bear the feelings tearing through him, pulling him apart.

Two feet away from Ty's left leg, stone chips exploded, spattering both of them with shards. From the valley below came the sound of rifle fire.

Ty dragged Janna up the trail and around an outcropping of rock until they were out of view of the valley. From ahead came the sound of stones rolling and bouncing as the mustangs scrambled on up the trail.

"When you get to the top, wait ten minutes," Ty said. "If I don't come, get on Zebra and ride like hell for the fort. Don't come back, Janna. Promise me. Don't come back. There's nothing you can do here but get killed."

"Let me stay," she pleaded.

"No," he said. Then he added in a low voice, "Please, Janna. Let me feel that I've given you something. Just once. Just once for all the things you've given to me. Please."

Janna touched Ty's cheek with fingers that trembled. He turned his head and kissed her fingertips very gently.

"Now go," he said softly.

Janna turned and walked away quickly, trying not to cry. She had gone no more than a hundred feet before she heard the harsh, evenly spaced sounds of Ty's carbine firing down into the valley below.

The remaining trail to the top of the plateau was more of a scramble than a walk, for the ravine that the path followed was filled with stony debris and a few hardy evergreens. The mustangs had left ample signs to follow—broken twigs and overturned stones and shallow gouge marks along solid rock.

The few steep pitches were mercifully brief. Within fifteen minutes Janna was standing on top of the plateau. She hadn't heard any sounds of shooting for the last ten minutes as she had climbed upward. She had told herself that that was good, that it meant Ty was on his way up the trail.

She also had told herself he was all right, but tears kept ruining her vision and fear made her body clench.

From where Janna stood on the plateau there was no hint that there might be a trailhead nearby, or even that the long, shallow gully she had just climbed out of was in any way different from any of hundreds of such gullies that fringed the steeper edges of the plateau.

The horses grazed nearby, wary of all sounds and shadows. All that forced Janna to mount Zebra was the memory of Ty's eyes pleading with her to be safe, and the gentle kisses that still burned on her fingertips, sealing her promise. Torn between fear and grief, rebellion and love, Janna mounted Zebra and waited, counting off the minutes.

Three minutes went by. Then five. Eight. Nine. Ten.

*I'm safe enough here. It won't hurt to wait just a bit more. The mustangs will tell me if anyone else is near.*

Twelve minutes. Fifteen. Seventeen.

Janna had reached eighteen when the mustangs lifted their heads and turned to watch the mouth of the gully with pricked ears and no nervousness whatsoever. Minutes later Ty came scrambling up out of the ravine.

"I told you—ten minutes," he said, breathing heavily.

"I don't know how to c-count," Janna said, trying to blink back tears and laughter at the same time.

Ty swung up on Lucifer, brought the stallion alongside Zebra and gave Janna a fierce kiss.

"Sweet liar."

Ty smacked Zebra hard on the rump, sending the mare into startled flight. Lucifer leaped to follow. Together the two mustangs settled into a ground-covering gallop. The plateau's rumpled surface flew beneath their hooves.

Twice Janna and Ty heard gunfire. Each time they veered more to the east, for the sounds were coming from the north and west. About every ten minutes Janna would slow the pace to a canter, allowing the horses to catch their breath.

Despite the itching of his backbone, Ty never complained about the slower pace. He knew that the mustangs might be called upon to outrun Indians at any moment; the horses wouldn't have a prayer if they were already blown from miles of hard running.

During the third time of resting, the distant crackling of rifle fire drifted to Janna and Ty on the wind. This time the sound was coming from the east.

"Should we—" began Janna.

She was cut off by a curt gesture from Ty. He pulled Lucifer to a stop and sat motionlessly, listening.

"Hear it?" he asked finally.

"The rifles?"

"A bugle."

Janna listened intently. She was turning to tell Ty she couldn't hear anything when the wind picked up again and she heard a faint, distant cry rising and falling.

"I hear it. It must be coming from the flatlands."

"Where's the closest place we can get a good look over the edge?" Ty asked.

"The eastern trailhead is only a few miles from here."

Janna turned Zebra and urged the mare into a gallop once more, not stopping until she came to the crumbling edge of the plateau where the trail began. Lucifer crowded up next to Zebra and looked out over the land, breathing deeply and freely, appearing for all the world as though he had barely begun to tap his strength.

Ty examined the land through his spyglass, sweeping the area slowly, searching for signs of man. Suddenly he froze and leaned forward. Six miles north and east of his present position, a small column of cavalry was charging over the land, heading south, sweeping a handful of renegades before it. Well behind the first column of soldiers, a larger one advanced at a much more sedate pace.

Ty swung the spyglass to look to the south, closer in to the plateau's edge.

"Christ almighty," Ty swore. "Cascabel's got an ambush set up where the trail goes through a ravine. That first group of renegades is the bait. He's got enough warriors hidden to slaughter the first group of pony soldiers before the rear column can get there to help."

"Can we get down in time to warn them?"

Grimly Ty looked at the trail down the east face of the plateau. It was even more precipitous than he had remembered. It was also their only hope of getting to the soldiers before Cascabel did.

"Would it do any good to tell you to stay here?" Ty asked.

"No."

"You're a fool, Janna Wayland."

Ty jerked his hat down on his forehead, settled his weight into the rope stirrups, gave a hair-raising battle cry and simultaneously booted Lucifer hard in the ribs.

The stallion lunged over the rim and was launched onto the steep trail before he had a chance to object. Front legs stiff, all but sitting on his hocks, Lucifer plunged down the first quarter mile of the trail like a great black cat. In helping the stallion not to overrun his balance, Ty braced his feet in the rope stirrups and leaned so far back that his hat brushed the horse's hard-driving rump.

When Lucifer stumbled, Ty dragged the horse's head back up with a powerful yank on the hackamore reins, restoring the stallion's balance. Surrounded by flying grit and rolling, bouncing pebbles, horse and rider hurtled down the dangerous slope.

Zebra and Janna followed before the dust had time to settle. As had the stallion, Zebra sat on her hocks and skidded down the steepest parts, sending dirt and small stones flying in every direction. Janna's braids, already frayed by

he wind, came completely unraveled. Her hair rippled and
wayed with every movement of the mustang, lifting like a
atin pennant behind her.

When Lucifer gained the surer footing on the lower part
f the trail, Ty risked a single backward look. He saw Zebra
ock-deep in a boiling cloud of dirt and pebbles, and Jan-
a's hair flying behind. The mustang spun sharply side-
vays, barely avoiding a stone outcropping. Janna's body
ioved with the mare as though she were as much a part of
he mustang as mane or tail or hooves.

Lucifer galloped on down the sloping trail, taking the
iost difficult parts with the surefootedness of a horse ac-
ustomed to running flat out over rough country. Ty did
othing to slow the stallion's pace, for each second of delay
ieant one second nearer to death for the unsuspecting sol-
iers in the first column. As soon as the trail became more
vel, Ty pointed Lucifer in the general direction of the ad-
ancing column, shifted his weight forward over the horse's
owerful shoulders and urged him to a faster gallop.

When Zebra came down off the last stretch of the east-
n trail, she was more than a hundred yards behind Lucifer.
ut Janna knew the country far better than Ty. She guided
ebra on a course that avoided the roughest gullies and
cky rises. Slowly the mare began to overtake Lucifer, un-
 finally they were running side by side, noses out-
retched, tails streaming in the wind. Their riders bent low,
ging the mustangs on.

Rifle fire came like a staccato punctuation to the rhyth-
ic thunder of galloping hooves. A lone rifle slug whined
ist Ty's head. He grabbed a quick look to the right and
w that the Indians apparently had abandoned the idea of
ading the soldiers into a trap. Instead, the renegades had
rned aside to run down the great black stallion and the
irit woman whose hair was like a shadow of fire. Even
scabel had joined the chase. Dust boiled up from the

ambush site as warriors whipped their mounts to a gallop
and began racing to cut off Janna and Ty from the soldiers.

Ignoring the wind raking over his eyes, Ty turned forward to stare between Lucifer's black ears, trying to gauge
his distance from the column of soldiers. Much slower to
respond than the renegades, the cavalry was only now beginning to change direction, pursuing their renegade quarry
along the new course.

It took Ty only a few moments to see that the soldiers
were moving too slowly and were too far away to help Janna
and himself, whose descent from the plateau had been so
swift that they were much closer to Cascabel than to the
soldiers they had wanted to warn of the coming ambush.
What made it worse was that the renegades who had waited
in ambush were riding fresh horses, while Zebra and Lucifer
had already been running hard for miles even before the
hair-raising race down the eastern trail. Now the mustangs
were running flat out over the rugged land, leaping ditches
and small gullies, whipping through brush, urged on by the
riders and by the whine of bullets.

Ty knew that even Lucifer's great heart and strength
couldn't tip the balance. The soldiers were simply too far
away, the renegades were too close, and even spirit horses
couldn't outrun bullets. Yet all that was needed was two
minutes, perhaps even just one. With one minute's edge
Janna's fleet mustang might be able to reach the soldiers'
protection.

Just one minute.

Ty unslung his rifle and snapped off a few shots, knowing it was futile. Lucifer was running too hard and the
country was too rough for Ty to be accurate. He hauled
the hackamore, trying to slow the stallion's headlong pace
so that he could put himself between the renegades and

Janna. Gradually Zebra began pulling away, but not quickly enough to suit Ty. He tried a few more shots, but each time he turned to fire he had to release the hackamore's knotted reins, which meant that Lucifer immediately leaped back into full stride.

*Dammit, horse, I don't want to have to throw you to make you stop. At this speed you'd probably break your neck and I sure as hell wouldn't do much better. But we're dead meat for certain if the renegades get us.*

*And I'll be damned in hell before I let them get Janna.*

Ty's shoulders bunched as he prepared to yank hard on one side of the hackamore, pulling Lucifer's head to the side, which would unbalance him and force him to fall.

Before Ty could jerk the rein, he heard rifle fire from ahead. He looked over Lucifer's ears and saw that a group of four horsemen had broken away from the column of soldiers. The men were firing steadily and with remarkable precision, for they had the platform of real stirrups and their horses had been trained for war. The repeating rifles the four men used made them as formidable as forty renegades armed only with single-shot weapons. The horses the four men rode were big, dark and ran like unleashed hell, leaving the cavalry behind as though the soldiers' mounts were nailed to the ground.

For the second time that day, Ty's chilling battle cry lifted above the thunder of rifles and hooves; but this was a cry of triumph rather than defiance. Those were MacKenzie horses and they were ridden by MacKenzie men and Blue Wolf.

Janna blinked wind tears from her eyes and saw the four horses running toward her, saw the smoke from rifles and knew that had caused Ty's triumphant cry: the speed of the four horses had tipped the balance. They were going to reach Ty and Janna before Cascabel did.

"We're going to make it, Zebra. We're going to make it!"

Janna's shout of joy turned to a scream as Zebra went down, somersaulting wildly, sending her rider hurtling to the ground.

## Chapter Forty-Three

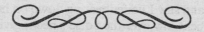

Before Janna hit the ground Ty was hauling back and to the right on the reins, forcing Lucifer into a hard turn. Despite the speed of Ty's reflexes, the stallion was galloping so fast that momentum alone swept them far past the place where Janna had fallen. Long before the stallion completed the turn, Zebra staggered to her feet to stand alone and trembling, favoring her left foreleg. Rifle fire erupted around her. She lunged to the side, seeking the cover of nearby piñons.

Ty saw the mare's three-legged motion and knew that she would be no help to Janna. A few yards from the mustang, Janna was struggling to her hands and knees, obviously dazed and disoriented by the force of her fall. A half mile beyond her, Cascabel and his renegades were bearing down in a cloud of dust and triumphant yells, certain that their prey was finally within their reach.

Measuring the distances involved, Ty quickly realized that Lucifer wasn't running fast enough to get Janna to safety before the Indians came within range. The stallion was straining, running with every bit of strength in his big body, but he was carrying more than three hundred pounds on his back.

Ty's knife flashed, severing the leather band that held the saddlebags full of gold on Lucifer's lathered body. The heavy pouches dropped away just as the mustang leaped a small gully. The gold vanished without a sign into the crease in the earth. Freed of the dead weight, Lucifer quickened his gallop.

"Janna!" Ty shouted. "Janna! Over here!"

Barely conscious, Janna turned toward the voice of the man she loved. She pushed hair from her eyes, forced herself to stand and saw Lucifer bearing down on her at a dead run. Ty was bent low over the horse's neck, giving the stallion all the help a rider could and at the same time calling for Lucifer's last ounce of speed.

Rifle slugs whined overhead and kicked up dirt around Janna. She noticed them only at a distance, as if through the wrong end of a spyglass, for she was concentrating on the wild stallion thundering down on her with Ty clinging like a cat to his black back.

A hundred yards behind Ty, four riders raced over the land like the horsemen of the Apocalypse, sowing destruction and death to any renegade within range of their rifles. The barrage of bullets slowed the charging Indians, who were unused to coming up against the rapid-fire rifles.

At the last possible instant, Ty twisted his right hand tightly into Lucifer's flying black mane and held his other hand out to Janna. He knew that he had to grab her and not let go—the momentum of the racing stallion would lift her quickly from the ground, allowing Ty to lever her up onto the horse's back.

"Get ready!" Ty shouted, hoping Janna could hear him.

His voice stitched between the war cries of the Indian behind Janna the erratic thunder of rifles and the drumroll of galloping hooves. She gathered herself and waited while Lucifer bore down on her like a runaway train. Despite the danger of being trampled, Janna didn't flinch or move aside, for she knew that her only hope of life lay in the man who was even now bending low over the stallion's driving body, holding his hand out to her.

Between one heartbeat and the next Janna was yanked from the ground and hurtled onto Lucifer's back just behind Ty. Automatically she scrambled for position, thrusting her arms around his waist and hanging on with all her strength while Ty hauled the mustang into a plunging, sliding turn that would take them away from the renegades. As the mustang straightened out again, Ty let out another chilling battle cry. Lucifer flattened his ears and his hooves dug out great clots of earth as he gave his riders the last bit of strength in his big body, running at a furious speed despite the additional weight he was carrying.

Ty's battle cry came back to him doubled and redoubled as the four horsemen bore down on him. They split evenly around the lathered, hard-running stallion. Each man fired steadily, making full use of the tactical superiority their repeating rifles gave. They were close enough now for accuracy, even from the back of a running horse. The relentless rain of bullets broke the first ranks of the charging renegades, which slowed those who were immediately behind and confused those who were on the sides.

A shout from the biggest MacKenzie sent all four horses into a tight turn. Soon they were galloping hard in Lucifer's wake, snapped at by sporadic rifle bullets from the disorganized melee of renegades.

There were only a few warriors who gave chase, for Cascabel had spotted the larger column of soldiers, which had been galloping hard to catch the smaller group since the first burst of rifle fire had come. Cascabel was far too shrewd to fight the Army on its own terms. An ambush was one thing; a pitched battle was another. The renegade leader turned his horse and began shouting orders. In a short time the renegades had reversed direction and were retreating at a dead run, preserving their arms and ammunition for a better battleground.

The first group of soldiers swept by Ty and then the MacKenzie brothers. Neither group broke pace. Not until the brothers were within sight of the larger Army column did they overtake Lucifer.

Knowing that it was finally safe, Ty slowed the stallion to a walk, stroked the mustang's lathered neck and praised him over and over. The biggest of the MacKenzie brothers reined in alongside.

"That's one hell of a horse you're riding. Am I to presume he's the fabled Lucifer?"

Ty's flashing grin was all the answer that was needed.

"Then that must be your famous silken lady riding postilion," the man said dryly.

Janna flinched and looked away from the tall rider's odd golden-green eyes. She knew instantly that this man must be Ty's brother, for surely no two men could look so alike and be unrelated. Tall, powerful, dark haired—on first glance he was Ty's twin. A second glance showed the differences; hardness of feature, a sardonic curl to the mouth, eyes that summarized what they saw with relentless pragmatism.

"Janna Wayland, meet Logan MacKenzie, my older brother," Ty said.

Janna's arms tightened around Ty's waist. She didn't speak or turn her face from its hiding place just below his shoulder blades.

"Sugar? You're all right, aren't you?"

"Yes," she said, her voice muffled. "Can we go back for Zebra?"

Logan's black eyebrows lifted at the husky, tantalizing feminine voice issuing from such a disheveled creature.

"No. Cascabel won't keep running. He'll split his force and double back to pick off scouts, stragglers or anything else he can get in his sights before the sun sets."

"But—"

"No," Ty said roughly, interrupting. Then, more gently, "I'm sorry, sugar. It's just too dangerous for you. Zebra will be all right. Mustangs are tough. They have to be. She was limping off to cover before you even got to your hands and knees."

"Zebra?" Logan asked mildly. "Were you keeping a zoo?"

When Janna didn't answer, Ty said, "Zebra is a mustang. Janna talked her into becoming a friend."

Logan gave Ty a slanting green glance. "'Talked' her into it?"

"That's right, big brother. Talked. No ropes. No saddle. Not even a bridle or stirrups. Just those soothing hands and that sweet, husky voice promising all kinds of things...and then delivering each and every one of them."

Logan's eyes narrowed at the seething mixture of emotions he heard in Ty's voice—affection, anger, bafflement, passion.

"Seems she caught herself more than a zebra mustang that way," Logan muttered.

If Ty heard the statement, he ignored it.

A renewed clash of rifle fire came from behind. The second column of soldiers had just come within range of the fleeing renegades. A bugle's wild song rose above the sound of shots.

"Hope whoever is leading those soldiers knows his business," Ty said. "Cascabel had an ambush laid that would have wiped out the first column before reinforcements could arrive."

"So that's why the two of you came down like your heels were on fire. Case heard something and put the glass on the cliff. He knew right away it was you."

"Surprised Blue didn't spot me first. He's got eyes that would put an eagle to shame."

"Blue was talking with the lieutenant at the time, trying to convince the damned fool that we might be galloping into an ambush."

"And?"

"Blue was told that when the lieutenant wanted a breed's advice, he'd ask for it."

Ty shook his head in silent disgust. "Well, at least he'll keep Cascabel busy long enough for Janna to get clear. Cascabel made some strong vows on the subject of her hair."

Logan looked from his brother to the auburn-haired girl who had refused to face the MacKenzies after that first brief look. Logan remembered the flash of pain he had seen in Janna's face before she turned away. He reined back slightly, leaned over and slid his hand beneath her chin. Gently, firmly, he turned her face toward himself.

"Easy, little one," Logan said soothingly. "No one's going to hurt you. I just want to be sure you're all right. That was one hell of a header you took."

Reluctantly Janna turned toward Ty's older brother. Long, surprisingly gentle fingers touched the bruised spot on her cheek and the abrasion along her jaw.

"Feeling dizzy?" he asked.

"I'm all right. No double vision. No nausea. I didn't land hard enough to get a concussion."

"She knows what she's talking about," Ty said. "Her daddy was a doctor."

Black eyebrows rose again, then Logan smiled, softening the harshness of his face. "You'll do, Janna Wayland. You'll do just fine." He turned toward the other three riders. "Listen up, boys. This lady is Janna Wayland. Janna, the big one is Blue Wolf."

"Big one?" Janna asked, looking at the men surrounding her. "Are you implying that one of you is small?"

One of the riders tipped back his head and laughed, reminding her of Ty.

"The laughing hyena is Duncan," Logan said. "The dark-eyed, mean-looking one on the chestnut horse is Blue Wolf."

"Pleased to meet you, Janna Wayland," Blue Wolf said in educated tones, and his smile refuted the very idea of "mean." He tipped his hat to her and went back to scanning the countryside for danger.

"The quiet one is Case. He's the baby of the family."

Case nodded slightly to Janna. A single look at his pale green eyes told her that Case might have been the youngest in years but not in harsh experience. There was a darkness in him that transcended words. A wave of overwhelming sadness and compassion whirled up in Janna as she looked at Ty's youngest brother.

"Hello, Case," she said softly, as though she were talking to an untamed mustang.

Ty heard the emotion in Janna's words, smiled rather grimly to himself and said in a voice too low to carry to Case, "Save your sweetness for something that appreciates it, sugar. Except for blood family, Case has all the feelings of a stone cliff."

"Why?"

"The war."

"You went to war, too."

Logan looked over at Janna. "All the MacKenzie men fought," he said. "Case is the only one who won't talk about it. Not one word. Ever. Not even with Duncan, who fought at his side most of the time. Duncan doesn't talk much, either, but it's different somehow. He still laughs. Case doesn't." Logan shook his head. "Damned shame, too. Case used to have the most wonderful laugh. People would hear him and stop and stare and then smile, and pretty soon they'd be laughing, too. No one could resist Case. He had a smile like a fallen angel.''

The clear regret on Logan's face changed Janna's opinion of him once more; despite his hard exterior, Logan was a man who cared deeply for his family. Rather wistfully Janna wondered what it would have been like to grow up with that kind of warmth surrounding her. Her father had loved her, but in a rather distracted way, never really stopping to discover his daughter's needs and yearnings, always pursuing his own dreams and never asking about hers.

"What a sad smile," Logan said. "Is your family back there?"

"Where?"

"In Cascabel's territory."

"Not unless you could call Mad Jack family," Janna said. "Besides, he ran off rather than hang around and be dragged to the fort. He knew how mad we would be about the gold."

"Gold?" Logan asked, looking at Ty.

"More than a hundred pounds of it."

Logan whistled. "What happened?"

"He gave us half and we promised to take half to his kids."

"Where did you leave it?"

"We didn't," Janna said. "It's in those saddlebags in front of Ty."

Ty and Logan exchanged a look.

"It was too much for Lucifer to carry," Ty said. "I cut loose."

Janna stiffened. "But that was how you were going to buy your silken la—"

"One more word, Janna Wayland," Ty interrupted savagely, "and I'm going to hand you over to that scalp hunting renegade myself!" He took a deep breath and struggled to leash his volatile temper. "Anyway, the gold isn't lost. Soon as I'm sure that Lucifer didn't hurt himself on that run, I'm going back for the saddlebags."

Janna wasn't surprised that Ty would risk his life looking for the gold once more, but she yearned to be able to talk him out of it. Hopefully she looked over at Logan. His smile didn't comfort her—it fulfilled the sardonic promise she had first noticed in the line of his mouth.

"So Janna isn't your silken lady after all?" Logan asked Ty. "Damned white of you to save her hide anyway at the cost of all that gold."

The cold, needling edge to Logan's tone didn't escape Ty. Nor did the censure in Logan's eyes, for he had realized that Ty was Janna's lover the first time Ty had called her sugar in a soft, concerned voice.

"Drop it," Ty said flatly.

Logan's smile changed indefinably, becoming almost sympathetic as he realized Ty's dilemma. For years Ty had been pursued by the finest that southern and northern society had to offer; he had turned everyone down in his own pursuit of a dream of the perfect silken lady. Now he found himself hopelessly ensnarled with a wild, gray-eyed waif whose voice could set fire to stone.

Logan leaned over and cuffed Ty's shoulder with rough affection. "Forget the gold, little brother. I'll turn Silver loose on your uncurried mustang lady. In a few weeks you'll never know she wasn't paddock born and raised."

Janna turned her face away, trying to conceal the red tide that climbed up her face as she thought of the unbridgeable gap between silk purses and sows' ears. Eyes closed, she held on to Ty, saying goodbye to him in silence, for she knew with bittersweet certainty that he would go after the gold...and she would walk away from the MacKenzies and never look back, freeing Ty to pursue his dream.

"You planning on taking her to Wyoming?" Case asked. Like his eyes, his voice was cool, passionless. He had been watching Janna with measuring intelligence.

Ty turned and glared at Case. "Yes. You have any objections?"

"Not a one."

Ty waited.

"She doesn't want to go," Case added matter-of-factly.

"She'll go just the same."

"Is she carrying MacKenzie blood in her womb?"

If anyone else had asked that question, Ty would have beaten him into the ground. But Case wasn't anyone else. Because Case had destroyed or walled off all emotion within himself, he didn't concede its presence in anyone else.

"She could be carrying my child," Ty said tightly.

"Then she'll be in Wyoming when you get there."

With no warning Case bent over, plucked Janna from Lucifer's back and put her across his saddle.

"Ty!"

"It's all right. Case will take good care of you." Ty smiled oddly. "Don't try running from him, sugar. He's the best hunter of all of us."

# Chapter Forty-Four

They must have magic mirrors in Wyoming," Janna said, looking in disbelief at her own reflection. "That can't be me."

Silver MacKenzie smiled, touched up the dusting of rouge on Janna's cheeks and stepped back to view the results. "It's amazing what three weeks of regular food and sleep can do for a body, isn't it?"

"More like four," Janna said.

Silver's ice-blue eyes closed for an instant as she composed herself; the thought of losing Logan made her heart freeze.

"I'm sure the men are all right," Silver said firmly. "It must have been harder to find the gold than they thought, that's all. Perhaps Ty couldn't remember precisely where he cut the saddlebags loose. You left rather in a rush, from what Case said."

Janna smiled wanly. "You could say that. At least, Ty was in a rush to get away."

"Speaking of getting away..." Silver began, changing the subject eagerly.

A flush crawled up Janna's cheeks as she remembered the night after she had arrived in Wyoming. Case had dropped her rather unceremoniously at the doorstep, told Silver that Janna had come to be combed and curried like a paddock horse for Ty and that she might be carrying Ty's child. Silver had been sympathetic, Cassie had been angelic, and Janna had gone out the second-story window the first time everyone's back was turned.

The next morning a very tight-lipped Case had brought Janna back, set her on the doorstep and told her that she could give her word not to run until Ty came back or she could spend the time waiting for him trussed hand and foot like a chicken going to market.

"...now you know why men like their women dressed in yards of silk," Silver finished. She blew a wisp of moon-pale hair away from her lips as she bent and adjusted the voluminous skirt of Janna's cream silk ball gown.

"What?" asked Janna, distracted by her memories.

"We can't run worth a darn for all the hoops and flounces, that's why. The best we can manage is a serene face and a dignified, very slow exit."

Janna smiled just as Silver straightened. The older woman stared, arrested by the sight Janna made. Her dark auburn hair was piled high in deceptively simple coils, which had been threaded through with strings of pearls. Pearls circled her neck in a delicate choker whose centerpiece was a ruby that had been in Silver's family for three hundred years. Earrings of pearl and teardrop rubies hung from Janna's ears. The ball gown's off-the-shoulder style dipped to a modest point in the front. The hint of a shadow between Janna's breasts was as seductive as the lines of the ball gown were simple. A brooch of ruby and pearls was pinned at the base of the gentle décolletage. With each breath, each movement, ruby fire shimmered, echoing the secret fire of Janna's hair.

"Shadow of Flame," Silver murmured. "The renegades saw you very clearly, didn't they? You're really quite stunning. The dress looks far better on you than it ever did on me, as do the rubies."

"It's very kind of you to say so."

"The truth is rarely kind," Silver said grimly.

Janna saw the shadows of worry on Silver's face and knew that she was concerned about her husband.

"I'm sure Logan is all right," Janna said. "He's a smart, tough man."

"All the MacKenzies are smart and tough. Even the women. You'll fit in just fine."

There was silence, then Janna said huskily, "Ty wanted something different in his wife."

"Ah, yes, Ty's famous silken lady." Silver saw Janna wince. "Don't worry, he'll take one look at you and see the woman of his dreams. He may be MacKenzie stubborn but he's not stone-blind."

Tears ached behind Janna's eyes at hearing her own secret dream spoken aloud. The hope of having Ty turn to her and see his silken lady was so overpowering that she was helpless against it. That, as much as Case's threat, had held her in Wyoming.

Silver's hand rested lightly on Janna's cheek. "Does he know how much you love him?"

Janna nodded slowly and whispered, "It wasn't enough. His dream . . ."

"It was the war, Janna. Each MacKenzie responded to it differently. Logan wanted revenge." Silver's mouth turned down in sad remembrance. "He found it, but it wasn't what he thought it was. I think Ty will discover that silk isn't what he thought it was, either."

A call came from the front of the house. Both women froze in wild hope before they realized that it was Case greeting guests rather than Case announcing the return of Blue Wolf and the MacKenzie brothers. But Janna had to be sure. She ran to the window and looked out. The first of the guests were indeed arriving.

"I still find it hard to believe that there are lords and ladies running loose about Wyoming," Janna said.

Silver smiled wryly. "Unfortunately, it's true. What's worse, I'm related to most of them by blood or marriage." She looked out the window. "Those specimens are Cousin Henry's guests. They don't actually live in Wyoming. They just came here to hunt." She sighed and shook out the folds of her skirt so that it fell properly. "I'd better go meet them. Case has impeccable manners, but he tires of the game very quickly. I don't want Melissa to drive him away before the ball even begins. He's a marvelous dancer. Almost as good as Ty."

"I can't imagine a woman driving Case anywhere."

"It's my fault, really," Silver said as she hurried out the bedroom door, her ballgown billowing gracefully. "I made him promise not to hurt Melissa's feelings. Case takes promises very seriously. Come down as soon as you're ready, but don't be too long. Everyone is dying to meet you. Women are so rare in this place. Especially young and pretty women."

Janna looked in the mirror for a moment longer. A stranger looked back at her, a woman not unlike her mother in elegant appearance, but a stranger all the same. Janna wondered if she would ever become used to dresses and rustling folds of cloth. Even after nearly a month, she was still aware of the muffling yards of material swathing her legs and the contrasting snugness of bodice and waist. Even if the cloth had allowed her to run, the tight waist would have made deep breathing impossible. The shoes were the hardest to bear, however. They pinched.

She looked toward the armoire, where her father's hand-me-downs hung. She had washed and mended the clothes very carefully, for they were all that she could call her own. Her moccasins were patched as well, using doeskin she had traded a few of her precious herbs to obtain. Her canteen medicine pouch and ragged blanket roll were set aside, waiting to be picked up on a moment's notice.

*Maybe I won't need them. Maybe Ty will look at me and see a woman he could love. Maybe . . .*

With hands whose creamy softness still surprised Janna from time to time, she reached into the medicine pouch and pulled out the sketch of her mother. Broodingly Janna looked from her reflection in the mirror to the sketch and then to her reflection again.

*Will what he sees please him? Will he turn to me out of love rather than duty?*

After a few minutes Janna set the sketch aside and went downstairs through the huge ranch house, which had been restored after a fire had all but razed it. She walked through rooms whose furniture had been shipped from England and France and whose rugs had come from China. She barely noticed the elegant furnishings. Nor did the sparkle of crystal reflecting candle flames catch her eye. In her mind she was once again in the secret valley, where Ty was holding out his arms to her with a smile on his face and love in his eyes.

Janna went through the ritual of introductions and polite words, moving with a natural grace that enhanced the seductive rustling of silk around her body. Men were drawn to her, both because of her restrained beauty and the natural thirst of men in a rough country for that which was soft and fragile. Janna was like the ruby between her breasts—clear yet enigmatic, sparkling yet self-contained, the color of fire yet cool to the touch. When the violins played she danced with men from neighboring ranches, men both titled and common, men who shared a common interest—Janna—and a common complaint—her lack of interest in them.

"May I have this dance?"

With a subdued start, Janna focused on the man who was standing between herself and the blaze of candlelight from the buffet table. For one heart-stopping instant she thought that Ty had come back; then she realized that the familiar, broad-shouldered silhouette belonged to Case.

"Yes, of course," Janna said, extending her hand to take his.

Moments later she was whirling and turning to the stately strains of a waltz played by Silver on the grand piano. The music was rich and civilized, a brocade of sound embroidered upon the wilderness night. Case danced with the casual perfection of a cat stalking prey.

"I've been watching you," he said.

Janna looked up at his pale green eyes. "That's not necessary. I gave you my word. I'll keep that word."

He nodded. "I wasn't worried about that. I was afraid that you'd get to believing all the polite nonsense Silver's cousins and guests are pouring into your ear."

With a smile that hovered on the brink of turning upside down, Janna shook her head. "I know what I am and what I'm not," she said huskily. "I'm not the 'fairest flower ever to bloom on the western land,' among other things. Nor am I a fool. I know what men hope to gain by flattering a woman." She met Case's eyes and said evenly, "Your brother didn't lie to me in any way, even that one. He always stated quite clearly that my feminine attractions were . . . modest."

Case looked at the proud, unhappy set of Janna's mouth. "That doesn't sound like Ty. He always had a line of flowery speech that was the envy of every man around."

"Flowers and silk go together."

"And you weren't silk, so he saved the flowers and got right down to business, is that it?"

Janna's eyelids flickered. It was the only sign of her pain, but Case saw it. As Ty had warned her, Case was the best hunter of all the MacKenzies. Nothing escaped his cool, dispassionate eyes.

"No, I wasn't silk," Janna agreed huskily.

"But you are now."

She smiled sadly and said nothing.

One of Cousin Henry's guests cut in. Janna tried to remember his name, but nothing came to her mind except the memory of the young man's intense, hungry eyes watching the ruby brooch shift and shimmer with her breaths. She prayed for the waltz to end, freeing her.

"Are all western women so charmingly quiet?"

Janna opened her mouth to answer. Nothing came out except a soft, startled sound when the waltz ended in an abrupt jangle of notes. She looked over at the piano in time to see Silver lifted into Logan's arms for a kiss that conceded nothing to silk or ritual politeness.

"They're back!" Janna said.

She looked around frantically but saw only one tall, roughly dressed man mingling with the guests—Blue Wolf, not Ty. Then she felt a tingling all the way to her fingertips. She turned and saw Ty standing at the doorway. He was leaning against the frame, his arms crossed over his chest and his eyes narrowed. Slowly he straightened and began walking toward her. As he closed in on her, there was no welcoming smile on his bearded face. There was only anger.

"Willie," Ty said coldly, "your nanny is looking for you."

For a moment the young aristocrat holding Janna thought of taking the insult personally; then he shrugged and handed Janna over to Ty.

"Apparently this dance belongs to the rude frontiersman?"

When Janna didn't object, the man bowed and withdrew. Ty ignored him completely, having eyes only for the *bruja* who stood before him gowned in silk and shimmering with gems.

The waltz began again, played by four hands. Ty took Janna into his arms, holding her too close for propriety. He moved with the graceful, intricate, sweeping motions of an expert dancer. An equally expert partner could have followed him, but Janna was new to ball gowns and dips and whirls. Inevitably she stumbled. He took her weight, lifted her, spun her dizzyingly until she had to cling to his arms for support.

"Ty, stop, please."

"Why? Afraid those fancy Englishmen will see you holding on to me?" Ty's narrowed green eyes glittered coldly at Janna through his black eyelashes. His voice was equally icy. "Not one of those titled fops would touch you if they knew your past. When they see past the silk they'll be furious at the joke you've played on them."

"Men never look past the silk."

"I've looked, Janna Wayland. I know what's beneath all the finery—and it sure as hell isn't a fragile silken lady."

The words sank into Janna like knives, killing the last of her foolish hope. A feeling of emptiness stole through her as she realized that no matter how she dressed she would never be Ty's dream, for he would always look at her and see the ragged waif dressed in men's clothes.

*Silk purse. Sow's ear. Never the twain shall meet.*

Janna tried to turn away from Ty, but his fierce grip on her never wavered. She would have fought despite all the people around, but even if she had won free she would still have been trapped within swath after swath of silk. Silver had been right: men preferred silk because it prevented women from running off.

Janna was in a silken prison. There was no escape, no place of concealment for her but deep within herself. Yet even then her tears gave away her hiding place.

Case tapped Ty firmly on the shoulder. "This dance is mine."

Ty turned on his younger brother with the quickness of a cat. "Stay out of it."

"Not this time," Case said matter-of-factly. "I brought her here, forced her to stay here until you came back, and now you're spoiling the Thanksgiving ball Cassie has looked forward to all year. Your family deserves better than that, don't you think?"

Ty looked beyond Case and saw Blue Wolf starting through the throng in Ty's direction. He knew that Blue was even more protective of Cassie than Case was. Then Ty spotted Duncan and Logan closing in on him with grim expressions.

Silver began playing a waltz again. Its slow, haunting melody recalled formal summer gardens and elegant dancers glittering with gems. Calmly, Case disengaged Janna from Ty's arms. As Case whirled Janna away, he said over his shoulder, "Go take a bath. You aren't fit company for anything but a horse."

Without a word Ty turned and stalked off the dance floor, shouldering aside his brothers.

Behind him Case and Janna danced slowly, gracefully, for Case matched his demands to his partner's skill. When the final strains of the waltz dissipated among the candle flames and rainbows trapped within crystal prisms, Case and Janna were standing at the doorway. He held her hand and looked at her for a long moment.

"Cassie told me you aren't pregnant," Case said finally. "I'm sorry. A child with your grit and grace and Ty's strength and fancy speech . . . well, that would have been something to see."

Janna tried to smile, couldn't, and said simply, "Thank you."

"There's a fiesty zebra dun in the corral. That fool brother of mine packed more than a hundred pounds of gold all over Utah Territory for three weeks looking for that zebra mare. Sixty pounds of that gold is now in a bank waiting for you to draw on it. The MacKenzies will honor Ty's promise to see that Mad Jack's half gets to his kids."

"Half of my gold is Ty's."

Case shook his head. "No."

Janna started to object again. Case watched her with the patience of a granite cliff. She could object all she wanted and nothing would change.

When Case saw that Janna understood, he bowed to her more deeply than custom required and released her hand.

"You're free, Janna. All promises kept."

# Chapter Forty-Five

The oil lamps in Janna's room turned her tears to gold, but that was the only outward sign of her unhappiness. Cream leather shoes stood neatly next to the armoire. Pale silk pantalets were folded neatly on the chair. Hoops and petticoats were hung out of the way. Earrings and necklace and brooch rested in an open, velvet-lined box. All that stood between Janna and freedom was the maddening fastenings on her ball gown. The dress had been designed for ladies who had maids in attendance, not for a mustang girl who had nothing but her own ill-trained fingers and a burning need never to see or touch or be reminded of silk again.

"Allow me."

Janna spun so quickly toward the door that candle flames bowed and trembled.

Ty stood in the doorway watching her, but he was a different man. Gone was the rough frontiersman. Ty was clean shaven except for a black mustache. He smelled of soap and wore polished black boots, black slacks and a white linen shirt whose weave was so fine it shone like silk. He looked precisely like what he was: a powerful, uncommonly handsome man who had been born and raised to wealth and fine manners, a man who had every right to require that the mother of his children be of equal refinement.

Janna turned away and said carefully, "I can manage, thank you. Please close the door on your way out."

There was silence, then the sound of a door shutting behind Janna's back. She bit her lip against the pain ripping through her body.

"A gentleman never leaves a lady in distress."

Janna froze with her hands behind her back, still reaching for the elusive fastenings that held her confined within a silken prison.

"But I'm not a lady, so your fine manners are wasted. Nor am I pregnant, so you needn't feel dutiful."

The bleakness of Janna's voice made Ty's eyes narrow. He came and stood behind her, so close that he could sense her warmth.

"Case told me," Ty said.

His nostrils flared at the fragrance of crushed roses that emanated from her skin and hair. Memories blazed for an instant in his eyes. He brushed her hands away from the fastenings that went down the back of her dress.

"You're a satin butterfly," Ty said, unfastening the dress slowly, feeling a hunger to touch her that was deeper and more complex than a desire, a hunger that tightened his body as each tiny hook silently gave way, revealing a bit more of Janna's skin. "And I'm going to release you from your cocoon."

Ty's long index finger traced the graceful centerline of Janna's back. She made a stifled sound as the dress fell away, leaving her naked. Ty had never seen anything quite so beautiful as her elegant feminine curves. He traced her spine once more, following it to the shadow crease of her hips.

"During the war, Case kept his sanity by walling off his emotions," Ty said quietly. "I kept my sanity in a different way. I swore that I would never see such ugliness again. If I survived, I vowed to surround myself with fine and fragile things that had never known even the shadow of violence and death. Every time grapeshot ripped through living flesh, every time I saw young children with empty eyes, every time one of my men died . . . I renewed my vow."

Eyes closed, body trembling, Janna felt the lingering caress of Ty's fingertip tracing her spine; but it was the pain in his voice that broke her heart and her control. She had loved him recklessly, without regard for the future cost. Now the future had come to demand its reckoning.

"It's all right, Ty," she said huskily. "I understand. You've earned your silken lady. I won't—"

Janna's voice shattered as Ty's hands caressed the length of her back before smoothing up her torso until her breasts were cupped in his hands.

"Run away?" Ty offered, finishing Janna's sentence for her. The feel of her nipples hardening at his lightest touch made blood rush in a torrent through his body. "That's good, because touching you makes me so damn weak that I can hardly stand, much less run after you." With aching gentleness he caressed the breasts whose textures and responsiveness never ceased to arouse him. "So soft, so warm. No, hold still, love. It's all right. We're going to be married just as soon as I find the strength to leave this room and round up a preacher."

"Ty . . ." Janna's throat closed around all the tears she hadn't shed, all the dreams that couldn't come true. "You have to let me go."

"Why?" His long fingers shaped her, caressed her, made her tremble with a wild longing. "You want me as much as I want you. Have I told you how much I like that? No games, no coyness, just the sweet response of your body to my touch."

Janna bit off a telltale moan and asked desperately, "Did your parents love each other?"

Ty's hands stilled in surprise. "Yes. Why?"

"Think how you would have felt if they hadn't. Think how a child would feel growing up and knowing that his father felt a combination of desire and duty and disappointment toward his mother. Your child deserves better than that. So do you. And," Janna added softly, "so do I. Seeing you, having your body but not your heart... It will break me, Ty. Is that what you want?"

Gently Ty turned Janna around. She met his eyes without evasion despite the slow, helpless welling of her tears.

"Janna," he said softly, bending down to her, "I—"

She turned her head aside and spoke quickly, interrupting Ty, words tumbling out in a desperate effort to be heard. "No. Please listen to me. Please. I may not be fine or fragile, but even mustang ladies can be broken. You said once you owed me more than you could ever repay. You can repay me now. Let me go, Ty. *Let me go before I break.*"

Eyes closed, hands clenched into fists at her side so that she wouldn't reach for the man she loved too much ever to cage, Janna waited for Ty to leave. She heard him make a hoarse sound that could have been anger or pain, sensed currents of air moving as he moved, and she trembled with the violence of her emotions.

Tears touched the sensitive skin between her breasts, and she was shocked to know how hot her own tears were. Then she felt Ty's cheek against her body, saw him kneeling at her feet, felt his arms close tightly around her waist, and she realized that the scalding tears weren't her own.

Moved beyond words, Janna stroked Ty's hair with trembling hands, feeling as though she were being torn apart. She had thought she could leave him, but every instant she was with him told her how wretched life without him would be.

"I won't let you go," Ty said finally. "Don't ask me to. Don't beg me to. I can't do it, Janna. I need you too much."

"Ty, don't," she whispered achingly, trying to still the trembling of her body, failing. "I want so much for you to have your dream."

"I dreamed of you every minute I was away. You're my dream, Janna. I went back to get that gold for you, not for myself. I couldn't close my eyes without seeing you, couldn't lick my lips without tasting you, couldn't sleep for wanting you. Then I walked into that ballroom and saw the perfect silken lady of my dreams dancing with the perfect silken man. *And I wasn't that man.* I went—crazy. I wanted very much to kill that high-nosed son of a blue-blooded bitch for even looking at you."

"But you said—you said that you'd seen past the clothes, that I wasn't a fragile silken lady."

"Yes, I'd seen past the clothes, and I thank God for it."

Ty turned his head slowly, kissing the smooth breasts that smelled of roses.

"Listen to me, Janna. There's far more to being a lady than silks and bloodlines. A true lady is more concerned with the needs of the people around her than she is with the state of her wardrobe. A true lady gives succor to the sick, laughter to the lonely, respite to the weary. And to one very, very lucky man, a true lady gives herself . . . and asks nothing in return but that she be allowed to give the gift of her love."

Ty smoothed his cheek between Janna's breasts, absorbing the beauty of her living warmth. "That kind of gift is so rare that it takes a man by surprise."

He kissed the velvet tips of Janna's breasts, smiled to hear her breath break and tremble even as her body did. His mouth caressed the smooth skin of her stomach and the auburn cloud at the apex of her thighs.

"My sweet satin butterfly," he said in a low voice. "Let me love you again." His hand eased between her legs and he groaned to feel her heat once more. "Janna ... please, let me."

Janna's knees gave way at the first gliding penetration of his caress. Ty's arm tightened, holding her still for a searing instant while he was still within her warmth. Her breath unraveled as he slowly released her, leaving her body shimmering and without the strength to stand.

With a dark yet oddly tender smile, Ty caught Janna and came to his feet, taking the warm weight of her in his arms once more. He walked the few steps to the bed, put her on the fur coverlet and kissed her lips gently before he stepped back and unhurriedly removed his own clothes, watching her with smoldering green eyes the whole time.

When he was as naked as she, he lay next to her on the bed, gathered her against his body and kissed her as tenderly as though she were a frightened maiden. The caresses he gave her were equally restrained, almost chaste, but his words were elemental fire.

"Your body is all satin, strong and hot and sleek. You're perfect for a man who is more rawhide than silk. For me, Janna. Just for me. You are ... perfect."

Janna's breath caught, then broke when Ty's hand smoothed down her body. She didn't deny him the intimate warmth he so gently sought. She could no more have refused him than she could have told her heart to stop beating. Nor could she hold back the shimmering pulse of her pleasure, the heat that welled up and overflowed at his touch; and she cried out his name with each pulse.

The evidence of Janna's need for him was an exquisite shaft of pleasure so intense that it was also pain. Ty groaned and sought her secret warmth once again, and once again she didn't deny him. Eyes closed, he bent and kissed her lips, her breasts, the taut curve of her belly, trying to tell her things for which there were no words. And then her finger threaded lovingly through his hair and the words came to him.

"Once," Ty whispered, "I saw Lucifer go to you, put his head into your hands with such trust that I was reminded of the legend of the unicorn and the maiden. It made me . . . restless, baffled, angry. I felt sorry for the unicorn, trapped by his reckless love.

"And then the maiden opened her hands and let the unicorn go, for she loved the unicorn too much to hold it against its will."

Janna's fingers stilled until Ty's head shifted against her palms, asking to be stroked once more, asking to be held by her touch even as the unicorn had been held.

"The unicorn ran off and congratulated himself on his clever escape, and then . . ." Ty turned slowly, covering Janna's body with his own. He touched the hot center of her just once, slowly, drawing a long, broken moan from her. "And then," Ty whispered, watching Janna's eyes, "the unicorn realized what a fool he had been. There was nothing in the forest as exciting as the maiden's touch, no beauty to equal her companionship, no pleasure as deep as the ease she had given his soul. So he went running back and begged to be given the maiden's gift once more."

When Ty neither spoke nor moved to join their bodies, Janna's heart hesitated, then beat with redoubled strength.

"What did the maiden say?" she whispered.

"I don't know. Tell me, Janna. What did the maiden say to the unicorn?"

Tears magnified Janna's eyes. "I love you," she said huskily. "I'll always love you."

She felt the emotion that shuddered through Ty's strong body as he bent and kissed her tears away.

"Yes," Ty said, watching Janna's eyes. "I want you to be my wife, my mate, my woman, the mother of my children, the keeper of my heart, the light of my soul. I love you Janna. *I love you.*"

Janna reached for Ty even as he came to her. Their bodies merged, softness and strength shared equally, defining and discovering one another in the same elemental moment. Ecstasy blazed as they lost and then found themselves, man and woman forever joined in the reckless incandescent union known as love.

\* \* \* \* \*